THE PREQUEL:

IT HAPPENED HERE

A Novel By John Kingston

THE PREQUEL:

IT HAPPENED HERE

A Novel By John Kingston

AN ALTERNATIVE TRUE HISTORY

Copyright © John Kingston 2017

The author was responsible for the design of the three covers and SpiffingCovers.com produced the artwork.

The work has been printed in Arial fount script size 10.

First published in England by John Kingston Publishing Ltd.2017

VOLUME TWO OF THREE

ISBN: 978-0-9955703-1-3

9 780995 570313

STATEMENT

With the exception of Mr. Michael Randle, Mr. John Wrighton and Mr. Lawrence "Larry" Questad all characters appearing in this work are fictitious. Any resemblance fictitious characters' bear to real persons, living or dead, is purely coincidental.

DEDICATIONS

I WISH TO THANK DOCTORS PHILIPPE RIBET, ROBERT GREENBAUM AND ESPECIALLY MR. STEPHEN EDMONDSON FOR GIVING ME A 'SECOND CHANCE' IN MAY 2007 AND THE OPPORTUNITY TO FINISH THIS WORK.

MY PERSONAL GRATITUDE TO MR. SHERIF HABASHI, DR. NEIL KITCHEN AND PROF. MICHAEL GLEESON FOR SAVING THE LIFE OF MY YOUNGER DAUGHTER, LAURA.

TO EVERYONE, AND ESPECIALLY MY DEAR FRIEND ROGER BALL, FOR THEIR HELP AND SUPPORT IN MY JOURNEY THROUGH LIFE.

INDEX

VOLUME TWO

THE PREQUEL: IT HAPPENED HERE

AN ALTERNATIVE TRUE HISTORY

THE ORIGINS AND BIRTH OF THE
NEW ORDER

ONE

At the end of the Second World War, National Socialism, both as an ideology and even as a pseudo religious creed, except for a miniscule hard core, was internationally discredited. The world wide projection and influence of what was described as 'Americanisation' throughout the globe and the confrontation with their economic, military and political opponent, the extreme form of Socialism - Communism - led under the banner of the Soviet Union and then in nineteen forty-nine, supported by the new communist regime in China, overshadowed all other events.

In the United Kingdom only a small band of supporters survived, in denial of the true nature of the horrendous consequences of National Socialism's policies.

The life and career of Sir Oswald Ernald Mosley summarises the rise and fall of Fascism in the United Kingdom. He was the 6th Baronet of Ancoats, distantly related to Queen Elizabeth the Second, educated at the Royal Military Academy, Sandhurst, who served with honour, on the 'Western Front' in the First World War. He became the youngest active M.P. in the House of Commons, aged twenty-one, serving the constituency of Harrow for the Conservative Party' however he fell out with the party over the issue of Irish policy, crossing the floor to become an Independent M.P, retaining his seat twice in subsequent General Elections. By nineteen twenty-four he was growing increasingly attracted to the Labour Party and in March he joined the Independent Labour Party and allied himself with the left.

In December nineteen twenty-six he won a by-election for Labour at Smethwick and his then current political philosophy was symbolised by his close, ardent association with the Fabian Socialists

In the Ramsey MacDonald Labour government of nineteen twenty-nine he became Chancellor of the Duchy of Lancaster, but had expected higher office and ultimately resigned as he had been given the responsibility to solve the unemployment problem and his radical proposals were rejected. He then founded the New Party based on his corporatist economic policy which became more radical and authoritarian. Following a study tour of Italy and its leader Mussolini and other Fascists he founded the British Union of Fascists in nineteen thirty-two.

The party surrounded itself with a corps of black uniformed paramilitary stewards, nicknamed Blackshirts, and the party was frequently involved in violent confrontations particularly with Communist and Jewish groups. In October nineteen thirty-six, Mosley and the British Union of Fascists attempted to organise a march through an area in the 'East End' of London with a high proportion of Jewish residents.

Following scenes of violence and a dramatic and valiant defence of their neighbourhood, the Commissioner of the Metropolitan Police disallowed the march from going ahead. On January first nineteen thirty-seven the Public Order Act 1936 came into force inter alia banning political uniforms and quasi military style organisations. The Party went into decline as the threat of Nazi Germany became more apparent and on May twenty third nineteen forty, as the disaster in France unfurled and the evacuation from Dunkirk was underway, he was interned under Defence Regulation 18B and soon afterwards the British Union of Fascists was proscribed. The war ended what remained of his political reputation but supporters persuaded him, post war, to found the Union Movement, however in nineteen fifty- one he left for Ireland, subsequently moving to Paris, returning in nineteen fifty- nine to offer himself in the General Election at Kensington North, losing badly.

TWO

In March nineteen sixty-four, Great Britain was beginning to recover from the trauma of war and adapting itself to the new social and economic climate. Despite alarmist forecasts from both the *Daily Mail* and *Daily Express*, the National Coalition government under Harold Wilson did not declare Martial Law after the nuclear attack on East Anglia by Soviet bombers. What the Press did not announce, or furtively imply, was that the wartime military censorship had voluntarily been accepted by all the national newspapers and also the regional and local newspapers and would continue, including, because of the temporary shortage of newsprint, a reduction in the number of pages published. This situation would permanently continue and was the first step in the erosion and ultimate end of Democracy.

Rumours spread in the absence of a definitive government statement, but the truth was that the Soviets, in the dying days of the war, and within twenty-four hours of the American nuclear counter first strike had specifically attacked U.S. bases in East Anglia to pre empt a further American nuclear strike on the exhausted, victorious Warsaw Treaty forces who had been clandestinely assisted at the end of the campaign by Soviet troops and equipment. Subsequently it was agreed by analysts that Khrushchev`s actions (they were not then aware that he had mentally and physically collapsed and in what was in fact a *coup d'état*, Brezhnev had assumed power) were not solely or primarily a military action but to show both the resolve and continued capability of the Soviet Union. But these factors were no longer of prime importance to the British Prime Minister Harold Wilson, who was assailed by problems that were overwhelming the capability of the makeshift Cabinet and indeed would have been insurmountable to any government.

Parts of East Anglia and an area broadly defined as surrounding the Humber estuary were a waste land following the indiscriminate use of nuclear devices, as military observers commentated, "broadcast like corn being sown in the fields", the medical services were inundated with casualties but above all the most optimistic analysis was that the area would not be agriculturally productive for at least five years and that there would have to be either a voluntary influx of labour or a new 'Direction of Labour Act' to restart agricultural production on a limited basis. A decision would have to be made, literally within days, to 'raid' the secret food reserves to maintain the existing supply of food. It was pointed out, by experts, that for example, in the London area, the reserves stored under Hyde Park (with access from Park Lane) and Hendon in Aerodrome Road might only delay the inevitable, that was the reintroduction of rationing and the draconian application of a food allowance of 1500 calories a day even for heavy manual workers, though they had the foresight to suggest and recommend that pregnant women be exempt. The fear was of a national backlash of inestimable ferocity.

Trade between Great Britain and the European mainland had ceased to function and the only contact was the declining, pitiful stream of refugees who were both braving the Channel crossing and evading the ever vigilant and increasingly efficient supervision of the coast. However as the stream dried up, so did the intelligence which they brought, but in essence the information was consistent and uniform.

Like Hitler and the Third Reich nearly twenty-five years before, the coast was being increasingly militarised and inland the military presence, especially at the aerodromes was rapidly intensifying. The civilian population of the occupied (or liberated lands, depending if one listened and believed the occupiers) was becoming subject to what one refugee graphically described as 'the new Gestapo', prominent people were disappearing and that food was in short supply.

Nationally, led by exhortations from the press of all persuasions was an incessant demand for the release and repatriation of 'our boys', that were the British forces who had either been captured or who had surrendered in the tidal wave that had swamped the N ATO forces, combined with unsubstantiated reports, which were played down in the press, of the terrible injuries that had been suffered following the vicious use of chemical and nerve weapons.

Internationally, the old Empire not only remained loyal but deferred payment for its goods. Thus food supplies were being shipped from New Zealand, Australia, Canada and South Africa but the vast distances and the political uncertainty was an ever worrying concern. In a portent of 'Things to Come' the South African ambassador had privately and secretly intimated, with Pretoria's insistence, that their continued support would depend on a public declaration by the Prime Minister that:

"The British government respects the integrity and independence of the government of South Africa and in consequence understands and accepts their policy relating to the separation of the races."

The word apartheid had been cunningly omitted and Wilson knew that despite a decimated Parliament that, since the tragic and horrendous massacre, had infrequently been in session, Labour supporters would not tolerate such a declaration and that a Conservative government, under a new leader might be re-elected.

His senior civil servants had persistently raised the subject of the economic and commercial climate. The pound was coming under pressure, mainly from a rump of speculators in the United States and, it was suspected, by unofficial representatives of the South African authorities, and whilst the export of goods, especially to the North American continent was rising, the Stock Exchange was losing confidence and this was reflected in the continuous, inexorable decline in share prices. Wilson, with an optimism born out of hope, reminded them that football had continued without interruption, but in a telling and withering reply he was reminded that the Winter Olympic Games had been cancelled two weeks before their official opening by the International Olympic Committee meeting in Switzerland, and that only forty eight hours before, the same organisation had announced, with great regret, that the summer games scheduled for October, in Tokyo, Japan, had been postponed for two years but the nineteen sixty-eight games scheduled for Mexico City would go ahead, as planned.

But overshadowing all these problems was the military situation. The United States government had issued a public demand for the Warsaw Pact to return to its pre November the twenty- fifth borders but the demand was ignored, indeed intelligence reports and anecdotal evidence indicated that imprisoned N A T O troops and especially U.S. forces were deliberately being kept on Warsaw Pact military bases effectively as hostages.

What Wilson did not know was that a major rift had developed within the small clique at the heart of the U.S. government: it was led by Robert McNamara, who was championing the strategies of Herman Kahn who had suggested the initial, devastating and successful first(nuclear) strike and then holding the defenceless Soviet cities as hostages and finally, if in the absence of Khrushchev's capitulation, a second but immense thermonuclear strike would be launched which should break the Soviet's will and finally end the plague of Communism.

Wilson had only recently learned, in a memo *HAND WRITTEN* [author's emphasis] by the ambassador in Washington, so confidential that it had not been encrypted and transmitted, just in case it was routinely decoded by their' friends and major partner', but delivered by special courier, was the truth about Johnson, his health and above all his paranoid anger at the British and the 'traitor' Wilson. The Americans now knew that Wilson had 'caved in' to Khrushchev's pressure and had moved the British 'V Bomber' force and its precious cargo of nuclear and thermonuclear weapons out of the European theatre and had not confided in their friends and ally especially since Johnson had announced his new 'Monroe 'Doctrine.

What Johnson had forgotten, conveniently, was that at *HIS* request, communication between the two nations' Intelligence Services had been previously temporarily terminated because he blamed the British for mishandling and misinterpreting the secret approaches which now clearly exposed themselves as a grandiose deception. Furthermore Wilson could not be trusted since he had deliberately deceived his own country, personally and publicly announcing that the' V Bomber' force had successfully participated in the assault...

"On the Soviet Union",

and that even now his bodyguard of lies, by the continued deception of the British public continued to hide the truth.

Wilson's reaction was to both try to undo what had been done previously and to literally reverse his actions. To this end as an absolute priority he ordered the R.A.F. to make arrangements to bring back the fleet of aircraft together with their Yellow Sun cargo of thermonuclear weapons but fate and circumstances were to combine and conspire against him.

David Bruce, John Kennedy's appointment as the United States ambassador to the Court of St. James, was invited to a private dinner at 10 Downing Street with the emphasis both on privacy and informality such that the invitation stressed that the meal was to take place in the private apartment of the P.M. It was surprisingly and promptly accepted since the Cabinet Office had commented that they had recently found a distinct chill in their daily dealings with the ambassador's senior staff.

Before the dinner Wilson decided to make an unscheduled visit, by train, to his constituency of Huyton, in Liverpool, not only to gauge local opinion but to ascertain the economic climate in the City. To that end, in his capacity as Prime Minister, he decided to host a lunch for local business leaders and representatives of the Chamber of Commerce, most of whom he knew and knew were politically his opponents but recognised that their mutual respect and the privacy of a relatively intimate meal could illuminate and clearly expose the current business climate.

He would balance the position by inviting local Trade Union leaders to a 'Beer and Sandwiches' reception later in the day to find out their concerns and worries which cynically he intended to ignore unless the threat of strikes was raised but he already had a plan for cooperation which he believed that they would swallow and which he called 'In Place of Strife'.

There was one other task that he had set himself and that was the modernisation of the role and style of the Prime Minister. He had observed the youthful approach of the slain President and compared it to the style of his predecessors, especially to that of Roosevelt and his 'fireside chats' during the Depression. In his opinion Harold Macmillan had displayed an anachronistic and aristocratic approach which he felt was patronising and he intended to consign this style of communication to the dustbin of history. He knew that he did not have the youth and glamour of Kennedy but he believed that even though the climate was grave he could present a new image of leadership and authority .His intimate associates knew of his intentions and had suggested, very discreetly, to obtain coaching by amenable T.V. directors skilled in the art of communication.

Not only that, a different method of communication could enhance his relationship with the press and to this end the journalist Gerald Kaufman was recommended .Highly intelligent with a M.A. at Queen`s College, Oxford University in philosophy , politics and economics and currently a political journalist on both the Daily Mirror and New Statesman he was a superb choice, but the other additional candidate to act as Wilson`s assistant and liaison with Kaufman (if he accepted the post) was a complete surprise , an unknown quantity and an additional reason for the P.M.'s visit to his political stronghold.

In nineteen fifty, when he became M.P .for the new constituency of Huyton , a secretary was required and an unknown local activist named Gold very timidly volunteered and later ,whilst he admitted certain mistakes caused solely by ignorance and inexperience for his task, his indefatigable application created an efficient and effective operation that his permanent successor continued, but without any acknowledgement or appreciation of his inheritance, though Wilson noted Gold's additional qualities of alacrity and cheerful readiness. Gold continued as a valued member, even spurning the annual opportunity to visit the House of Commons as the guest of his M.P. Little was known of his background or financial status though he appeared of independent financial means which contradicted his support for a Labour M.P.

Wilson read the M.I.5 report as he sat in the first class compartment bound for Liverpool accompanied by his private secretary and his personal detective.

When he finished he stared into the infinite void ahead of him, tapped his pipe against the window ledge and as if dumbfounded by the contents stated that:

"This is either a poor concoction in very bad taste, or a pastiche of a nineteen thirties novel by the man that wrote Lost Horizon, whatever his name was. "

The erudite detective looked up from his paperback and responded knowingly...

"Jimmy Hilton".

At which stage Wilson concluded the review by observing that the author's Christian name was, in fact, James and that, as a matter of priority, and to satisfy his interest, he required by means fair or foul, urgent sight of the Court records, Mandel Goldburgh's prison records and above all his complete M.I.5 file. He was now aware of the man's true, full name, the fact that he had been charged under the Official Secrets Act and with uttering counterfeit currency. Heard, in camera, at the Central Criminal Court in September nineteen forty-eight, charges under the Official Secrets Act were dropped at the last moment but he received the draconian sentence of nine months for the currency offence, leaving for the United States shortly after his release and returning two months later.

Goldburgh met the P.M. in his hotel room, ravaged by time, economic neglect and thoughtless abuse, where no visitor could relax, though Wilson endeavoured to calm his guest with the offer of a whisky and soda which was declined with good grace. Wilson got straight to the point and informed his surprised visitor that there was, possibly, the opportunity of a position in his private office.

"Would you be interested?"

Goldburgh reacted with, what would be expected in such a situation, surprise and shock, and Wilson sensing the man's response, framed his next question, to calm his nerves, as a humorous joke.

"Had he been or was he now a Soviet spy?"

Then all three men, including the detective, burst into a gale of laughter when Goldburgh stated, 'off the cuff', having obviously considered his reply that:

"He had never been a Soviet spy and was a loyal British subject, however in nineteen forty-eight, because he had been blackmailed by the N K V D, he was instructed to ingratiate himself, however long the period would take, into Harold Wilson's immediate circle of trusted friends and advisors and a recommendation of his Machiavellian qualities could be obtained, on the Prime Minister's behalf by M.I.6, by application to the K G B (the successor to the N K V D) and Lavrenti Beria, who, as he realised that Wilson must know all about him, he had met on two occasions, but since he had been dead for over a decade, a personal recommendation might be difficult to obtain."

For the first time since Wilson became aware of the existence of the man, he detected an impish and wicked sense of humour but could not conceive that his reply was not only true but also, he had been effectively blackmailed by the N K V D using the threat of the letter delivered by the official from Yerevan to Beria via Kaganovich.

Wilson subsequently, more as a diversion from official duty than a prudent investigation, did peruse the requested files but he had already made his flawed decision, based on his judgement and the candidate's repartee. Goldburgh's ultimate loyalty was perhaps to himself, forged by the pressures of his experiences, when like a pupa, he had shaken off the idealism and naive values of youth and had donned the armour of pragmatism, self interest and cynicism.

Goldburgh had also been confronted, shortly before his appearance in court, with a threat of the unbridled wrath of the establishment who were still convinced that he was a traitor and that they were certain that the account of his time in the Soviet Union was a false concoction. The press, barred from reporting the case, and the democratic procedures of the court could not save him and he could face imprisonment for at least twenty five years. Even at this last moment, if he told them the truth, the trial would be adjourned and a gentleman's agreement negotiated. He categorically declined but pleaded guilty, on his Counsel's advise, to the currency offence and was given nine months imprisonment but the judge decided to adjourn court until the following day to deal with the extremely serious offences under the Official Secrets Act. It was therefore with great surprise, both to the Defendant and his Counsel and also the Judge that when the second part of the trial begun the next morning, that the prosecuting Counsel announced that all charges were to be dropped because of insufficient evidence and the absence of any witnesses.

He was initially imprisoned in Wormwood Scrubs being subsequently transferred, without explanation, to Pentonville, where he served the balance of his sentence. He used the prison libraries with a voracious appetite for increased knowledge and whilst he was never held in solitary confinement he gained the reputation of a 'loner' and an intellectual. This brief interruption in his life was a time and period that he used to assess his future, realising with cold objective reasoning that he had no true loyalty to the institutions of Britain and to his Majesty, King George and that the authorities had effectively callously discarded him and that he would also find a method to rid himself of the continuing burden of blackmail that had been imposed upon him by the Soviet embassy in London. He looked across the Atlantic for his future after his release and the golden nuggets of information that he could trade with Mr. Maddox perhaps even for a new life in the United States.

The period after his release was an unnecessary frenzied rush. Having first travelled by underground to Kings Cross he endeavoured, by telephone, using the special method of communication, to leave a message for the man who, he believed, might offer him both payment for his knowledge and sanctuary. Three days later an anonymous voice that he did not recognise contacted him and arranged to meet him in the Dorchester hotel.

The appointment was amicable and brief.

"He had certain information that, for a price, and assistance he wished to make available to Mr. Maddox who he wanted to meet face to face and supply the information and not through an intermediary."

Within days he received a reply that was not wholly what he expected or wanted. At his own expense, he was to travel to New York and register at a particular hotel where he would be contacted by Mr. Maddox personally

Within a week, carrying the three diamonds which he had recovered in a great hurry, he had travelled to Liverpool, caught a liner very shortly before its departure and enjoyed the lazy pleasures of second class travel and a life not dictated by the Victorian regimentation of the prison staff.

He registered at the hotel, only venturing out for his meals and newspapers and once to visit the so called 'diamond district' where he found his long latent knowledge of some Yiddish a commercially positive bonus as he introduced himself and his goods to astute orthodox Jewish traders. He had learned the art of hiding his emotions but was pleasantly surprised at the offers he received and resolved, by some means, to contact the Jewish dealer in Istanbul, to thank him for his honest trading. He did not consummate a deal but prevaricated and haggled, concluding the negotiations by the promise of an early final answer to the best and most lucrative offer that he received.

The following morning he received a telephone call, not from Mr. Maddox, but from his assistant, who requested that Goldburgh be ready for ten fifteen and that he be collected, by taxi. True to his word a taxi drew up exactly at the appointed time and a rather well groomed and athletic man exited and entered the vestibule where Goldburgh was waiting in anticipation. The introductions were brief and friendly, Goldburgh joining Maddox's assistant in the taxi which sped off towards Times Square and when they arrived they briskly walked to the nearest subway where they took a train for two stops before alighting and then taking another taxi to the Waldorf Astoria. Goldburgh thought that he was a participant in a Film Noir such was the manner of the journey but concerned himself with, what he hoped, would be a face to face meeting with a memory from his youth.

THREE

As he entered the room he immediately recognised Mr. Maddox who was sitting on a settee in an exclusive suite on the third floor of the hotel. He appeared more mature, even avuncular and was sipping a cup of coffee but he immediately rose, simultaneously putting the cup on a table and offering his hand in friendship, then he asked his guest if he required a coffee and receiving an affirmative answer then courteously enquired if he took milk and sugar. The formalities completed, he was the paragon of good breeding and etiquette, beginning the dialogue in such a way that his news, of the most distressing nature, was conveyed in such a manner that its content did not have the dramatic effect than if carelessly delivered by a messenger without sense or compassion.

"If you remember, when we last met, that you requested me to make enquiries concerning your parents' fate which I did and in consequence, when I had the answer, I endeavoured to contact you in the Portobello Road but you had moved on and it was not prudent for me to make contact.

I would have told you that they were murdered by the Gestapo, in Lyon, your father by Klaus Barbie personally and your parents were buried in an unmarked, anonymous and to this day still an unidentified grave. The British authorities knew this information and should have informed you on your return from the Soviet Union and I believe you wish to tell me of your adventures, but to be blunt, at a price I have found the art of haggling an embarrassment and an accomplishment that I have not mastered; I have satisfied those with whom I have dealt with, based on mutual trust. No doubt you have already prepared a summary of your experiences which perhaps you could tell me about bearing in mind that the information must have already been supplied to our friends and allies in London."

The shock of his parents' fate was mitigated by the fact that some time before he had reconciled himself to their deaths since he had rationalised the situation that they had made no contact.

He was being blackmailed by the London embassy of the Soviet government. He had worked for nearly a year in the Ukraine at a secret camp run by the N K V D preparing a group of twelve young men and women to be infiltrated into the United States as long term spies but he couldn't be certain of this fact as the camp commander did not confide in him. He believed that he was too executed on his return to Moscow but, with the assistance of a Soviet army officer who had worked with him at the camp, he had escaped and managed to reach neutral Turkey. Natalia and the American residents were not mentioned and he intended to expand on his brief summary if and when he was further questioned.

Then a silence fell over the three men in the room, like a Victorian fog. Goldburgh wondered what response would greet his story.

"My dear friend, where have you been for the last year or so and for what reason?"

Goldburgh immediately sensed that Maddox knew perfectly well where he had been and the story behind his trial and he framed his answer appropriately, generating a further unexpected enquiry.

"Since your arrival in New York have you made any unusual visits?"

He was inclined to respond almost sarcastically but tempered his reply with tact, conjecturing also that like a criminal he had been watched since his arrival, admitting he had attempted to sell some diamonds and hoped to consummate the deal within a day or so.

The next question clearly followed his last answer.

"Where did you obtain the diamonds?"

He could have lied and said his mother but truthfully answered the question in two words and promptly anticipated the next question as his mind raced ahead wondering exactly what Maddox knew and, most likely, what the British authorities had told him. He was correct in his assumption and this time was more specific and exact.

"I was given money, to be specific and accurate, about nine hundred U.S. Dollars by my Russian Army officer friend."

The dialogue which was turning into an amicable interrogation, continued.

Why did he give you all that money and where did he obtain such an amount of foreign currency?"

He was slowly, inexorably beginning to reveal the real truth of his time in the Soviet Union and felt shortly that he would have to fully disclose the whole story.

"From where he obtained the money I do not know, why he gave me all that money was to help me leave Russia and possibly because he did not wish to be found with foreign currency which might well be a crime."

Suddenly and unexpectedly Maddox suggested that:

"They stop for lunch, relax and resume when refreshed."

The hiatus probably gave them all the opportunity to take stock of their positions and to consider the best way forward and Goldburgh resolved to explain his deceit to the British authorities.

He noted, with interest, that Maddox and his assistant were not making any notes and begun what was for him, a confession.

"I would like to tell you the complete story (he could have used the word truth but thought it would be inferred that his earlier statement was a fabrication and a concoction of lies), but feel certain that you would wish to make notes for it will take some time to tell the whole story."

At which juncture Maddox`s assistant, for the first time, actively involved himself in the meeting.

"Please do not worry or concern yourself as all that interests us is your honest account of your stay in Russia."

"The British authorities were correct in their analysis that I did not tell the truth and my reason at the time was because the Soviet authorities were specifically, and is this phrase suitable, targeting America and not Great Britain? My justification and assessment at the time was that it was of no direct interest and concern to the British. Even then I had little loyalty to what was my adopted country and now with my recent experiences, especially my imprisonment, what loyalty remained has now been extinguished (he stopped, not only to prepare continuation of his statement, but to give the others an opportunity to raise any questions, but they remained silent).

If you are prepared to accept the integrity and honesty of my statement, my loyalty is to the United States."

At which moment the assistant intervened and commented...

"At a price!"

Immediately Maddox interjected and calling his assistant by his surname, with a diplomatic tact which stopped short of chastising him, stated...

"I think it only fair that Goldburgh be allowed, in his own time and in his own manner, to fully tell his own story and to explain his reasons."

Goldburgh began his tale with his introduction to Natalia and Kashkarov, their initial meeting with the first camp commander, the train journey and arrival at the camp.

He then began a broad description of the American residents, explaining that they never regarded themselves as prisoners or inmates and that they lived, within the confines of the camp, well, and that all the residents ate the same diet as if they lived in a suburban or Mid West town of the United States. He knew that all the Americans had previously been inmates in Soviet labour camps and were grateful for their transfer since he understood that their continued incarceration would have resulted in their premature deaths such were the conditions that prevailed and he believed that invariably their only crime was to have been American.

Central to the camp were the twelve young men and women, all of whom were, at the beginning, unable to speak any English at all.

He saw that Maddox suddenly became extremely interested when he mentioned that one of his responsibilities, along with Natalia, who had lived on the West coast, was to teach the group about life in the United States and educate them how to blend in. As an example of the facts that they had to learn he cited that they were taught the names of all the previous Presidents, the names of the States of the Union and their capital cities and the titles of many baseball teams.

He mentioned, in passing, the incident when they were woken at night and the punishment that they suffered for exhibiting their knowledge of Russian.

Time figuratively flew until Maddox interrupted Goldburgh with a comment that he had given them so much to absorb that he felt a second meeting would be required and asked his assistant to give Goldburgh two hundred and fifty U.S. Dollars and confirmed that he would telephone the hotel the next morning with instructions.

That evening Goldburgh decided to clear his head and go for a long walk before eating. It would also give him the opportunity to consider and review the day's events. He had clearly been followed as how would they know he had been to the 'diamond district' and they were aware not only that he had been to prison but more importantly he had been to Russia though that information could have emanated not from the British authorities but from the American embassy in Moscow. He felt uncomfortable as he navigated past other pedestrians walking in his direction and against him. He sensed that he was being followed but did not give in to an irrational emotion and act as a character from, and again he thought of the analogy, a film noir. He ate very well, far, far better than if he had dined in London, overslept and was woken, not by the early morning dawn but much later by the insistent tones of the telephone.

He recognised instantaneously the voice of Maddox`s assistant who informed him that he was to be collected at noon, by taxi, that he was to pact his effects, pay his bill and to inform the reception that he intended to visit Lincoln, Nebraska but would return in some six weeks and ...

"Could they hold any incoming mail."

He felt very uncomfortable in the taxi since it took a circuitous route to its destination and Maddox`s assistant looked ill at ease even compounding the tense atmosphere, not by talking of irrelevant trivia, but apologising for his hasty comment the previous day.

The train journey to Washington was smooth, uneventful and enhanced by the comparative luxury of the first class carriage but whilst it revived memories of the journey from Moscow to the Ukraine, it could not and would not stand any comparison, though the simple fact of the journey allowed forgotten memories to resurface.

FOUR

They drove past sixteen hundred Pennsylvania Avenue and the Lincoln Memorial, finally arriving at their destination which was a small nondescript hotel typically used by travelling salesmen and tourists visiting the Capital on restricted budgets, so anonymous that in hindsight he could not even remember if it displayed its name but the room and bed were clean and every day, at his request, the staff changed the linen and the bathroom was not only adequately stocked with every convenience to satisfy his hygiene but the shower was very powerful, giving him an invigorating and cleansing experience .

Later that afternoon, after he had settled in, he was met by Mr. Maddox who drove him to his club, where years before he had entertained the man`s parents, and at his invitation lodged themselves in a small alcove hidden from the other members and regularly, but discreetly and efficiently visited by an attentive waiter who always addressed Maddox, as Sir.

"I am inclined to believe your story absolutely but your motives are somewhat dubious, indeed there are doubts about your integrity, however my associates and I, and the man that even I report to, consider that your story and its ramifications are so potentially damaging that it has been decided to investigate, in depth, the story of the camp where you were based and the events which took place there.

Your claim that you are being blackmailed by the Soviets is a convenient aperture into their motives. You must report to my staff in London details of their demands and interests and they will inform you of the information that you should give them. Do not, under any circumstances, meet their representatives abroad, for obvious reasons. Before you return to the United Kingdom we will help you set up a bank account and you are to inform the bank staff that at irregular intervals, transfers are to be made to your account in England, in U.S. Dollars on the instructions of your New York attorney which will be converted into Sterling locally.

Furthermore I will set up a payment facility for your services which will be paid again, in U.S. Dollars, on a regular basis and transmitted by another firm of attorneys to your bank, described as funds from investments made by your late parents (Maddox then stopped to allow his agent, for that was what Goldburgh had become, to absorb the instructions).

It is unlikely that we will meet again and contact will be through my personal representative and before this meeting is over I will tell you how to contact him. As well, I will give you the names of four or five attorneys who can act on your behalf and who are in no way connected with me, or the organisations that I act for. Before you return to England sell your three diamonds and deposit the funds with your new attorney.

From tomorrow onwards you will be collected each day by taxi and taken to a private house where you will be thoroughly interrogated about all aspects of the camp and possibly about events once you left, up till your arrival in Istanbul."

He fell silent as if he was contemplating a matter even more important than Goldburgh`s story, finally concluding with the remark that:

"As you commented yesterday, this does not concern the British authorities."

Which he inferred and construed as a subject not to be disclosed to any British authority.

Neither knew that they would not meet again for nearly twenty five years and that one would actually save the life of the other, but this event was hidden behind the veil that obscures our view of the future.

Maddox invited his guest to the members` private dining room where they both enjoyed a rib of medium rare beef and an excellent claret. After the taxi dropped him off at his hotel (Maddox had informed the doorman at the club of the name of the hotel) Goldburgh realised that whilst their conversation was both stimulating and far reaching, his host had contrived not to disclose any personal information but had been able to delve into his guest`s personal details.

The following morning and for the next thirteen mornings, including the following two Sundays, he was collected by the same taxi driver and driven to the same unpretentious detached early twentieth century wooden house where he met Maddox`s assistant (who years later, Goldburgh, as he became more knowledgeable of the Intelligence Service jargon, would describe him as his 'handler') and another, very studious, young man who strove to impress his associate by the acuteness of his questions and the shrewdness of his observations.

He had never previously experienced such an intensive and rigorous investigation and was ill prepared for what was a journey into his past. In his career he had undergone the pressures of examinations, mainly written but also oral, and had stood alone in the dock of the 'Old Bailey' and pleaded guilty to uttering forged currency but had never been asked to make a journey of the mind to remember people, facts and events that had taken place over five years before. Vivid memories of the court and its cast of officials flooded lucidly into his mind because the first anniversary of the hearing was virtually coincidental to his interrogation. In his mind`s eye he could clearly see counsels both for his defence and prosecution dressed like university tutors in black robes but also in archaic wigs, the latter sensing blood and the judge, aware of his alleged crimes, eager to don, metaphorically, the dreaded black cloth on his head. Would he be led by two shepherds to uncover and illuminate the information or would he be coerced and dragged back through the darkness of history to revive his experience of a time gone by?

Perhaps the first day was an anti–climax spent investigating the American occupants, especially their names and experiences in the prison camps. He actually admitted how little he really knew about them or their lives, but the more he spoke and, as the questions became more probing, small pieces of the puzzle melded together and as the day drew to a close, a number of inmates had been identified and their histories, if not in depth, began to emerge.

On the following, second day, a third man was present, holding a sketch pad, and he began to draw, using Goldburgh`s descriptions, faces of some of those camp inmates that his memory could visualise. By lunch time on that second day a rapport had developed and sometimes he was unable to control, if not his excitement, then his enthusiasm as he increasingly corrected and recommended improvements to the artist who created more and more accurate drawings.

The third day was almost a religious epiphany for him, as the two men concentrated on portraits of Natalia, Kashkarov and the two camp commanders. If there was a scheme or purpose behind the formulation of Maddox`s plans then yesterday had been arranged to prepare him for the task of creating a resonance between him and the artist as he accurately remembered details of the four senior members of the camp hierarchy. By mid afternoon the artist`s flair and natural talent had created almost lifelike portraits of both Natalia and Kashkarov which he admired both for the way the artist had captured their personalities, but also as a reminder of her beauty. The association had come at a price as cooperation between the artist and his advisor had been conducted amidst great emotion, ranging from anger and frustration to great euphoria as the portraits slowly evolved and became more accurate and close to completion.

The final, completed works were an inspiration for him and revived memories that had burrowed deep into his mind. He was so electrified and supercharged that a vast reservoir of recollections cascaded deep from in him and he twice refused requests to terminate the meeting, which ended close to ten p.m., an uninterrupted session of nearly eleven hours.

Late that evening the two representatives had before them an abundance of information, especially about Natalia concerning her early life on the West coast of the United States, her father`s *ALLEGED* occupation and her duties in the camp. Their joint opinion was that she would rise to high office in the N K V D whilst Kashkarov`s military record and his pre war support of Marshall Tukhachevsky were all noted.

The next four days concentrated on the nine remaining trainees since it was mutually agreed that the three trainees who had been allegedly sent to the prison complex were most unlikely to be reinstated. He was under considerable pressure, on one hand he was endeavouring to work with the artist and they were both shifting from one portrait to another and he was juggling with the two investigators, supplying them with miniscule items of information when it was agreed that he concentrate only on the portraits and when finished, the three of them would use each drawing as the basis to create individual reports.

He confessed to the artist when only about three portraits were anywhere near completion and the other six were in an embryonic state that he had suddenly lost all inspiration and, if he was honest, enthusiasm. With the joint approval of the two investigators (he thought the definition, interrogators had a malicious and malevolent overtone) he left early that day and treated himself to a twenty ounce New York strip steak (medium rare), apple pie a la mode, three Coca Colas and two generous slugs of Jack Daniel`s (which he promptly regretted because whilst he enjoyed and savoured the flavour and texture it was too much for him to absorb).

He went to bed at dusk and was soon asleep.

Suddenly he awoke. Disoriented, he momentarily had to search for the light switch and then in the artificial light which forced him to squint he looked at his watch which shocked him declaring a time of ten past two and then he rummaged through the drawer at the side of his bed. He quietly and reverentially thanked the Gideon`s Bible for its help and located a supply of notepaper headed on each sheet with the title and address of the hotel, which he ignored.

He began to make notes and even infantile, childlike portraits of the trainees.

The dream had been so vivid and clear. He was back in the camp teaching the twelve students weights and measures. Some were laughing, others rigorously making notes as they all repeated by rote...

"Sixteen ounces, one pound. Fourteen pounds, one stone. Two stones, one quarter. Four quarters, one hundred weight. Twenty hundred weight, one ton!

Ray, Bobby, Ira and Betty stop laughing, stand up and recite slowly the measurements of weight! Ira, slow down, your pronunciation is too rushed. We will stay late to try to improve your accent.

Dave, Mike! Twelve inches make, what? How long is an inch? Show me by the distance between your thumb and index finger!"

He remembered. He was almost frenzied in the way he wrote and wrote, anything and everything, stopping briefly either to relieve himself of the excellent steak and apple pie or the beverages or to draw or sketch some minor or insignificant part of each student`s face as it appeared to him.

He must have dropped off to sleep about six o`clock for he was roused and woken at nine fifteen by the insistent, emphatic knocking of the morning reception clerk.

"Your taxi has arrived and the driver is hooting with impatience."

"Tell him I`ve overslept and will be fifteen to twenty minutes and oh, could he go round the corner to the diner and get me a coffee and cheese roll which I`ll eat on the way."

He began to read his voluminous notes as he munched the roll inside the taxi. Even he was excited and knew instinctively that the three men, who, no doubt, would be concerned at his late arrival, would be pleased with his labours.

Such was the cornucopia of information that the allocated four days went into a fifth as dossiers on the nine, headed by each member`s first name, gave a schedule of personal details, including regional accents that they had picked up whilst being lodged with certain families and those facts enabled him to identify even more American names.

Later, analysis of the information confirmed that four men and the girl Betty had New York Bronx accents, two, Mid -West and of the other two, one Texan and the remaining one, West Coast, Californian.

That dream had also revealed what the two investigators had appreciated as gems. Off the cuff observations about certain idiosyncrasies, foibles and peccadilloes. Betty had, what Goldburgh tastefully described as a very ample pair of bosoms and tended, he felt unconsciously, to run her hands through her long blond hair and at the same time arch her back to amplify her femininity.

The artist was requested to redraw her portrait and to show her upper torso which in the execution caused some male mirth and ribald comments.

Ira, might, if under pressure stammer and was coaxed to speak slowly and deliberately. Yuri was attracted to Natalia and indeed Kashkarov had mentioned to him one incident which both men construed that the two had furtively met in the forest but they mutually decided to forget the matter.

Goldburgh had been informed, though there was no evidence to support the allegation, that Yuri was also extremely competent, accurate and fast when it came to the use of a rifle but it was forbidden to discuss or think about their past lives from that moment, on their first day, when they had been informed that it was henceforth forbidden to speak Russian.

The next two days were spent delving into the operation of the camp. The baseball game had previously been mentioned and the investigators were keen for Goldburgh to estimate from the time the idea of the competition was suggested, the time lapse till the arrival of the equipment. And the newspapers: how old were they, were the only papers available, *The New York Times, Washington Post, Los Angeles Times and The San Francisco Examiner?* On average were they one, two even three weeks late? The food. Was he absolutely certain the produce was from the United States or perhaps had some been produced in say, neutral Sweden? Did he see any tins, whether unopened, opened or empty or boxes or even wrapping paper which might have confirmed their origin?

How regular were the deliveries, did any of the nine frequent the ice cream parlour?

Without even thinking he mentioned that Ray must have had an allergy to nuts as he had to have medical attention after a visit to the parlour.

The second investigator, shrewd and clever, immediately pounced and asked who had attended to him.

Again, without thinking, Goldburgh answered that one of the American women was a qualified doctor and had access to a limited supply of medicine available in the pharmacy. He suddenly, without prompting, remembered the doctor's name (who, he added, they were forbidden to consult, for security purposes) and the trivial but in reality, important fact that she had worked in a particular hospital in New York, shortly before she had emigrated, with great expectations, to the Soviet Union.

The following day and the early part of the next, was spent in the company of a fourth man, recreating both in a diagram and drawings, the layout of the camp and visualisations of the community centre.

His inquisitors seemed to have exhausted all their avenues of enquiries and spent the last days going over much of the information that had previously been raised generating some additional facts, mainly about the Americans.

On what had been scheduled as the final day and it did, in fact, turn out to be the last day, Goldburgh was asked a question, so simple, that its response created an atmosphere of concern and intense interest. Before the question was asked he had not even thought about the matter.

"What happened to all the Americans when the camp was closed?"

He thought very carefully. For the first time he was actually confused and perplexed and then he reached a profound and frightening conclusion. If, as they had been promised, they were repatriated through neutral Turkey, with the assistance of the American Red Cross then such a question would be superfluous, because they would have informed their saviours that a number of Americans had decided to remain in the Soviet Union.

"When I originally arrived at the camp, we, that is Natalia, Kashkarov and myself, understood that the American contingency had been informed that when the purpose of the camp had been fulfilled, those who chose, could be repatriated to the United States, of course subject to the current military situation. At the very end about seventy percent opted for repatriation, the others, who wished to stay, were to travel to Kiev to help rebuild the shattered city. (He then again mentioned the party and the fact that the twelve trainees were deliberately allowed alcohol and that was how three of them failed).

He assumed that they would have made the journey to the Turkish border partially by train, but he was not certain of the railway facilities."

He was then given the Washington telephone number of his contact and informed that the first part of his debriefing was completed and was handed, in used notes, two thousand U.S. Dollars and told to go on vacation, even to visit Lincoln, Nebraska and he was to return to New York and the same hotel that he had previously used, not only to collect his mail, but to accidentally leave a local Nebraska newspaper to validate his original advices. He should leave, for safe keeping with them, the three diamonds which could be collected, on his return, together with a cheque for the balance of monies that he was owed. Arrangements would be made to introduce him to the attorney of his choice, have a private conversation and then sell the diamonds at the best current price, in dollars, and finally to open a bank account, if necessary in conjunction and in the presence of his new attorney.

Lincoln, Nebraska, was an anti climax. His English teacher and inspiration had prematurely died, the high school's principal had moved on, out of State, and in the dozen years or so since his departure the image and ethos of the high school had altered and like the rest of the post war world looked forward to the nineteen fifties and not backwards to the nineteen thirties.

He travelled on to the West coast and spent ten days enjoying the weather of California and Santa Barbara, returning, by train, to New York though he missed the first train since his taxi was involved in a rear end shunt, which in itself was not only inconvenient but if he had caught the first train he would have come across a recently graduated student who was beginning her business career as a travel journalist, which legitimately would cover her regular and apparent random trips across America. Thus the paths of Mandel Goldburgh and Miss Deborah Levy (as she was now known) did not cross.

FIVE

On his arrival in New York, he made a call to Washington and arranged to meet his 'case worker' the following day outside of a particular attorney that he had chosen, at a time which would give him adequate opportunity to complete the initial contact and if asked, would advise that he obtained the attorney's name from the telephone book.

After the meeting, and satisfied with the man's integrity and competence, he met his case worker who he knew only as Harold, or years later as Hal, collected the three diamonds and proceeded to the diamond district where he completed his transaction, finding, most pleasantly, that since his original approach, that he was offered and gratefully accepted an increased payment receiving in total an amount of seven thousand, four hundred and fifty dollars.

He phoned his new attorney, who had in the interim period contacted his bank, and made arrangements that same afternoon for his new client to visit the bank, open an account, make a deposit and to confirm that irregular payments would be made into and from the account on his behalf by his attorney as he would be based in England and that currently he did not have a permanent address but...

"Would let them know."

Combined with a crumpled cheque for the not so insubstantial amount of two thousand three hundred and seventy five dollars representing the balance of his remuneration he calculated at an exchange rate of just over four dollars to the pound, that his account stood at an equivalent value of just over two thousand, four hundred pounds.

Harold then announced that:

"There had been a development and that he was required for an additional debriefing which should only take about three days and that, again, of course, he would be further remunerated."

The three meetings were held in the Waldorf Astoria, not in the same suite, but in a smaller, but still well appointed room.

The group sat round a reproduction antique oak table and a new member (perhaps a better description than investigator) produced from his briefcase what appeared to be playing card size photographs, which he placed face down on the table before reaching again into his briefcase, this time producing a rather elegant almost antique magnifying glass which seemed to be out of place in that particular room and the type of meeting being conducted.

"Take your time and use the magnifying glass, when necessary."

The first three pictures probably were taken at the same location, a boardwalk or promenade on the coast, in summer, as those pictured were wearing appropriate clothing. The first two pictures were both discarded but only after Goldburgh had thoroughly perused them.

The two agents looked at each other when Goldburgh, whilst carefully examining the third picture, suddenly reached for the magnifying glass and began such an intimate assessment that his eye was only inches away from the picture.

"That is Natalia, without doubt, but much younger, I can see by the clothes that the photo was taken in about nineteen thirty-seven. Look at the way she holds her hand: I did not realise that it was such a characteristic. I don't know who the other two are, possibly her parents. Where did you obtain the picture?"

Harold gesticulated that Goldburgh continue his perusal of the photographs.

Only two more pictures caught his attention, the latter perhaps included to confound and surprise him. The former was of a high school year group and Goldburgh realised that again Natalia might be identified, unless the picture was an intentional diversion to trick him. He was meticulous and even a tad punctilious in his examination of the document. Doubts clouded his judgement. No one in the picture fulfilled his expectations, except one girl, who was in profile, as if she had not expected the photograph to be taken at that particular moment and had turned to talk to her adjacent fellow student. He wouldn't bet his life or shirt on a positive identification but, there was something familiar, yes, he would take a chance.

With a reticence that exposed his lack of confidence he stated...

"I think that's her again."

Harold's assistant went once more to his briefcase, this time producing a folder that obviously had been frequently used and abused many times over a long period and took out its latest content, a photograph, enlarged to A4 size, which he passed to Goldburgh.

This picture was totally out of place with all the others. He immediately must have seen the subject that was of interest to him and burst out laughing, controlled himself and asked...

"When was this taken?"

The answer was not curt or specific but a single, succinct word only.

"Recently."

Pointing to a seated Red Army officer flanked on either side by two pairs of two other officers, and facing a similar number of other seated men who were unidentifiable as only the rear of their heads could be seen, the picture having been taken both at an elevated height and at an angle.

Goldburgh had never before been as confident as he was at that moment and his voice, though restrained, clearly expressed his assuredness.

"This is, without doubt, my dear friend Kashkarov. Only slightly older than when I last saw him five years ago."

Harold then interrupted him and stated that:

"It was an opportune moment for Goldburgh to recount his experiences once he left the camp, for the final time, along with Kashkarov, up to the time he reached Istanbul."

During the following three and three–quarter hours the two agents sat riveted, listening to his story, though on two occasions they did interrupt him to confirm the sequence of events, for on his own admission he had confused and contradicted himself but the overall impression, looking back, was a tale taken from a boys' adventure book. They confirmed that whilst the parts involving the two smugglers was interesting that it did not further their enquiries but his experiences in Yerevan since it involved N K V D officers was to be pursued.

The following day was to be the final day of his meetings and terminated in a convivial late lunch that only ended as other diners began their dinners. Goldburgh had two questions and intimated that their answers were of great importance and interest to him.

Harold sensed that he might be compromised or that he might not be permitted to directly answer his questions and therefore responded that he would do his best which he believed would cover any eventuality.

"You never made any notes but always appeared to remember everything that I mentioned?"

"A confession (replied Harold): we had two microphones very discreetly positioned about the room, leading to engineers in the next room recording the conversations and every half hour or so, the recording was passed to experienced typists who would transcribe your statements and our discussions. Indeed the day which ended late at about ten p.m. concerned us greatly because we thought our engineers would exhaust their tapes and that was why we tried to end the meeting. "

"The photographs. How did you obtain them or know that Natalia would be of interest to you more than a decade after being photographed and my dear friend Kashkarov, who, as I told you might be dead following our staged fight - where is he now?"

"I do not think that my superior, Mr. Maddox, will chastise me for my honest reply as it was not Natalia that was of interest to us, but her father and mother who, we still believe, acted as a courier for him and incidentally we are not allowed to tell you their real family name as we now know, with absolutely certainty, that the name that was used in San Francisco was an alias. We also have another picture taken outside the Fairmont hotel, a venue that they regularly frequented. As regards your friend, and you must not try to contact him, he is currently based in East Berlin and acts on behalf of the Soviet delegation as one of the four powers governing the City and liaises with the three Western powers.

I think that I have been more than helpful and informative and must stress that absolutely no action be taken to contact your friend."

SIX

Liverpool was covered by an early morning mist and the dampness of autumn as his vessel moored on that September Monday morning. He had spent the entire journey in his cabin suffering, and then recovering, from a stomach infection which had abruptly curtailed his hopes of an epicurean experience in the liner`s superb restaurants and had also deprived him of contact with his fellow passengers and news from the outside world.

For no logical reason he was determined to reach London, without delay, and took a taxi to Lime Street Station where he was buffeted and jostled whilst attempting to weave past the local commuters and he had no time to purchase either the *Liverpool Echo* or *The Manchester Guardian*.

There were three other passengers in the train compartment and he decided to rest for the duration of the journey but was distracted not only by various background noises, the frequent interruptions in the pace of the journey (as, without apparent reason, the train regularly slowed down) but also snippets of conversation between two passengers which utterly interested him. He slowly pierced together the news, ultimately, requesting sight of the *Echo* which one of the two men was avidly reading.

Monday, September 19th 1949

He quickly turned the pages until he reached page 6 and the dramatic headlines: -

The £: Plight of British Tourists:

Gold Shares Jump

Holidaymakers queue in vain at banks

Turn to Consulates for Cash to Pay Hotel Bills.

He looked up and without asking was handed *The Manchester Guardian*.

Monday, September 19th 1949

He again quickly turned the pages until he reached page 5 and the more informative headlines: -

POUND DEVALUED 30 PER CENT

FROM $4.03 to $2.80

NINE COUNTRIES FOLLOW:

BANKS CLOSE TODAY

Price of Bread to Go Up

And glancing across the page he noticed a further headline:

EXTENT OF DEVALUATION THE BIGGEST SURPRISE

The shock slowly dissolved as he suddenly realised that his account in New York was in Dollars and that conversion into Sterling would appreciate the value of his funds. He returned the *Guardian* but accidentally held on to the *Echo*.

His attention was diverted from the important subject of money when the third passenger engaged him in trivial conversation and raised the matter which had originally held his attention and would now be answered by the man opposite.

"Don't you agree the Country is going downhill? This journey, according to the time table should take just under five hours, but with the delays will take over six. It`s claimed that necessary maintenance of the track and the rolling stock is the reason for the delays but all I know is that before the war, in nineteen thirty-eight, the journey was faster and that before the First World War the regular journey was even quicker. I blame the authorities and the poor quality of the coal that they burn!"

He phlegmatically agreed as he was in no mood to either argue or concur with the man's argument.

When he reached London, exhausted by the journey, his first act was to purchase the *Evening News* and absorb the latest news.

London Monday, September 19th 1949

GOLD SHARES BOOM IN THE CITY

THOUSANDS OF BROKERS, JOBBERS, JAM THE STREET MARKETS

COPPER, RUBBER, TIN, OIL RISE

BIG DEVALUATION DEALS

He saw no mention of the price of bread and wondered if the population would now eat gold or copper!

He deliberately settled into a cheap hotel near Kings Cross and the following day telephoned his Russian contact who he met the next afternoon near Speakers Corner, close by Marble Arch. They walked innocuously together down Park Lane, speaking quietly in Russian, and he confirmed that he was prepared to move to the 'North West' and begin to cultivate a connection with Harold Wilson, but it was a question of money. He had just returned from America where he had settled his late parents' financial affairs (implying that he now knew that they were dead). They had bequeathed to him an amount that would scarcely pay for a deposit on a house and he would need an amount to increase his meagre deposit. He had in his hotel room, a copy of the *Liverpool Echo* and he needed (it was at this stage that he inwardly drew his breath, threw caution to the wind and stated emphatically) ...

"Three hundred and ninety five pounds."

He waited optimistically for a response which was not forthcoming and continued (believing that all was lost and that if he was to sink then an additional demand would not alter his fate).

"I need money to live and am not prepared to enter into trade or commerce. After a reasonable time settling in I would wish to teach part time and perhaps write. I could manage on twenty two pounds, ten shillings a month (they had just passed some American tourists and he had inadvertently overheard the wife or girlfriend talking to the much older man and she had mentioned that amount in a different context)."

They shook hands and agreed to meet in two days time when an answer to his request would be resolved. Fortune favours the brave! Or perhaps, as he postulated, the Russians had a great long term interest in the President of the Board of Trade.

At their next meeting his contact announced...

"We will make a payment of only two hundred and sixty five pounds towards the mortgage deposit and a monthly payment of twenty pounds, five shillings, administered by a firm of unimpeachable attorneys based in Zurich, ostensibly monies left by your late parents, however the payments will be in Swiss Francs and will have to be converted by you at a possible loss."

He initially moved to Leigh, in Lancashire, and temporarily secured accommodation in an economically priced hotel which he discovered, with great interest, was frequented by members of the entertainment profession, especially those in repertory theatre and he spent many a pleasant morning listening to their experiences and was able, with great success, to fend off and evade questions about his life.

A local bank was most keen to arrange an account for him once they learned that his income would derive from Switzerland and he was most careful to maintain and continue the account once he moved to Liverpool where he set up an entirely new account with a different bank who were even more keen to act on his behalf when he informed them that his income would derive from a firm of attorneys in New York and would be paid in dollars.

He purchased a beautiful property in the Fresh field area of Liverpool shortly after the nineteen fifty General Election when adequate funds arrived from the United States and with the help of his solicitor he was able to arrange a most advantageous mortgage funded by the Soviet embassy and the Intelligence Community in the United States.

His first act was to join the Huyton Labour party and to volunteer his services to the new M.P., Harold Wilson, though at that time Wilson was surrounded locally by acolytes and sycophants eager to be associated with a famous national figure.

He apologised that he had been unavailable to assist the party in its General Election work but promised to make up for his absence by giving his time to assist setting up the local office (it was a new constituency) and a donation of eight pounds and fifteen shillings worth of stamps was gratefully acknowledged, personally, by the M.P.in a letter from the House of Commons which was the first time that the name Manny Gold was known to Harold James Wilson.

Gold, as he was known both to the local party and to the community at large, but not to his two banks and his solicitor, deliberately did not cultivate his tenuous connection with the local M.P. who was now in opposition, preferring to become appreciated and a recognised valuable worker, indeed like so many voluntary organisations, Gold realised that others were not forthcoming to volunteer their help since they knew that he would always be relied upon to take on the task at hand. His reputation was based on his commitment and hard work, so much so that his associates in the local party and his neighbours never interested themselves in his history and since he deliberately never mentioned his past or his knowledge of Russian that no one ever questioned him.

But this did not unduly concern or worry him for he knew instinctively that inevitably it should draw him closer to Wilson. He was however both assiduous and meticulous communicating information to the Soviet authorities in London, approximately every three or four months visiting the capital where he would pass his notes, normally at the same rendez–vous where he had last met the Soviet representative in Park Lane. He thought that the value of his information was worthless and that a higher grade of information could be found quite legitimately in the political columns of the national newspapers, though peripheral 'gossip' such as the political orientation of the local party management committee appeared to be of great interest. The fact that certain members held Marxist viewpoints or that there was a clique with Trotskyist tendencies actually drew a response at a subsequent meeting. Each report was carbon copied, the carbon being destroyed and the copy delivered to an associate of his handler 'Hal' before his return to what he was fast perceiving as the boredom, greyness and banality of Liverpool.

It was only in nineteen fifty-six with the 'Suez' catastrophe and the unsuccessful uprising in Hungary that he recognised locally a deepening cynicism both about the nature of Communism and of the

Socialist view of the Soviet Union. In a meeting in either March or April nineteen fifty-seven he was surprised that his new handler was excessively interested in the opinions of the management committee concerning the ideological nature of Marxism and the Soviet Union's attitude to its satellites. Furthermore, for the first time, he was actually asked to further his connection with the M.P., initially to ascertain his private opinion of the Soviet Union and not the public posture that would not antagonise the party's different wings.

It was about this time that he decided to contact his old friend in Russia, despite the warning nearly seven and a half years before, which he now thought was obsolete. He reasoned that there could be unfortunate consequences both for him and his dear friend and he therefore judged, deviously, that he should write anonymously to the address in Moscow that had been given to him when they jointly left the camp and to give and use a Post Box address that was not in London or Liverpool. His first letter was sent in February nineteen fifty–eight from Brighton which meant that he would have to make a special return journey each time to collect any response. In his letter, he adroitly and obliquely referred to Kashkarov's bravery at Kursk and in the vaguest of terms to the injuries 'suffered in the most unusual circumstances' and hoped that 'he understood that his sacrifice had not been in vain'.

In July nineteen fifty-eight, on his next journey to London, he took the opportunity to visit Brighton, in the hope that a reply was forthcoming, but no reply had been received and he sent a further and final letter. In April nineteen fifty–nine he repeated his visit, again without success, and it was only in May nineteen–sixty on what he thought would be his last visit that he retrieved a reply from Kiev.

It was clear that Kashkarov recognised the true identity of the sender of the second letter - but he made no reference to the original correspondence - and that he appreciated his caution. Interest in his war time exploits was noted, but there many more of his comrades whose bravery would be of greater interest to him, however if he was interested, then a meeting could be arranged in Finland. He awaited a reply.

A prompt, urgent acknowledgement was sent specifying a town and a hotel in Finland, close to the border and a period towards the end of September that would give both parties adequate opportunity to make arrangements.

Their reunion was not dramatic, but emotional. 'Gold' had prepared himself for a stay of some twelve days but his friend arrived on the third. Age and time had hewn their superficial appearances but in each other's eyes time had stood still. They agreed to speak in English and quietly for the unspoken word was that the eyes and ears of Moscow extended far beyond its borders. No mention was made during their first meeting and subsequent encounters of Goldburgh's knowledge that Kashkarov had been based in Berlin in nineteen forty-nine or more importantly how he could live an existence without employment but since his friend could only understand the communist theory and practice of labour it was a matter that was soon forgotten. His dearest friend never alluded to or mentioned the currency that his friend had 'stolen', being excited and spellbound by the partially fabricated tale (mainly consistent with the story that he had repeatedly told the British authorities other than the amount and use of his American dollars) of Goldburgh's escape and journey to Istanbul, using the American dollars to bribe the N K V D in Yerevan and to pay the smugglers.

Kashkarov had escaped censure for his failure to deliver his companion to the headquarters of the security service in Moscow (even now he was not certain as to their intentions about his friend) and by the time he had recovered his health following his shooting injuries, Berlin had been captured and he understood that the authorities were more concerned to impose their political will and to destroy any democratic or socialist opposition to their plans.

Natalia had disappeared from both their lives (Goldburgh said, of course, nothing) and Kashkarov had climbed the ladder of the army hierarchy such that could legally leave the Soviet Union subject to stringent conditions, but he always had to be cautious. Their friendship was sealed when he announced, with great pride, that his son had been named deliberately with the Russian version of Mandel and his daughter after Natalia, who he knew they would both wish well and that sometimes he wondered, but kept his thoughts to himself, whatever happened to the camp or its inmates to which, in reply, Goldburgh commented that he shared his interest but wanted to look to the future and not back to the past.

They agreed to meet again, in Turku the following spring, possibly with his wife and two children but since he now held a senior position (and he told his friend that he could trust him absolutely with his news) responsible for the allocation of tactical nuclear weapons to certain highly trained branches of the army artillery division, that he had a far better standard of life, but if Goldburgh met his wife, no mention should be made of his responsibilities.

SEVEN

The Boeing 707 military transport arrived at Andrews Air Force Base and safely delivered its valuable cargo of the United States ambassador to the Court of St. James, David Bruce, who had urgently been summoned to Washington by his President and instructed to hide his absence from London by every means possible. Thus, the news and subsequent official statement that he was suffering from an unspecified infection which would incapacitate him for a few days was accepted, without investigation, especially as his doctor visited twice daily at his official residence in Regents Park to give substance to the illusion.

Every precaution had also been taken to transfer him from the embassy unobserved, to a military air force base therefore avoiding London Heathrow Airport and this meticulous attention to detail was continued when transferring him to the White House and entry through a rear service access.

He kept an open mind as to the reasons for his summons but anticipated, as a dedicated Anglophile, that he was to be notified of bad news to be presented to the British Government.

The Oval Office was dominated by the President, Lyndon Johnson, sitting behind his impressive desk and as Bruce walked up to him, the Commander in Chief rose, and to his visitor's surprise, placed his arms around him in a gesture of filial friendship. He observed that the President had lost weight (a good thing but whilst his face was gaunt it had a healthy glow) and he made a snap decision not to mention his observation, lest it might cause distress or offence.

Seated around the room were Bob McNamara, Bobby Kennedy and two men that Bruce had known for some years, John McCone, head of the Central Intelligence Agency and – he couldn`t believe his presence-an old family friend and intelligence agent.

The President perceptively noted Bruce`s surprise and commented that:

"He was unaware that he knew Mr. Lennox."

The ambassador responded with a half truth delivered with the sincerity and confirmation of one who was prepared and able to hide the whole truth behind a facade of apparent integrity:

"Our families had similar roots in Virginia but our paths first officially crossed when as members of the O.S.S. we had intelligence duties in liberated France."

Unspoken was that in the privacy of their homes, the two Davids could use Lennox's real family name, not even known to the President and that Bruce could, without disrespect, be addressed by his wartime title of Colonel.

The formalities completed, Johnson immediately commenced an anti British and especially anti Wilson tirade. There is no benefit capturing in this work his Texan accent, but more importantly to report, if not verbatim, the thrust of his opinions and demands.

Crucial to Johnson was the fact that in six months' time he was to face the electorate on the first Thursday in November for re election as President, a post that he had inherited on the death of his predecessor and not by election.

The euphoria of the American people following the massive and successful nuclear strike against the 'commie bastards' [sic], which had substantially put back their military expansion and capabilities, was still noticeable both in the visual displays of patriotism but more importantly in the latest opinion polls, but the 'fucking shits' [sic and apparently said with much venom] were using captured American troops as hostages at tactical and strategic locations to deter further use of nuclear weapons against them.

Although the Republicans had yet to confirm their candidate, Johnson's political advisors had warned him that the repatriation of U.S. troops and civilians could form an important arena of debate in the forthcoming campaign and could lose him the election. Not only that, secret reports via the Red Cross in Sweden, had given what was an horrendous and frightening summary of the appalling condition of those troops who had been the victims of nerve gases.

In the six months since the outbreak of hostilities and the wanton, indiscriminate use of a variety and cocktail of chemical and nerve agents, those who had survived were succumbing, following inadequate medical attention, to a callous disregard for their condition and more importantly to the fact that they were deemed pawns in a global exchange of retribution and deliberate procrastination.

That procrastination was believed intentional when the President cited the latest and most secret intelligence provided by the C.I.A.(most likely by the continuing and ever increasingly dangerous 'U2' reconnaissance flights) and evidence that Mr. Lennox had recently obtained by his own endeavours and sources that he kept secret even from his own superior, but since his reputation was historically based on the most dramatic and unexpected information then it was deemed accurate especially since it fitted into a logical and sensible progression of military technology.

The Soviet Union had made a massive effort to accelerate its development of Intercontinental Ballistic Missiles and their deployment was imminent. That their accuracy was in doubt was now immaterial, the frightening possibility that U.S. cities could be targeted would cause such a political backlash that the Democrats could be ejected from power.

What happened next is shrouded in contradiction and disinformation. What is certain is that Johnson became not only hysterical and apoplectic in his condemnation of the British and especially their Prime Minister but almost contemptuous in his analysis of the power and influence of the United Kingdom.

David Bruce realised that if a special relationship had existed, it had now been consigned to history.

The foundation of Johnson`s assessment was that British Intelligence had been duped and should have taken a more cynical and less sanguine approach and certainly recommended a more cautious response, the immediate consequence being not only a military and political disaster in Europe but a body blow to the confidence of the American ground forces.

Wilson was a coward and a liar. The language and invectives used cannot be repeated. What Johnson had conveniently forgotten and with the effluxion of time, was that he had personally instructed his Intelligence Services to break off contact and had the association been in operation then Wilson would have been aware of the new' Monroe Doctrine' and would not have essentially 'caved in 'to the Soviet`s demands and withdrawn the 'V Bomber' force. And to quote in this particular instance, verbatim, a remark which was noted contemporaneously by 'Mr. Lennox' that:

"Then this trumped up former civil servant had the balls to claim to his allies and the British people that their' V Bomber' force had been part of the assault on the Russians, inflicting much damage."

45

Johnson had clearly been in discussion with a spectrum of advisors who were objective in their analysis which converged into a realistic and pragmatic interpretation of the *REAL* relationship between the two nations, indeed Bruce noted that the President referred to a briefing paper and he was able to read, upside down, an analyst's observation that had been circled in red ink clearly noting the phrase...

"Monumental ineptitude."

The 'Polaris' agreement was dead and buried though the United States was prepared to take over existing or planned naval bases on the coast of Great Britain to service their expanding fleet.

In the short to medium term the use of bases in Great Britain for their B52 bomber fleet was to be expanded and could be later used for mobile launchers and hardened missile silos.

The United States would effectively take over the defence of the British Isles creating (as they would use Japan) a super, unsinkable floating 'aircraft carrier' crucially a first line of defence for the North American continent.

With a frightening echo of Hitler, nearly a quarter of a century before, Britain could retain its political independence, Empire, Commonwealth and currency (the 'Sterling Area') but would have to pay for its defence.

Johnson then stated that he intended to ask his friends on 'Wall Street' to *screw* the British and just as in September nineteen forty- nine when the Attlee government (including the President of the Board of Trade, one Harold Wilson and his Chancellor, Sir Stafford Cripps), had been forced to devalue the pound then he intended again, without qualms, to squeeze the British government and its economy.

Diplomacy, loyalty and respect for his President's wishes were put aside as Bruce tried to propose a more rational and conciliatory position directly asking him what olive branch or act the British could perform to resolve this colossal breakdown in their relationship.

McNamara then intervened, suggesting that the only option, in his opinion, was to repatriate their bombers together with their weapons and be prepared, whatever the consequences, to join with their allies in a planned second strike that would also destroy what was left of the Soviet naval capability in the Far East leaving America unchallenged in the Pacific and able to exploit the two super 'aircraft carriers' of Japan and Formosa. Sensing he had caught the President's ear he then continued, almost patriotically to state that:

"There would not be another 'Pearl Harbour'"

And then finished by stating that their B52 bomber force had now, by replacement, cannibalisation and repairs, reached three hundred and thirteen D to H class operable variants and that Herman Kahn's strategic plan that the Soviet cities (West of the Urals) were to become hostages, after an additional 'European' second strike which would again exhaust the Soviet's defensive capabilities, could further allow the destruction of their embryonic missile system and..

"Whatever we can vaporize."

It was at this stage that most unexpectedly 'Mr. Lennox', having allowed McNamara to outline the proposed military action, then announced that within the previous twenty four hours he had obtained through what he described as ...

"The most reliable source that he had ever used, preliminary details of the deployment of the first production line of Intercontinental Ballistic Missiles which could be verified and that (turning to his superior and C.I.A. chief McCone), he had obtained the first definitive photograph of Markus Wolf."

And he proceeded to hand a picture to McCone and a sheaf of papers to McNamara.

The photograph showed clearly and sharply a man in his forties, exiting from a car, his face slightly turned away from the direction of the camera but still fully visible and the sheaf of papers were in Cyrillic including two maps both of an area around the North Pacific rim.

It was at this moment that Johnson, having allowed the discussion to promote the British cause, intervened and made an offer that was both constructive and offered a compromise.

"Only a fool won't change his mind. We cannot afford to delay a second strike for fear of discovery or if Khrushchev launches his existing medium range missiles against our military facilities in Southern Europe. I will give Wilson twenty one days to ready his bombers for a joint second strike. If he fails then Wall Street will begin to tie a noose around his neck."

"David Lennox" then threw the meeting into confusion when he caught the eye of the President and announced that:

"It is not Khrushchev you will have to deal with but Leonid Brezhnev. Khrushchev fell in December when his first strike bomber assault was shot out of the sky and even before our first counter-strike had penetrated Soviet territory, the Politburo summarily deposed him in favour of Brezhnev who had been plotting his predecessor's fall from power for some time. Khrushchev is now just a figure head and a broken man. The Politburo are using him as the focus of the military's dissatisfaction until the autumn when he will be retired either on health grounds or in disgrace."

That evening the two Davids were able to enjoy a rare private dinner and Bruce learned that the ethereal and almost legendary Joel Ben Yitzhak had been the source of his friend's contributions to the meeting.

"The Jew, Ben Yitzhak, trades knowledge but never for gold or financial reward but for materials that can vary, dependant on the circumstances, this time it was supplies of the most latest medicines for what is left of the decimated homeland of the Hebrews."

EIGHT

David Bruce could offer the British Prime Minister a life line to save him and the British people from the consequences of political ostracism and subsequent economic collapse; the price was low and required a commitment and the ability to provide a credible and operative bomber strike force.

Wilson's prescience and foresight both (following intelligence) inviting the ambassador to a very private and intimate dinner and more importantly giving instructions to make ready the 'V' force could yet turn disaster into even a pyrrhic triumph.

But Wilson was soon to harvest both the cost of his mistake and haste when he succumbed to the threat of Soviet aggression.

The fleet of approximately ninety planes was scattered, with varying degrees of damage, but mainly to their undercarriages (caused by landing on runways which were both unable to bear their weight and which were too short), across a number of South African military aerodromes and in the absence of satisfactory servicing - and necessary repairs - were deteriorating rapidly. Furthermore some bombers were damaged, beyond repair, and lay, liked beached whales, on the edges of the runways.

A bird's eye view or more interestingly from an orbiting United States spy satellite or U 2 reconnaissance flight would observe the almost random pattern of parked V bombers, both the four jet Mark Two Victors and Vulcans, some Mark One Victors converted to a refuelling role and a few Mark One Vulcans that were now in reserve. The greyness of the scrubland vividly contrasted with their metallic shells which glistened in the hot sun and that simple comparison conveyed the enormity of the lack of planning and foresight.

In summary, the prime and overwhelming consideration of the British Prime Minister had been national survival and then to secure the delivery system and their thermonuclear and nuclear weapons. Little thought had been given, not only to the continuous 'up keep 'of the devices but also maintenance of the planes.

The warm dry air, combined with the relentless sun had effected the delicate technology of the bombs, temporarily emasculating them whilst the planes themselves starved of maintenance crews had deteriorated and needed major overhauls which logically required trained engineers and time, time that the British government did not have.

As a man, Wilson did not impress the ambassador, indeed Bruce maintained the minimum of contact with him necessary for the conduct of relations between the two nations, despite being an avowed Anglophile. 'Lennox', with the approval of the head of the C.I.A., had briefed his friend that the British embassy might have already warned Wilson of Johnson's displeasure but were unsure what action he had authorised concerning the bomber fleet. Bruce, in uncharacteristic desperation, even considered communicating, behind the back of Wilson, the situation with the now in disgrace officials Sir Hugh Stephenson and Sir Kenneth Strong, but they were now, if only temporarily, emasculated of power or even influence.

Wilson greeted the ambassador with those contradictory, superficial attitudes of fawning obsequiousness and overconfidence that had repelled Bruce in the past. In the privacy of his private apartment and in the absence of prying eyes he felt confident enough to light up a Dominican cigar, being courteous to offer the ambassador the same, pointing out, almost diplomatically, that they were not Cuban.

"The meal would soon be ready, your favourite: Scotch Beef, hung for twenty–one days and medium to well done."

Bruce could detect that Wilson's overconfidence was undoubtedly based on his intelligence of Washington's posture and he was surprised when Wilson, without further preamble, threw into the meeting the dramatic statement, which was untrue that:

"On the advice of his military planners, he had authorised the temporary withdrawal of the' V Bomber' fleet but repatriation could be organised within days and the fleet made available in partnership with their American allies."

Bruce spontaneously decided that it would not, at that moment, be necessary for him to deliver his President's ultimatum and the threat of economic blackmail if Wilson could fulfil his promise and suggested that the matter be pursued over dinner. Wilson's cigar extinguished, they entered the humble inner sanctum of the P.M's. private apartment to enjoy a private and intimate dinner.

It was during the meal, after the host had disclosed that he intended to go to the nation in October for a mandate and election of a Labour majority, that his guest, in the most tactful way that he could express himself, summarised what was required of the British government:

"You have no more than twenty one days to make ready your complete' V' force, fully armed, for possible use in partnership with the Strategic Air Command. I understand that globally every available base will be at your disposal together with refuelling facilities."

Wilson, his confidence inflated by the knowledge that he had already given instructions for the return of the grounded armada, and his ego and arrogance projecting like a peacock 's plumage confirmed that:

"In days, the Grand Alliance will be ready to deliver a hammer blow against the forces of despotism."

NINE

Around the same time, Nikita Khrushchev could be found at his dacha sitting in his favourite wicker chair, alone on the veranda, looking North West towards Moscow, wearing his panama and in the early evening, his old grey trench coat. Summer was imminent and the well maintained lawns, newly mown, scented the gardens as the apple and cherry trees began to grow their fruits. In the not too far distance the forest which encircled the estate was also coming into season having shrugged off the winter mantle of snow.

Superficially nothing had changed, the elite guard of K G B troops marched around the dacha with the accuracy and exact regularity of a metronome, an officer meticulously saluting the First Secretary on each revolution and discreetly hidden, security officers to protect their titular leader for this was a man whose power and authority existed in title only.

He was, in reality, a prisoner unable to leave the estate and subject to the whim of the Presidium that he had so recently commanded. Whilst his wife dutifully carried out her household responsibilities and still, with the sincere appreciation of the soldiers that guarded her husband, provided hospitality for them, her husband secretly, persistently and obsessively still pursued his thoughts, wondering how his foe had been able to determine the location and purpose of his country home and how his beloved grandchildren and his wife Nina had been made pawns. Such was his obsession that after nearly six months there still lay, in an old cookery book that had belonged to his treasured first wife, the draft of his political statement cut vertically into three sections.

No longer did he receive the twice weekly intelligence report, indeed he received no information or interest from his erstwhile associates in the Kremlin. The only information that he gleaned was from the pages of *Izvestia* and *Pravda* which he knew to be false for they not only extolled his role in the rebuilding of the nation but published falsified and doctored photographs of him and some including his wife.

Visitors were permitted, but obviously very carefully lectured as to their behaviour and matters that were permissible to discuss. Therefore, one of the few allowed to visit him was his old mentor and Stalin loyalist, Lazar Kaganovich, and their time like for so many old men, was spent reminiscing.

Those who now ruled the Soviet Union were following a policy hastily conceived with absolute ruthlessness and single mindedness which had begun with the assassination of the American President.

The Soviet people, living in a 'closed' society, had been told that their arch enemy, the United States, without a declaration of war, together with their allies, N A T O, had first attacked their Warsaw Treaty allies vindictively using chemical and nerve agents, initially penetrating to the borders of Poland but the brave soldiers of the Warsaw Treaty, supported by the workers, had rallied and pushed back the invaders who had suffered catastrophic losses (both in men and materiel) and that the supremacy of Socialism and the brotherhood of the workers against the Capitalist Oppressors had finally been proved. Then, again without warning, the Americans had launched an insane and reckless assault using bombers to deliver nuclear devices, most of which had been destroyed by Soviet fighter pilots and the outstanding superior quality of their planes.

Only the threat of a devastating retaliatory strike that would effectively immolate the United States in a conflagration of unimaginable horror had forced their enemy to withdraw and agree, with great humility, to pay reparations. But great damage had been done and the Presidium asked the people, once again, to sacrifice themselves for the beloved Motherland.

The falsification of history was substantiated by selective and 'doctored' film and journalistic reviews of the great victory whilst prominence was given to Khrushchev's leadership during the early part of the titanic struggle, the massive strain put on his health and then, with ever increasing prominence, the later role played by Leonid Brezhnev.

The truth was that the Soviet leadership was using delaying tactics in their negotiations with the United States, who were utilising the Swedish government in Stockholm as intermediaries to compel the Presidium to fulfil the conditions of the oral agreement that McNamara had imposed upon them.

The punitive and draconian terms had been accepted to avoid further crippling damage and whilst Brezhnev and his fellow members had never any real intention of carrying out their side of the 'bargain' and effectively to renege on the agreement, it was a hazardous course to follow, which COULD result in the resumption of military action.

The anger of the United States hierarchy (symbolised by McNamara supported by Kahn), which had been for some time both rudderless and leaderless in the vacuum of ultimate authority, led to conflict as to the course of action to be pursued, combined with delays created by the cumbersome involvement and representation of the Swedish government. The American people were starting to become disillusioned for they were beginning to learn that Warsaw Pact forces had not returned to their former borders, that Europe was still occupied, that APPARENTLY the repatriation of their military forces had stalled and above all no information was forthcoming about the whereabouts and repatriation of their families, friends and business colleagues.

A Presidential Election was only six months away and cynically their own government had suppressed information that captured civilians and troops were not only prominently held at key tactical and strategic targets but their presence was clearly made known to both the Swiss Red Cross and representatives of the Swedish government.

With callous indifference and also in deliberate contravention of the promise made by Brezhnev, allied troops injured by the chemical and nerve agents were allowed to suffer, being given the absolute minimum of medical attention and drugs, justified by the spurious and dishonest reason that their major pharmaceutical factories had been obliterated in the vindictive American bomber attack.

However the prime reason for the Soviet's campaign of delay was to continue producing, installing and arming their first generation of Intercontinental Ballistic Missiles which would instantaneously nullify and neutralise the Americans' overwhelming superiority in bombers. Only then would Brezhnev begin what was for him meaningful negotiations which would include the permanent annexation of the occupied countries and he decided with some flexibility that the maximum advantage would be gained shortly before the American Presidential Election when Johnson would cede the most to gain a pyrrhic victory but would allow him to claim a victorious resolution of the conflict and in consequence the support of the voters.

The Limited Test Ban Treaty had been signed in Moscow by the foreign ministers of the United States, Soviet Union and Great Britain on August fifth nineteen sixty-three and entered into force on October tenth of the same year. The signatories to the Treaty pledged not to carry out any nuclear explosions in the atmosphere, in space, or under water and not to conduct underground tests that might [leak and] cause the spread of radioactive debris outside the territorial limits of the states party to the treaty.

Whether or not the Khrushchev regime intended to honour the treaty will never be known but since the Geneva Convention was flouted by the use of chemical and nerve agents indicates a degree of cynicism and bad faith.

On March fifteen, nineteen sixty-four at ten fifty-nine and fifty-eight seconds local time, the Soviet Union legitimately, to test weapon effects, exploded a subterranean nuclear device at their testing centre at Semipalatinsk and on May sixteenth, a weapons development test was carried out at fifty -eight seconds past nine a.m. local time, again at Semipalatinsk. Subterranean testing at the Novaya Zemlya range was scheduled to begin in mid-September.

TEN

Gold and Kashkarov met in the spring of nineteen sixty-one in the Finnish city of Turku but to the disappointment of Manny Gold his friend was unable or unwilling to bring with his family. Gold had little new news for his friend who was most effervescent and informative. He had received a major interim promotion, an acknowledgement of his expertise and abilities, and he hoped to bring along his family to meet his old and dear friend when they next met, but details of his old duties and now his promotion to an elite planning department should remain a secret as was the possibility of a further promotion to the Defence Council where, in his own words...

"He was being groomed to act as a special advisor to no less than the Minister of Defence."

And he possibly had news of Natalia!

"There was a rumour, highly speculative and at best vague that she- "

He visibly stopped himself and neither of them mentioned her again.

In the few days they had together they went for long walks, initially in the city, the shops abundantly filled with goods that were not available in Moscow and in any event Kashkarov could not afford to purchase them, so that his gratitude was unbounded when, without a second thought, Gold asked if he could pay for a pile of presents for his friend to take home, though Kashkarov admitted his concern that their importation to the Soviet Union might be difficult.

It was on the fourth and final day of their reunion, as they strolled in a local wood, that Gold confessed the real reason paying for the presents was prompted by a sense of guilt and he explained that his previous story, when they first met, was partially untrue, and then he told his friend about the diamonds, but had difficulty explaining the economics of the windfall when he returned to London and the devaluation of the Pound. Kashkarov then asked his friend for a favour and help though he was under no obligation whatsoever and it was a matter completely outside of his knowledge...

"His specific role was to plan a variety of defensive options and counter strikes to an American assault against their Warsaw Treaty partners and against the Motherland which he knew the Presidium feared, especially since the young, new American President was untested and they had to be prepared for any unexpected action that he might foolishly take. His expertise in tank warfare and tactics foundered because they calculated that the Americans, either in desperation or ruthlessness would introduce battlefield tactical nuclear weapons as a preliminary to an escalation to more powerful nuclear weapons.

He wanted a fresh, independent and novel viewpoint on battlefield tactics and political supervision looked at from either side however unusual, and could his friend research such a scenario. Could they meet later that summer for a joint holiday and perhaps he could bring some information?"

On Gold`s return to Liverpool he mulled over the dilemma that confronted him. He knew nothing of military tactics or where to seek such information, however their meetings had provided him with an abundance of intelligence that Maddox might appreciate, though he had contravened a specific request not to communicate with his friend. He had to balance loyalty to his friend who had helped, with almost mortal danger to himself, to gain him his freedom, against his loyalty to the United States and its representative, Mr. Maddox. However Gold (or Goldburgh) had already begun a journey corrupted by financial greed and his moral obligation towards his friend was overwhelmed by his desire for financial reward and security.

On his next visit to London he contacted Harold in the prescribed manner and a meeting was arranged, this time at a down at heel cafe in Clerkenwell, where Gold first confirmed that he had not been in recent contact with his connection at the Soviet embassy for he had no news to impart and in response he was advised by his American handler to make contact if only to show them his continued commitment.

With the discretion and self control of both a well trained agent and of a poker player dealt an extraordinary hand he listened unemotionally to Gold`s story and above all details of Kashkarov`s career and his hopes for a further promotion. This was the first time he had heard of the secret Defence Council and personally was fascinated to learn of the Presidium`s opinion of his new President and above all their concern and fear of possible American military action.

Within forty eight hours of Maddox receiving what he assumed to be another bland, unexciting, litany of trivia he summonsed his agent back to Langley, Virginia, and advised him that Kashkarov`s future possible access to the highest echelons of power had to be cultivated and that if necessary, if possible, Goldburgh (or whatever name he gave himself) should meet his old friend as soon as possible, however the greatest caution should be observed, lest his 'handler' in the Soviet embassy based in London became aware of his visit and that his superiors in Moscow found out about his revived friendship and fatally, his ultimate loyalty to the C.I.A.

Unilaterally and without reference to the head of the C.I.A., Maddox arranged for the preparation of various military scenarios but more importantly that Gold or Goldburgh (he was unable to understand Goldburgh`s desire to Anglicise his name) could be tutored in military tactics and science being given a list of manuals and books to read and absorb so that in the event of him being questioned he could cautiously air his acquired knowledge and coincidentally, as a sign of Maddox`s appreciation ,his monthly salary was substantially increased and he was instructed, if possible, to raise his profile and relationship with Harold Wilson.

It was arranged by Gold that he and Kashkarov (together with his family) would meet in July of nineteen sixty-one again in Finland but this time in the town of Porvoo, on the Gulf of Finland, North East of the capital City Helsinki and Gold, on his arrival, as a sign of friendship, purchased gifts for the two children, prudently spending amounts that he thought compatible with his friend`s likely salary since any excessive spending might be noticed, with potential repercussions. He even purchased locally a Leica camera which he intended to give to his friend, once, on the specific instructions of his handler, 'Hal', he had taken photographs of Kashkarov and also his family, retaining the roll of film, not realising that the developed pictures would be compared to the sketches penned a dozen years before and the photograph taken of him exiting a vehicle.

Gold had with him a personally typed report that he had copied from a document supplied by his handler and in which he had made a number of deliberate typing mistakes to give the document added authenticity.

It was his intention to thank his friend for the opportunity to assist in his work which had surprisingly given him a new interest and with the cooperation and assistance of the main library in Liverpool he had read a number of diverse books on military history, weaponry and battle field tactics and intended to visit the British Library to expand his knowledge of the subject.

The report also contained 'HIS 'observations and comments summarising his thoughts and he asserted that surprise and ruthless unremitting action when the enemy least expected such a move was as potentially successful as an overwhelming force of arms whose preparation, if discovered, would forewarn their enemy.

He finished his brief paper with a cryptic and unusual request if...

"He had any qualms about violating the terms and moral conditions of the Geneva Convention?"

But propitious fate intervened. He was not unusually concerned when his friend did not arrive on the agreed date, but after a further three days Gold began to be worried, however on the following day he unexpectedly received a letter postmarked Helsinki and franked two days earlier, cancelling the meeting, without excuse or explanation and requesting a new rendez–vous on September seventeenth in the town of Pyhasalmi near the coastal city of Oulu.

The delay had an unexpected benefit, for on his return to London and a meeting with his handler, and by then they were on first name terms, Hal informed him that by the beginning of September and certainly before his departure he would have available a more up to date and comprehensive report to hand to his friend which yet again he should copy, inserting some deliberate errors, and in the meantime he was recommended to read certain specified military material.

Kashkarov's wife was, in Gold's opinion, sweet, domesticated and pleasant but had no fire or personality that would cause him to be interested in her company which was convenient, as she played with her son and daughter whose enjoyment of the gifts that he had previously purchased, greatly enhanced his standing with the children. Their mother was clearly and obviously inexperienced in the luxurious pleasures of life for on the first night, he entertained the family to dinner, at what would be described as a 'family 'restaurant and embarrassingly after each course, she promptly and efficiently cleared up the plates, leaving the confused waitress the job of only taking them away.

Gold did not expect such an excited response to his poorly typed report and suggestions that had been composed, not in the dry analytical terms of many of the books that he had recently read, but as a personal opinion drawn from common sense and historical experience.

Kashkarov could not conceal his almost childlike excitement and shock at the plan which he realised was a composite of previously simulated strategies. He read out what were to him the highlights and Gold responded with his comments:

"Inform your enemy that you intend carrying out major defensive manoeuvres and invite their observers to witness the build up and even the war games themselves."

Gold continued and explained that a furtive and secret build up might be identified and correctly interpreted as the prelude to an attack.

"Previously prepare secret supply dumps of munitions that could be quickly brought to the front."

Gold also suggested that the observers could even be shown some of these dumps whose use would be explained as to create a more realistic battlefield experience for some of the more inexperienced troops.

"Destabilise the enemy by assassinating their political leadership and shock your own forces with the news that the enemy had launched a pre emptive first strike somewhere so far away that verification would be impossible."

Because the whereabouts of the Western leaders was generally well known and foolishly publicised, with planning and good fortune they could be murdered either in a plane 'accident' or by the use of an exotic rare poison which could not be identified.

"Utilise civilian light aircraft normally used for agricultural purposes to broadcast chemical and nerve agents to cause panic and chaos amongst their opponents."

Gold stressed that use of these weapons of terror should only be on their enemies' territory and if the operation was led by their allies, the Warsaw Treaty States, then the task should be delegated to their Polish' friends' sarcastically referring to the Poles' defeat of the Red Army in nineteen twenty.

Kashkarov clutched the brief document with the fervour of a man possessed with some absolute truth. His appreciation was almost limitless as his friend, concealing its true origins and his passive contribution, insisted that he build on *HIS* basic plan but more importantly they temporarily set aside matters of duty and plan a joint holiday...

"If possible I would like to join you in the land of my birth and the home of my parents, visit Moscow and jointly travel to the holiday centre of Sochi."

It was quickly agreed that they would meet in Moscow late in September or early October the following year but they both recognised that communication might be difficult and Kashkarov hinted in the strongest terms that he understood that mail to the 'West' was intercepted, read and might be misinterpreted. They therefore contrived to write to each other using their hotel to forward on each other's letters, Gold easing the inconvenience to the obliging manager with four five pound notes. Telephone numbers and addresses were confirmed by the three parties, Gold, Kashkarov and the manager.

Gold handed his friend the Leica camera as a parting gift but asked, whilst inserting a new roll of film, if he could take a number of different 'shots' of them all and of him and his family and of him by himself and when the photography had been completed Gold took out the partially used roll. He stayed on in the town for long enough to have the film developed and to write a letter which he posted from the airport in Helsinki giving his address as the hotel, not expecting to receive a reply.

ELEVEN

The post, that early February morning in nineteen sixty-two, comprised an invitation from the local Labour party to meet their M.P.(cost two shillings and six pence) including fish and chips, a letter from the British Library confirming that he was entitled to an admission card which could be issued on production of evidence of identity (and they suggested, for example, his passport), confirmation from the main library in Liverpool that the novel Random Harvest(incidentally partially based in the City) was ready for collection and a hand written brown envelope in an unusual script which he perused meticulously noting a foreign stamp which on closer inspection was identified as Finnish.

He inquisitively opened the envelope to find inside a further letter addressed to him, care of the hotel where he had previously stayed, with a Russian stamp and he realised that his friend had been able to contact him. He excitedly opened the second envelope to find a poorly typed letter from Lazar Kaganovich who he had never expected to reply to his speculative earlier correspondence.

Moscow, January 20th 1962

My dearest Mandel,

With surprise and great pleasure I received your letter and photographs (including a full face portrait) only last week. You look so much like your father and there is also a hint of your beloved mother. I had always hoped that their tragic murder in France by that evil beast Barbie might still be avenged. As you may know the Soviet Union has changed so much and not only am I no longer a member of the Politburo (it is currently called the Presidium) but also of the Party and I am unable to exercise the power and influence that I previously held. But my protégé, Nikita, is the First Secretary and the deputy head of the K.G.B. (it was the year after Stalin's death and the barbaric murder of Lavrenti [Beria] that the title was changed from the N K V D) and he is still grateful for the support I gave him and through him I may be able to help you.

Last October, with very little notice, like Capitalist landlords, I was evicted from my apartment where I had lived since I became a member of the Politburo in July nineteen thirty and it was only, following my plea, that Nikita arranged to have me re-housed in a smaller but more modern apartment which is very [sic] warmer during these bitter winter months. The new tenant in my old home is that swine Viktor Grishin but I will not spend any more time upsetting myself about this cock sucking sycophant whose supreme ability is to toady up to those who control the organs and levers of power and influence. I suspect that his malevolence deliberately delayed your letter being forwarded.

I will write to you again if I have been able to make arrangements for your visit.

Please promise me that if you come to Moscow that you will not only stay here, in the apartment, even though it will be cramped, but that you will keep me company for it is very lonely being an old man and my former colleagues shun me because I have never recanted my principals and to my last breath I am a Stalinist. Others may have changed their values and opinions but I saw, first hand, how he dragged the nation from being an agrarian backwater to an industrial giant. Yes, a few thousands suffered, but what about the failures of Hoover and Roosevelt? The poverty and humiliation of the proletariat in the United States was a crime against civilisation and it took a great American, Steinbeck to tell the truth.

I can show you where your parents first made their home together and possibly the bar where they first met which was a hot bed of intrigue in those pre revolutionary days. I do look forward to your company and perhaps you could bring some strong expensive coffee which, because of my humble status, I am unable to obtain?

Your beloved "uncle" Lazar

Moscow, April 7th, 1962

Dear Manny,

It took only twelve days from when you posted your letter in Liverpool, to reach me via your friends in Finland! It took, even by special courier, three days for the letter from the Boss to reach the local N K V D head, instructing him to issue the deportation order for that shit bastard and criminal Trotsky whose final act, as he left the Motherland that he had defiled, was to threaten that he and the elusive Hebrew, Joel Ben Yitzhak would have their revenge. They were empty words and febrile threats especially as the Yid had double crossed the atheist!

My family accuses me of living in the past but we achieved so much and I do not think it wrong to remember what the Party gave to the nation.

I have little news for you but can you explain why you wish to be known as Manny Gold and to consequently deny your heritage and the patronym of you father and his small contribution to the Party?

I managed to secure an appointment with one of my few remaining friends in the Presidium and he was most attentive and friendly but there was no reciprocation for the help that I had given him in the past. Believe me, it is when you no longer possess something that you realise and appreciate its worth. My only hope is First Secretary Nikita Khrushchev. Even though we are diametrically opposed over the interpretation of Marxist -Leninism there still is a friendship and when we meet (every three months or so), whilst he does not confide in me, he speaks freely, openly and I suspect solicits my opinion.

Spring is coming and I do hope that we can meet again. Please remember the coffee.

Your dear family friend

Lazar

Moscow, May 26th, 1962

Dear Manny,

Some good news. But first let me tell you that two days ago I went for a long walk from my apartment that is cool and pleasant in this period before the heat of summer and much, much more manageable than the old place which was literally archaic and a relic from the days of Tsar Nicholas the Second.

Grishin, the shit, is welcome to freeze in winter! Anyhow, my walk. Following your letter and I still do not understand why you wish to 'Anglicise 'your name to become more acceptable to those around you and to 'blend in'. You argued that Stalin and Trotsky were not their birth names but their *noms de guerre'* which they maintained but neither, even the criminal and traitor, denied their origins.

Anyhow the walk took over three hours and I felt tired and distressed when I reached the address that you stated in your letter. A woman answered and was somewhat confused and then defensive when I introduced myself by my name and my former status, however as soon as I mentioned your name – *NOT* Manny Gold, she understood why I had called upon her and her hospitality was very friendly. Her husband was away and her children at school so we had a long chat and I told her all about you, when you were a baby and she laughed so much when I told her the anecdote about you and Trotsky and how the Boss, who for once allowed himself to show his emotions, burst out laughing. Anyway, that story has been repeated enough times to make it stale and boring. They have no telephone so I promised to write or visit them as soon as I have news about your visit.

Lazar

P.S. Remember the coffee!

Moscow, June, 22nd 1962

Manny,

The best news possible. When I thought that I was unable to help you, a kind word from Nina must have persuaded Nikita to authorise the issue of documentation to facilitate your journey to, and throughout Russia.

You have been given a seat on flight AY 108 on Monday the fifteenth of October from Helsinki to Moscow and a return passage (flight number AY 107) on Friday the ninth of November which is very close to the anniversary of the Revolution.

I have been given certain instructions to pass on to you and have been categorically told to emphasise that you *MUST* comply exactly as follows:

You should arrive in Helsinki no later than the preceding Friday and register at the hotel Kamp on the Pohjoisesplanadi and sometime on the Sunday collect an envelope which will contain a numbered key.

On the following day, the Monday, you *MUST* be at the Helsinki railway station (it is called the Helsingin rautatieasema) with all your luggage by six a.m.

I will contact your friends to tell them when you will arrive and would you please write back to me and confirm not only that you have had my letter but also, for the documentation, if you wear glasses (and the measurements) and your feet size!

I was present at your *Briss,* so I know what religion is to be inserted on your documents (probably like me you do not practice religion which I think is anachronistic and a creation of the ruling hereditary elite to control the proletariat).

I am very excited to be seeing you and would you please not forget the *COFFEE!*

Lazar

P.S. I have found pictures of your parents and a photograph of you very soon after you were born! As I was about to fold up this sheet of paper I realised that today is the twenty first anniversary of Hitler's betrayal and the invasion of our Motherland. I still vividly remember the chaos and an almost electric, even incandescent atmosphere in the Kremlin as the Politburo received an ever increasing flood of dramatic and catastrophic news.

TWELVE

The concierge, without question, substituted the expensive Fortnum and Mason bag with an innocuous and sturdy brown paper bag that had contained his own personal shopping and for the third time that Saturday morning checked and confirmed that no messages or documentation had been received for Mr. Gold.

As there was little to do but wait and to wile away the time he went on an unplanned and random walk which he abandoned because the chilly afternoon was no longer pleasant, and he caught a taxi back to the Kamp hotel, hoping on his arrival that in his absence a message or an envelope had been delivered but he was to be disappointed.

He did not sleep well and awoke late. After he bathed, shaved and dressed he went downstairs for a late breakfast and read the previous day`s *Times* which must have arrived earlier that morning from London, before reading *Pravda*. Whilst immersed in the editorial (which attacked the young American President following recent events in Cuba) he subconsciously sensed a presence and folding his newspaper, saw the duty concierge standing close by, who announced that overnight an envelope had been delivered for his attention which he duly gave him, much to his gratitude.

He paid little attention to the addressee on the envelope and crudely opened the document only to retrieve a numbered key.

He remembered the instructions and exhibited some self control otherwise he would have rushed to the Railway Station and the left luggage cubicle to collect its contents, however he was not to know that the contents were to be delivered later, during the night, using a duplicate key.

By the time he had reached the station the following morning, minutes before the deadline, it was still dark outside and he excitedly fumbled with the key before successfully opening the door to see a suitcase and an envelope which he recognised as identical to the one that had contained the key.

Inside was a typed letter with absolute specific instructions, a Finnair one way airline ticket and a further document, which he temporarily ignored, promising himself to read on the flight but he noticed it incorporated a portrait photograph of himself.

He took both his own and the new suitcase to the toilets where he completely undressed, placing his clothes in his suitcase and then dressing in the clothes that had been provided for him, including a pair of glasses, the frames when later he looked at himself in a mirror made him actually appear like a Soviet politician; and the shoes, both unfashionable and coarse were, at least, very comfortable.

His passport, along with any documentation that might identify him and any foreign currency were to be left, again in his suitcase which was to be placed in the locker and on his return to Helsinki the procedure was to be reversed.

The instructions confirmed that on arrival in Moscow he would be met by a car and taken to the home of Lazar Kaganovich, supplied with Soviet currency but any unused money would have to be repaid before he returned to Helsinki and that the enclosed document, which was to be retained by him at all times, would serve not only as an internal passport but as an authority for the bearer to be granted *EVERY* (the author's emphasis) possible assistance and would also guarantee any costs that he might incur.

The Finnair Ilyushin 14 flight was without incident and once he got used to the noise of the two radial piston engines he was able to drift off to sleep and recover the lost time of the previous two nights.

He was reunited with his suitcase and proceeded to a vast rectangular room (which at some time in the past must have been an aircraft hangar), along with most of the other passengers and was confronted with an almost infinitely long trestle table behind which stood a number of uniformed officers whose appearance and demeanour, as they literally interrogated the passengers, was dictatorial.

He was dealt with by a particularly aggressive, and in Gold's own summation, noxious man, whose attention was immediately drawn to the paper bag and its contents. Gold answered his enquiry with the only answer that was applicable and confirmed that it was a gift for a family member, deliberately not identifying a person who, in effect, was a disgraced politician.

Caution tempered his attitude when, in no uncertain terms, he was informed that his gift, for hygienic reasons, was to be confiscated and that he should produce his passport which should have been tendered immediately on his entry into the hall.

The folded document was handed over, opened up and obviously read by the man who suddenly, without explanation, turned red in complexion, looked at Gold as if to compare the photograph with his actual appearance and then turned away, walking urgently to a private room. Gold suddenly became concerned for his safety and even his liberty but after some minutes his interrogator returned with another uniformed officer who, by his confident attitude, was undoubtedly his superior.

His tone, attitude and above all his single question were in stark difference and contrast to his junior...

"Are you comrade Bernstein?"

Gold was unused to be addressed as comrade and by the name that was undoubtedly on the unread document. He only nodded.

Unexpectedly the man put out his hand to shake that of the visitor and then in the most deferential of terms asked...

"If there was anything that could be done to assist him on his visit and that someone of his status was an honoured guest in the Soviet Union?"

Without a request, the once arrogant junior officer, with a forced insincere smile, produced the previously confiscated goods and shuffled away, no doubt to reap his superior's wrath.

Gold took the opportunity to read the document in the Zil limousine en route to his uncle. It was brief.

The printed heading was a statement of fact, without any baroque embellishments and the information that preceded his photograph (glued, stapled and embossed to the paper) incorporated an implied warning signed by the First Secretary, Nikita S. Khrushchev. He now understood the absolute cooperation of the almost grovelling senior official.

THIRTEEN

The apartment was smaller than he had imagined but was artificially reduced by the many shelves of books (some of which were banned - including Doctor Zhivago - which was on the equivalent of the Holy Roman and Universal's Index of Prohibited Books) and piles of old newspapers.

His uncle was ecstatic at the arrival of his visitor and almost, but not quite, astonished at the supply and quality of the coffee. Under any other circumstances Gold would have declined his invitation of hospitality but could not bring himself to disappoint his host and anyway...

"It would only be for two or three days."

He was able, the following afternoon, to summons the Zil limousine and its accompanying driver, which he had unexpectedly discovered was at his disposal, and arrived unannounced at his friend's house where the door to the apartment was opened by his shocked friend. He was invited to stay both for dinner and the evening but insisted that his uncle also be invited and he arranged for the vehicle to return to the apartment and for Kaganovich to be collected. When he arrived, there were tears in his eyes which rather embarrassingly he explained as...

"Not since he was a member of the Politburo had he experienced the unmitigated luxury and the convenience of being chauffeured like a plutocrat or a member of the aristocracy."

Everyone enjoyed each others' company and the table was laid with wholesome food which was more than adequate for the six diners and whilst it was not luxurious it truly expressed the festive cuisine of the Russian people. Kashkarov's two children were visibly upset that their 'uncle' had not brought them any presents and in response they were told that a surprise awaited them, even though Gold had no idea how to fulfil his rash promise.

It was in fulfilment of that promise and through an unusual combination of circumstances that Gold set into motion a series and train of events that a decade later would destroy his career and jeopardize his life.

Manny Gold could clearly observe the reignited previously long extinguished pleasure and happiness in the face of his uncle, temporarily and perhaps for one night only the centre and focus of those around him, as the host and hostess, especially the host, listened to his intimate observations and anecdotes as Stalin's trusted personal assistant. Interest focused on that horrendous period, commencing on June the twenty second, the day of Hitler's invasion of the Motherland and how the Boss had, through the strength of his determination, organised the strategic withdrawal of his battered army but above all inspired the nation's generals and the political leadership to reject the option of defeat and to support the soldiers in their valiant defence of the soil of Mother Russia and of the workers and peasants.

Lazar dominated the evening, even playing with the two children, but in hindsight Gold realised that that his hosts had not even questioned him about such important matters as the change and direction of the Party's policies after the death of Stalin and the disappearance of his henchman, the chief of the N K V D, Lavrenti Beria and that whilst they had a unique opportunity, which might never be repeated, that they did not raise the matter of 'The Great Terror' and an explanation for the purges.

The following day Kaganovich insisted that they use the opportunity to visit his parents' first home and then to try to locate the old cafe and bar where his parents originally met. The Zil limousine took them to a suburb of the city and a discreet road where they saw an old dilapidated three-storey mansion which on further investigation turned out to be a home for retired nurses.

The two men gained access to the building and Kaganovich, from memory, located the two rooms where Goldburgh's parents had made their first home and their son visualised the bedroom and living room but realised that there were no other facilities; Kaganovich had to explain to him and took him along the corridor, to show him where they used a communal toilet, bathroom and a joint kitchen. Lazar, temporarily displaying the arrogance of power that had been rescinded some years before, then instructed the driver to take them to another address expecting and hoping that it would bring them to the location of the former bar and cafe where Joel and Leah had originally met over forty-five years before, however they were to be disappointed since the building had clearly been razed and was now the site of a rather bland utilitarian Stalin era block of flats occupied by industrial workers.

The next day, at the suggestion of his driver, Goldburgh arranged to take Viktor and his wife to what he was reliably informed was the most opulent and luxurious hotel in Moscow, the Metropol. That afternoon Kashkarov and his wife enjoyed the pleasures of the West as the hotel was a meeting place for the diplomatic service (who, of course, realised that the hotel was staffed by members of the K.G. B .and that therefore they had to be discreet about their comments). By 'Western' standards the hotel did not have the cuisine and facilities of a five star hotel but in the barren oasis of Socialism this was, by far, the best that was available.

Following his very recent promotion (which his wife did not know about) Viktor was dressed in his new ceremonial military outfit and across his chest he prominently displayed rows of medals including the one that had been given to him personally by Marshall Zhukov after the battle of Kursk.

Three Western diplomats entered the lounge and since Goldburgh had his back to them he was totally unaware of their presence as they walked to a nearby, but not too close, table. They were celebrating the imminent return of one of their number, a Swiss diplomat who had completed his tour of duty and was about to fly back to Switzerland and he was accompanied by a Swedish military attaché and a British diplomat specialising in trade matters, but the truth was that he was an MI6 intelligence officer and this fact was known not only to his two associates but also to the K.G.B.

Duggan had given the officer a fleeting, almost cursory glance as he walked past, only paying attention to his dress uniform and medals; his immediate analysis was that the man was in the top echelon of the army and his medals were consistent with service during the Second World War. It was only his professional commitment which compelled and obliged him to continue his observation of the man who was with a woman and opposite them another person who was obscured by a high backed chair. Duggan continued talking to his associates whilst photographs were being taken of each other, individually and as a group but he found it difficult to listen to the officer across the room though, as the room slowly emptied, he began to find it easier to eavesdrop. His name was Viktor Kashkarov, who together with his wife, were meeting an old friend who they had recently met in Finland.

Duggan was about to terminate his interest in the trio and especially the man, because it was clear that they were not discussing any matters that were of interest to him, when most unexpectedly, the man obscured by the high backed chair called out, in perfect English, for the restaurant manager to attend their table. Duggan was aware that the restaurant manager spoke reasonable, but broken English, and he endeavoured to listen to the conversation which appeared to be rather unimportant as the guest was asking if a party could be arranged for his friends' children the following day and if they could provide the best ice cream. It was the manner in which he was addressed that was of interest.

"Comrade...stein (it was at this pivotal moment that a waiter dropped some plates therefore unfortunately obscuring the full name of the man) it would be my honour and my duty to help a valued friend of the Soviet Union and may I say a man who is held in such high esteem by the First Secretary."

Then the army officer also most unexpectedly spoke in excellent English...

"Mandel, your kindness is greatly appreciated but it is not necessary for a you to go to such lengths to fulfil your promise to the children. "

The conversation reverted to Russian and the other man, still hidden, declared that:

"Had it not been for your kindness and sacrifice during the war I might not have been able to return to England and that act will never be forgotten and it was the least I could do to show my gratitude."

Duggan realised that it was imperative to obtain, if possible, photographs of the two men and he therefore suddenly seized from his Swiss friend the camera and urgently requested that his two companions sit in a particular position where he was able to take a furtive photograph of the army officer. He then endeavoured to photograph the other man but it was not possible from his present position and he therefore walked round the room in order to obtain a clear view of the man now known as Mandel...stein but it was again impossible take a photograph. Very shortly afterwards the two men and the woman got up to leave, permitting Duggan to rapidly take two photographs and he followed them to the front door, noting that they were collected by a Zil limousine bearing KGB number plates.

For Mandel Goldburgh or as his friend was beginning to call him, Manny Gold, his journey home was to take a surprise direction. Kashkarov requested that he be dropped off before his apartment as he wanted to take a walk to clear his head and Goldburgh must have realised that his companion wished to talk to him privately and not in the presence of the driver or even his wife.

What he had to say was both exciting and potentially explosive: he began by apologising that he would be unable to join his wife and dearest friend together with the two children on holiday in Sochi because he had earlier that morning been ordered to take on his first duty for the Minister of Defence. Within forty-eight hours he had to visit a secret factory and make a report on the efficiency, effectiveness and the quantity of weapons production...

"A location so secret that twenty four hours before he was not even aware of its existence and the nature of the weapons that were being produced. He had obtained the agreement of no less than the Minister of Defence to take Goldburgh with him only in view of his assumed close connection with the First Secretary and would he like to accompany him on this most secret and important trip, indeed he would appreciate his assistance drawing up the report?"

For Duggan, the next twenty four hours were a period of intense anticipation and hope: he had not explained to his Swiss companion why he had urgently needed use of the camera but insisted that the photographs be developed in the security of the embassy and he would personally collect the developed photographs.

He was to be partially disappointed for whilst one photograph of Kashkarov was quite clear, only one of the other photographs had captured the subject of his interest and unfortunately the picture of the man was partially obscured but he had now some definite evidence of his appearance. He spent the next two days drawing up a report of the events and his concerns. He added a postscript that was ultimately to prove his concern and worry. He felt certain that during his career he had come across the man but more important, one name definitely was known to him. It would be necessary for him, on his return to London, to begin a journey through the archives and hopefully to identify the two men.

Duggan was not due to complete his tour of duty until the spring of nineteen sixty-four but with the intervention of the war that began in November nineteen sixty-three he, along with the other members of the embassy, protected by representatives of the Swiss Embassy, left Moscow early in January nineteen sixty- four.

Sometime later during his stay in Moscow Duggan remembered his meetings with Goldburgh, the interrogations, but above all his doubts about the veracity of his story. He kept the discovery to himself and undoubtedly went through the archives of the embassy to confirm when Goldburgh was based in Moscow, prior to his secondment to the Soviet government.

He prudently brought back with him documentary evidence from the embassy archives and during the summer of nineteen sixty -four he was able to locate the original files concerning the investigations carried out in Istanbul and Cairo. With great interest, he noted that his report from Moscow had caught the eyes of his superiors and that copies of the pictures, along with the two names had been passed to the offices of the C I A in Langley, Virginia for their help despite the sudden chill that had been imposed upon them by the 'White House'.

They had received a prompt acknowledgement and some six months later a Mr. Menzies wrote back to say that despite extensive enquiries no further identification was possible of either man.

Duggan would never know that Menzies had again successfully completed a major intelligence coup and had obtained a report from Goldburgh summarising his visit to Arzamas 16.

FOURTEEN

The two men met at a military airport on the outskirts of Moscow and were escorted to an area clearly reserved for the political hierarchy and high ranking military officers. Their flight took about an hour and during that period Kashkarov literally opened up to his old friend in a manner that was most unexpected and divulged information of the most secret nature.

The reason that he had to cancel their reunion the previous year in Finland was because he had been sent on a special course which culminated in a visit to the islands of Novaya Zemlya and with palpable fear recounted that he had been an official observer at the testing of a thermonuclear device on October 30, 1961...

"We were about thirty kilometres from what was ground zero in a specially constructed, heavily reinforced subterranean bunker mainly staffed by scientists with equipment to measure the power of the weapon. The power was unimaginable. The scientists calculated that the force was between 50 and 57 megatons. The building shuddered and for a few moments I thought that the whole unit was going to collapse in on us. I heard later that the flash had been seen one thousand kilometres away. Moscow, New York or London would cease to exist if one of these bombs hit them. Even a twenty megaton air burst would completely wipe out any of the major cities on Earth."

Mandel turned to his old friend and asked why he was being told this and in response was informed by Viktor that:

"We are being taken to the most secret location in the Soviet Union, approximately four hundred kilometres South East of Moscow which is the main design laboratory and warhead production and assembly facility for thermonuclear devices. My first assignment for the Minister of Defence is to submit a brief report with my comments. Your notes and recommendations describing a possible United States surprise attack using chemical weapons and nerve gases followed by a tank assault has been welcomed by my superiors with extreme interest and my associates are secretly developing a programme based on your recommendations and I will be seeing them in a few weeks to discuss progress. I had hoped that you could prepare for me a concise paper summarising my observations and comments for the Minister who incidentally, I understand, does not suffer long reports. I would be very grateful for your help in this matter."

TOP SECRET

ORIGINAL AND TWO COPIES ONLY. REPORT OF

MAJOR VIKTOR KASHKAROV

DESIGN LABORATORY ALL – RUSSIAN SCIENTIFIC RESEARCH INSTITUTE OF EXPERIMENTAL PHYSICS (VNIIEF)

KNOWN AS ARZAMAS-16 (KREMLEV)

LOCATION - 55 DEGREES 23 SECONDS NORTH, 43 DEGREES 50 SECONDS EAST.

SAROVA, NIZHNIY NOVGOROD OBLAST.

Your instructions were to visit the above facility which is the main centre for the design of thermonuclear devices, the production of warheads and their assembly.

Arzamas-16 is associated with the component factory of Penza-19 and the subsidiary design laboratory and component factory of Zlatoust-36 which I had no instructions to visit.

SECRECY

I understand that the name of this centre is based on a location between 50 and 100 kilometres distant and the 16 is a post code. The proximity of an airport and residential complex in such an isolated area, if observed by our enemies, might invite interest in the purpose of the facilities. Furthermore, the high volume of communications between the three centres both by telephone and radio might further arouse the interest of our enemies. An immediate review to secure communications is recommended.

You personally authorised the visit of Comrade Bernstein but whilst security surrounding the perimeter of the complex was of the highest standard, once we entered the administration area and were received by one of its leading scientists, who escorted us on a full tour of the administration block, then the weapons` production complex and finally the assembly plants, answering every enquiry freely in, as far as possible, laymen's terms, security clearly and visibly deteriorated. Specifically internal entrances and exits were not guarded and in the actual weapons production area, whilst safety must be the prime consideration (because, I understand, of potential radiation leaks), access was allowed as it the whole area was a public thoroughfare or a university research centre! Knowledge of my arrival meant that I was able to immediately enter the complex and whilst there was no record of comrade Bernstein, he was also allowed entry, solely on my word. This is totally unacceptable. Urgent action is demanded.

OPERATIONAL EFFICIENCY

Each completed weapon is given a unique identification including details of its mega tonnage. I asked for the last twelve months production figures, per month, both in terms of the number of weapons produced and their mega tonnage and was very efficiently supplied with documentary evidence which I am pleased to state was taken from a locked safe. A cursory review of the figures by my good friend, revealed that during the winter months, that is October to April, production fell by about forty percent, blamed by our guide on difficulty in the delivery of constituent parts, supply of weapons grade Plutonium and Uranium and heavy water or tritium (which apparently sometimes was delivered in a frozen state!).

Prefabricated equipment is continually arriving at the airport which services the centre and the *COMPLETED* manufactured weapons are transported, again by aeroplane, for onsite deployment. Security was excellent to the extent that when I demanded unfettered access to the weapons I was stopped on the correct grounds that a special procedure was in force and could not be circumvented.

It is imperative that the logistics of supplying the centre be urgently investigated.

(The brief report was signed and dated by Kashkarov on November the second nineteen sixty- two).

FIFTEEN

The two men would very briefly meet one more time after Goldburgh's departure from the same airport where he had originally entered the Soviet Union and he would never again walk on the soil of his beloved Russia or smell the pine trees in bloom. Their last conversation confirmed Viktor's gratitude for his friend's help preparing the report and how the Minister of Defence was so impressed with the brief (and in his own words) objective report that in consequence the recommendations would be immediately implemented.

Between the time that the limousine dropped off the two men and Mandel's departure, Viktor also confided in his friend that the Minister was so satisfied by *HIS* analysis of the Arzamas complex and his succinct review and recommendations that he would shortly have to travel to the Kola fjords close to the mouth of the Barents Sea to review and inspect the various bases of the nuclear powered submarine fleet. But before that, he would take his family to Sochi and on his return and before his fact finding journey to the Barents Sea he would see his associates and jointly make further and discreet enquiries concerning the nation's chemical and nerve gas capabilities especially now he had access to highly confidential documents.

By early December, Mr. Maddox and then the C I A had received a treasure trove of intelligence including a reconstituted copy, from Goldburgh's memory, of the report.

SIXTEEN

It was early afternoon on Monday, May twenty- fifth nineteen sixty-four and a few members of the general public were entering Downing Street from Whitehall, some even marvelling at their proximity to 'Number 10' and also hoping for the front door to open and for a well known figure to emerge before they continued their walk towards Green Park.

An anonymous, almost insignificant Ford Zephyr drew up to the front door and even before the solitary police officer could open the rear door and permit the exit of Harold Wilson, such was his urgency that he opened the door himself, intending, *post haste* to rush inside for a very important meeting. However he was waylaid by an eager young sightseer and was obliged, like an actor, to feign interest and was compelled to sign his autograph book and then be cajoled into being photographed by the boy`s parents.

A matter of state awaited him and as he entered the lobby he thought that two more votes had been secured for the Election that he intended to call in October. Before one of the staff could relieve him of his coat, he dropped the Gannex raincoat on the antique and unique black Night Watchman`s chair, which was located diagonally opposite the front door in the right hand corner of the vestibule.

It had been twelve days since David Bruce had given to him what was, in effect, an ultimatum and he hoped, expected and secretly wished that the report would confirm the immediate availability of the 'V Bomber' fleet.

His Private Secretary was sitting in his, the Prime Minister`s private office, on the first floor, two doors away from the Cabinet Room and was engaged in the Times ` crossword. As the P.M. entered he slowly and with care put down the journal without implying haste and stood up in respect.

A large envelope was lying on the table and was the exclusive subject of Harold Wilson`s interest and attention.

He tore open the Manila A4 envelope and his fingers fished out the enclosure which was an A3 size, thick sheet of paper folded in half to create a folder and carelessly stapled at the folded edge so that the Prime Minister accidentally caught the tip of his finger which he cut.

He opened the folder and was confronted by a few sheets of white A4 paper and as he glanced through the six or seven pages he noticed that the typing was double spaced which created adequate space to make notes and annotations but also inflated the limited information that was provided.

The opening page scheduled the twenty seven members of the team, listing their composition by either membership of the Royal Air Force or the Army but also specifying not only their ranks but their areas of technical expertise. The next page confirmed when they were instructed to visit the various sites in South Africa and also the nature of the instructions.

The third page caught the eye of the P.M. and was a summary of their preliminary investigation and for the purposes of the Prime Minister made the subsequent four pages irrelevant and redundant. The highlights were a damning commentary on the consequences of his now rash decision. The summary confirmed that in the opinion of the investigating team no more than twenty seven V bombers' *MIGHT* [sic] be in a fit state for combat and even then with the insufficient equipment that they had been able to take with, they were not certain if the Yellow Sun thermonuclear weapons loaded on some of the possibly operational bombers and others loaded on non operational Victors and Vulcans had substantially deteriorated in the absence of adequate maintenance or protection from the climate and weather. It was emphasised that some weapons would have to be removed and transferred to the limited number of operational bombers but they lacked the equipment to effect the transfer.

Had Harold Wilson concerned himself with the minutiae of the remaining four pages and had he carefully read the contents he would have realised the hopelessness of his situation and the futility of expecting an early resolution of the immense problems that would confront the engineers in South Africa. The fourth page had begun with a guide confirming that items of importance were in capitals and that the extremely important matters were also doubly underlined which explained why the document had been prepared with double spacing between each line.

The problem was partially logistical but fundamentally a matter of engineering and technology. Both ground and flight crews would have to be assembled in the U.K. and then flown over together with specialist engineers who would first investigate the operational condition of the bombers. Fuel would have to be brought in together with sundry equipment and also the special trolleys to transfer weapons from the non-operational to operational bombers.

The crucial problem regarding the bombers and their weapons, much of which in the report was both in capitals and doubly underlined, had been a complete lack of maintenance and the almost wilful neglect which had allowed the planes to be exposed to the sun and the excessive heat; seemingly the only consideration being the security of the bombers and their weapons and that was by specialist teams from the South African Air Force. From the time that maintenance crews and specialist engineers arrived together with their equipment it was estimated that it would take approximately one month to prepare 20 bombers back to full operational status provided that the availability or the delivery of parts could be promptly organised.

It must have been when Wilson completed his review of the brief interim report that he realised how desperate his position was and how he was unable to meet the American ambassador's deadline and ultimatum. He passed the brief report to his Private Secretary and requested that he also review the document and convey to him his comments in the matter perhaps believing that:

"A problem shared is a problem halved."

His considered response was not what Wilson expected or wished to hear since it was suggested that the matter be reviewed and debated by a full Cabinet meeting which could be convened within twenty four hours.

In reality the Country was being run by an exclusive cabal of Ministers, being Harold Wilson, the Home and Foreign Secretaries and the Minister of Defence all of whom were privy to the secret concerning the nation's defences or its lack of a credible first strike or retaliatory counter strike force.

The Cabinet (unlike the National government of the Second World War under Winston Churchill, which although having different social and economic priorities and methods was united in the crucial purpose of survival and ultimate victory) was in effect, a coalition that had rarely met and was not a complete representation of the various departments since not all the posts had been filled. In truth, and not for any dishonest purpose, it was a temporary and interim measure to maintain the facade and aura of government and to bolster the morale of the nation.

It had been drawn from the survivors (who, for various reasons, were not present at the time) of the November 25th massacre and represented expediency over merit and ability thus some of the various government departments and Ministries had been operated, possibly more efficiently, by the permanent civil servants and their elite meritocratic senior staff, either in the absence of a Minister or with the tacit agreement of an inexperienced, therefore untested ,docile and easily manipulated Cabinet member.

That evening Gerald Kaufman and Manny Gold were called to the P.M`s. private office for an unscheduled, unrecorded, private conversation. Harold Wilson urgently required their comments and observations on the situation and he desperately hoped for inventive recommendations and suggestions. He had to confide in the two men that the bulk of the 'V Bomber' force had temporarily been moved to South Africa because he had been forced to reach an understanding with the Soviet government to take them 'out of the equation' in order to forestall an all out Soviet strike against the nation`s major cities, and he then mentioned to the two men that these events had occurred before President Johnson`s announcement of a new 'Monroe Doctrine'.

By different routes the three men constructed a slightly biased and flexible review of the events that had led up to the present situation which, in itself, could be looked at from a very different perspective, though Kaufman, a man of great integrity, was inflexible in his opinion that the P.M. should, in his own words...

"Come clean".

Manny Gold, on the other hand, was most constructive and creative in his interpretation of recent events and their presentation to the impending Cabinet meeting.

The Cabinet met on Tuesday, May 26th and of the eleven present (other than the Cabinet Secretary and two secretaries) only the P.M. was aware of the subjects to be discussed and when he began to raise the matter of the United Kingdom`s defences did his three senior Ministers then realise what probably was to be divulged, though two other major matters caused even them to be shocked.

Like the Prime Minister, all those present would be convicted of High Treason or conspiracy to suppress knowledge of the act of treason (some, in the earliest 'Show' trials) and executed by the New Order other than Sir John MacLeod, the Minister of Agriculture, Fisheries and Food and Conservative M.P. for Ross and Cromarty (though since nineteen fifty he had described himself as a Liberal and Conservative), who was sentenced to eight years hard labour and was believed to have committed suicide such was the severity of the prison regime.

Present, other than John MacLeod, were the following:

Prime Minister, First Lord of the Treasury

> Mr. Harold Wilson, Huyton- Lab.

Home Secretary

> Mr. Harold Lever, Manchester, Cheetham-Lab.

Secretary of State for Foreign Affairs

> Mr. Patrick Gordon Walker, Smethwick-Lab.

Minister of Defence

> Mr. Edward Heath, Bexley-Con.

Lord Chancellor

> Sir Reginald Manningham-Buller, South Northants-Con.

Chancellor of the Exchequer

> Mr. Denis Healey, Leeds, East-Lab.

Minister of Housing and Local Government and Minister for Welsh Affairs

> Mr. John Rankin, Glasgow, Govan-Lab. and Co-op.

Minister of Education

> Sir Hendrie Oakeshott, Bebington-Con

President of the Board of Trade

> Sir David Campbell, Belfast, South-U.U.

Minister of Transport

> Mr. James Griffiths, Llanelly-Lab.

Lord President of the Council and Secretary of State for
Commonwealth Relations

Mr. K. Zilliacus, Manchester, Gorton-Lab.

The Prime Minister, continuing tradition, entered the Cabinet room last
and sat in his chair which, again to comply with tradition, had been set
at an angle. He began by making an announcement that the Minister of
Agriculture, Fisheries and Food, Sir John MacLeod, the Conservative
Member of Parliament for Ross and Cromarty was absent through
extended illness and on behalf of the Cabinet he wished him well and
hoped that he would make a prompt and full recovery.

His absence was both convenient and fortunate because the Prime
Minister was able to begin and base his recommendations on biased
and spurious information and the deliberate misinterpretation of
statistics.

Harold Wilson announced that information had been provided by the
Ministry of Agriculture, Fisheries and Food within the last 48 hours,
which confirmed that the country's reserves of food could not be
maintained by the intermittent importation of food from the
Commonwealth, Empire and the United States.

Indeed, the behaviour of the United States government and especially
the President, in their recent meeting, had cast grave doubts on their
good faith, integrity and willingness to support the British government
and people. Consequently, he had reluctantly come to the conclusion
that it would be necessary, without delay, to bring in rationing not only
of food but also of petrol and that it might be necessary to invoke the
1920 Emergency Powers Act or a new Act which the Home Office had
been urgently reviewing in the unfortunate absence of enough M.Ps. to
make up a committee.

It was at this stage that Wilson requested the Chancellor of the
Exchequer, Denis Healey, to briefly summarise the country's current
financial position. In essence he confirmed that the nation's Gold and
Dollar reserves were being eroded at an alarming and accelerating
rate and that in his opinion major action should be taken to protect the
currency. At this moment Wilson decided not to mention the question
of devaluation but wished to pursue vigorously the imposition of
rationing of food and petrol.

The P.M. then began his summary of events commencing with his
predecessor`s tenure and Home`s reckless and almost treasonable act

of acquiescing to his advisors' craven suggestion that the 'V' bombers and their Yellow Sun thermonuclear weapons be moved...

"To protect them against a surprise Soviet assault."

Completely overturning the Government's primary duty to protect its citizens and also strategically to confront its potential enemy, indeed since no peace treaty had been signed, the Soviet Union was, *de facto*, still a belligerent adversary.

"Indeed, if recently some of you detected any animosity towards my predecessor, it was not because of party or even ideological differences but because his action had betrayed the very foundation of his duty to Parliament and had left me and my colleagues with a burden that was now almost impossible to shoulder and that was why the situation was now being openly disclosed 'in Cabinet' together with the apparent withdrawal of support and cooperation by our so called ally and partner, the United States"

Wilson then stopped as if to permit the reality of the situation to be absorbed and understood by those present.

John Rankin, through and through a 'man of the people' summed up the nation's precarious position, with the eloquence of a man whose reputation was based not only on his upbringing and cultural background but his education at Glasgow University...

"Home helped Chamberlain betray us at Munich and if we all go with a bit less food and have to walk more then it won't do us any harm!"

Before turning to the P.M. and if, as an aside, and with a twinkle in his eye he remarked that:

"My people will take most things but don't ration the beer or tell those Capitalist bastards to water the stuff down to increase their profits!"

What Wilson had feared could be a potential disaster had become a triumph, even to the extent that in the euphoria of patriotism over rationality, no one had raised the fate and the government's intentions concerning the repatriation of the' V Bomber' fleet, a subject which now could be pursued by an alternative time scale and a diplomatic approach to the President and his Administration.

SEVENTEEN

The President was woken at approximately 5 17 a.m. on Tuesday June 2nd, 1964 and was confronted with the potential apocalyptic scenario that the United States might shortly be under nuclear attack by the Soviet Union. He had gone to bed a bitter and angry man for that previous evening he had met Harold Wilson, the United Kingdom Prime Minister, who had all but begged for cooperation and equal status even though he had been forced to concede and admit that the British 'V Bomber' force was in effect impotent and was not able to support a potential strike in partnership with its American allies, if the situation ever arose to...

"Once and for all destroy the bacillus and plague of Soviet Communism,"

which President Johnson thought not only excessively dramatic, but hypocritical and dishonest since he had been briefed prior to the meeting and shown certain highly confidential documents that shed a new light on Wilson`s real political philosophy and intimate connections with certain Soviet 'front' organisations in England, culminating, despite his excuses, in the withdrawal of the' V Bomber 'force therefore gaining the Soviets a massive strategic advantage.

Approximately twenty-four minutes earlier NORAD had not only detected the launch of a missile from somewhere in Kazakhstan but ten minutes later a second and then after another five minutes, a third and final launch. Unusually their trajectories were determined to be in a North Easterly direction over Soviet territory.

Wearing a dressing gown, the President was unceremoniously hustled into a nuclear bunker somewhere beneath the White House by his Secret Service staff where he awaited a preliminary report from NORAD whose first analysis was that the Soviet Union was launching a strike against its ally China but this was promptly withdrawn when they confirmed the plotted course of the three missiles .Shortly afterwards they confirmed that the three missiles had been launched from Tyuratam in Kazakhstan (also known as the Baikonur Cosmodrome) and that their estimated target was the nuclear testing grounds at Novaya Zemlya. The President decided to return to his apartment to dress and have a very early wake-up coffee and his favourite beverage, a Doctor Pepper.

He was, of course, in constant contact and twenty-five minutes later he received confirmation that the three missiles had all crashed somewhere in the bleak permafrost of the two Novaya Zemlya islands It was only a further twenty–five minutes later that he received notification that instruments had detected strong seismic activity in the areas of the crash landings and that three ground level thermonuclear explosions had been recorded, each in the region of five megatons and in absolute contravention of the Treaty that had been signed, with great hope for the future, less than a year before and it was only then that the President requested the attention of his senior advisors and of the Secretary of Defence, Robert McNamara.

NORAD was instructed, without any delay whatsoever, to place the Strategic Air Command and ground based missiles on the highest level of alert.

On the following Sunday, broadcasts were monitored from the Soviet Union announcing that on the Monday, First Secretary Khrushchev and President Brezhnev would jointly address the people on a matter of national interest and its political future. President Johnson, when informed of the intended broadcast, after intense discussions with the National Security Council, ordered the country's military capability be ready to launch either a counter first strike or a retaliatory first strike.

The real truth was somewhat more prosaic and Machiavellian. Brezhnev and his closest advisers, well aware that their actions were in absolute violation of the Treaty, needed more time to build up their fleet of Intercontinental Ballistic Missiles and the construction of their hardened silos.

The major purpose of the exercise, for this was not solely a test of the missiles, was to completely mislead their enemy. The three R-16U (SS7) ICBMs had been launched from test silos built on Pads number 81/24, 90/20 and 110/38 and loaded with dummy warheads. The plan had been hastily but brilliantly conceived and coordinated with great technological expertise (and some little luck). The coordination being the detonation of three thermonuclear devices that had been previously set up and were ready to be exploded as close as possible by physical distance and time to the crash landings, one of which would be one hundred kilometres East of Mityushikha Bay in the Novaya Zemlya test range.

At 9 p.m. Moscow time Nikita Khrushchev appeared on Soviet television, on national radio and a recording was subsequently shown in the Republics' many cinemas. Had television been in colour it would have shown how well the First Secretary appeared, indeed his whole appearance expressed his excellent physical and mental health. The programme was preceded by blatant and overt propaganda showing first of all Soviet achievements in space, especially highlighting the bravery and success of the first two Cosmonauts, Yuri Gagarin and Gehrman Titov, and then proceeded to show a film of the Soviet counter offensive and advance into Nazi Germany in 1945, ending with shots of the latest Soviet military technology including fighters bombers and tanks. The message was clear: Soviet technology and the power of its armed forces.

Nikita Khrushchev announced that during the previous week, engineers had simultaneously test launched multiple ICBMs known as R-16Us, each loaded with a five megaton thermonuclear warhead and so confident were they of the launch of their weapons and of their efficiency that they had flown over Soviet territory and landed...

"Somewhere within the Arctic Circle."

The operation had been a complete success.

He continued by confirming that the country was rapidly arming itself with a host of R-16Us Intercontinental Ballistic Missiles able to reach any target in the United States and that new, more powerful missile systems would soon enter service. He reminded the nation that they have been betrayed by...

"The Capitalist warmongers and their military and industrialist paymasters. "

With almost callous and chilling ruthlessness (remembering that he knew that as a politician he was, in truth, powerless and impotent) he promised that retribution would ultimately be unleashed against their mortal enemies but he, like the people of the Motherland, had no enmity towards the people of the United States, it was the leadership under President Johnson, a man who had not even been elected and was untrustworthy.

National security and the defence of the very soil of the Motherland was the prime foundation of the Communist Party's responsibility towards the people but had to come at a price and that price, for the immediate future, would mean a sacrifice in the ever increasing living standards that the people were now enjoying.

He reminded his listeners and viewers that his loyalty to the Party and to the nation had begun before the revolution and that he had seen great changes and an improvement in the life and freedom of the people. He then announced that he was passing, in four months time, in October, the leadership of the nation to his great friend and ally, Leonid Brezhnev, and he then proceeded to introduce the future new First Secretary.

As Brezhnev entered ,Khrushchev stood up and the two men embraced each other before they jointly sat down, looked at the camera and Brezhnev promised that he would defend the nation and, repeating his predecessor's promise, chillingly stated that he would avenge the premeditated and vicious assault on the soil of Russia that had caused the deaths of husbands and wives, sons and daughters, friends and Comrades and had torn into the very fabric of every citizen (conveniently still not yet indicating the casualty figures).

Khrushchev hid a secret smile as he remembered the past, especially events that he had been a party to. No longer would a purged leader be subject to a secret trial, or a 'drum head' court-martial or worse still a show trial all of which would end in a bullet in the back of the neck. He had been a signatory that had authorised not only the execution of Lavrenti Beria but that his lifeless body be consumed by fire.

He would be able to withdraw from public life, retain his dacha, his staff, have the protection of the KGB and not be their prisoner and be able to enjoy the pleasures of his family and above all his four grandchildren. Superficially the leadership had travelled a long way since the epic show trials of 'The Terror' from 1936 to 1938, no longer would a man like the Prosecutor Vyshinsky destroy a man as he did Krestinsky, perverting the truth and his association with that swine and enemy of the people, Leon Trotsky, or his secret, perfidious ally who had 'double crossed' him, the Yid, Joel Ben Yitzhak.

And then, for the final time in his life, he remembered *THAT* night and Bukharin's desperate pleas for him to both intercede and mediate with the Boss.

Leonid Brezhnev had already formulated a new plan. Like Stalin before him, he would consolidate power and patronage but his vision was international and global. It was to be more than revenge against the Capitalists and the United States: it was to be both territorial and political expansion and initially he would temporarily ally himself with the Chinese and then, when expedient and convenient, deliver a hammer blow against Mao Tse Tung and Chou En Lai. A modern Comintern and Cominform would be created and a new Empire was to arise, by the people, of the people and above all, for the people. In that moment, the embryonic future New Order based on three dominant superpowers had begun to emerge.

Harold Wilson returned to London a chastened figure, his sole consideration being the retention of power and influence. The Cabinet, *de facto,* was weak, generally inexperienced, and ineffective and emasculated and like the inner core of Ministers, who made the only important decisions, would be allowed to continue, like the country, to be misinformed and misled about the outcome of his talks with the American President. Until such time as the British government and the people were confronted with a contradictory truth, the image of the 'Atlantic Alliance' and 'Special Relationship' would continue and once the' V Bomber' force was repatriated to the United Kingdom and became, once again, a significant element in the military equation he could then return to Washington and both' patch up' and renegotiate his relationship with Johnson, who he had been reliably informed by the British Ambassador, would win the forthcoming Presidential Election.

It had been nearly fifteen years since Stafford Cripps had devalued the pound against the dollar by about 30% and Wilson, literally on the back of an envelope, had calculated that a further devaluation of about the same amount would reduce the exchange rate from U.S. Dollar 2.8 to the pound to U.S. Dollar 2.0 and therefore make British exports to the United States more competitive and consequently revive the British economy.

Although essential foodstuffs and oil were still reaching the United Kingdom, supplies were becoming even more intermittent and irregular and he focused again on the urgent reintroduction of rationing, an act close to his heart since he had always believed in the central control of the economy by the state. Also updating of the 1920 Emergency Powers Act had again been raised by the Cabinet Office who vigorously recommended that the 'Bill' be rushed through Parliament and the Lords and that the 1936 Public Order Act could be strengthened.

With almost frenzied action and determination a new Emergency Powers Act was literally rushed through despite objections that it was...

"Ferocious, draconian and above all (and how prescient were the objectors), potentially dangerous to democracy."

It received the Royal Assent and became law on June tenth, 1964.

The British Isles were in the middle of a turbulent storm and he could not see it abating in the near future. The democratic processes of the nation might have to temporarily curtail and the people asked to make the same sacrifices that Winston Churchill had asked of the nation in

May 1940. He still intended to call a General Election in October but believed his greatest enemy was the press that he could slowly emasculate and control by the simple expediency of substantially reducing the supply of newsprint and continue the wartime control of press censorship.

The next six weeks were a period of intense activity both by President Johnson and, secretly, by the many and diverse branches of the United States' intelligence community. Johnson begun actively campaigning for re-election as President in his own right and was buoyed by the support that was expressed across the nation who had responded to *HIS* decisive strike on the Soviet Union and his advisors recognised that a further attack to destroy Soviet Communism once and for all would be accepted by the nation even though losses might be suffered following a Soviet counter strike.

Every available means of intelligence gathering was utilised to determine the number and location of the R-16U (SS 7) Intercontinental Ballistic Missiles. All available U2 spy planes repeatedly overflew the Soviet Union seeking launch sites and missiles as did the first generation spy satellites, whilst on the ground human spies (they were very few and far between) unsuccessfully pursued their trade as did the electronic gathering facilities, since the Soviets were very parsimonious in the information that was passed over the airwaves. The truth was that the programme was behind schedule and that there were very few missiles in place and not enough to deliver even an inadequate blow against the Continental United States.

The Soviet deception achieved its goal and it was decided that the country could not chance an all out attack by the Strategic Air Command and the submarine launched Polaris missiles because of the potential of a retaliatory strike by the Soviet Union using SS7 Intercontinental Ballistic Missiles. It was only some months later, in the spring of 1965, that the first actual intelligence was received which proved, beyond doubt, that a window of opportunity had been lost and that they were no longer able to inflict a devastating and catastrophic blow on their enemy who had now been able to deploy sufficient missiles to cause such damage to their enemy as to justify the policy of 'mutual assured destruction'.

EIGHTEEN

For Great Britain ,a misnomer, since Britain was no longer great as its thermonuclear military capability was supine and its economy in decline, partially caused by weak management in the face of intensive and virulent trade union activity, the descent into the abyss of the totalitarian state would commence with the introduction not only of food rationing but the compulsory issue of documentation(in the interests of national security) combining a joint photographic identity card together with the bearer's ration card. The corporate state would soon be born and the individual submerged in a terror where both natural justice and the rule of law, cast aside in a cynical ploy, would cease to protect the individual.

The lessons of history, either forgotten or ignored, such as the rabid hate of a demagogue or the idealistic Jew caught in a Kafkaesque nightmare were portents that the last free man or woman could not perceive or worse still, halt.

THE OPENING OF, AND EXTRACTS FROM:

CHANCELLOR ADOLF HITLER'S ADDRESS TO THE REICHSTAG,

BERLIN, APRIL 26th 1942

RECORDED BY THE FOREIGN BROADCAST MONITORING SERVICE,

FEDERAL COMMUNICATIONS COMMISSION

"The 11th of December of 1941 when I last spoke to you it was my privilege to lay before you an account of the course of events of the preceding year. In their historical magnitude and lasting political significance they are such as may not be recognized to the full extent for centuries to come. After a few weeks the suppression of the uprising in Belgrade which had been instigated by Britain and Moscow, Europe for the first time in perhaps centuries to come became aware of the common danger from the East, upon the successful warding off of which the very existence of the whole of our continent had so often before depended. For many people the causes of this terrible war into which we were forced in 1939, began to be more clearly recognized, for this war did not bear the characteristics of the previous conflicts among the European nations to which we were accustomed. To an ever increasing degree it began to be generally realized that the reasons for this conflict were no longer to be sought in the usual interests even if plausible of the various nations, but that in reality it was one of those elementary struggles which shaking the foundations of the world but once in a thousand years, introduce a new millennium...

When on the third of September, 1939, after Germany had made countless efforts in the cause of peace, France and Britain declared war on the New Reich, after these states had shoved Poland into the foreground by giving her authority to act as a means of starting the conflagration, one was compelled to doubt the common sense of a world, which instead of averting the terrible misfortune of such a mad war literally forced this catastrophe to happen without any apparent reason.

Now we all know that ever since the internal disruption of the European states Britain had entered into a conspiracy based upon a political doctrine which saw in the disintegration of the continent the essential conditions for the prosperity and growth of the British Empire. No doubt this thought which dominated British policy was in itself very alluring. While Europe was exhausting her strength in numerous internal wars, Great Britain succeeded in burning [?, Author's note] up a world-wide structure with a minimum of sacrifice of blood. The title of "Empire" was given to this structure deserved to be compared with that of imperial Rome as little as an international business concern for the creation of cultural values.

It is an overestimation of the British statesmanship as well as of the political and military capacities of the British to assume that these are the causes for the decay of Europe. Here the origin of the condition is confused with its exploitation. For Europe's decay is due partly to the natural senility of the continental power pre-eminent after the collapse of the Roman Empire, and partly to the deterioration of the elements which had provided the Western centre of that time with its racial and constitutional foundation. The dissension between the classical Roman conception of the state on the one hand, and the no less imperial claims of the Roman church on the other brought about the gradual destruction of the foundations of the central state in Europe. To this was added the profound earnestness with which the world then treated questions which were suited to involve Europe in endless internal religious status, while the same problems are today recognized as being completely unimportant as far as the state is concerned, and treated accordingly.

Thus, the collapse of the old German Empire and consequently of the centre of the dominant internal European organization was just as little brought about by the British as the collapse of Rome was brought about by the Germanic tribes. In both cases, however, internal conditions of weakness resulted in situations which enabled external forces to intervene, thus imposing a new course on the history of the world for many centuries to come...

Only a fool can overlook or deny the fact that, like every political organizing process, this process too confers its benefits on the human race, but it is just as foolish to assume that the British Empire could forever maintain the so-called balance in Europe. The racial elements of this continent linked together by blood and outlook who were striving to establish unity could not in the long run be prevented from combining. It was, moreover, completely foolish to assume that on the appearance of a danger forming an equal threat to the existence of all the people in Europe they could prevent the union of the countries thus threatened...

With whomever England allies herself, she will see at the end of this war her allies stronger than she is herself or ever will be. Her arch-capitalists and the Bolshevist statesmen may greet each other with the greatest possible deceptive friendship, her archbishops may embrace the bloody spectre of Bolshevism as fervently as possible, the more lies, deception and corruption have to be used in order to hide the unnatural coalitions of this Empire from her own people or from humanity, the less they will be able to deceive the nations with a vision and to hinder the natural progress of a forced historical development.

There is a wise proverb which says that the gods strike blind those whom they wish to destroy. I do not know whether every Englishman today still thinks that Britain acted with wisdom and inspiration when she declined the innumerable proposals for an understanding which I have made since 1933. Nor do I know whether every Englishman today is as convinced that it was wise to refuse my offer of an alliance renewed as late as September 1st 1939, and to repudiate my peace proposals at the conclusion of the campaign in Poland and France...

The hidden forces which incited England already in 1914, in the First World War, were Jews...

In this tremendous and truly historical uprising of the nations we are all now taking our part, some of us as leaders, others as actors or performers. On one side we find the exponents of democracy, that is Jewish capitalism with all its deadweight of obsolete political theories and parliamentary corruption, its out-moded social order, the Jewish brain trust, the Jewish newspapers, stock exchanges and banks, a concern of mixed political and economic profiteers of the worst order, arm in arm with the Bolshevist state. Those powers of a perverted humanity are ruling, over them the Jew, who brandishes a bloody scourge in Soviet Russia...

That I am determined to do everything in this direction in order to do justice to these problems, you, my old party comrades will not doubt. However, there`s one thing I shall expect, namely that the country will give me the authority to immediately intervene and take personal charge whenever unconditional attention is not paid in the service of great and vital tasks. The front and the homeland, transportation administration, and our agriculture (?) must obey only one thought and that is to win the victory...

But if in England the idea should prevail of carrying on air warfare against the civilian population with new methods, then I should right now to state the following to the whole world: Mr. Churchill began this warfare in May 1940. For four months I warned him and waited. Then the time came in which I was compelled to act. The person who was alone responsible for this kind of fighting began to complain. Even now my waiting is no weakness. Let this man not complain and whine again when I find myself compelled to give an answer which will bring very much suffering upon his own people.

From now on I shall repay blow with blow until this criminal himself and his work are crushed."

PROCES S PROTISTATNIM SPIKLENECKYM CENTREM

RUDOLFA SLANSKEHO

"In the end every gangster will get his just deserts, everyone will get his well deserved punishment. The conspiring gang standing in the dock today is a nest of rats who were caught. They are hated and despised by all honest people of our country. Citizens, you who are in the position of people`s judges, in the name of our nation, against whose freedom and happiness these conspirators were subverting, in the name of peace and against the dastardly conspiracy, I demand for all accused the death sentence."

Thus Josef Urvalek, the Czechoslovakian state prosecutor addressed the Court on November the twentieth, 1952, at the...

"Trial of anti –state conspiracy centred around Rudolf Slansky."

In the dock was the Jew Slansky, former General Secretary of the KSC and thirteen other Communist leaders or bureaucrats, ten of them also Jewish. They were accused of participating in a Trotskyite-Titoite-Zionist conspiracy and in the service of "American Imperialism".

Their route to the Court was primarily the consequence of the independently minded Yugoslav leader, Josip Broz Tito who had broken away from the domination of Joseph Stalin who then decided to impose his will throughout the Soviet Union's 'satellite' allies but also to purge national Communist parties of their Jews and finally, most tragically, probably Slansky was betrayed by Klement Gottwald, his long time ally and President, who was prepared to sacrifice his friend.

They confessed to all crimes (under duress or after torture) and eleven were executed and three sentenced to life imprisonment.

Now, *YOU* the reader, who regards freedom as a right, remember that Slansky was hung in Pankrac Prison on December third, 1952, his body cremated and the ashes scattered on an icy road outside of Prague. Guard your freedom carefully and also the liberty of others!

Whilst these events, like certain others, were years and hundreds of miles away, the British people had a profound trust in the democratic system that had evolved literally over hundreds of years even if superficially there was a cynicism and resentment of Parliament and, inter alia, the perennial problem and application of taxation. The 'Mother of Parliaments' was allowed to continue unsupervised though the 'Fourth Estate' (that is the free and unfettered press) was by an unspoken word granted the responsibility and task to freely report and comment on their proceedings and work.

NINETEEN

When rationing was announced and the additional, conditional requirement to have available a passport sized photograph, tens of millions of citizens were more concerned with the anticipated chaos obtaining a photograph from a studio than the consequences of rationing and above all the economic reasons for its imposition, having experienced the equality that rationing guaranteed during and after the Second World War.

For the 'older generation 'memories of the 'Blitz' caused them to be excessively concerned with their future safety and a possible Soviet nuclear attack.

The most significant and obvious change to day to day life, had been in the size of newspapers which had been cut down to some four sides, however the sports coverage appeared to be unaffected and made up half the contents excluding the cartoons and crossword puzzles. Everyone realised and commented that the press had been censored since there was very little adverse news, whilst the press openly exhorted the Country to carry on' as usual '.

Little was heard from the government and the new Prime Minister, Harold Wilson, which many people considered to the benefit of the nation, but recently, with increasing frequency, rumours were circulating and more importantly, from various independent (and also 'unimpeachable') sources, that East Anglia and specifically the American air force bases had been hit by Soviet tactical nuclear weapons and the ensuing radioactive fallout had destroyed the agricultural production of the whole region and no one knew when, or even if, any crops could be grown or livestock reared and milk, for example, produced. Since the shops were full of basic produce and there had been up to then, no rationing, most dismissed the rumours.

On Wednesday, August twenty-sixth, nineteen sixty-four, the limited B.B.C.1 and 2 television programmes were interrupted by Richard Baker, the well known and above all highly respected and trusted announcer, at approximately eight–thirty p.m., who stated that at nine p.m. the Prime Minister would speak to the nation and that his statement would also be broadcast on Independent Television and all B.B.C. radio stations. An announcement, at the same time, was broadcast on Independent Television by Kenneth Kendall. The immediate fear was that the nation was again on the verge of war and that, this time, it might an uncontrollable thermonuclear holocaust.

TWENTY

In hindsight, or in retrospect and with wisdom, the events of that evening, the introduction and the P.M. 's address, were subtly and ingeniously produced and crafted (and indeed may even have included a primitive subliminal message hidden in the presentation), however the immediate public response was of confidence and support for the

Government, its bold decisions and of the broadcast, drawing comparisons to such war time classics as 'The First of the Few', 'The Way Ahead' or 'Went the Day Well?'

The introduction was clearly constructed to catch the attention of the audience who were unaware of the content and purpose of the subsequent address. The soundtrack was the music of Edward Elgar and William Walton, fervently patriotic and blended with a series of montages commencing with a photograph of the successful conquest of Mount Everest and then continuing with the Queen's Coronation and her tumultuous reception when she left Westminster Abbey. Following that was the final lap of Roger Bannister's epic first sub four minute mile, after which were various scenes of British achievements including action shots of the new Jaguar E-type, finally ending with dramatic film of the British 'V Bomber' force depicting a wing of twelve Vulcans and then, spectacularly, a panoramic view taken from (presumably the cockpit of a Vulcan) concluding with the pilot ominously announcing...

"Target in sight."

An anonymous voice then introduced the Prime Minister...

"The Prime Minister, the Right Honourable Harold James Wilson, will now speak to the nation."

There then followed a panoramic view: on the right hand side sat the Prime Minister in an armchair and to the left and slightly behind, a magnificent fireplace and above the fireplace a portrait of her Majesty the Queen and Prince Philip whilst to its right was a photo of former Prime Minister, Winston Churchill.

The Prime Minister looked relaxed, confident and assured as he enjoyed his pipe which after a moment or so he put down in an ashtray. Slowly the television camera focused and concentrated on the Prime Minister whose attitude and demeanour was that of the wise and venerable uncle inviting his friends and family to a 'fireside' chat.

"My dear friends and fellow countrymen. I am speaking to you now from a room in ten Downing Street with news and in order to tell you of my hopes for the future. The Cabinet has confirmed my democratic intention that in October, subject to the political situation, a General Election will be held in order that the wishes of the nation are fulfilled (he paused for a moment, if only for his opening statement to be absorbed and understood by the viewers and listeners).

The last few months have been filled with mighty events and uncertainty, however I am pleased to inform you that following the assistance of the Swiss Red Cross and the neutral Swedish government in Stockholm, that we have nearly concluded negotiations with representatives of the Warsaw Pact and the Soviet Union to repatriate our troops from occupied Europe and ours boys, their heads held high, should start to come back within the next six to eight weeks and this operation should be concluded by the end of the year when I personally hope that they all will be reunited with you and their families to celebrate Christmas, (There then followed another short pause).

The circumstances of the unprovoked attack on NATO only strengthened the resolve of your government and of our loyal ally, the United States, and our joint retaliatory counter strike delivered such a blow to the heartland of the Soviet Union that I am again pleased to announce that the Soviet government have agreed to pay substantial reparations in gold, material goods and medical assistance in recompense, however any reparation will be inadequate to counter-balance the human suffering and the traumatic way that many lives were lost."

At this juncture the Prime Minister temporarily stopped, recovered his pipe, slowly and with obvious enjoyment placed the end to his lips, took some puffs and deliberately held the instrument in his curled fingers before recommencing his speech.

"Many of you have been concerned that little information has been released by the government or has appeared in the nation's newspapers and indeed I have learned from many sources how disappointed you all are about the massively reduced size of the newspapers and it might erroneously be believed that vital information has been withheld from the national press. One consequence of the events of recent months has been a reduction in the supply of paper from Scandinavia which the government hopes will shortly be rectified."

Wilson again temporarily halted, put down his pipe, then took a small sheaf of papers that had been precariously resting on the left hand side of the leather chair and which he then appeared to peruse, made a note by pen on the second or third page which he had viewed, finally putting the sheaf down and resumed his address.

"The fortitude of the British people since that dreadful weekend last November has been magnificent and whilst the matters discussed during my regular audiences with Her Majesty must, by tradition, remain confidential, I feel both obliged and almost humble when I confide in you Her Majesty's admiration for not only your fortitude but also your strength and support for all those values which have made this Country great.

Your victory has come at a price, a price that I believe is only temporary, for our trade links have been interrupted and are not yet secure and whilst our allies in North America, the Empire and the Commonwealth have rallied round us and have given their support, far in excess of anything that we expected, it is not possible to expect them to continue their sacrifices, yes sacrifices, that they have previously and are currently making.

It has therefore been decided that the fairest option is to temporarily bring back food rationing from the end of September, that is Monday the twenty-eighth and from midnight tonight an immediate price and wages freeze will also come into force.

In the next few days everyone who has reached the age of sixteen should begin to register for their new ration card and this document will combine an identity card including a photograph of the bearer. Notices will be displayed in all public buildings and, I am assured, in every street, explaining how the system will work including details about the arrangements for children and babies and most importantly for pregnant women, but it will be necessary that every eligible person obtains an up-to-date passport sized photograph to be included in their identity card. In the period leading up to the commencement of rationing the trust that you have put in the government of your nation, we hope will be reciprocated in our trust in you and you will not take advantage of the situation and either irrationally stock up or buy food and goods in panic.

Shops will be informed, irrespective of their size and the amount of their stock, only to sell what is deemed a fair and reasonable amount of any item to any customer. It is not intended that staples such as milk, eggs, flour, bread or beer and cider will be rationed, however spirits over a specified strength will be subject to a special additional duty which, to comply with the wages and prices freeze, will apply from eleven p.m. tonight.

The freedom which we all so jealously guard and cherish was the same freedom that was abused by our enemies and allowed them the unfettered opportunity not only to infiltrate this country but to nearly but, thank God, fail to destroy the very foundations of our democracy. (he paused and then dramatically ended his speech with the unexpected statement):

God Save the Queen. Advance Britannia."

First, the viewer or listener was aware of a silence and then, for the viewer, the picture appeared to dissolve into blackness when the appropriate announcer took over and confirmed the new time table. For B.B.C. One and Two, the respective announcers confirmed that Sportsview and the Polish epic of the Second World War, 'Ashes and Diamonds' would be concluded, whilst on I.T.V., London Rediffusion, the delayed news would be broadcast, followed by a discussion, in the studio, about the P.M.'s statement.

The speech contained blatant lies, half truths, distortions and two ad hoc inclusions that unilaterally Wilson had decided to include without reference to the Cabinet and only after Goldburgh, whose obsequiousness (which was beginning to irritate and annoy the more loyal Kaufmann) and increasing influence, had suggested in passing, as a method to increase central control of the economy.

The original speech had been prepared by the Cabinet Office and the patriotic conclusion, "Advance Britannia", had been uttered by Churchill when he broadcast to the British people announcing the end of the European war in May nineteen forty-five and the first draft circulated, late that afternoon, to all the members of the Cabinet for their approval or comment. Negotiations were only at a preliminary stage with the representatives of the Warsaw Pact and Soviet Union, however the weak objections of the more 'junior' and inexperienced members of the Cabinet were rejected by Wilson and his 'inner circle', whilst logistical objections to the enormous procedure photographing and registering some thirty to thirty-five million people in a little over four weeks and maintaining adequate food supplies against an avalanche of panic buying was again denied by those for whom the retention of power was becoming a more important consideration.

TWENTY-ONE

When and where the 'Right' or more specifically, as they had been historically labelled by the 'Press', the 'Extreme Right', began its renaissance or emergence from the odium of public rejection and obscurity can now never be determined, even if it is possible to identify a location or time, since the fragments of information that are still available and more importantly reliable, only indicate that 'cells' or groups spontaneously arose, formed in response and opposition to 'Left Wing' Trade Union groups who vehemently opposed the Government's price and wage freeze. However, this is only reasoned conjecture since the primary factor was the chaos and uncertainty that resulted from the original implementation of national registration and the intended imposition of food rationing.

By the following evening the promised official notices were prominently displayed throughout the country, mainly due to the unprecedented, efficient cooperation of the Post Office and the Railway authorities though it is probable that the more isolated hamlets in Scotland and Wales and the outlying islands off the coast of Scotland did not receive their posters for a further forty -eight hours.

In great haste the satirical B.B.C.T.V. programme, 'That Was The Week That Was' was resurrected for a special show with superb professionalism, orchestrated and led by David Frost and Ned Sherrin and not only lampooned the government but showed extraordinary and meticulous attention to detail, pointing out not only spelling and grammatical errors in the poster but inconsistencies and also contradictions in the instructions.

Thus, within days of the registration procedure beginning, the public's actual practical experience resulted in widespread dissatisfaction and concern for the fairness of the rationing system and more importantly, the inefficiency organising the registration.

Unused and possibly archaic contingency plans facilitated the prompt release of suitable film stock and the necessary chemicals which were distributed to photographers who, not unexpectedly, were overwhelmed by the initial surge in demand.

Whilst there was still a reservoir of experience in the Home Office regarding identity cards and in the Ministry of Agriculture, Fisheries and Food, currently rudder and leaderless in the absence of an appointed Minister but led by incumbent permanent civil servants with limited knowledge of the rationing system, there was no inter -ministry arrangement or coordination for a revolutionary joint identity and ration card. With great urgency, reminiscent of the darkest, dire days of June nineteen forty, a meeting was held, dominated by the Home Office Minister and his senior civil servants, where, within hours, and on the same day, a document acceptable to all parties was designed including reference and identification numbers that each Department could independently use and jointly coordinate.

However, it was when the matter was delegated to the lower level civil servants who would be responsible to organise and operate the system, that their visualisation completely underestimated the sheer magnitude of the procedure. Like so many other government initiatives, the theory behind the operation was not only sound, but sensible. In reality, even though a vast pool of civil servants in the lowest echelons were assigned and delegated to process the human avalanche, the system could not cope and was engulfed in a tidal wave of paper work.

The preparation and design of the information poster had been completed, under great pressure, within a matter of hours, resulting in a number of basic errors that would have been readily detected and corrected had not stringent time constraints not been imposed.

Likewise, the same pressures resulted in decisions which, in hindsight, were both flawed and ill considered, since for reasons that superficially were logical it was decided to operate the registration process through the national network of general practitioners, in their surgeries, where the patient was known, could be identified, their photographs verified and then processed by the assigned civil servants temporarily based in the surgery. Unfortunately the reality of the procedure was that the system was inundated and effectively collapsed under the weight of numbers. The population was to be processed alphabetically and those missing their allocated place or 'slot' were to be dealt with at the end. Not only was the system overwhelmed but the inordinate haste setting up the system was exposed when the administrators realised that no request had been made for a duplicate photograph for the system's records. The official public notices had to be reprinted and redistributed (including corrections to the spelling and grammar) requiring the bearer to produce a copy photograph, many of whom accidentally or deliberately overlooked the requirement or whose photographs were never married to their files or were incorrectly or wrongly assigned.

For the government and the highest echelon of the civil service who monitored the ongoing and ever increasing chaos and frustration of the population, concern grew as they considered, if not the political consequences but the potential social unrest. In a second and more scathing and acidic commentary during a further special edition of 'That Was The Week That Was' the situation was described as an unmitigated disaster and debacle dwarfing the catastrophes of Dunkirk and the fall of Singapore. Furthermore, within days of the programme being broadcast, documentation was exhausted (about the time when the letter 'H' had been reached), causing not only administrative chaos but public anger and the infectious, contagious fear that families without documentation would be ineligible for rations. The consequence was an unprecedented rush for food virtually clearing the shelves of the nation's stores and fermenting near panic.

Even earlier it had become self evident to the government that the operation could not be completed before, or on, or even within a reasonable period after rationing was due to commence leaving many without documentation on September the twenty-eighth.

To postpone the commencement of rationing was not considered an option, since a delay would be in contradiction to the government's public assessment of the economic situation.

It was then that Manny Gold, unelected and unaccountable to the people and in his position solely by the whim of an unelected Prime Minister and on the fringes of power with, without doubt, the intention of furthering his own career, perceived a course of action that would resolve the problem but above all would regain the confidence of the people, enhance the reputation of his mentor, the P.M. and strengthen the Labour party's chance of Election victory. The metamorphosis of Goldburgh to Gold symbolised the change from an idealistic and solitary Cambridge University student and currently minor administrative assistant with potential, but untried ability, to a realist without conscience; cold, calculating, cunning, even (though he did not yet recognise the latent traits) a penchant for unrepentant cynicism and capriciousness. He would not even impertinently request a reward for his analysis and suggestion, only the opportunity to express *HIS* appreciation for the trust that had been placed in him, for the opium of power had corrupted him and destroyed the natural qualities of integrity and morality.

He was a member of the official party that accompanied the P.M. in an exclusive railway carriage that formed part, but was independent and isolated from the rest of a main line train, en route from London Euston to Blackpool and the Trades Union Congress. Some weeks before, Gold since he had been notified of his inclusion in the official party, had decided to use the opportunity to visit his home outside of Liverpool and to renew some now unimportant personal contacts, however the recent events and the Prime Minister's problems created a new situation from which he could personally profit and perhaps even enhance his position and influence.

The Prime Minister was alone in his carriage wrestling with two problems: his reception by the General Secretary of the T.U.C., George Woodcock and 'Conference`s' response to the imposition of a wage and price freeze and secondly, and most probably the more intractable, the ongoing and escalating problem of the introduction of a joint identity and ration card. Every hour seemed to bring news of further problems. Gold decided figuratively to 'take the bull by the horns' and make an approach to the Prime Minister suggesting a bold and daring course of action potentially dangerous and even politically fatal in the event of an unsatisfactory outcome but promising a resolution of the administrative problem and potentially enhancing both the Prime Minister's reputation and his hope that he could win a dramatic and possibly a massive and emphatic victory in the forthcoming General Election.

TWENTY-TWO

Gold had carefully investigated and analysed the background to the ongoing and ever increasing chaos which he initially interpreted as administrative incompetence caused by inadequate preparation, the actual volume of work involved in the registration process and unreasonable time constraints, mainly the result of the P.M.`s own urgency though Gold knew he would be wise to deflect any blame to the civil service and its staff who were expendable.

The proposition and argument was sound, he was confident that he could lucidly and convincingly describe a plan that could, no would, resolve what was becoming a disaster, though he felt that that particular word might incense Harold and that he should play to the P.M.`s ego, possibly even suggesting that his deputy, the unstable George Brown, recently recovered from an ongoing 'problem' appear as the figure head therefore shielding the P.M. from the immediate direct consequences of failure, which was unlikely but he, Gold, wanted the P.M.`s authority and imprimatur to oversee and control the whole operation, and if it failed then that would be the end of Gold`s career. He was confident of success but only if he was allowed absolute and total, even authoritarian power.

The Prime Minister's private detective opened the carriage door and assumed that Gold had prior instructions to deliver to the P.M. a cup of tea together with some digestive biscuits. The Prime Minister looked up, smiled at Gold, thanked him for his initiative and beckoned him to sit down. For some minutes Wilson continued to write, apparently oblivious to the presence of Gold, then stopped, immersed two sugars in the cup of tea and then, without shame or regards to etiquette, dipped a digestive biscuit into the cup which overflowed and then most surprisingly asked...

"Please could you get me two rounds of toast, lightly grilled and with plenty of butter?"

Gold immediately left the carriage and returned shortly with his master`s order, much to the appreciation of Harold Wilson and he watched the Prime Minister consume, with obvious pleasure and relish, not only the toast but the final biscuit crisp and fresh, uncorrupted by the now lukewarm, if not cold tea.

It was now or never as he took a deep breath, which Harold Wilson could not fail to notice:

"I believe that I can help you resolve the problems of rationing, registration and victory in the election but you must be both humble and ruthless and above all brave."

At one stage Gold believed that he would be summarily dismissed from the carriage and told never to communicate with the Prime Minister again, however Wilson listened intently, sometimes gesticulating to Gold, by flapping his hand, to slow down, allowing him to make scribbled rough notes whilst twice interjecting to ask the same question:

"Have you thought this through?"

When Gold finished, Wilson responded with a laconic and almost resigned statement of inevitability..:

"I know of no Prime Minister that has ever made such a formal acknowledgement as you suggest. It is suicide."

But this response was what Gold had expected and he had planned and prepared his answer which he believed would confirm his argument.

"Churchill did in May nineteen forty: he told the truth and the people followed him. You must remember Low's famous cartoon in the 'Mirror'."

Gold sat in his hotel room in anticipation of a Prime Ministerial summons and could tangibly sense the power and influence that was slowly coalescing around him and would be in his grasp. He confidently asserted to himself that shortly the phone would ring and he would be summoned to the Prime Minister's private suite where he would be confronted with Harold's (then he stopped himself from being too over familiar) - the Master's enquiries - which he would answer with his well rehearsed, plausible and reasoned response. The late afternoon, like a boring book or film, had dragged on into early evening and then into the final hours of Saturday September fifth as his earlier confidence and self assuredness were beginning to evaporate in a series of personal recriminations and increasing bouts of self doubt and analysis, when at about 11 o'clock, as he was about to concede failure, he was unexpectedly shocked back into his former self assuredness. He received a telephone call, not from the P.M. but from Gerald Kaufman who requested Gold's urgent attention and presence in the Prime Minister's suite where the three of them were to have a private conversation without the P.M.'s. Permanent civil servant and would not therefore be recorded.

Wilson was relaxed and in the privacy of his suite had dispensed with his pipe and was enjoying what could only be an expensive Cuban cigar which he held in his right hand whilst in his left was a whisky and soda.

Wilson was absolutely blunt to such an extent that Gold believed that his career was in jeopardy and it was apparent that Wilson was racked by doubts and was unable to make a decision, one way or the other. It was at this juncture, at this critical time, that Gold confidently reminded the Prime Minister that humility and honesty and the promise and explanation that he had suggested earlier that same day in the railway carriage would gain the public's support. Gold knew exactly how he intended to proceed. A hiatus, a delay, but above all a period in which the whole procedure could be efficiently organised and in the meantime the shops and their shelves had to be restocked and replenished, an early Christmas. The Government would have to authorise and permit their strategic emergency supplies of food to be raided and made available.

He had been given access to the warehouses in Aerodrome Road, Hendon, North West London and had been told of other locations in the London area and a summary of other 'dumps' scattered at various anonymous sites across the country.

"Wilson must appear on television, admit that the Coalition government had let the people down by the incompetent way that the administrators had, and were currently processing the registration procedure, but it was in his power, with the support of the country, with the support of the Unions, with the support of the employers, and above all with the support of the people that, (and Gold by the tone of his voice, by his gesticulations, emphasised how the P.M. was to express himself) they could, and the following word had to be stressed, *TOGETHER,* overcome the crisis. Implementation of registration and rationing would have to be delayed and no child, no widow, no orphan or the weak would go without or suffer because of the incompetence of those who had been delegated to bring in registration and food rationing (Gold told him not to identify them as civil servants but as 'those')."

Gold ended his presentation, looked at Kaufman who smiled, and then at the P.M., who took a deep inhalation of the nearly finished cigar and then clearly was about to come off of the fence and 'the horns of a dilemma' and make an absolute decision:

"Tomorrow we will meet the' Brothers' who dictate the policies of the T.U.C., they will demand a change in the law following the Rookes versus Barnard High Court decision, which, for the convenience of our discussions and negotiations was and will be deemed unfair."

TWENTY-THREE

The 'Brothers' (as Wilson sarcastically described the delegates in the confidence of his private circle of intimate friends and advisors) were mostly arriving on Sunday, September sixth and it appeared almost random, even haphazard, that certain delegates or union leaders never received or were passed the telephonic invitations or were so focused on previously made arrangements that they did not have the interest to pursue the subject, since the invitation was not from the P.M. but from the leader of the Labour party.

The invitation was to a private meeting hosted by the leader of the Labour party, Harold Wilson, to confirm the party's solidarity with 'Congress' and in the privacy of the meeting to solicit and exchange ideas and suggestions that would strengthen the movement, show support for its members and in the current climate improve the social and economic conditions of the nation.

The 'Press' was not invited and in their later conference reports no mention was made of the event and most important of all the comments of those who were present. Thus the conference report in The Times on Monday, September seventh included the following:

"The Associated Society of Locomotive Engineers and Firemen agreed meekly today to withdraw their motion calling for the removal of the Polaris base at Holy Loch and opposing nuclear bases in Britain.

The National Union of Public Employees, decided to withdraw a motion on the Contracts of Employment Act."

Harold arrived early at the hotel conference suite accompanied by Gerald Kaufman and 'Manny' Gold who were to be his 'eyes and ears', passive and receptive to their guests' comments and remarks. Kaufman was generally well known and intellectually and politically well respected - a potential power in the party - whilst Gold was both something of an unknown quality and strangely perceived, not for his Semitic origins, but for the apparent haste of his elevation within the party's hierarchy of power and unsubstantiated rumours not only of his financial status but of his wartime record.

The document on which Wilson had been making notes when Gold had entered the private railway compartment was the second, and a more devastating report from South Africa which, and Wilson was only interested and concerned with the overall situation, was a damning summary that it would take no less than four months to organise teams of engineers, mechanics, heavy duty equipment and the delicate and sophisticated equipment to repair some (Wilson's own mental annotation) of the bomber force and to correct the sophisticated technology of the thermonuclear and nuclear devices. It would be a major operation and logistically would require a tremendous application of money and labour. Furthermore, and the report alluded to the political and military aspects of the return journey which would have to be planned in a hostile world, where friendly and reliable allies had to be identified and secured, in order to guarantee emergency landing and refuelling rights, access to airspace and the protection of their precious, dangerous cargo.

At best, including refuelling planes, the latest estimate was that only sixty planes could be made serviceable and that only forty-five would be loaded with the 'Yellow Sun' thermonuclear devices and nuclear weapons.

Temporary and ad hoc measures had, and were being taken, to protect both the planes and weapons from the intensity of the climate but each day exponentially increased the damage.

Thus Wilson was slowly being suffocated by his error of judgement, but he convinced himself that the effluxion of time might solve the problem, even, and he remembered his Roman history, Livy book XXIII, Hannibal's defeat of the Romans at Lake Trasimene and how the Decemviri had decreed the military tactic of delay (was it, he mused, in Latin, cunctator, the delayer?) to enable Rome to prepare adequate defences. Whilst Wilson had been shocked, he had had the supreme confidence, or arrogance, this time to make a correct strategic decision. The cost was irrelevant, it would be amortised over a decade, a lifetime, and he had to have a viable and potent deterrent that would give him a negotiating posture with both the United States and the Soviet Union.

Perhaps the unions, at long last, were seeing common sense and the Locomotive Union's decision was not only sensible but also showed that the Government's greatest secret was still secret, but he was not confident that the truth could be hidden for much longer. He was also reaching a personal, unilateral and undemocratic decision regarding the forthcoming General Election.

Actually the roast beef sandwiches were succulent and generously filled whilst the only other option, egg, salad and cheddar cheese were the best that he had tasted for a long time. As the 'Brothers' began to arrive he grabbed another roast beef sandwich, filled his pipe (flaunting a cigar would damage his image) and began the ritual and facade that each 'brother' was important both to him personally and to the future of an elected Labour government.

Wilson would personally receive and greet every delegate irrespective of the size or influence of their Union but he would concentrate on the major power brokers before discreetly ascertaining Kaufman's and Gold's analysis of their conversations. He intended to make a short speech in response to the general tone of the gathering.

The free, but limited bar 'lubricated' the gathering and the guests were not backwards in coming forward to sate their unquenchable thirst, though the excellent, but restricted, buffet was generally ignored by the visitors. It was not necessary to loosen the tongues of the delegates as both Kaufman and Gold were very soon to discover. Their first discussions signalled the prime interests and concerns of the delegates; Kaufman was surrounded by representatives from the National Union of Sheet Metal Workers and Coppersmiths(Messrs. Buck and Barr), the British Actors Equity Association (Mr. P. Plouviez) and the Tobacco Workers Union (Mr. P Belcher) whilst Gold had, in his company at a similar time, Mr. G. Hook of the National Union of Agricultural Workers, the blunt, but sincere J. O`Hagan of the National Union of Blast Furnace men and George Elvin, Secretary of the Association of Cinematograph, Television and Allied Technicians.

For some, their concerns were expressed in the language of the factory floor whilst others were more eloquent, though however distilled, refined and summarised their worries, had a common and selfish theme. Little mention was made, even less concern was uttered regarding the government`s attempts and negotiations to repatriate the nation`s forces from occupied Europe, indeed no mention was made by any delegate regarding its liberation, as if the British Isles were a 'Churchillian' fortress, both in military and economic terms. Above all the common denominator was the almost paranoid, near hysterical fear that following the Rookes versus Barnard decision, political but above all union power and influence would be legally curtailed. The law had to be changed. The delegates held diverse opinions about the forthcoming General Election, considering that the Tories had 'shot themselves in the foot' or as one plain-spoken delegate stated, and fortunately his identity was lost in the later summary, that:

"Yet again a Tory was caught 'on the job' when he should be on the job."

But most delegates stated, or implied, that the forthcoming Election was 'In the bag' and confirmed that funds would soon reach the Labour party but rather chillingly also announced, as if the matter had already been debated in Congress, that they intended to publicly and vociferously publicise their demand for new legislation to reverse and correct the House of Lords` decision.

Had Kaufman and Gold thought that the unions would be satisfied with just new legislation then the thorny matter of the 'Wages and Prices' freeze was also raised. They had, in principle, no objections to a joint identity and ration card, even supporting the whole idea since they remembered how, during the war, it had guaranteed a fair distribution of food, but a wage freeze! It was abhorrent, an anathema and would undermine the democratic principal of collective bargaining. It was, and they presumed, a tactic and suggestion of their political enemies in the Cabinet, the Conservative–Liberal coalition! They would fight 'tooth and nail' this new assault on their hard won freedom to negotiate and bargain.

These opinions and the general posture were repeated again when both Kaufman and Gold jointly met representatives from the Laminated and Coil Spring Workers Union, the United Patternmakers Association and the Sign and Display Trade Union, whose representative described (his words are paraphrased)...

'... The intellectual concept of a wages freeze as a call to arms for the workers to rise up against the capitalist vermin...'

Though his exact words are unprintable and are best left to the imagination of those who have listened to the unexpurgated language of the 'shop floor'.

Wilson had deftly organised a meeting with the three major powerbrokers within the T U C hierarchy. As a postscript, The Times in its issue of Saturday, September twelfth, listed the membership of the Transport and General Workers Union as 1, 373,560, the National Union of Public Employees as 230,000 and the National Union of General and Municipal Workers as 791,940.

Surrounding him were the General Secretary of the T.G.W.U., Frank Cousins and his associate Jack Jones (at his trial for high treason Wilson was confronted with the incontrovertible evidence that within 48 hours of the meeting Jack Jones had betrayed the contents and substance of the 'private' meeting to' Moscow '), Alan Fisher of the National Union of Public Employees and J. Cooper of the N.U. of G. and M.W.

During their conversation, Mr. H Taylor of the National Union of Mineworkers courteously introduced himself (and surprisingly did not object to his apparent earlier exclusion from this ad hoc meeting) and took the opportunity to also make known to the meeting an up and coming young trade union official who appeared somewhat overawed by the authority and power of those surrounding him.

The summary of their message, which was uncompromising, but wrapped in the message of 'fraternal' support for their political wing, the Labour party, was that legislation had to be promptly passed to protect the Trade Union movement and to eradicate and wipe out any Act or Acts of Parliament that supported the *Rookes* versus *Barnard* House of Lords decision. A wages freeze was absolutely unacceptable and would result in both industrial action and disruption, including secondary and tertiary picketing. Mr. Taylor's young protégé then blurted out, as if the potential forces of energy suddenly were released from within him, in a kinetic eruption that:

"The betrayal of the miners in nineteen twenty-six would not again be tolerated and although patriotic and loyal to the flag they would pursue their democratic rights to the bitter end."

Harold Wilson was believed to have said some hours later, in the confidentiality of his private room, that he was not certain if the young man meant the Union Jack or the Hammer and Sickle and that as well as enemies on the coast of Western Europe who were confronting democracy he could see that now there was an internal, even fifth column, who might even be' hell bent' on destroying the very foundations of British society.

When this confrontation ended, Wilson decided to consult his' eyes and ears', when he was 'waylaid' by Mr. W. Mowbray of the Scottish Union of Bakers and Allied Workers, who, perhaps emboldened by the surprise meeting with the British Prime Minister reminded him that the...

"Struggles of Willie Gallacher (including an obtuse attack on the evils of alcohol and the 'abundance' of free alcohol at the gathering) would be repeated and the workers would sacrifice their liberty and even endure imprisonment for their beliefs."

He had hoped to meet the Secretary of the Fire Brigades Union (Mr. T Parry) and the representative from the Civil Service Union (Mr. J Vickers), however having spoken to Kaufman and Gold he realised the enormity of the task that confronted him, especially summarised by Mowbray's and the young miner's emotional outbursts. As a duo, the two circulated in the room purely on a social basis allowing Harold Wilson the opportunity to mentally consider the contents of an ad hoc speech.

TWENTY-FOUR

The speech was brief. He had been unusually bruised and shaken by the mood and intensity of the delegates' sentiments and demands and did not wish to inflame or exacerbate the situation further. His few words were prudently chosen and designed to enhance and strengthen their support and not to confront them with the pressures of the real world and their impossible Socialist utopian visions.

"He had sensed the mood of the meeting, that his intentions had to be trusted, that it was blatantly obvious that legislation would have to be brought in as soon as possible to regularise the status and to give legal protection to the Union movement and that, in conclusion, he believed that he would have to be 'flexible' about a 'Wages' freeze (he had deliberately not included mention of a 'Prices' freeze and at the final moment he refrained from reminding them that he hoped that their common sense and wisdom would comprehend that short-term financial gains would be cancelled by a political backlash and more important of all by the ever lurking and pernicious enemy of inflation)."

The following day Harold Wilson was due to speak to 'Conference' before an assembly of delegates estimated to have reached the landmark figure of one thousand and it was widely expected, and anticipated, that his speech would be the first salvo in the forthcoming General Election campaign and indeed the P.M. had originally decided not only to launch his campaign but had already drafted a provisional speech which was eagerly awaited by supporters and opponents alike. Not only the party activists, but also the party faithful, informed by the press, radio and television, anticipated with great interest what was expected to be a damning review of 'thirteen years of Tory rule'. Naive visionaries, whether on the shop or factory floor through to the erudite and articulate 'Intelligentsia' hoped, and expected, a statement, a rousing speech of substance together with a programme listing details of economic and social reforms. Surprisingly, little interest was expressed in the reality of the current European military position and the fate of the imprisoned British forces, since their simplistic and myopic concerns were inward looking and their opinions were influenced and moulded by the voluntary censorship operated by the Press who were unanimous and consistent in avoiding reference to, and comment, concerning the situation on the European mainland.

The previous evening's reception and his secret thoughts about the forthcoming General Election (he had decided to obtain the Cabinet's agreement to delay the election until the following spring of nineteen sixty–five, on the grounds that it was imperative, first to bring in the joint identity and ration card and then also 'Wages' and 'Prices' controls) meant he had to play a trump card utilising part of Gold's intended plan which he felt confident would persuade the weak and supine Cabinet to accept his argument for delay. That delay of some six months would allow the' V Bomber' force or a substantial part, to be repatriated therefore strengthening his hand in any negotiations with 'Washington' and 'Moscow'.

Wilson was not only obsessed by his intention to impose a freeze but also to implement the compulsory joint identity and ration card, though Gold's persuasive argument had tempered his fervour. His intended postponement of the Election was a strategic error that unbeknownst to him would ferment and finally cause his downfall and tactically a disaster since virtually all the Opinion Polls confirmed that he would win, albeit with a small, possibly only a single figure majority. His intentions harkened back to the post war Attlee government, of which he was a member, and the Socialist desire for centralised control of the economy.

In fact his speech had been hastily drawn up and was focused on a number of slogans that had been composed, constructed, compiled and collected together, specifically to obtain the broad support of the delegates, and to create unspecified vague areas of policy that could be amplified and clarified at a future time. He began by referring to the (false) umbrella of the country's defence in the form of the (nonexistent) 'V Bomber' force, of the new technologies described, perhaps with indirect reference to the steel and allied industries, as the 'White Hot 'heat of the fusion of science and industry which would revolutionise the factory floor, citing the marvel of the electrical (sic) computer.

Playing to the audience's Socialist fervour, like a Stalinist economics minister, he united the strength of the workforce together with the trade union movement (no mention was made of the employers and their joint interest in any industrial and commercial success) perceiving, in the future, a substantial improvement in the standard of living but managed to include a statement that a major initiative was to be launched within a few days concerning both the identity and ration card and the price freeze (but no mention was made of a wages freeze). He concluded his speech with an almost theatrical grim reference to the High Court decision concerning *Rookes* versus *Barnard* and his desire and urgent intention to bring in legislation.

The response to his brief speech confirmed to him that he had recognised and was in tune with the mood of the assembled delegates which was immediately confirmed when they, *en masse*, rose and applauded him, or more important of all, what they believed were his imminent and future intentions.

Gerald Kaufman was delegated to remain in Blackpool for the duration of the conference specifically to monitor any political developments whilst Wilson returned with Gold, the latter hoping that his recommendations and suggestions would be approved and that he could take action that would not only further his career but would improve his mentor's chance of winning a resounding victory at the forthcoming General Election.

TWENTY-FIVE

Election fever had begun to grip the country and when it was announced that a Cabinet meeting was to be held the following Monday and that Mr. George Brown, deputy Labour leader, and recently recovered from an extended and unspecified illness, had been asked to attend, purely in an observer status, all branches of the media for once concurred that the General Election was to be formally announced. Opinion was also uniform that Thursday, October fifteenth was 'favourite' and it was reported that 'certain' bookmakers had accepted bets for this date but had ' closed their books' such was, if true, the deluge of money.

Common, but well informed gossip had it that 'books' had been opened at 'three to one' and had been closed at 'ten to one on'.

Even those Cabinet members who were due to attend had no doubt as to the purpose of the meeting and two were anonymously quoted in three newspapers that:

"It was in the bag",

but more importantly they commonly regarded the end of their short Ministerial careers not only with relish, but hoped that:

"The mess that was the introduction of a joint identity and ration card and the proposed freeze should be left to the incoming Government which probably would be led by Harold (Wilson)."

But Harold Wilson had no immediate intention of requesting an audience with the Queen to set in motion the procedures to dissolve Parliament and to call a General Election. He had constructed a forceful argument supported by documentation and he intended to seek the Cabinet's support, or if they wavered, or objected, he would be ruthless in compelling them to back him up. This was Churchillian in purpose as his famous predecessor had neutralised the 'Appeasers' and formed a government that would stand up to naked aggression.

The following summary of the two Cabinet meetings that took place is in part based on an anonymous review of a statement believed to have been made by an assistant to the Cabinet Secretary, who had been called in to assist her superior, and additionally her answers during her trial, which was held in camera, on charges that have never been made public, however it is believed to be an offence of knowingly permitting an act of treason.

Apparently she was convicted and sent to prison for only eighteen months (the logical inference being the minor nature of the actual conviction) but died in her sleep following a severe epileptic fit, though her husband claimed, but later withdrew his statement, that his wife had never been epileptic, had never displayed any symptoms and he had known her intimately for twelve years.

A reconstruction of the first meeting based partially on her statement and her purported answers begins after she had been requested to assist her 'boss' and she joined him in the Cabinet room and it would seem that the P.M. had only just requested the Cabinet `s approval for his political deputy to sit and observe from the Table itself, as distinct from sitting behind the Cabinet members.

Wilson must have surprised everyone in the room when instead of announcing his intention of visiting the Queen and requesting the dissolution of Parliament, he confirmed that he had, over the weekend, been supplied with estimates by the Ministry of Agriculture, Fisheries and Food with their forecasts for the summer harvest. It was already known that even if there was a bumper harvest, because of the damage inflicted in East Anglia following the Warsaw Pact strikes on the U.S.A.F. bases, that there would be a considerable shortfall.

"Our Commonwealth and Empire friends", as he had said before, were supporting them but the cargo ships were still not delivering adequate supplies from across the 'High Seas', which were becoming much safer as evidenced, as he had been informed only that morning by the Board of Trade, that the 'Lloyds marine war rate' was nearly back to pre crisis times, that is before the assassination of the U.S. President; but he was disinclined to comment, even in the privacy of the Cabinet room, concerning their allies in 'Washington' who had not supported them in their hour of need, an admission that came as a shock to those members that up to then had been denied knowledge of the true relationship with the nation that previously had been believed to be Great Britain`s most loyal ally.

"By the skin of their teeth they would get through the winter provided it was mild, but it was necessary and imperative to implement not only rationing but a temporary freeze to protect the economy. It would be like rats leaving a sinking ship, a dereliction of their duty and a scandal, if they reneged on their responsibilities and not only demanded a General Election but allowed the situation to deteriorate whilst they were campaigning."

And then Wilson got up from his chair, walked round the Table, over to the window and looked down on the immaculately kept garden and with his back to the Cabinet stated that:

"I have no alternative but to again address the nation and admit, though it was the incompetence of others, that I must be personally held responsible for the debacle which has been the chaotic and inefficient attempt to bring in the joint identity and ration card, even though, in the greatest of secrecy, since before my return from Blackpool, a team led by my political associate, George Brown, has developed a new streamlined plan for the registration which would be simpler to implement and even fairer when being operated. It could even be working by the New Year when, combined with a control of wages and prices, an Election could be called for late March or early April. Although there has never been a formal declaration of war by us or our enemies, we are, *de facto*, still in a state of war which might flare up, with dangerous consequences, at any moment."

Why Wilson had innocuously and cunningly ended his remarks with a reference to the state of war did not immediately make any impression on those in the room but he was now ready to hear any comments or remarks in response to his statements in order to draw out any potential objectors and then asked if:

"There was anyone or a group or clique who was prepared to put narrow party politics before the national interest?"

Wilson expected that Edward Heath, a former officer in the Second World War, and the formidable Sir Hendrie Oakshott, not on any party political, but on constitutional grounds, to strongly and forcibly endeavour to persuade their fellow members - irrespective of their political affiliations – to confront Wilson`s apparent attempt to maintain his now increasingly authoritarian and dictatorial control but they remained surprisingly silent. Craven and impotent.

Wilson was about to legitimise his intentions and will when one member of the Cabinet unexpectedly, unexpectedly because the P.M. had regarded him as weak, pliant and malleable, if at first falteringly, began to speak. Sir John MacLeod, Conservative M.P. for Ross and Cromarty, Minister of Agriculture, Fisheries and Food, appointed only to 'make up the numbers' and for his perceived physical weakness, began to speak eloquently, with a beautiful regional Scottish accent that was both unique in a sea of 'Upper class English' but above all was sincere and compelling.

"He was confused and uncertain. As the Minister, despite an ongoing and debilitating illness, he had not received from his Permanent Secretary, within the last few days, any papers in connection with estimates for the summer harvest and that the plan to bring in 'Cards' and a freeze had, in his opinion, not been dealt with correctly, had been foolishly rushed, inadequately debated and that they, the Cabinet, were only now reaping the consequences of the P.M.'s perhaps ill conceived attempt to push through *HIS* [both the speaker's and the author's emphasis] policies."

Finally, with a conviction that clearly was swaying even those who might be, for party political purposes, expected to support Harold Wilson, he declared that:

"He would unswervingly back the Prime Minister provided that the Cabinet was unanimous in their support which would be obtained if Harold [he used the P.M.'s first name with that beguiling and distinctive Scottish accent] could convince them of the economic, political and military situation, that is [and Wilson could see his whole plan disintegrating] there was a full and candid disclosure of the nation's state since it appeared that the Cabinet was most likely not in possession of all the facts."

A silence descended upon everyone in the room, only broken by the man that Harold Wilson had believed was even weaker than his Conservative Minister for Agriculture. George Brown, who, with authority, even though he had been introduced into the room as an observer, then opined:

"That it might be in the best interests, not only of the nation but of this meeting, that a further Cabinet meeting be held, as early as tomorrow, to give the Prime Minister the opportunity to present to everyone now present, information and documentation to support his position and in order that a decision be reached."

As the Cabinet exited 10 Downing Street through the famous black painted door and into the road that led to Whitehall, the assembled press and members of the public were surprised that no comment was made concerning the forthcoming election and their faces expressed a sense of acute despondency. It was only Sir John MacLeod, who surprised the press and spectators when, in contradiction to his image, he raised his right hand with his vertical thumb and called out:

"Good news will, I promise, follow"; but in reply to journalists' demands for amplification or clarification they were ignored and he remained, like the Sphinx, enigmatically silent.

TWENTY-SIX

Wilson could not contain his anger and bitterness, slamming the door to the Cabinet room and truculently and without any consideration for those in his path, like a battering ram, marched to his private apartment to emerge some twenty minutes later, still incandescent with rage, to demand a meeting with his now two trusted advisors, Gold and Kaufman (civil servants in hearing distance commented upon the new order of seniority) and:

"His f*****g deputy, whose was as loyal to him as... (he stopped completing the comparison when he saw the number of staff in hearing distance, milling around)."

Whether Kaufman had inferred any importance to Wilson`s priority of Gold over himself, will now never be known, but what was clearly evident was an increasing schism between the two men as they vied for the P.M. `s attention and favour. They were then both still unaware of all the events in the Cabinet room only that their mentor had suffered a rebuff and that a General Election was not to be immediately called, which the astute Kaufman had immediately recognised as a mistake of monumental strategic and constitutional proportions. Brown was cowed and intimidated not only by his superior`s outburst but by his perception that he had been eclipsed by two new rising stars. When confronted by a summary of the unexpected events and outcome in the Cabinet meeting, Gold suggested that the Cabinet be persuaded and not coerced into support by the arguments of patriotism but above all by the pragmatic necessity to avoid an even greater catastrophe if rationing was not brought in and additionally, in his own words:

"A lid was at least temporarily put on the surge in demand exceeding supply or inflated wages chasing insufficient goods, but leaving an adequate window of opportunity for expansion and wage increases."

Gold realised that the labyrinthine, almost maze like relationship of Wilson with the unions, meant that he would pay 'Dane Geld' to buy and secure their loyalty but at that moment he did not want to incorporate this dimension in the advice that he gave.

Gold had also refined and completed his programme to bring in a simplified card and argued that a carefully drafted and specious appeal to the nation by a humble P.M., could convince the people and swing their support behind him. Kaufman was less sycophantic in his advice but postulated that his master's political opponents could be swept aside if they did not support his argument which must be backed by as much evidence that his senior civil servants could assemble within the next few hours or, if necessary, they would have to work through the night, but in any event (and unfortunately he did not present his argument to Harold Wilson in the most diplomatic of terms, not understanding his obsessive desire for more central control of the economy):

"A General Election was constitutionally now due and that over five hundred constituencies were currently not represented by an M.P. and that any delay might be interpreted as purely a party political ploy to retain power."

The following day, the absence of George Brown (who had had an unexpected recurrence of his 'medical condition') at the resumed Cabinet meeting was noted with indifference, but the appearance of both 'Manny' Gold and Gerald Kaufman sitting strategically behind Harold Wilson and effectively 'shunting' the Cabinet Secretary to the 'side lines' (therefore, in consequence, restricting the freedom of movement of those Cabinet members on either side of the P.M.) was noted with ominous anger by his political opponents and Wilson's opening remarks further enflamed them with his comment that:

"He might require his special advisors to speak, on his behalf",

which was immediately greeted by a deluge of objections on the grounds of precedent or procedure to which he glibly replied:

"That in view of the national situation he considered any constructive information brought to the table would help those present to reach the best decision in the national interest."

The Cabinet Secretary had again brought in his assistant whose statement, at her trial in camera, was not therefore witnessed by her husband, speaks of an atmosphere that was from the outset, confrontational, acrimonious and vindictive, as those present at the Cabinet table appeared to split into almost tribal party lines without listening to or reviewing the information, which in certain cases was a revelation and drew immediate accusations of recklessness, especially when it was disclosed that the country's strategic food reserves had been effectively 'raided' to support the food supply, which also surprised the less knowledgeable who had never realised that previous governments had had the foresight to have created and kept stocked food dumps in the event of an emergency or war!

Whilst previous governments and cabinets had their own unique style and procedures, it is certain that traditions and habits developed, literally, over more than two hundred years had indelibly put their mark on the accepted procedure of this most august body of power, however even if Harold Wilson had the even handed qualities of an unbiased chairman, he was unable to maintain discipline, authority and above all fairness when at times, again according to the secretary's statement and corroborated by the Cabinet Secretary at his trial, where his secretary's evidence was used against him, the meeting descended into a battleground where dignity was debased in a flood of recriminations and counter recriminations.

In less than an hour, the legacy of democracy that had been accumulated since Magna Carta nearly seven hundred and fifty years before, was squandered in a vicious confrontation between two sides whose anger and animosity descended into naked hatred, the victors being the ones that were prepared to sacrifice the principles of democracy for their own short term gain.

TWENTY-SEVEN

At that same moment in time, not even Harold Wilson knew that he would bequeath a poisoned chalice to his successors, indeed he was to be the last British Prime Minister actually legally installed by the procedures of tradition and at the request and invitation of the Queen and by his actions and almost authoritarian dictatorial style of leadership, inaugurate events that would terminate in the callous asphyxiation and assassination of democracy. The Cabinet room would, for want of a better analogy, become a cockpit where two opposing sides confronted each other like fighting cocks, the end result being the survival of the victor, the vanquished symbolically mauled and left for dead, though in reality within minutes of what was to be a pyrrhic victory, Wilson had instructed the Cabinet office to impose a D Notice (Defence Notice) on any matters that had been raised in the supposedly confidential Cabinet meeting.

The Cabinet office had recently installed a number of the latest advanced Xerox photocopying machines and in front of each member of the Cabinet, with spare sets available for the advisors in the room, were copies of a document from which Harold Wilson, who opened the meeting, referred to and began to speak. It was a hastily produced updated document that senior civil servants had worked on overnight in conjunction with their associates in the Ministry of Agriculture, Fisheries and Food which gave an in depth analysis of the country's food reserves and the anticipated harvest that was beginning to be brought in. Its presentation immediately generated a vitriolic response from Sir John MacLeod who objected that:

"He had not been notified or informed of his civil servants' actions and categorically should have at least been supplied with copies of the documentation before the meeting."

Wilson was prepared for this anticipated objection and with an uncalled for tone of sarcasm stated that the document had been finally produced only minutes before the meeting commenced and that:

"Should the Minister wish to carefully peruse the introduction he will find a statement confirming that the contents had not been 'proof read' and therefore might contain errors, but a definitive version was in the process of being prepared and would be available by six p.m. that day."

Wilson painstakingly, slowly, meticulously and even at times punctiliously and sometimes intentionally to the obvious boredom and irritation of even his own political allies, went through the report even drawing the Cabinet members attention to obvious errors. The report optimistically estimated, in anticipation of a bumper harvest and no adverse weather interruptions, but taking into account the loss of agricultural production in East Anglia following the nuclear attacks by Warsaw Pact bombers against the United States Air Force bases and the secondary and residual damage to agricultural land, that the country would only have available ten to fourteen weeks stocks of food on the shop shelves, together with a further seven to ten weeks in reserve, the latter figures relating to warehouse stocks and the reduced supplies in the emergency food dumps.

Edward Heath, on completion of the depressing summary, hastily interrupted Wilson and commented that:

"The situation was critical and justified draconian action and that -"

He was in turn counter interrupted by the Secretary of State for Foreign Affairs, The Right Honourable Mr. Patrick Gordon Walker, who stated coldly...

"Exactly", but not allowing Edward Heath to continue his argument which would have been that it had been reckless to raid the strategic food reserves, purely for political capital.

Then the Minister for Transport, James Griffiths, speaking crudely in a Welsh accent, literally tore into the Minister for Defence Edward Heath, and without finesse and more important without grounds, accused him …

"Of being a party to thirteen years of decadent Conservative rule, of putting the wealthy before the weak and now, in the hour of the nation`s greatest adversity, putting his party before the nation`s best interests."

Wilson made no attempt to curb the invective or the polemical assault, because he saw his Labour party associate as a tool to subdue and control his adversaries when he then reported on the critical state of the fuel reserves from documentation which he announced was classified as 'Top Secret' since it had obvious military implications. He reminded all those in the room that overwhelmingly, supplies came from the Middle East where the political situation was still unstable and that whilst, in conjunction with their ally, the United States (crucially ignoring his comment of the previous day), they had reasserted their control and were still dominant in the Mediterranean, there was still danger from the Bay of Biscay onwards, necessitating a wide diversion to avoid Warsaw Pact and Soviet forces now entrenched in France.

In order to emphasise the potential danger, he reminded the Cabinet of his remarks made the previous day, that at no time had either side declared a state of war on the other and that military action might flare up at any moment and it was only (and he then chose his words cunningly) the potential threat and his willingness, in the final analysis, to use nuclear weapons and the ultimate weapon, the Yellow Sun thermonuclear device, this time against Moscow(actually believing the government`s own propaganda and continuing mendacity), that he believed that those in the Kremlin had seen reason. Reverting to the fuel stocks, strategic reserves for the military and the organs of law and order were more than adequate (in reality up to six months) but there was an unquantified shortage for civilian use (he was aware that if rationing was introduced and priority given to the transport and haulage sectors then there was at least three months stock).

It was then that the Lord Chancellor, Sir Reginald Manningham- Buller, with great dignity and courtesy but with clarity and coherence, requested that the P.M. not only quantify the strategic and tactical reserves of fuel but also give details of the Commonwealth`s contribution to the food reserves as mentioned in an earlier Cabinet meeting, then referring to his copy of the report, which he had briefly reviewed, which made no mention whatsoever of this relevant, but important element. But before Wilson could give a response (whether factual or evasive, indeed the compilers and statisticians in their haste had completely overlooked this relevant aspect) Konni Zilliacus, the Secretary of State for Commonwealth Relations, without justification, turned on the Lord Chancellor and demanded to learn if ...

"He was prepared to betray his country, like his political ally and co - conspirator Heath, for short term political gain when his only consideration should be the best interests of the country and not his plutocratic friends in the House of Lords or the degenerate aristocracy!?"

Later, after the meeting, a placid, almost humble Zilliacus introduced himself to Gold and mentioned, with great pride, that he had briefly met his parents when he went to Russia with Josiah Clement Wedgwood after the Revolution and like so many others was captivated not only by his mother's beauty but also her passionate support for her husband's (sic) research on the history of the Russian people. Strangely he ended the brief meeting with, at that moment, an unusual enquiry:

"Had he ever met a fellow Hebrew, or one of his representatives, Joel Ben Yitzhak?"

His patience exhausted, and to legitimise his intentions, the P.M. called for a vote to authorise whatever action the Cabinet deemed necessary to protect the nation and, almost as an aside, Wilson mentioned and confirmed that he intended to delay the General Election until the spring of nineteen sixty-five in order to urgently bring in a new revised joint identity and ration card. No mention had been made regarding the solution and the operation that George Brown was heading which prompted Sir Reginald Manningham-Buller, again with great dignity and courtesy, to raise the matter, when in response the P.M. contemptuously, leaning back in his chair, drew the Cabinet's attention to 'Manny 'Gold, who he said...

"Had, in conjunction with my political deputy, George Brown, who was unable to attend following a recurrence of his long standing medical condition, prepared an entirely new programme which only required the Cabinet's approval, and the necessary production and printing of documentation to complete and resolve the matter, effectively in the most simple terms, necessitating only a streamlined registration process and collection of the public's cards.

Gold was preparing himself to speak before the Cabinet when Wilson, displaying what was in fact his true nature and contempt for the democratic process, announced that unless anyone in the room could...

"Bring to the Cabinet table any constructive arguments, he felt that the time had come for decisive action and not short term political sectarian considerations

Those who had been raised on, and adhered to the democratic process, were subdued and shocked into a temporary silence by, what one who was present at the meeting later described as...

"This 'Stalinist' disregard for discussion and negotiation, but more ominously, the delay calling a General Election."

Wilson`s wishes, which he had effectively 'railroaded 'through, were approved by a vote of seven to five.

Thus Wilson, through coercion and bluff, had succeeded in his quest and stood unassailable, able to dictate and steer the nation`s path to fairness and equality. The defeated left the room, shell shocked and wondering what had actually taken place in the name of democracy and social equality.

TWENTY-EIGHT

Mandel Goldburgh, now commonly known as Manny Gold, was walking excitedly and briskly across Trafalgar Square, in a Northerly direction, with St. Martins In The Fields to his immediate right and Charing Cross Road ahead of him, with the intention of locating a public house where he could order some simple Anglo-Saxon sustenance and a ginger beer to celebrate the confidential news that the Prime Minister had just imparted to him in the privacy of his office. The second Cabinet meeting in two days had ended somewhat acrimoniously some three hours before with, in the verbatim observation of his 'boss' ...

"A victory, not for his convincing argument, substantiated by confidential documentation, or his strength of will, but a monumental victory for all the British people."

The roast beef sandwiches were not as fresh or even as succulent as the ones that had been available the previous week in Blackpool but his excitement and the hormonal euphoria following Harold's news neutralised any dissatisfaction and anyway the ginger beer had been served at exactly the right temperature, poured with care and bloomed with the flavour and bite of raw ginger. He savoured the ginger beer, but strangely felt, and he had never experienced the sensation before, that he was being observed, no something more, he was being watched. It was an unnerving experience but he resolved to ignore the sensation and soon decided to take a leisurely walk, not to Leicester Square Underground Station but a short distance further on to Piccadilly Circus or if the pleasant weather held, to Green Park where he would get a Piccadilly Line tube to Kings Cross and then change and make his way home on the Northern Line.

As Gold passed the statue of Eros and joined a throng of Londoners (and by their accents a small vociferous party of Americans) waiting to cross Lower Regent Street on their way to Piccadilly, the sensation returned, indeed he felt slightly frightened as if he instinctively knew that his pursuer already sensed that his quarry was aware that he was being stalked. He hoped that salvation would lie in his anonymous location deep within a crowd of sightseers and shoppers when suddenly, unexpectedly, he was assailed, discreetly in the beautiful language of Russian by the person who had been tracking him.

"My dear Mandel, though until now we have never met, I have, with great interest, followed your ever increasingly successful career, now here but previously in the Soviet Union and the United States, sometimes delving through the tortuous layers of deceit to understand and recognise exactly where your loyalties lay, again sometimes wondering if, like a whore or a politician, your ultimate loyalty was to yourself alone. But then I remembered once and once only, if only foolishly, when you committed yourself to print did you really disclose your true faith to Lavrenti Beria or was it some fraudulent attempt to cover your intentions to escape from the Soviet Union?"

He found himself in Fortnum and Mason, whether in a failed attempt to escape his pursuer or if his pursuer had deftly engineered an escape from the crowded street he would not know, but did enjoy the Ice Cream Sundae. His host ate three scoops of vanilla ice cream but he sensed that he had only eaten the dish to put his guest (or quarry) at ease. The man had switched to impeccable English, without any trace of an accent, actually talking in a manner as if to calm his guest about the Sword of Damocles that had been raised above his head and permit Gold to conjecture how he knew about *THAT* long forgotten letter.

Then strangely and unnecessarily the man began to speak in Yiddish, asking initially if Gold wished to speak in that archaic, anachronistic tongue which was even less likely to be understood by those around them, reminding him that if they conversed in Russian it might bring even more unwanted interest, such was the current climate of xenophobia.

For some the art of diplomacy or tact can be learned or even inculcated, a few are endowed with the virtue as a natural characteristic whilst for others it is an ability to communicate a demand in such a way that the recipient actually believes that their own wishes and desires have been achieved.

There are also those for whom the art or act of communication is a skill and virtue which can never be grasped.

"His career, now blooming under the Prime Minister could continue, indeed must; his relationship with their mutual friend in Washington (it was only after the meeting had ended that Gold suddenly realised the ramifications of the man`s comment) would not be in peril, and his loyalty whether genuine or spurious with his 'handler' at the Soviet embassy could continue uninterrupted or his whole devious existence based on financial greed and his egocentric desires would quickly collapse.

He had been circumcised as a Jew, indeed his first name had a special Yiddish meaning and now he must confront his heritage and responsibilities."

The host paid the bill and shortly afterwards Gold found himself walking and talking in Green Park. It was a magnificent late afternoon of probably the final week or so of a glorious summer, and for the first time he felt exhilarated as the sunshine warmed his face.

"International Judaism is not a secret society as caricatured and scurrilously and mendaciously portrayed in the Tsarist forgery, *'The Protocols of the Learned Elders of Zion'*, neither is it a body of Capitalists or Communists working to undermine and destroy the foundations of diverse societies now or in the past or future. Judaism, Israel and the diaspora will always be confronted by enemies, the latest being the author of a vicious work entitled *'The Authoritarian State'*, for sale at the paltry sum of one and sixpence. By his very nature the Jew is both a member of the wider community and at the same time isolated and separate.

Throughout history, the Jews have suffered ignominy and humiliation by those whose motives were based on ignorance or callous jealousy, even hatred or in more simplistic terms in the desire to steal that which they were not either capable or competent to earn by their own toil.

But there was and currently existed an organised group of likeminded Jews who were and always would be prepared to defend their fellows to permit them the freedom to pursue their faith and above all the higher values that set apart 'us' from 'them' but they never believed that they were better than the wider community only that a sacred or special duty had been imposed upon them.

The body was global and international in its presence and activities but there was no formal bond between those that pursued its aims, only the fundamental consequence of birth, being their Jewishness. Therefore there was no organisation that was registered or incorporated and those that had committed themselves never thought that they were members or associated with others such as the Lodges of Freemasons and there was no badge in the literal or symbolic sense to identify them, neither were there gatherings, only the transfer of information or instructions through intercommunicating cells like neurones in the human brain.

The secular interests of the Jewish people, despite their diverse attitudes, have coincided with the wider interests of the Western democracies and even the social and cultural aspirations of their Semitic Islamic brothers and it has been economically and politically convenient for all parties, through their representatives, to cooperate in harmony.

Judaism is not Zionism and vice versa. The aspiration for a national home has only recently been fulfilled at an almost inconceivable cost in human lives and whether it was one death, a million or six million, irrespective of the fate of the one or the many that suffered, is it right for the diverse factions to live their lives in conflict when, in harmony, that region which is called Israel could succour the rest of the 'Middle East' and create a vast area of agricultural and commercial wealth and plenty?

Its members were decimated during the years nineteen thirty-three to nineteen forty-five but the fundamental objective survived intact; however those based in the United States, Canada and Mexico were not affected and their connections and influence helped to secure a national home, at long last, for the Jewish people and, as an aside, their intelligence nearly thwarted the vicious assassination of one of its supporters, my former personal friend Lev Bronstein ,Leon Trotsky, who had been warned of the true nature of the man who had assimilated himself into the friendship of the Trotsky household."

The anonymous harbinger stopped, strangely bent down and proceeded to pull from the ground a small tuft of grass which he rolled between his palms which he then raised to his nose, clearly appreciating the smell.

"My name is Joel Ben Yitzhak. If only our lives were as simple and beautiful as nature, then the darkness of evil and the task of making difficult choices could be avoided. Your patriotic loyalty to Great Britain should transcend your duty as a Jew to Israel and Judaism even if it is in apparent opposition, though I have found that even decisions or acts intended or seemingly in conflict with our interests can be utilised to our advantage. Thus, for example, whilst the British government courts what is known as the Arab Middle East, primarily to secure and maintain the supply of oil, though the events of late last year have perhaps temporarily destabilised the situation and have given the appearance of denying Israel's interests, in reality the status quo continues, for the oil is handled by a 'Third Party' before it is shipped openly back across the Mediterranean to Israel.

We may never meet again as contact will always be through my associates who will make themselves known and will inform you of what is needed, be it information or the pursuit of some act or policy. "

Gold was about to respond cautiously and with caveats to accept the unspecified demands that had been placed on his shoulders when suddenly he realised that he was alone; he immediately turned through three hundred and sixty degrees to locate the man who for all intent and purposes had disappeared as if a magician had spirited him from the stage of life.

TWENTY-NINE

By early November two interconnected events had taken place which inexorably were propelling the world order to the brink of a new era which was the formation of three global superpowers where in two, any lingering, isolated flames of democracy would be extinguished and the rule of absolute totalitarianism and the end of the individual's rights would triumph; whilst in the third, 'the national Interest' would dominate and over-ride the' inalienable rights' of the individual and it was only in the countries that had comprised the old British Empire that was Canada, New Zealand and Australia, did democracy survive intact but in all three states, voluntarily under the protection, military 'umbrella' and will of the United States, certain national interests had to be jettisoned.

On October fifteenth, Khrushchev appeared on television to announce that due to ill health he was forthwith resigning from all his official positions including the Communist Party executive which he had loyally served for over half a century and was recommending to the Politburo (Soviet observers immediately noted that the title had officially reverted to its original name, though Khrushchev may have made a mistake) that his associate and dear friend, Leonid Brezhnev formally assume his responsibilities and official positions.

On October seventeenth, Israeli Army radio broke into its regular broadcast to announce that on the previous day, the sixteenth, the Chinese had exploded their first nuclear weapon at Lop Nor in Sinkiang Province.

Early in November, Chou En Lai arrived in Moscow on a hastily arranged official visit publicised as a long standing invitation from the Soviet First Secretary to his Socialist Brothers and consummated at the airport by an extravagant bear hug from Brezhnev for Chou.

What was discussed, in camera, and the tone of the two men's conversation was chillingly frightening. Brezhnev was aware of Khrushchev's promises and when pressed readily agreed to the transfer of fissionable material to construct up to the increased number of fifty nuclear devices but based on the Chinese design. The 'spheres of Influence 'was again discussed and agreed however this time given the formal status of a treaty by the issue of two bilingual maps each signed and dated by the leaders.

The Pacific Ocean was to be, in the words of Brezhnev:

"Liberated from Yankee hegemony",

and he insisted that with immediate effect berthing rights be afforded to submarines from their Northern Fleet which were to be redeployed in the Far East with the intention of roaming the Western Pacific and as far West as the Indian Ocean, initially cutting, by military action, commerce between Britain and her old Empire allies and later between the United States and Japan thereby reducing the military build up that was a threat to Socialism.

Furthermore Brezhnev hinted, but did not amplify or clarify that a new generation of high technology weapons would place...

"The Americans on the defensive and therefore more amenable to the expansionist policies of the Union of Soviet Socialist Republics and People's Republic of China and their policies of liberation."

Business was completed by a humble request from Leonid Brezhnev that in tribute to the Great Helmsman, Mao Tse Tung, henceforth he was to be described as the Supreme Great Helmsman.

At an intimate State Banquet attended by some six hundred guests, where Chou En Lai was the honoured guest, speeches were made extolling the Supreme Great Helmsman. An Albanian party of leading Communist cadres included a distinctly East European Semitic member who occasionally left the table to visit another table occupied by the much feted scientists who had created their nation's first nuclear bomb and who had secretly been given blueprints and technological expertise for this weapon by the same man, Joel Ben Yitzhak, clandestinely supplied by United States Intelligence thus allowing their government to constantly monitor Chinese nuclear capabilities.

It was shortly before these events that Prime Minister Harold Wilson made his eagerly anticipated television broadcast on Tuesday, October sixth, nineteen sixty-four, once again viewed sitting beside the fireplace, smoking his pipe, endeavouring successfully to create the impression of confidence and as his speech progressed he projected a new image of humility, integrity and self recognition of his fallibility culminating in an apology for the current situation concerning the distribution of the joint ration and identity cards.

The following morning the Press was equally divided in its analysis, not only of the P.M.'s presentation, but more importantly in the substance of his vision and intentions. If he had intended to be 'Churchillian' in his delivery or more importantly in the frankness of his message, reviews ranged from 'Statesmanlike' (*The Daily Mirror*) to 'A Second Hand Car Salesman' (*The Daily Mail*). He had announced, with gravity, that:

"Whilst it was still most important to bring in rationing, the procedure had been inefficiently organised and would have to be started again. Fortunately, his political deputy George Brown had been involved with the civil service for some weeks, completely reorganising the operation which would resume in November and would be completed by mid December. New documentation was being printed incorporating the facility for photographic identification, however it was not intended to include a passport picture [sic] as he personally considered it to be an unnecessary infringement of the individual's freedom and could not, or would not be used as an internal passport, the mark of a dictatorial state."

Emboldened by his deft presentation and confident in Gold's proposition and plan he consummately announced to the British people that:

"He personally had made a grave error of judgement when he had authorised the original registration system, not realising that certain [unspecified] senior Civil Servants had misinformed and misled him over their ability to handle the enormous task that the government had ordered them to deal with."

He then stopped, enjoyed his pipe, deliberately allowed his audience to appreciate his humility and honesty, then continued...

"No child, widow or the weak would suffer because of his error or by poor government (Gold had specifically advised him not to use the word incompetent on the basis that he did not want to inflame the Civil Service Union). The shop shelves were full of food and produce and there was no necessity for panic buying or more important of all fear that the absence of a ration card would deprive anyone of their fair share. Arrangements had been made and were ongoing to organise registration in an orderly and fair manner without the necessity of a registration photograph. Whilst the global military situation appeared calmer and Lloyd's marine rate for war risks (a benchmark and 'thermometer' of peace) was slowly coming down and approaching the pre crisis level he could not predict the future, but supplies, in ever increasing volumes were being shipped from Canada, New Zealand and Australia."

He stopped again, this time lighting his pipe, appeared to ponder over his next comments and finally projected an air of extreme gravitas...

"It is your right in our democratic society to elect those who you wish to represent your constituencies and for the majority of those elected through the party that they support to form a government. At this moment in time over five hundred constituencies remain unrepresented, a situation which is both unfair and intolerable. The Cabinet agonised about calling a General Election but considered its urgent first priority to implement the joint identity and ration card. We have therefore agreed to postpone and delay the Election until the spring of next year when a new Electoral Register will come into force based on the registration which will take place before the end of the year."

Shortly afterwards Gold joined the P.M. and Kaufman to put into force the implementation of his well conceived plan whilst coincidentally and concurrently beginning to outmanoeuvre and sideline Gerald Kaufman. Gold, having savoured the corrupting taste of power intended, if possible, to accumulate power and influence independently of his mentor and it would be initially expressed in severing and terminating the influence of his former superior, Kaufman.

George Brown was little more than an insignificant figurehead and cipher, primarily interested in the trappings of his sinecure and relieving the boredom of his official presence by the companionship of that which was the root of his illness.

For Gold, the next few weeks were a period of intense activity, sometimes alleviated by cursory meetings with his nominal superior, George Brown, who increasingly had reoccurring bouts of his illness.

In reality the new, revised cards differed only nominally from the original version but now included a facility to specify dependents under the age of sixteen (including their dates of birth), cross referencing the document to other documents issued for dependents and partners.

An analysis of the operation would deduce that Gold's scheme did not incorporate any radical or new methods to operate, streamline or even accelerate the administration but relied on the trusted and existing well tried system of polling stations that were set up at each election taking into account the current Electoral Register but this time instead of being open for one day only and from the usual seven a.m. to nine p.m. were to open including Sundays for two weeks and this time they would be supported by adequate competent staff from the banks and local government, assisted by civil servants who would create their internal registers in effect generating a mini census and an up to date record of the country`s inhabitants .

The police and M.I.5. were also interested in the potential of the new scheme.

THIRTY

Such was the simple efficiency of the new registration procedure that by early December every constituency had completed its work, delivered and recorded the documentation and submitted records which were stored, securely against fire or water damage or by unauthorised access, in each local Town Hall.

On Wednesday, December thirtieth, nineteen sixty-four, George Brown was admitted to a London teaching hospital and discreetly allocated a private room where his presence and the real reason for his admittance were not publicly announced. News of his tragic death early on New Year's day was broadcast first by the television channels and the following day by his loyal political colleague and long time friend, the Prime Minister. On that same Wednesday, Harold Wilson hosted for his immediate family and their most intimate friends and political allies a cocktail party in the previously sacrosanct private apartment at Ten Downing Street.

Both Gerald Kaufman and Manny Gold were on the invitation list and the announcement of George Brown's condition and hospitalisation was greeted by some of the guests with an unusual movement of their right hands, wrists and elbows. Manny Gold was, for some, a surprise guest but was specially singled out and both praised and congratulated by his mentor...

"For a job well done (and)...for my salvation."

Within three days this unimportant trivia was gratefully received, along with a list of all the guests (and other insignificant news) by a journalist who had previously a close association with the now closed Soviet embassy in London and within a further twenty four hours by those in Moscow who anticipated, in the future, more important items of intelligence.

When, five days earlier, Her Majesty the Queen broadcast her Christmas Day message, accompanied by her husband and supported by her two elder children, Prince Charles and Princess Anne, and interrupted by the occasional presence of her youngest child, Prince Andrew, she spoke not only of hope, but of a guarded optimism for the forthcoming year, contrasting it to the uncertainty of the year that was nearly over. This measured hope correctly mirrored the dominant national mood but also confirmed to Harold Wilson that his decisions, however confrontational or unilateral, undeniably were in the best interests of the country and also proved that the advice and assistance of Manny Gold would further his position.

At the end of November, a convoy of Swedish registered vessels (and others flying the Panamanian flag) had left Stockholm on route for New York, carrying an estimated twelve and a half thousand United States servicemen and women, repatriated through the intervention and negotiation of the Swedish and Swiss Red Crosses. In Great Britain, Pathe News, in cinemas, and the three T.V. channels, broadcast scenes of their euphoric arrival and reception clearly showing their good health and obvious relief.

What was not shown, as part of the draconian agreement negotiated by the two national Red Crosses and the Swedish government, were four fully laden hospital ships that had deliberately been held back and berthed in the dead of night containing the debris of war. The United States negotiators had been compelled not to publicise in any way the flagrant physical horror of the use of chemical weapons, the awful consequences and the horrendous suffering. It was to be some months before the American people would be confronted with the truth behind the initial military debacle.

The United States' President was re- elected in his own right following a massive pro Democratic Party landslide though had the voters known the real situation regarding the previous secret negotiations for the repatriation of U.S. military and civilian personnel in occupied Western Europe and the evidence of Russia's deployment of Inter Continental Ballistic Missiles able to hit (though their accuracy was still in doubt) any U.S. location, then perhaps they might have voted for the hawkish and aggressive Republican candidate. However, in any event, the die had been cast and the future direction set in a tablet of bitter recrimination.

The terms of the repatriation agreement, reluctantly accepted by the President, forced him to realise that he should have accepted the ruthless advice of the so called 'Hawks' against the 'Doves' to finally, in a second strike, hit and wipe out the Soviet Union as a viable military entity in one massive blow, as both militarily and strategically correct, and that the moral arguments were of minor importance. Now the window of opportunity had forever closed and his and his successors' only primary option was a policy of research, development and continued modernisation of military weapons which he recognised would continue long after his Administration had ended its tenure.

He therefore also had no choice but to cede the *de facto* occupation and annexation of those Western European nations which formerly were the homes of democracy and allies of the United States to the Warsaw Pact and the Soviet Union, leaving them to their fate and as for the 'Atlantic Alliance' with the United Kingdom, until their potential military capability was fully restored it would be their own responsibility to recover and repatriate their forces and stranded civilians on the European mainland.

British optimism (to be proved in vain) was further raised when the United States President personally announced that the rest of his country's forces would be home by the end of March and that a further Armada, en route to New York, at that very moment just off the coast of Greenland (the President meant Iceland, but confessed later that such was his genuine joy, that a tear of emotion blurred his vision) was carrying the vast bulk of American civilians (not mentioning with suppressed rancour that a price had been paid by the Companies that they had worked for in the forced 'sale' - or confiscation or 'liberation' - of their European operations and loss of all their assets).

Nineteen sixty-five therefore ushered in hope for the British people that they would also see the return of family and friends from the beleaguered European mainland and this sense of hope and a partial resolution of the traumas of war and its consequences would mitigate their doubts and fears of an uncertain future.

Nineteen sixty-five also ushered in great hope for Harold Wilson for in the early afternoon of New Year's Eve three' V' Bombers loaded with live thermonuclear and nuclear devices completed their arduous and long indirect flight back from South Africa ,landing at a base in Lincolnshire having first, at the specific demand of the P.M, flown over Southampton and then London in a hastily organised triumphal fly past, described in the national papers as a long time planned display of national confidence and a tribute to the British forces that had some months before wrecked havoc and retribution on their Soviet adversaries.

When the last of his guests had departed, Harold left for the relative tranquillity and solitude of the Cabinet Room where he could consider the problems that the New Year would undoubtedly bring, the most likely being Trade Union opposition to his intention to impose a 'Price' and 'Wages' freeze but he felt confident that the nation would support his actions along with 'rationing'.

On Wednesday, January thirteenth, Parliament was to be recalled in what no one knew was to be its final session in perhaps over seven hundred years. He had less than two weeks to prepare his response and strategy to any opposition to his policies and especially to the new Emergency Powers Act, the only Act that had been passed since he had become Prime Minister and which had come into force the previous June, hurriedly (an understatement) rushed through Parliament and the Lords (at the behest of the Permanent Secretary to the Cabinet Office) in two days in June when both 'Houses' were sitting and where the Commons was under the authority of the newly elected and above all pliant Speaker.

Its critics, mainly in the national press, had raised muted questions, muted because of the voluntary censorship agreement, especially concerning its brevity and intended interpretation, but the initial interest had, like so many other causes, gradually subsided until the matter had euphemistically 'died a natural death'. What the Press did not know that on becoming 'The First Lord of the Treasury' Wilson had been confidentially informed of the draconian and almost totalitarian arrangements that had been put in place and were constantly being refined and updated to control the nation in the event of a nuclear war or major emergency, but he had put this knowledge and the potential situation to the back of his thoughts. He, of course, anticipated that those who had voted against his policies, in Cabinet, would continue their actions, possibly persuading those assembled to force a vote of no confidence, bringing down the interim government and forcing a General Election which was the unspoken wish of the nation.

Negotiations, utilising the Swedish Red Cross and government, continued at a painful, almost snail like pace with the Soviet representatives, who were described as having hearts colder than Siberia and whose very posture implied an intention to humiliate their opposite numbers and to secure an agreement on the most shameful and vindictive of terms, no doubt as a response to the suffering of the Soviet people following the nuclear attack, almost forgetting the previous suffering caused by the use of chemical and nerve agents. Wilson, impatient for a resolution of the negotiations, signalled to the negotiators, in Stockholm, to accept the conditions - or any terms (most likely with an eye to the resumption of Parliament and the forthcoming Election) - but either ignored or did not comprehend the final conditions of the agreement, therefore making a further catastrophic decision which would soon rebound against him with grave consequences. Thus he was able, when Parliament convened, to be able to announce that on Sunday January twenty- fourth the first batch of repatriated troops would arrive at Tilbury and he hoped that the nation would unite together, not only to greet them, but to end a period of trauma and mourning.

This had been an area of policy that had not involved Gold but when he next contacted his handler he was informed, with little tact, that 'Moscow' had expected some information, however insignificant (no doubt in order that even more harsher terms could be extracted and imposed as a response to Britain's so called nuclear assault on the Motherland).

The Prime Minister would also announce that rationing would commence on Monday, January twenty-fifth and that special arrangements would now be made for pregnant women and children under two years of age...

"If I and this government is to be remembered, its lasting legacy would be of compassion for the weak and care for those unable to defend themselves."

Government scientists and nutritionists had devised a diet and a spectrum of rationed foods which would give a level of fourteen thousand two hundred and ten calories a week, though staples such as bread, milk, eggs and cheese would be included in the total.

Although Gerald Kaufman's status and usefulness was diminishing in the eyes of the P.M., Wilson still saw him as a useful agent and decided to employ him as a conduit to the Press and the ever increasing role of Television as an 'anonymous source close to the Government' to divulge details of rationing so that he could gauge public reaction and he resolved to use Gold to contact Jack Jones, whose connections with the Trade Union movement would be, as an understatement useful, should they continue to object to the imminent "Price' freeze.

Before Parliament reconvened, by the same methods of contact, 'Moscow' was informed by two separate sources of the P.M.'s proposed approach to the Unions and whilst one of the sources also requested 'instructions' the other source revived his connections with his friends at the American Embassy also indicating that:

"He now felt able, after a period of silence, to provide information which he believed would strengthen the bond between the two nations."

When Parliament reconvened (unknowingly for the last time ever) in the magnificent and great Westminster Hall, conversation centred, not on the death of George Brown (with many members unwittingly repeating the almost Masonic like hand, wrist and elbow action) but of the news that the life of Winston Churchill was rapidly coming to its end, indeed the P.M., for once with genuine humility and with the full cooperation of the new Speaker, began his address to the 'House' which temporarily united all those present and permitted him to deliver his subsequent pre prepared speech and undermine what would have been the opening salvo of his political opponents .

The subsequent debate in response to the P.M.'s statement conveniently ended on the Friday afternoon permitting those assembled to disperse and return to their constituencies for the weekend and to gauge the local mood to the events.

The new Act was retrospectively reviewed and M.Ps. assured that the spirit, intention and purpose of the Act was only to apply in the event or imminence of nuclear war or of some dire emergency. Satisfied with the explanation (and Wilson conveniently did not go into details of his briefing and the ferocious, draconian nature of the authority that would replace the existing democratic system), he also selectively used the latest definitive report of the Country's food stocks but not, for security purposes, information regarding the strategic fuel reserves and supplies. Without a vote the government reached approval and agreement to bring in rationing but with the Government's Front Bench promise that the matter be reviewed in six months and that if any reduction in the calorific level be considered necessary then Parliament's approval had to be obtained.

The Prime Minister's original unilateral declaration to raise the salaries of the Armed Forces and the Police were debated with only some minor objections coming from an insignificant group of Labour Cooperative M.Ps. who referred to the intended freeze but were effectively overruled by the Speaker, a man of little experience, originally promoted and recommended by the Cabinet for his pliancy.

The same group of M.Ps. were vocal in their objections to the intended wage freeze, their arguments ranging from the pragmatic...

"The Union leadership would find it difficult justifying their acceptance of such a restraint on workers' rights and to maintain support beyond the spring or early summer might not be possible."

To the cogent and convincing...

"Whilst, in the current economic and political climate, personal economic sacrifice was an option, the very recent generous salary increase allowed to the Armed Forces and the Police should be extended to the workers who also had made great sacrifices in the coal pits, in the docks and on the railways."

And also the emotional, expressed by one belligerent M.P. in a rhetorical question as...

"The people in the other House will not go without, so why the hell should my constituents suffer?"

A motion of support for a "Wages" and "Prices" freeze for a minimum period of six months was passed, the majority being irrelevant since Wilson knew that a confrontation was inevitable and would require all his guile and a compromise shrouded in a fog of obfuscation.

THIRTY-ONE

The imminent confrontation between the government and the more militant unions was to be complicated by what then was regarded as an irrelevant and insignificant political force, but who would ultimately, in a few short months, change the destiny of the nation. Only the more visionary readers or soothsayers would have considered as relevant or important an item on page six, column four of The Times, Tuesday January fifth...

MR. GORDON WALKER

CALLED TRAITOR

Mr. Colin Jordan, leader of the National Socialist Movement, burst into a press conference Mr. Gordon Walker, Foreign Secretary, was holding at Leyton yesterday and shouted:

"You are a disgusting racial traitor."

In itself it was a futile and worthless act, virtually unreported and therefore ignored by the country at large and interpreted by those present as the unimportant opinion of a hothead and of a discredited and spent political ideology. Events however and the extreme Right`s almost lucky ability to recognise the mood of the country and their response to the nation`s concerns would create a seismic change in Britain.

Jack Jones met his 'handler' at their latest current *rendezvous* and was not surprised by her instructions which, not unexpectedly, were to ferment industrial anarchy, by strikes encouraged by marches of non union supporters expressing their concern at the iniquitous imposition of rationing, whilst the Campaign for Nuclear Disarmament(which even he had suspected was a Communist front organisation) would 'independently' begin a programme exposing and publicising the suffering of the Soviet people, highlighting the injuries suffered following the 'joint' American and British nuclear assault. He was handed a bulging, battered, brown briefcase, anonymous and nondescript whose weight surprised him and he immediately correctly realised its contents but it was only later that evening, in the privacy of his flat, was he astounded at the amount of old, grubby and therefore untraceable one and five pound notes. Only once before had he seen such an abundance of money and that was when, in Spain, during the Civil War, whilst fighting for the International Brigade, he had volunteered, for his new N K V D masters, to courier British currency to Madrid and to the sworn enemies of the P.O.U.M. which would finally facilitate their destruction.

He was enjoying the film and stayed long after his handler had left.

At the highest level of the Trade Union movement there was anger tempered by pragmatism that their 'brother and ally' had not made, in his speech to the Commons, any mention of legislation as promised at the Trades Union Conference, to protect the movement following the 'Rookes' versus 'Barnard 'decision of the House of Lords. Wilson's omission was in fact solely an error of memory but had he pursued the matter he would have recognised the potential opposition from the remaining rump of the decimated Conservative party which would have resulted in a protracted and potentially long and exhausting use of Parliament's time (and it was not convenient or in his interests to have Parliament in session) and in any event by the spring, the postponed General Election would take place, hopefully resulting in an overall majority.

THIRTY-TWO

Those Trade Union leaders and senior officials who were at the centre of what was subsequently described, early in the life of the New Order, as the 'perpetrators and architects of insurrection' are no longer alive to explain or justify their actions or to describe, from their viewpoint, the events in which they were active participants and more importantly, instigators, that is from Wednesday January thirteenth, when Harold Wilson made his statement and speech to the assembled House of

Commons and which was widely reported that same evening on radio and television, first to Friday January twenty second and then subsequently to the events which petered out early in February.

Conclusive and corroborated evidence confirms that as early as Thursday January fourteenth, George Woodcock, leader of the Trades Union Congress, and generally regarded as being to the right of the Socialist spectrum, telephoned the Prime Minister who arranged an unofficial and unrecorded meeting at a mutual acquaintance (probably Gerald Kaufman, who still had his uses) in order to discuss the movement's immediate and anticipated grievances and the probable actions of certain constituent members in the absence of any reference to the Trade Union movement in the statement of January thirteenth .

Wilson genuinely apologised for his oversight but reminded Woodcock that on consideration he would not be able to steer the required legislation through Parliament and that, with the *SENSIBLE* support of the Union movement he could secure a General Election victory and then deliver to the Unions a fair deal in return for their compliance with a prudent and realistic economic policy.

The meeting was probably on the evening of Friday January fifteenth when, coincidentally and most likely concurrently, David William 'Bill' Martin (the young 'firebrand' who had recently been introduced to the P.M. at the Labour Party reception) addressed a group of miners following the end of their shift. His impromptu, *ad hoc* address, was only reported in the local newspaper but far from being 'impromptu' was undoubtedly not only thoroughly conceived and crafted, but the following morning was delivered by post to over five hundred national pits on headed National Union of Mineworkers' paper and included an introduction confirming the source of the circular, background details both of the author and the reasons for his statement.

The two page address and his speech can be summarised by one sentence extracted from the document which even in isolation expresses the inflammatory intentions of his actions...

"He had absolutely no intention of allowing his members to be persecuted and used as economic fodder or pawns, as were their fathers and grand fathers in nineteen twenty-six during the General Strike and their struggle against the mine owners who had wanted to reduce their wages; now the clarion call of defiance might lead them to raise the 'barricades' to defend their basic and fundamental rights because otherwise they would be overwhelmed and destroyed by a new tyranny."

From the contents of the extract the reader can be in no doubt confident of the manner in which the 'ad hoc' address was made but subsequent speeches clearly showed that Bill Martin was a shrewd demagogue who knew exactly what he wished to impart and his ulterior motives.

On the Saturday morning any thoughts of a quiet or stress free weekend were dashed for the P.M. when he received an unexpected telephone call from Sidney Greene, general secretary of the National Union of Railwaymen and more ominously the man who had led the only official national strike, albeit for one day only, in October nineteen sixty-two.   Any repetition would perhaps be fatal, however the substance of his approach was both conciliatory in tone and intention...

"An industrial crisis of major proportions is brewing. My executive have been baying for strike action since Thursday and this morning they have been talking about their brothers in the mine workers` union and a clarion call to defend their basic and essential rights."

Greene arrived, characteristically in accordance with his moral and ethical values, on public transport, accompanied by an assistant, in his early forties, who he introduced as a fellow Sidney, but with the surname Weighell, who during the course of the afternoon, whilst temporarily absent, was described as the man who he was intending to recommend as the new assistant general secretary and perhaps one day might be his successor. Wilson`s spirits were raised, as the three men enjoyed homemade Ham and Cheese sandwiches (and bottled pale ale) since they were unanimous in their opinion that the country could not afford strike action and a drain on its resources whilst the P.M. was fascinated by Weighell`s recollections of his brief time as a professional footballer with Sunderland and how his career was eclipsed by a certain Raich Carter. Wilson asked the fundamental and only pertinent question which was...

"Could Greene control or persuade his executive and avert official or unofficial action or would the members start wildcat strike action at the grassroots?"

Ominously at that very moment, with almost theatrical timing, just as he awaited an answer, a definitive answer, his telephone burst into life and his private secretary announced an imperative call from Frank Cousins, general secretary of the Transport and General Workers Union. Usually such a call would be taken in a private office, recorded by a secretary and most important of all out of earshot, but the P.M. decided that he could not only trust his guests but use the situation to begin a process of reconciliation and no doubt, if absolutely necessary, compromise.

However Cousins was not in a mood to compromise, indeed his very attitude was aggressive and the sobriquet, trade union baron, consummately and perfectly described his tone as if he considered the power of his union above and beyond the authority of the government or any government.

"He had been democratically elected, unlike the Prime Minster whose reticence to stand before the Electorate and seek a mandate was clear and transparent evidence of his disregard for the democratic process and lack of confidence in his own policies. On the contrary, he had the absolute and overwhelming support not only of his executive but also and more important, his members, who numbered in excess of one million, three hundred thousand and (Wilson would find out the following day that Greene and Weighell had been observed walking along Whitehall and entering Downing Street by an observant T.G.W.U. executive member and Cousins` acolyte) whose patience was now at breaking point."

As much in anger as contempt he continued...

"The Union Movement no longer expects excuses but your active public support. Alan Fisher of the National Union of Public Employees and senior members of the National Union of General and Municipal Workers have made it clear to me and my executive that a line has now been crossed and that only the ultimate sanction, a policy that I have never abused, can be our only way forward. It is now up to you to consider the interests of the workers and not, apparently, your own interests."

At his trial, Greene confirmed that the P.M. was for a moment apparently completely unable to formulate any answer or riposte to the' Baron`s' statement and implied threat (in fact what fleetingly and initially went through Wilson's mind was the thought that Cousins had not mentioned a ballot of his members to confirm strike action). The silence allowed Cousins to continue, however he had exhausted his prepared statement and was unable to exploit his damning argument. Wilson seized the initiative and suggested that:

"Both parties meet, as soon as possible, to examine ways for the government and the Union Movement to constructively and jointly move forward within the parameters of an equitable and realistic agreement."

Unfortunately, what Wilson had in mind and offered was no longer an option for Cousins since his intentions were no longer open to negotiations and in any event, he was the prisoner of his own rhetoric but also he would be swept along by the demands of his fellow leaders.

THIRTY-THREE

These events had taken place earlier that day allowing Wilson to summon Gerald Kaufman, not only to solicit his observations and opinion, but to permit him' anonymously' to brief the press, with the express intention of giving various industrial and political journalists Harold Wilson`s view and in order to break the news in the Sunday papers of an imminent and potentially vicious confrontation between the government and the Trade Union movement.

We can never determine the Prime Minister`s true motives and intentions even taking into account the statement of Gerald Kaufman at the now notorious treason trial, but Wilson`s defence, at the trial, appeared feeble if mendacious, as he promoted the explanation that he wished to warn the nation of what he saw as a confrontation between unbridled union power and a duly elected government despite the obvious facts that personally he not had the endorsement of the Electorate and that damningly he had delayed and deferred the General Election.

Whatever his real motives and intentions and however Kaufman expressed and conveyed his patron`s arguments, the 'leak' generated scant coverage. The front pages of the Sunday journals were unanimous in their coverage of the declining condition of the former war time leader and statesman, Sir Winston Churchill, as he fought what was shortly to become his final battle.

The Prime Minister was already aware that arrangements had been made and were in hand to grant Britain`s defender of freedom in the darkest days of 1940, a State Funeral, the nation`s tribute to a man and a tradition of sacrifice going back to Sir Francis Drake and the defeat of the Spanish Armada nearly four hundred years before and Admiral, Viscount Nelson, who had given his life in the cause of freedom, on the twenty first of October 1805 off the coast of Spain when his force of warships destroyed the peril of a French invasion fleet off of Cape Trafalgar.

The headlines in the newspapers were consistent and a variation on a single theme. Thus the *Sunday Citizen* led with...

World's eyes on his battle

CHURCHILL

"Weaker" after a day of peaceful sleep

The Sunday Times...

A little weaker but Sir Winston fights on

The Observer...

Sir Winston a little weaker

still sleeping peacefully

And finally, *The News Of The World...*

As the flame flickers low at No 28

THE OLD WARRIOR FIGHTS ON

Where the 'leak' was reported, coverage was poor and did not have the impact as was intended. The political and financial correspondent 'Scorpio' of the *Sunday Citizen*, could not be reached whilst James Margach of *The Sunday Times*, the political columnist, in conjunction with David Divine of the Business News weaved a brief one paragraph report which by fate, or error, or even the malevolence of the unionised compositors never made the final edition though it appeared in earlier editions. Interestingly the greatest coverage was in the *Sunday Mirror*.

The stark warning and even the sentiments of the P.M. were reported exactly as intended, and were skilfully included in an article co–written by Charles Wilberforce and Anthony Shrimsley which continued and expanded on an article originally published on January the third headed...

BLOODY-MINDED, SELFISH, ARROGANT

What is the Dockers' reply to this verdict?

Which essentially was an attack on the Dockers' working habits which were dramatically effecting the country's export drive.

Strangely and coincidentally, the most significant article also appeared in *The News of the World*, on page four and was headed...

Ron Mount talks to the female Fuhrer of Notting Hill

The most OUTRAGEOUS woman in Britain

She's tall, blond, blue – eyed and dressed from head to foot in kinky black leather. But she's no Cathy Gale.

She is Francoise Suzanne Marie Jordan...and presently wife of Britain's self styled Fuhrer Colin Jordan.

Of the Jews...

"When we come to power, as we hope to, they will be deported along with all the other non Aryan foreign trash in Britain."

Her solution to the colour problem is equally simple:

"Within 24 hours of taking over we would stop any more Niggers coming in", she says.

Frighteningly, her dream of power was more imminent than she ever hoped, or expected, the catalyst being the unbridled demands and expectations of the extreme elements of the Trade Union Movement and those who stood up to, and opposed them, originally a small group of now anonymous members and supporters of a far right Fascist or National Socialist group who, for the better good of their leaders have been air brushed from the history of the New Order, the incident and participants changed for the convenience of the ultimate, final victors of the struggle.

The first unofficial strikes began on the Monday and although there is now no evidence to confirm where they originated, it is generally agreed that they centred on those pits where the personal influence, aura and growing power of Bill Martin was effective and like the ripples in a pond the strike spread nationwide. National Union of Railwaymen concurrently also began unofficial action and their withdrawal of labour was the first inconvenience to the general public. Vauxhall Motors also suffered from industrial action, however whilst the majority of workers, by their *de facto* withdrawal of labour, supported the unofficial wildcat strikes, there was a substantial minority across the whole labour movement who continued or attempted to work despite growing and more physical action to prevent them ,though unexpectedly, a public announcement from George Woodcock for those on strike to abide by the procedures of their unions and consideration for the public had little effect or influence.

The leadership of the N.U.M. and the N.U.R. was thus confronted with the consequences of their own threats and Machiavellian intrigues and whilst , at their trial, it was actually proved that secretly they were not only supporting the 'rank' and 'file', but by a devious and by the normal standards of evidence, only at best circumstantial, was it 'proved' that monies supplied by the T.G.W.U. representative, Jack Jones, was being utilised to bolster the many strikes, all of which had or were to become official. National Union of Public Employees joined on the Tuesday creating an ever enlarging rolling snowball that must have satisfied Jack Jones and his ultimate masters, where his true loyalties lay.

It was on the Wednesday morning, the twentieth, that to compound his difficulties and problems, during a meeting hurriedly convened by Harold Wilson, that specifically included the Home Secretary, Secretary of State for Foreign Affairs, fortunately the Minister of Defence, the Lord Chancellor and Chancellor of the Exchequer, held in the luxurious and comfortable setting of one of the reception rooms, on the first floor of 'Number 10', that most unusually the Cabinet Secretary was approached by an assistant and they both exited the room with that tact and discretion which was the hallmark of the consummate art of the highest levels of the Civil Service.

Shortly afterwards the Cabinet Secretary returned alone, allowed the current speaker to conclude his statement and make his point, which in fact was to suggest that the Army be put on standby to take over the Railways - an act of great provocation and futility since they did not have the expertise for the mammoth task - when Wilson's attention was drawn to a small sheaf of paper that the Cabinet Secretary had brought with him. Wilson apologised for the interruption, began to read the document, passing each page to the Minister of Defence, and when he finished he buried his crestfallen face in his hands, in obvious despair, allowing Edward Heath to complete his own analysis of the document. When the P.M. finally began to speak, his voice quivered before he managed to control his composure.

"Colleagues, news has just been received that within the last four hours, during a flight from Australia, where we had dispersed six of our bombers for strategic purposes, a 'V' bomber returning to the United

Kingdom and loaded with a thermonuclear device and at least three nuclear weapons has crashed close to the Canadian – American border, approximately at the juncture of Idaho, Montana and British Columbia and the remaining other five bombers have made, whilst carrying a diverse load of thermonuclear and nuclear weapons, an emergency landing at an unspecified base and it is currently unknown whether the base is in Canada or the United States. However, there is other news to compound what is in reality a grave crisis, for like the tragic crash has also not yet been made public.

My greatest fear has been and is still that our trade links and the supply of food which have appeared to have been unaffected by military action over the last ten months now seems to be in peril and like 'The Battle of the Atlantic' we may now be witnessing a new assault on our freedom.

The Foreign Office, through our secret intelligence and listening services, have just within the last thirty minutes received reports of the sinking in the Pacific of three vessels, and in two cases messages were sent to confirm that they had been hit by torpedoes. I fear that it is only a matter of time before our mercantile fleet is subject to attack."

Within twenty four hours the identities of the three vessels were known: the Kotei Maru en route from Los Angeles for Yokohama, the Olga Maersk from San Francisco for Japan and lastly the Caledonia Star from Seattle for London. Within a further four days the list would swell to include the Polyxene C also from Seattle but bound for Calcutta, the Bengal Mail from Vancouver, bound for Japan and the Krishna Jayanti bound for Bombay from San Francisco.

The 'Battle of the Pacific' had begun and in terms of ferocity and intensity would last for some time, though with changing alliances would intermittently decline, as were the natural dangers of the vast Ocean.

THIRTY-FOUR

By mid day on the Thursday it was reluctantly decided to release the minimum of information to the press, television and radio, with a discreet request to emphasise that fortunately no British bound vessels had been attacked, but Wilson and the 'Inner Cabinet' believed that it was only a matter of time before the inevitable took place and on the

Friday the national newspapers, by consensus, endeavoured to minimise the severity of the situation, confirming the fact and identities of the sunken vessels and, with the emphasis on the word 'understood', stated that they understood they had all been sunk by torpedoes (conveniently the number of pages of every paper were reduced, therefore justifying the brief and scant coverage). A postscript additionally referred to an aviation accident in Canada involving a British bomber which had crashed on a reported 'training' mission emphasising that the fate of the crew was presently unknown.

The strikes were increasing in number and ferocity across a wide range of manufacturers and industries whilst the various union leaders were quick to make them official despite a further ineffectual plea from George Woodcock who now was both marginalised by the leadership of the participating unions and derided by the national press who themselves were under pressure from the printing unions who had gone out on official strike at six p.m. on the Thursday night.

Limited editions were produced of every national newspaper, with the assistance of the management and co-opted non union printers (and even some former, now retired staff) though the *Daily Worker*, where, despite its proclaimed support for Socialism and consequently the struggle of the workers, continued to be produced normally and published by its staff, arguing in a large banner headline on Thursday January twenty-first that:

The Struggle Has Reached

A Crucial Moment.

"The imminence of a National Strike to express the workers' right to free and collective bargaining, and to confirm the inalienable right to food and sustenance without its supply being controlled by the land owners, casino operators and spivs in the Stock Exchange and [the following was most provocative] their craven lap dogs in Downing Street, brings forward the time when this nation will truly be led by a government of the workers!"

Worst still, a lengthy article written by the editor that same day referred to and chronicled the anarchy in post First World War Germany and the abortive Left wing coup in April nineteen-nineteen, when the 'Bavarian Socialist Republic' was founded, initially ruled by USPD (Independent Social Democratic Party of Germany) members such as Ernst Toller and Gustav Landauer, however [the chronicle continued...]

within a week it had collapsed and was replaced by the Communists led by Eugen Levine who created his own army, the Rote Armee (Red Army) but within a month the 'Right' regained control following bitter street fighting after a force of nearly forty thousand troops of the Freikorps and 'White Guards of Capitalism' triumphed.

As a postscript it is relevant to note that Levine was executed and that years later the sub division of the Freikorps which had captured Levine was incorporated into the Nazi S.A.

Rosa Luxemburg was specially idolised and extolled by the editor in his extensive article as an intellectual and unmitigated revolutionary (which was to cost her life in January of that momentous year, nineteen-nineteen, when she was murdered by the right wing Freikorps) and whose writings were an inspiration to the workers, citing especially her seminal work...

"Freiheit ist immer die Freiheit des Andersdenkenden",

The English translation being...

Freedom is always the freedom of the one who think differently.

Again, as an additional postscript, it is interesting to note that in 1907, after being imprisoned on three occasions for her political activities, she went to the Russian Social Democrats' Fifth Party Day in London, where she met not only Vladimir Lenin but Joel Ben Yitzhak whilst she stayed in Mortimer Crescent, Kilburn.

The tone and implication of the article could not be expressed in more pellucid terms. It was a call not only to bring down the unelected coalition but to incite insurrection!

Adjacent to the article was a separate column of readers' and strikers' comments, their identities conveniently hidden by their initials and the absence of their unions' names though each was given a vague geographical location. The two opening comments incited treason, the first suggesting that the armed forces 'lay down their arms' and join the workers whilst the second demanded the arrest of 'The Ruling Classes' and their trial for genocide and murder of over twenty million men, women and children in Russia and the Ukraine following the British involvement in the nuclear assault the previous year.

Friday, January twenty-second, started well for the P.M. and the now daily meeting of the 'Inner Cabinet'. Canadian officials in the capital, Ottawa, confirmed that the five remaining V Bombers were shortly to depart from the Canadian air force base where had made an *EMERGENCY LANDING* [Author's emphasis] and arrangements had been put in hand for them to be refuelled and provisioned en route for the United Kingdom (no details were supplied as to the location but Air Ministry experts conjectured that it would be in either Newfoundland or even Greenland) and Edward Heath remarked with his unique laugh that so irritated the P.M...

"Their return means, at last, the foundations of a credible military force and consequent political influence both with our ally and more importantly the Soviet Union."

The P.M. silently concurred.

It was at that very moment, with almost theatrical coincidence, that the P.M. was notified by a discreet note handed to him by his Personal Private Secretary that the United States Ambassador, David Bruce, had requested a most urgent meeting.

It was agreed that the 'Inner Cabinet' reconvene on the following Monday when they would have a clearer picture of the 'cancerous contagion' which was spreading throughout the labour movement, most likely in response to the government's lack of action which was no doubt perceived as indicative of their procrastination when the situation demanded action and not a passive, supine reply to the engulfing storm.

Harold Wilson greeted the ambassador at the front door of 'Number 10' in full view of a number of invited press photographers and members of the general public some of whom were using the short cut through Downing Street to reach St. James's Park though most were unaware of the identity of the important visitor.

The night watchman's chair symbolically noted his arrival in the lobby and further down the passageway Winston Churchill's favourite leather armchair awaited, in vain, for its old occupant to once again assume his rightful place. The two men walked upstairs and entered the P.M.'s private office where, with great foresight, an antique tray had been placed on Wilson's desk on which sat a jug of fresh hot coffee (containing a brew known to be particularly enjoyed by the important visitor), its inviting aroma overpowering any emotions of the two men, though the ever alert P.M. immediately sensed the gravity of the situation and a message from Washington that might not be as palatable as the beverage.

Without hesitation the visitor poured himself out a cup of coffee and a large measure of decadent double cream which he insisted upon calling 'heavy' cream, but Wilson was not concerned with trivia for as time progressed he increasingly began to fear the contents of the plenipotentiary`s message.

The message, when it was delivered, was a bitter blow to Wilson`s hopes for an improvement in the transatlantic bond upon which he knew the country`s future lay.

"Mr. Wilson, Mr. Prime Minister, my position as Ambassador to the Court of St. James and my personal situation as an Anglophile makes the following message even more difficult to deliver and such was its importance and tone that unusually a messenger was dispatched by Washington to hand me what in fact was a statement made by the President. The imperative nature of the President`s, and I stress emphatically the actual word, demand, has meant that Vice President Hubert Humphrey, when he should be basking in the afterglow of the Presidential Inauguration was flown by a military jet to one [sic] of our bases in Mildenhall, Suffolk, where I met him, indeed such was the secrecy surrounding his visit that until I actually shook hands with him I really believed the President himself was the visitor. At this moment he is at the Dorchester Hotel, his anonymity currently secure and awaits an urgent meeting which I have suggested be at my official residence down the street [sic] in Regents` Park. I am not fully aware of the exact purpose of his visit but he did say that (Lyndon) Johnson was so angry that both he and a team of doctors, who now are permanently available, cautioned him lest he triggers a further major heart condition.

I am instructed to hand to you an edited, sanitised, Pentagon briefing paper, prepared within the last twelve to eighteen hours which clearly is at the root or is one of the President`s major cause of great anger. No doubt when you meet Hubert you will be able to fully respond to the contents and I must warn you that under the present circumstances you should address him formally, not in deference to his position as normally he is very easy going, but in view of the President`s ire and wrath."

It was then, as the ambassador enjoyed the luxury and richness of his coffee, that two emphatic knocks pregnant with possible further, unfortunate overtones punctuated the chilled and slightly tense atmosphere. Yet again the P.M.'s Personal Private Secretary entered, to pass a message, but this time uniquely diverging from protocol, and surprisingly using his own initiative, he stated that he had the gravest news, which, he felt the Ambassador should know as a friend of ...

"Our country in its most darkest hour."

It was self evident and only needed to confirm what the two men in the room must have realised.

"All hope has ended for the continuing life of Sir Winston and it is only a matter of hours before the end, however I am honoured to say that shortly before he fell into unconsciousness he weakly whispered to his wife, Clementine, whom he addressed in semi delirium as Clementine Hozier, that he was proud that he was to be granted a State Funeral. I have taken the initiative, on your behalf, discreetly to set in motion the many strands which will make up the nation's tribute."

There is a tide in the affairs of men when decisive action, initiative on the spur of the moment, is the answer to problems that demand solutions and Wilson, grabbing at that moment, without hesitation, suggested that:

"It was therefore essential that a meeting be arranged without any delay, when a comprehensive response would be given to matters raised in the Pentagon document and other matters that might be raised, however, as the ambassador realised, he must now attend to the most tragic event that was now unfurling."

Within minutes of the ambassador's departure Wilson had perused the dossier, summonsed Edward Heath, in his capacity as Minister of Defence and the Home Secretary, Harold Lever. Two photocopies were made, one of which was dispatched, under rigorous security to an urgently convened *ad hoc* assembly of some of the country's anonymous and highest ranking intelligence officers including Sir Kenneth Strong and Sir Hugh Stephenson. Any previous animosity or blame following the disastrous analysis of the false and spurious intelligence that had been a major contributory factor in the catastrophic military defeat on the European mainland had to be, at least, temporarily put aside to deal with the contents of the dossier and the anticipated problems that the Vice President would raise on behalf of the newly inaugurated President.

The dossier reported on the crash of the V bomber just inside United States territory. It contained two maps, the first, displaying the states bordering Canada and the second, more detailed, of the State of Montana and specifically the location of the town of Eureka, eight miles

South of the border and on Highway ninety- three, nestling in the heart of the Rocky Mountains, between the Whitefish and Purcell mountain ranges and surrounded by a (National) forest and adjacent to a river.

Accompanying the two maps were the brief reports of two eye witnesses, the first based in Whitefish - a town South East of Eureka and also on Highway ninety-three (a local doctor of impeccable reputation) who stated that he had first witnessed the plane flying at low altitude and in apparent difficulty, come in from the West and then attempted to gain height as it turned North West towards, in the distance, Eureka when he lost sight. The second witness, was a twenty one year old engineering student (at California`s Stanford University whose name was also given - Lawrence Questad- on a hunting expedition) whose statement continued the first as he reported that the stricken aeroplane appeared from the South East, nose up, when it suddenly lurched down, missing the Highway, *SOUTH* (emphasised in Capitals) of the town and crashed in the forest but did not explode or burst into flames. The second witness concluded his report by confirming that he abandoned his expedition to get to Eureka and to raise the alarm, only to find that the crash been reported, by local residents, to the police.

The document continued with a terse statement that President Johnson had been advised by the Pentagon that whilst they had been informed, by their Canadian opposite numbers, of the intended flight by six nuclear armed bombers it had been agreed that they would not enter United States airspace *UNDER ANY CIRCUMSTANCES* (again emphasised in capitals).

First to arrive at the crash site was a party made up of local law enforcement officers together with members of the local voluntary rescue squad, comprised of specially trained firemen and some medically trained local residents one of whom was a local science teacher, carrying a Geiger Counter. They found the crew, still strapped into their seats, dead.

Extremely high readings of radioactivity were being recorded when the local police decided to abandon and quarantine the area, pending the arrival of the National Guard who had contacted the Pentagon for instructions.

THIRTY-FIVE

The British government and their intelligence services had been starved, on the specific orders of President Johnson, of the bi lateral transfer of intelligence for nearly a year and personal connections, which in some cases had been built up over nearly a quarter of a century, had begun to 'wither on the vine', leaving specialists like Strong and Stephenson unable to fulfil their potential and proven expertise, but once they had familiarised themselves with the contents of the dossier and discussed the matter with their associates it was decided to urgently strive to revive old friendships and associations in the United States in order to exploit their crucial hidden knowledge. The British intelligence officers had met in their exclusive London 'club' in the heart of the 'West End' where discretion and, as always, a consistent high standard of catering existed but as one of the elite members sententiously commented that:

"This was no time for the pleasures of life but for national duty and the chance to restore our impugned reputation."

The United States and Canadian embassies would shortly be closing for the weekend and utilising every available telephone and an archaic switchboard they endeavoured to contact the Canadian ambassador but more importantly the 'desks' of their former opposite numbers in the United States embassy.

The Canadian ambassador was immediately contacted, perhaps with good fortune, and without delay instructed his helpful air attaché to both contact Ottawa and above all the base in British Columbia where the remaining five V bombers would imminently be departing on their long journey back to the United Kingdom.

Initially there was less success contacting the 'desks' of the intelligence departments located strategically in the bowels of the United States embassy, compelling Strong and Stephenson impetuously to walk the short distance to the embassy where, on arrival, they were unsuccessful gaining access when luckily they were literally spotted by one of their quarry and within minutes the so called 'Old Boy Network' swung into operation and contact was made with their old friends in Washington.

Discretion was imperative since it was made abundantly clear that such was the anger of the President, that any direct help or cooperation would incur the wrath and ire of the Executive and of the President himself. Careers were literally put 'on the line' as a picture emerged of a leadership that had believed that it would lose the recent Presidential Election because of the military disaster and fiasco on the European mainland even though support had been overwhelming following the nuclear strike on the Soviet republics of Russia and the Ukraine and the earlier ambush and then the annihilation of the incoming bomber assault off of the West Coast.

The jig-saw picture which appeared and was pieced together early that evening when the members reassembled was of an ever increasing cynicism and disillusionment by every successive President beginning with Truman in nineteen forty-five, observing the decline of British military and economic power as the armed forces were slowly and consistently reduced and starved of equipment whilst commerce and industry were racked by industrial disputes and the growing influence of so called 'Left wing 'politicians, policies and Trade Union leaders as they became more and more ascendant.

This view was supported, secretly, by the State Department and those who had 'the ear' of the Executive indeed it was clear that the more ruthless proponents of American hegemony had from an early stage advocated the emasculation of British military technology, therefore making each successive British government more reliant on the United States military umbrella and her industrial – military complex.

Scorn was placed on the British delusion that the nation was still a major global power both militarily and economically and its archaic patriotism expressed in such fervent renditions of 'Pomp and Circumstance' and 'Rule Britannia' hid the fact that inexorably and inevitably real power was rapidly declining and her standing, for many other reasons, was diminishing.

An experienced secretary was summonsed, permitting the members to schedule and itemise their very recently acquired 'nuggets 'of information, cross referencing and confirming what had been gleaned independently by the others and at about six ten p.m., Sir Kenneth Strong telephoned the Cabinet Office to inform them that following contact with Washington and Ottawa, two reports were currently being prepared, without any copies, for the eyes of the P.M. only and it was estimated that they would be in his hands before nine o`clock and at twenty to nine the task completed, Stephenson turned to the small, exhausted group and announced ...

"All credit was due to their secretary for her calm patience dealing with two complex documents of such importance, compiled in an extraordinary manner in such a short time."

He made no comment on the damning contents of the two reports.

Their American counterparts had indeed been discreet in the manner in which they had conveyed the information (probably, instinctively realising that their phones were routinely 'tapped'), never once, consistently, confirming that either the President or any of his predecessors had ever made or enacted such statements as policy or had been formally advised by their most intimate counsellors, but always referred to private gossip and informed conjecture by many people 'in the know'.

Harold Wilson did not want to postpone or delay his nine thirty appointment with Hubert Horatio Humphrey, the Vice –President, but he was waylaid on the stairs leading down from his private apartment and not for the first time did the mantle of courtesy slip as Manny Gold met him at the foot of the stairs, his face gleaming with excitement and satisfaction. Wilson brushed the man aside without reason, apology or explanation only to be tactfully and respectfully challenged by Gold's initiative and important message.

"I've just come from the Cabinet Office which has been notified that at about ten a.m. tomorrow, three vessels flying the neutral Swedish flag will dock at Gravesend with the vanguard of repatriated former British prisoners of war!"

The Prime Minister turned, and if in an undertone whilst quietly reciting some prayer, half thanked the messenger but made no mention or even alluded to what he knew was to be a meeting pivotal to the future of his career and the nation's destiny.

He returned to his private office where he both read and digested the contents and ramifications of the two documents and by the time he had absorbed the devastating contents and then hurriedly, without consultation, decided on his immediate response it was already twenty-five to ten.

During the fifteen minute journey to Regents Park, Wilson had both the time and relative quiet to again mull over and consider the events that had culminated in what was the end of the so called 'Special Relationship'.

The report from Canada was an indictment of his disastrous decision to acquiesce and 'knuckle under' to Soviet pressure and blackmail. Even more so were the words of a Second World War hero, speaking from the flight deck of the doomed bomber.

The wing of six planes had scrupulously adhered to the flight plan and the admonition to avoid, at all costs, United States territory ,flying in a Northerly direction off the coasts of California, Oregon and finally Washington State until they were some seven minutes or so North of the Canadian and American border where they commenced their manoeuvre, veering and turning towards Canadian sovereign territory, when the outer starboard Bristol Olympus 102 turbojet engine of the ultimately doomed V bomber began to show signs of failure and just after the six aeroplanes crossed the Canadian coast the engine did fail just as the two port engines showed the same symptoms. It would then have still been possible to make a controlled landing at a number of Canadian bases close to the West coast but then terrifyingly the pilot began to lose control as the last remaining engine caught fire simultaneously as the two other engines failed and the electrical systems began systematically to shut down.   These events were faithfully being reported calmly and objectively from the flight deck by Group Captain Hugh Everitt, a tenacious wartime bomber pilot and former commander of a V bomber station in Gaydon, Warwickshire, temporarily seconded to Australia from his posting in Ghana and returning to Great Britain.   Till the final moments he described the pilot's valiant attempts to gain height, to avoid United States territory and maintain control, as allegations of hurried and botched maintenance to meet the politicians' demands could be heard in the background coming from the pilot.

The recording ended and radio contact ceased as the unnamed pilot sarcastically confirmed that their hydrogen bomb was still in operational condition.

It was unfortunately the contents of the other report, which clearly showed the delusion that the United Kingdom could still sit as an equal with their ally, the United States, at the table of the major super powers, indeed it was self evident that they no longer had the force of global power to warrant them still to sit with their superiors.   The journey in the anonymous chauffeur driven Rover ended just as he painfully recognised that:

"The game was up."

His late arrival did not sit satisfactorily with his host and valued guest and he could clearly see that he had annoyed his host and angered the representative of the most important and powerful man in the world.

His apologies were profusely offered (therefore immediately weakening any negotiating posture) and insincerely accepted, the choice of English tea genuinely made, accepted and enjoyed and the unimportant enquiry regarding the journey from Washington to Suffolk promptly answered with the minimum of detail and superficially noted by the enquirer.

"To put it bluntly Lyndon is extremely angry. We are now sitting on a volcano which is about to erupt. There is a load of radioactive material pouring from the crashed bomber and already it has seeped into the local river."

Harold Wilson had no response to this allegation or statement of fact. The truth was that the crew had most likely sacrificed themselves and the report of their final minutes would never be accepted in this inflamed atmosphere.

A summary of the other even more damning report flashed through his mind before H.H.H. could continue or expect a reply from Her Majesty`s Prime Minister.

It had begun shortly before Christmas nineteen fifty-three when President Dwight D. Eisenhower had read and had been revolted by the contents of a secret report. It concerned a British project codenamed Operation Cauldron shrouded in the highest secrecy and events between May to September nineteen fifty-two off of the coast of the Isle of Lewis in the Outer Hebrides when tests took place infecting animals (specifically Rhesus Macaque monkeys and guinea pigs) with bubonic plague.

The operation on the deck of a sloping pontoon was controlled from a vessel erroneously named or incorrectly typed as the Ben Loch Loman (the correct title being the Ben Lomond).

In nineteen fifty-six, following the nationalisation of the Suez Canal by President Gamal Abdel Nasser of Egypt, France, Israel and the United Kingdom colluded secretly to attack Egypt and take back control of the canal. In an act which Wilson could now see as clear evidence, not only of the perfidiousness of President Eisenhower, but as an example of the true relationship between the former war time allies, the then British Prime Minister, Anthony Eden, was literally threatened with unethical, undiplomatic pressure, including the threat to undermine the

Pound Sterling causing a 'run' on the currency. Eden had to back down and shortly afterwards resigned, his health broken.

Similarly the three nations had also to back down, humiliated, and thus for France and the United Kingdom they were both seen in the eyes of the world as no longer major powers.

Eden was replaced by Harold Macmillan, who in December nineteen sixty-two, at Nassau in the Bahamas, agreed with Eisenhower's successor, the soon to be assassinated President, John Kennedy, to be supplied with the new super weapon, Polaris, a submarine launched two stage solid fuelled missile. Again, Wilson conjectured that Britain was being inexorably drawn into the whim and power of the American government and the rapacious and extortionate clutches of the American Industrial-Military complex especially since the British government had recently been promised the (ill fated) air launched Skybolt missile which had encountered technical difficulties and was cancelled, without reference to the British government.

Now Kennedy's successor had either found further excuses or valid reasons to dissolve what was left of the 'Special Relationship': The intelligence fiasco surrounding what was in fact a massive deception and then its immediate consequences, the overwhelming military defeat and the awful suffering of the United States forces (let alone the suffering of their allies).

The British government's (and his) overt lie that British planes had been involved in the nuclear attack on the Soviet Union and finally the spectre of a potential nuclear disaster on the soil of the Continental United States caused by their incompetent ally must have been, euphemistically 'the final straw'. Wilson was characterised as a liar, following his and the British government's false claims to have been involved in the attack on the Soviet Union but above all Johnson regarded Wilson as a coward because he had 'caved in' to the Russians' threats which was inexcusable and consequently the so called 'Special Relationship' was at an end.

Also, a potential environmental disaster might have to be confronted and he understood that the leader of the United States did not wish the American people to ask awkward questions about the transportation of nuclear weapons across their homeland by their own Air Force.

THIRTY-SIX

"Harold, Mr. Prime Minister, are you all right ?!"

Harold James Wilson, Her Majesty's Prime Minister and holder of other symbolic titles, was aroused from some intense mental concentration as the United States ambassador both spoke to him and also placed his right arm around the man's shoulders.

H.H.H. had already mentally made his report of the meeting and was about to inform David Bruce that:

"He saw no point in continuing this futile exercise."

It was only the ambassador's intervention and deep love of the United Kingdom that persuaded the Vice–President to continue this most pivotal of meetings.

Ever adept at manipulation or juggling with the truth and striking an emotional chord which resonated with his hosts' sympathy and compassion, Wilson glibly concocted a lie to hide his late arrival and apparent strange behaviour...

"An inconvenient bout of minor flu which I hope you will not pass on to Lyndon. I was delayed because my doctor was late arriving and I had to argue with him for permission to attend this critical meeting. I had earlier received a report on the last few minutes of the V bomber's flight before the disaster which I truly believe proves that whilst the aeroplane crashed on United States soil, it had made every attempt throughout its journey to avoid U.S. territory."

He then gave a report based on the radio messages. The response from the Vice–President was lukewarm at best, indeed his attitude suggested that he was incredulous of the explanation. What Wilson and Bruce did not know and would never know was that H.H.H. already knew the true story for the flight messages had been routinely monitored and recorded by American listening stations and the transcriptions passed from the 'Pentagon' to' Washington'. Humphrey had a sinister reason for his visit as an emissary of the President and he now challenged Harold Wilson not about the intelligence failure but about his overt lie and British claims concerning their active involvement in the nuclear strike.

At his trial for High Treason held before a Military Tribunal, in camera, but recorded by a battery of film cameras, Wilson was unusually candid and frank, even disagreeing, correcting and sometimes rebuking the uniformed military officer who represented him. Since his arrest and impeachment, he had been initially surprised by the pleasant, even luxurious nature of his confinement and treatment and the respect and courtesy shown to him which dramatically changed shortly before his trial. Whilst he was denied access to visitors during his stay on a private estate, he received visits from his court appointed defender but Wilson recognised the man's limited competence and the daunting task that confronted them. The main charge against him included reference to the meeting at the United States ambassador's residence, his conversations with the ambassador, David Bruce, and with the Vice-President of the United States and above all the subsequent secret agreement.

However, the most damning evidence would be the hand written observations that he was compelled to read by the prosecuting counsel.

Wilson's statement to the court concerning the meeting was concise and brief and had notes been taken at the residence in Regent's Park they would, most certainly, have tallied with his statement.

He admitted that he had succumbed to Soviet pressure in the absence of American support but had their new 'Monroe' declaration come twenty–four or forty–eight hours earlier or had the British government or their intelligence services been made aware of their intended policy declaration then he would have strongly rejected what was the threat of blackmail and what he later knew as a new policy dictated not by Khrushchev but by Brezhnev. Furthermore he reminded his hosts that in order to maintain national morale (and to quote the words of a U.S. politician) ...

"In war the first casualty is truth."

"The country was, he had been informed at the time, both excited and pleased, because it reminded the British people of the war time bombing raids on the cities and factories of Germany in response to the earlier German Blitz, at night by the R.A.F. and by day, their American allies and it had raised national morale and the country's support for the President and the United States."

Humphrey confronted the British Prime Minister with little finesse or tact and certainly without the art of diplomacy. A few days later, David Bruce conjectured to Harold Wilson and after the arrangement had been completed, that his personal knowledge of the V-P. was such that he was tempted to believe that Johnson had sent him on this mission both as a test and to do his 'dirty work' especially as he was incapacitated in a hospital bed in Washington suffering from a bronchial infection.

"Britain was finished as a global super power. The United Nations, like the League of Nations before them, was no longer competent as a forum to resolve disputes between the two super powers and the nation that was estimated to be the new emerging third super power – China. Disputes between minor nations would be solved by any of the three super powers since they were both directing their client countries' actions and at the same time acting as external 'colonial' powers: for example, China was responsible for North Vietnam, Cambodia and Albania and the Soviet Union for its neighbour Finland, the Warsaw Pact and the recently conquered nations of Western Europe.

Israel, the agent of the United States and now re-armed with the latest military technology, slowly recovering from the nuclear assault and no longer prepared to hand the olive branch of peace to any of their neighbours, was mandated to maintain and control access (at prices determined by the United States and not the vendors) to the vast reserves of energy in the Middle East."

The future was clear. Obviously, Johnson's advisors had carefully analysed potential trends and perceived a new World Order where its former ally was no longer considered either an equal or more importantly capable of industrially or militarily matching the other three's power. Wilson wondered what would be offered and on what terms, which when listed he found to be generous but unpalatable.

"The President's advisors doubt that if and when a new Parliament was elected that it would agree and pass the necessary legislation or that Her Majesty would put her signature to such an Act of Parliament, so we suggest a memorandum of understanding between the President and the Prime Minister and their successors.

We are not concerned with your internal politics or usurping your leadership and authority over the 'British Commonwealth of Nations', indeed the Pound Sterling and the 'Sterling Area' should continue and as an independent sovereign nation you would continue to act internally and externally in any manner that your government deems appropriate however the government of the United States of America reserves the right to supersede your policies in matters of military and global political affairs. We would, as an ally, consult you and 'take on board 'your opinion and concerns however ultimately we would make the final decision and expect your support.

To guarantee your continued independence and freedom from the Soviet Union and their allies, the Warsaw Pact, we would require to increase and expand our military presence on British soil and as a sign of your good faith we would require a contribution towards their upkeep and your security together with trained British troops to support us containing any global aggression against our joint interests.

I leave on Monday evening and quite bluntly the President expects an answer on my return."

His tea tasted unusually bitter and the atmosphere felt tense, unfriendly with a distinct icy chill. Wilson could not remember how and when the meeting had ended or indeed if he had shaken his hosts' hands but he had himself been shaken to the very foundations of his senses. He next found himself in the chauffeur driven Rover which was trying to negotiate the junction of Baker Street and Marylebone Road but the traffic lights were faulty and since the staff had gone on strike it was literally everyone for himself though rather strangely a man waving a Union Jack and shouting (though he was barely audible)
...

"Britain stand up and fight union tyranny!",

was unsuccessfully endeavouring to direct the traffic and it was convenient and fortunate that the P.M. decided, on the spur of the moment, that he needed time to think and the chauffeur, worldly wise, took two right hand turns in rapid succession.

Minutes later he was being driven slowly around the Outer Circle of Regent's Park when the Rover was stopped by an unmarked police car for kerb crawling and the chauffeur questioned on his motives. The Prime Minister, sitting in the rear, was illuminated by a powerful beam from one of the officer's torches and temporarily blinded. Who was more surprised, the P.M. or the officer is of historical unimportance however the police men offered the suggestion of a nearby quiet lay by which they would monitor in response to Harold's statement that he had matters of State of such importance that he needed peace and quiet.

THIRTY-SEVEN

The Prime Minister slept badly that night; restless, sleep was punctuated and interrupted by regular and ever longer periods of waking when he craved the refreshment of sleep, but ironically he was able to focus his mind, his intellect and above all his shrewd astute qualities of political leadership and some of the dark arts, so adequately described by Machiavelli, to unravel and resolve most of the problems that had, all at once, confronted him.

He was totally unaware that at six nineteen a.m., a U.S. reconnaissance plane, on a routine flight, traversing a wide sweep across the English Channel and the North Sea, had identified a Soviet Kynda class cruiser travelling rapidly South, having evaded previous identification.

Mentally refreshed and confident, and even exhilarated in his ability and his alone, to weather the storm of adversity, he was dressed by half past six when he ventured downstairs to the tiny office on the right hand side of the reception hall as any visitor will notice on their arrival at 'Number Ten'. His judgement and timing was sound for as he arrived the staff were 'brewing up' and the police officer on duty outside, simultaneously brought in a large pile of the 'Sundays'. This was not the first time that he had 'sounded out' the junior, if not menial staff, for they were more in touch with what he knew to be the 'real world', whilst his senior civil servants seemed to exist in a more rarefied, detached environment. The reception staff, always overawed by the intimate presence of the P.M. were honest and candid, deferential and clearly, if not articulately, expressed their disapproval and those of their friends and families, of the rash and senseless ever spreading strikes which in the words of one receptionist, the most junior, was...

"Beginning to become more than inconvenient, as his wife, Tracy Jane, had told him that the corner shop was putting up the price of bacon rashers, claiming the shop keeper had told her that fuel prices were rising."

The smell of bacon, egg, beans and sausage heralded the arrival of overly filled plates which were brought up from the canteen and liberally flooded with H.P. sauce (and for some, additionally tomato ketchup!) and soon afterwards the residue on the nearly empty plates were wiped clean with bread lavished with butter. He felt almost invincible, mentally and physically able to deal with the problems of leadership.

Winston Leonard Spencer Churchill, symbol of an anachronistic Empire but above all the defender of freedom died on Sunday, January the twenty–fourth, just after eight a.m. at 28 Hyde Park Gate, Kensington, following a stroke.

Coincidentally, at about the same time, three vessels berthed in the Thames, two at Tilbury (following late instructions from the Port of London Authority) and the third vessel at Gravesend exactly in the same spot that in November nineteen sixty- three, a Polish registered ship had docked before disembarking a group of men who would soon be instrumental in changing history.

Harold Wilson was informed of the former event within minutes, and of the latter, by ten a.m.

He had decided to approach his old friend and the influential trade union official Jack Jones, to put out 'feelers' to the leaders of the striking unions to gauge their reactions to a formal request, in the interests of national unity, to end their industrial action and also now citing the death of their wartime leader and the nation`s tribute which would be effected if the unions and especially the Railway Unions continued their action, indeed when he spoke to Jones he even suggested a temporary hiatus as a sign of good faith. A few minutes later, around ten fifteen a.m. he contacted the private secretaries of the Archbishops of Canterbury and York and the Bishop of Durham, requesting their discreet intervention and diplomatic approaches to the unions, again suggesting that they emphasise national unity in a time of national grief which should supersede the unions` short term demands.   As an afterthought he then rang back Jack Jones and characteristically, with labyrinthine motivations, suggested that he had permission to inform the press, radio and television, anonymously, as a source close to the government and the Trade Union movement, that leading figures were endeavouring to resolve the industrial crisis.

Jack Jones did not need to notify his real masters that he would further inflame the anger of the unions citing Wilson`s 'intention' both to mobilise the army and then ruthlessly impose the wages and prices freeze.

But the one problem, titanic in proportion, was the independence of the country and its ability and will to control its own destiny. He knew instinctively, without seeking the opinion of Edward Heath, that he would not, under any circumstances, countenance the abrogation of

Great Britain's independence and that Harold Lever, Patrick Gordon Walker and Denis Healey, his Labour party allies would be, at best, lukewarm and above all would demand that such a change be debated by Parliament who would undoubtedly reject the proposition and that the Queen would never put her signature to such a dereliction of her sworn duty. He resolved that he would therefore confide in no other politician.

The repatriation of the first party of British prisoners of war and the arrival of the five V bombers could be a matter of national rejoicing, however it would tragically coincide with the death of the iconic and nationally revered leader, Winston Churchill, and he firmly made up his mind to make as much political capital since the General Election was less than three months away. At eleven seventeen a.m. he contacted both Manny Gold and Gerald Kaufman, interrupting their weekend rest with a demand that they go directly to Gravesend and Tilbury and to utilise the publicity for *HIS* (author's special emphasis) maximum benefit, however remembering the solemnity of this most event filled day.

At nine minutes past twelve the Soviet Kynda class cruiser was seen to temporarily slow down and meet a second Kynda class cruiser before jointly continuing South on their journey, oblivious to the ongoing tracking by British and American reconnaissance planes.

Gerald Kaufman, well known to the press, arrived at Tilbury around twelve forty -five p.m. where television cameras had, and were, taking live images of the disembarking troops and which were currently being 'beamed' nationwide, as crowds of civilians and families unconcerned with the public display of their emotions embraced their returning kin.

At frequent intervals coverage switched to Central London and contrasted the joy of those meeting the returning prisoners of war with the public's expression of grief on the death of WLSC as many people openly wept in Trafalgar Square and many more locations not covered by the television cameras.

Kaufman adroitly used the opportunity, with sublime opportunism, to confirm the Prime Minister's personal genuine loss, not only of a great national leader, but, amongst his outstanding achievements, his contribution as a Parliamentarian; also mentioning on behalf of the P.M. that shortly it would be officially announced that the Queen had graciously agreed, some time ago, to grant the great war leader a State Funeral and that speaking on behalf of the P.M. he felt sure that:

"Winston would have been pleased at the return of our brave soldiers."

Conveniently, press and television coverage was much less intense and evident in Gravesend. Manny Gold had reached the docks at five past one and initially found great difficulty obtaining access both to the vessel and the docking area though he finally achieved access through the intercession of a journalist who had in turn demanded a statement in response to a rumour that was circulating and was gaining ever more credence in view of the arrival of a fleet of ambulances both civilian and military.

Once his status had been acknowledged by the police and the shock of the nature of the rumour absorbed, he knew that he would have to contact the P.M. or the head of the Cabinet Office both for advice and instructions. He realised that he was neither competent or willing to handle a situation that was both tragic and had political consequences that might get out of control.

All he could see was the crowd being held back, some distance from the gangway, and that soon, if there was any foundation to the rumour, they might witness an unacceptable face of warfare. He felt the gentle tap of a hand on his shoulder and turning round observed an elegantly dressed man who addressed him with a superb, refined English accent and who introduced himself as the Swedish ambassador. His message was expressed in the language of the diplomat but the undertone was ominous and sinister.

"...Our duty and responsibility is, as quickly as possible, to transfer as many who are fit to travel to hospital and to maintain their dignity even at the expense of denying them access to their families, who I believe, will be traumatised at the appearance and medical condition of their loved ones. Do you feel strong enough to go below where the men and a few women lie on rudimentary bunks? I could never believe that man, as an intelligent species, could be as cruel to other human beings as these poor wretches who are suffering."

Even before Gold had begun his descent into the bowels of the hospital ship his sense of smell had detected an odour that immediately and automatically made him search and reach for his handkerchief which instinctively he positioned over his mouth and nose in what was to be a futile attempt to both ward off the smell and to control himself as...

suddenly he retched, tried in vain not to embarrass himself but was promptly sick.

"You're not the first and won't be the last today", commented the ambassador.

"The smell is, I think, a combination of a strong disinfectant used by the Russians to clean their hospital wards, vomiting of God knows what and the stench of rotting flesh. How anybody could exist in this world is beyond my comprehension. Good luck."

The lighting was subdued, the temperature pleasant, contrasting with the cold outside, but the sound of the ventilation system dominated the room. The smell of disinfectant suddenly triggered childhood memories of his upbringing in Moscow but he felt that it was much more intense and concentrated than that used, all those years ago, in his school.

Doctors and nurses appeared in abundance scurrying back and forth never appearing to spend much time at any one bed or bunk. The ambassador spoke, in his native tongue to one of the doctors who looked at the two men and made a statement in rudimentary English but the message was clear and unequivocal.

"The patients were possibly the last remaining survivors of those who had been the victims of the chemical warfare assault. As far as he could construct the situation from the information that had been passed to them by certain Soviet authorities, the patients on the vessel had only suffered minor inhalation or body contact and that their condition had taken some months to develop. The unlucky (or lucky) ones, dependent on one's point of view had died, many in excruciating pain, as from the information he had gleaned, the Soviet government had withdrawn most medicines and medical coverage after the joint U.S. and U.K. nuclear attack on Russia and the Ukraine citing the priority of their own civilians following the barbaric and vicious attack.

Treatment had been rudimentary and medical staff insufficient, having been prioritised to treat their own nationals. Very few patients had any medical records which in any case were unprofessionally completed and supplies that they had brought on board were quickly used up. The sights that they would see were harrowing and comparable to the suffering of those who were inmates of the camps administered by the Nazis such as Auschwitz and Belsen. "

Turning round one hundred and eighty degrees he lifted the sheet covering a young girl of twenty two or three, their eyes focused on her right leg and the obvious development and stench of gangrene.

"I brought with me a few bottles of schnapps which I had hoped to enjoy on the journey from Stockholm to London. I used the drink to partially protect this young girl from the pain. She needs an amputation within hours to have any chance of saving her life. The man, to her right, the one laying by the side of the pillar, breathed in a minute quantity of Chlorine gas. He could have been saved if he had been given treatment over a number of months. He will die in seven to fourteen days.

There are one hundred and seventy five patients on board together with thirty five who have died during the journey or who might have been dead before the journey begun and were dumped by the Soviets."

THIRTY-EIGHT

I am, as the author of this book, indebted to Joel Ben Yitzhak for the following background information concerning the history of Soviet work in the field of chemical warfare but am not qualified to attest to the validity and accuracy of the following and that furthermore I was not and never have been in direct contact with the primary source:

Despite the horrendous suffering of the Soviet people during the Great Patriotic War and the initial disastrous setbacks in nineteen forty–one and two did Stalin and the Politburo ever resort to the use of chemical weapons even though they had access to reserves of various weaponry.

On April fifth nineteen twenty-eight the U.S.S.R. acceded to the Geneva protocol and under international law the country was henceforth banned from the use of chemical and bacteriological weapons. Whilst initially the chemical attack in nineteen sixty-three was operated by Warsaw Treaty forces, specifically Polish and D.D.R. army and air force units, there can be no doubt that the Soviet leadership or First Secretary Nikita Khrushchev were active participants, indeed the authority, or any permission to release their stock could only be granted at the highest level.

Even before the Soviet Union acceded to the protocol the soon to be disgraced politician, then the first Soviet Commissar for War, Leon Trotsky had ominously stated...

"...wars can be avoided only if we fill the hearts of the imperialists and capitalists with intense fear of our strength of arms... For the attacks of enemy forces to be repelled, we must be armed with all the latest means of defence which modern war technique can produce. The use of poison gas in the last war requires us to keep even this means of warfare in reserve for the defence of our nation against the enemy."

There have been great strides forward in the development of chemical and biological weapons (and their antidotes) since their dramatic and effective use in nineteen sixty-three, including, in two thousand and three, the 'VX' attack on the State of Israel by Palestinian 'freedom fighters', which was immediately, with devastating and comprehensive consequences, countered by a nuclear strike from the IDF (Israel Defence Force) and had the new global order not existed, then the initial attack would have been internationally condemned, however with changing fortunes and fluid political allegiances only Peking and Tirana described the Palestinian action as...

"A blow for freedom by the oppressed against the Zionist Fascist Colonialist war mongers."

The following list, though not comprehensive, are of various groups and types of chemical weapons available in the early nineteen sixties and for some, descriptions of their use and consequences.

I would like to apologise, in advance, that details of their production methods have been deliberately withheld.

NEUROTROPIC TOXIN AGENTS including;

Botulin, Staphylococcal Enterotoxin, Ricin and Bungarotoxin.

IRRITANT AGENTS including;

Chloroacetophenone, CS and CR Tear Gas.

PSYCHOTOMIMETIC AGENT

BZ Hallucinogen

ASPHYXIANT/LUNG AGENTS including;

Phosgene and Chlorpicrin.

VESICANT/BLISTER AGENTS including;

Mustard Gas and Nitrogen Mustard.

BLOOD and GENERALLY TOXIC AGENTS including;

Hydrogen Cyanide and Cyanogen Chloride.

Finally if there can be any degrees of evil or viciousness the...

NEUROPARALYTIC AGENTS including;

Tabun, Sarin and Soman.

Sarin, an organophosphate, was initially developed in the nineteen thirties in (Nazi) Germany following investigative work on pesticides; it is a colourless liquid which attacks the nervous system when inhaled or absorbed through the skin and an inhaled dose of 0.5 milligrammes will cause death within one to ten minutes. Amongst the symptoms are shrinkage of the pupils to pinpoints, tear secretion, vomiting, diarrhoea, urinary and faecal incontinence, sweating and muscle weakness and relating to the central nervous system, giddiness, amnesia, seizures and respiratory depression.

Actual death would be by suffocation as the victim`s diaphragm and the muscles of the chest froze.

Hydrogen Cyanide again is a colourless liquid (which smells of bitter almonds) and in military conditions can only be fatal through inhalation. It is ideal for use in rocket launched artillery. The symptoms are sickness, headache and lack of breath. The actual chemical process is the inhibition of enzymes controlling cells in the nervous systems especially those effecting breathing.

Mustard Gas is a colourless oily liquid and is heavier than water. Intoxication is through the respiratory organs, skin and intestinal tract. The symptoms of cutaneous intoxication are reddening of the skin, then the formation of blisters followed by the formation of lesions where the blisters have burst. The eyes become inflamed which can result in blindness. Death is mainly consequent with necrosis of the tissue of the central nervous system after, yet again, inhibition of many enzyme systems.

Neurotropic Toxins have an affinity for, or localizing selectively in nerve tissue. Their injurious effect come through their ability to inhibit the receptors of the membranes responsible for the transmission of nerve signals.

Phosgene is a gas smelling of mouldy straw. Similar in effect to Mustard Gas, it effects the lungs, death results due to oedema of the lungs.

VX Nerve Gas is a colourless and odourless liquid acting very effectively against the respiratory organs in the form of a thinly dispersed aerosol.

If *YOU* now wish to judge *MY* values, first consider the depths to which the so called civilised human race can descend.

THIRTY-NINE

Harold Wilson had hoped for a quiet Sunday, during which time he could have endeavoured to resolve the U.S. ultimatum and drafted a hand written response or even personally typed a reply, such was the secrecy of the matter and his deliberate intention to hide the ultimatum from the Inner Cabinet or anyone who might disclose the facts, but events dashed his hopes. The more conscientious of his senior staff had been arriving ever since the news of the death of WLSC had been broadcast and they were dealing with an increasing flood of telephone calls and visitors paying their respects and offering their official and personal condolences. Thus the P.M., strengthening his ties with a number of dignitaries, ambassadors or their emissaries, was not able to attend to the problem which now absolutely dominated his waking hours since, ominously, the departure of the Vice President was coming ever closer. He could not conceive that the ostracism or breakdown in their relationship was so vast and deep, to the extent that both Reuters and the Press Association had both, in telex statements, confirmed that the President had publicly announced, from his hospital bed, that he wanted...

"Very, very much to attend Sir Winston Churchill`s funeral."

The Cabinet Office had not only received a brief message from Jack Jones, for the P.M. to contact him, Manny Gold`s harrowing enquiry, which due to the current situation had not been deemed of such priority as to interrupt the P.M., but also an intelligence report confirming the identification of two Kynda class cruisers which were shortly anticipated, from their current course and speed, about to enter the English Channel.

Amongst the P.M`s. visitors was the Canadian ambassador, and the senior staff manning their stations conjectured that, utilising the situation, the P.M. would appeal for urgent supplies of wheat to store in the nation`s granaries and warehouses.

Faced with isolation, the absence of any assistance, support or instructions from the Cabinet Office, the knowledge that the disembarkation of the patients would shortly commence and that the patience of the assembled press and media was rapidly evaporating, Gold realised that he would have to use his own resources and initiative not only to give the unsuspecting crowd forewarning of the spectacle that was shortly to confront them but to give the press and media an indication of the government's position and intended response .

He allowed himself the opportunity to temporarily withdraw, or to be honest, hide from his responsibilities, citing the need again to refer to 'Number Ten which he did on a special line once again provided by the police, but was unable to contact anyone who could resolve his problem.

He reasoned that he could and should adopt the conventional anodyne, banal and colourless uninformative style that was traditional and actually expected or he could confront the restless crowd and therefore the nation with the squalid, monstrous truth that their kith and kin had been the victims of a vicious and heinous attack and that...

For a few moments he lost the thread of his thoughts, the outline of his intended statement and suddenly he felt very vulnerable.

At three forty–five the Prime Minister received a telephone call from the personal secretary and confidante of Dr. Ramsey, the Archbishop of Canterbury, a man whose reputation for diplomacy and action outshone those of his master. The usual courtesies were promptly dealt with and Wilson's urgent demand for news, tactfully and efficiently parried, as it was announced that the miners' leader was pleased to...

"Talk, through a third party, to resolve a situation whose outcome was not in the best interests of his members, the Trade Union movement and the nation generally, however he confessed that he had lost control of his members who were being influenced and led by a firebrand and self seeking junior official."

At three fifty–three, Wilson spoke to the Bishop of Durham ...

"The leaders of the Railway Unions would be pleased to end this strike but to maintain their public image, especially with their rank and file, they have asked that the government made the first public concession, which would be immediately acknowledged. "

"Perhaps", Wilson conjectured, "He could find some precious time to consider how to handle his response to the bully in the White House", but first Jack Jones would be next on his list of priority telephone calls and his intuition indicated further success in ending the industrial dispute.

At nine minutes past four (London time) the commanders of the two cruisers each received an encrypted order to begin the next and crucial stage of their mission and when completed, under cover of a carefully timed fighter escort, proceed to the port of Le Havre.

The reconnaissance plane continued its surveillance, surprisingly still unobserved, but did not spot the frenzied but well rehearsed and practiced activity on board the two vessels.

A four fifteen p.m., just as the Sun was about to set and light rain began to cover the assembled crowd, the police announced that a representative of the Prime Minister wished to make, on behalf of the Prime Minister, a brief statement, prior to the belated disembarkation of the repatriated prisoners of war.

The announcement was greeted by an undercurrent of barely audible comments but promoting their presence, a knot of half a dozen men who had been standing in the rear of the crowd, each waving a fluttering Union Jack in the light wind, suddenly, in unison, shouted out brazenly...

"Britain: stand up and fight union tyranny!"

Gold was too immersed in stage fright to hear the crowd jeering at the men who were told, in no uncertain terms, to...

"Go back to bloody Adolf Hitler!"

Gold's debut as a public orator was only briefly and incidentally reported in one morning paper the following day with the terse observation that:

"As the P.M.'s representative began to speak..."

Gold and no one else present could have anticipated the event that was about to take place. Notwithstanding the imminent event he began well, commencing at four thirty–five, inadequately lit by the wharf's archaic lighting, catching the attention of all those around him, especially the group of right wing extremists led by a then virtually unknown John Tyndall.

"You must all be prepared for a terrible shock, for those that you love and for whom many of you have been awaiting patiently for some hours, for you will now see the horrendous sacrifices that they have made defending you against the tyranny of Communism and the evil of Socialist anarchy and Bolshevism-"

Gold stopped, realised that what he had said was not what he had intended to say and was about to backtrack when...

FORTY

For a few seconds the Northern sky literally exploded in a blinding white flash of light, then seconds later an eerie warmth rushed past the assembled gathering, followed by, after a longer break, the sound of rushing wind, so strong that the Union Jacks that had been previously only fluttering in a mild wind were now gripped in the vice of a tempest and appeared rigid as if instantaneously frozen.

Like the needle of a compass, without exception, everyone turned to the North and perceived in the distance a mighty mushroom cloud rising from the ground.

A minute later the spectacle and events were repeated, this time in the North West as now fear, panic and conjecture seized the crowd. Wild guesses and assumptions were made, however those with a basic knowledge of geography and trained in the art of navigation estimated that the targets were Chelmsford and the new town of Harlow. Whatever locations had been hit the consequences were frightening.

The speech was conveniently and immediately aborted and probably forgotten by those present, the crowd urgently dispersed and the orderly procedure of disembarkation begun, however since the destination of some of the patients were to be hospitals in Chelmsford and the Harlow area the best laid plans of mice and men had to be urgently revised.

John Tyndall, rabid anti Semite and Nazi sympathiser had intently listened to the unfinished statement and had a revelation as blinding and profound as the two bright flashes of light that had just changed history. He had, at that moment, his own epiphany.

Jack Jones tried once more, at four fifty-seven p.m. to speak to the P.M. but again was unsuccessful, however he continued to undermine the government, speaking to and perniciously poisoning the minds and opinions of a number of trade union leaders, influential officials, or selected journalists and the increasingly powerful and ambitious Bill Martin.

The seeds had been broadcast and sown and it would take the destruction of the fabric of society to fulfil its consequences and usher in the New Order.

When Gerald Kaufman and Manny Gold returned to central London, the roads and streets were unusually, but not unexpectedly, quiet and nearly deserted.

At the junction of Baker Street and Marylebone Road, the still broken traffic lights looked down on a lone but confident figure waving his Union Jack in defiance of the unions but now in control of the light volume of traffic.

All along the Euston and Marylebone Roads, from Kings Cross to the Edgware Road, a string of Union Jack waving men efficiently controlled the flow of cars, buses and a few lorries.

"Tomorrow Belongs To Me."

FORTY-ONE

The public's vision and perception of 'Ten Downing Street' was, until the rule of the New Order, of an iconic black front door, a terraced town house occupied by the P.M. and his family and the hub of power where politicians and their immediate officials came and went like the ebb and flow of the tide but in truth it was, in fact, only the visible sign of a vast operation comparable to the peak of an iceberg protruding from the sea, warning of a vast submerged bulk.

Ten Downing Street and the adjacent government buildings, including Whitehall itself, hid a warren of diverse secret complexes including the facility of a railway underneath Whitehall and bunkers probably adequate to protect its frightened inhabitants against a nuclear strike but not sufficiently strong enough to offer any defence or survival against a direct five megatonne or even a one megatonne thermonuclear hit.

The Inner Cabinet met at seven thirty precisely accompanied by three other Cabinet members, Sir Reginald Manningham-Buller, John Rankin and Sir Hendrie Oakshott, the three last named having been in central London in anticipation of their Cabinet responsibilities in the week to come. Despite the efficient ventilation system and the effective heating, set at a constant 68 degrees, the smell of fear was palpable, indeed every time a scrambled telephone burst into sound or an official entered the room, each and every man sitting round the table, clearly and without embarrassment flinched in anticipation of further terrible news.

They received the first definitive and absolute information just before eight p.m., following helicopter and air reconnaissance and it was confirmed that indeed the targets were Chelmsford and Harlow New Town. The epicentre of the former had been the County Cricket ground but because of the many fires which raged and clouds of dust, a more detailed assessment of the damage could not be made till the morning.

'Ted'Heath announced to an emotional response that five more 'V' bombers were scheduled to return to the U.K. and it was unanimously agreed that they be diverted over central London, the Houses of Parliament and then along the Thames for a short distance as a sign of the country's tribute to Churchill and more importantly to bolster national morale. Heath added that he had been informed that that the five planes were to be dispersed to different sites to avoid a Soviet first strike which could take out all the bombers and leave the country virtually defenceless.

For three hours the members of the Cabinet debated what action be taken against the Warsaw Pact and their masters, the Soviet Union, especially when they received a comprehensive report, at nine twelve p.m., that first chronicled the voyage of the two Soviet cruisers and secondly confirmed that, without doubt, the targets had been hit by two sea launched SS-N-3b anti ship and land attack transonic missiles (with the N.A.T.O. designation Sepal and an estimated range of 150 nautical miles).

With the assistance of a senior civil servant, Heath was able to describe the missiles as modern versions of the infamous German V 1 Doodlebug but in answer to the important question as to the power of the nuclear weapons detonated he was only able to extricate a vague general answer from the same official who estimated the force at 30 kilotonnes, compared to the 'Hiroshima' bomb, and the official was uncertain of the figure which would have to be verified, of 20 kilotonnes.

It was unanimously agreed that the first official government statement would be, for convenience vague, but would estimate the power of each bomb as ...

"Less than the 'Hiroshima' bomb of twenty kilotonnes."

By ten–thirty they had made, in reality, no progress agreeing a military or political response to the blatant act of aggression but it was self evident that the nation was incapable of mounting a credible or potent counter attack which might then provoke a second strike of incalculable magnitude including the ultimate nightmare of a 'Doomsday' scenario of an all out thermonuclear assault which would mean the end of the United Kingdom. John Rankin and Sir Hendrie Oakshott, in different times on opposite ends of the social and political spectrum, both questioned the definition of the so called 'Doomsday' scenario and on being graphically informed of the outcome they were, for once, in total harmony and agreement.

It was the Chancellor of the Exchequer, Denis Healey, clearly grasping 'the nettle' or 'taking the bull by the horns' who injected reality and objectivity into a meeting that was literally going nowhere, when, with a tired laconic tone, he commented that:

"There is no doubt, no shadow of a doubt, that we must shelter under the protective canopy of our old friends and allies, the United States."

Harold Wilson said nothing, expressed no visible sign of emotion, but realised that the Cabinet had capitulated and it only needed a simple plan to place the burden of responsibility onto the shoulders of the Inner Cabinet and create an arrangement that neither needed or required the consent of Parliament or Her Majesty's signature.

The new 'Monroe' doctrine had been forgotten in the confusion and events of recent months.

The meeting ended close to eleven p.m. with an agreement that they would all meet again at eleven a.m. the following morning when they would also consider the unresolved and still expanding industrial unrest.

At eleven–thirty or thereabouts Wilson was presented with a list of previously considered unimportant enquiries. Two telephone calls immediately caught his eye and he resolved that first thing in the morning he would contact his old and trusted friend, Jack Jones.

FORTY-TWO

He enjoyed breakfast and even managed to eat, whilst imbibing a mug of very sweet tea, four slices of lightly buttered, piping hot toast with jam though he sensed, correctly, that the day would be long and the problems many, and some not immediately soluble.

The headlines and leading articles in each paper from the pile that the porters brought in, vied between the death of Churchill and the double nuclear strike.

With the restriction on newsprint very little else was reported and only the spreading industrial dispute was given any attention.

The Daily Mirror was minutely scanned if not for editorial comment as for objectivity in its reporting of a momentous day and all that he could discern was a challenge to the government...

"To stand up to the Russians as would have the departed British bulldog, Churchill."

Interestingly, an 'eyewitness' report in the *Sun* caught his attention, not because of its description of the two nuclear explosions, but because of the preamble which surprisingly, because of the limited newsprint, the sub editor had not struck out and which commenced with ...

'As the P.M.'s representative began to speak...'

Before a graphic and vivid word painting of the two detonations.

He did not have time to closely peruse all the newspapers for exact details of the coverage and made a hasty pencilled note on the *Sun* for a civil servant to thoroughly read all the papers and to report back to him. Furthermore, if time allowed, he would ascertain from Gold and Kaufman their reports.

His first telephone call of the day was to Jack Jones as he had resolved the previous evening and the response was satisfactory and consistent with the two reports that he had received on the Sunday. Jack (it was good to have political allies that one could not only trust but rely upon for sound advice) suggested that since the attack he had received many reports and that his overall impression, which no doubt could be independently confirmed, was that shock had now changed to fear. He should speak to the nation reminding them of the strength of their resolve, her military capability and the single minded intention of the government to maintain essential services, as they did in the war, to confront the enemies of democracy, even if troops were deployed to man important services including the railways and London underground whose services had been disrupted following the attack, including unsubstantiated reports that last night some stations had remained open thus permitting people to sleep on the platforms.

Wilson judged that the time was now ripe for him to ask permission, at the imminent meeting of some of the Cabinet members, to institute negotiations to break the 'log jam' of the industrial dispute.

Jack Jones spent the morning speaking to his various union 'comrades' imparting the news that he understood that Wilson intended to speak to the country and would probably announce that the Cabinet intended to bring in the armed forces which would effectively break the railway strike, adding...

"Wilson may even contact you before his speech, however he should be judged not on what he says to you but his words to the nation and his actions."

His conversation with Bill Martin was recorded by M.I. 5.and ultimately reached the ears and custody of its chief and his deputy.

Jack Jones's information and suggestion was indeed correct, for the London underground was under great pressure to service an increased volume of traffic and a spontaneous demand for permanent access to the platforms of an increasing number of subterranean stations whilst 'open air' stations such as Cockfosters (such a quaint, unusual name) at the end of the Piccadilly line and a gateway to the countryside was beginning to see an increasing flow that might best be described as the vanguard of a stream of refugees!

At the other end of the political spectrum John Tyndall made a profound decision that in a few months would propel him and his ilk into the seats of power and destiny. His provenance and origins for the moment can be ignored but what is important is to understand his ultra right philosophy and his inspired decision to temporarily discard his warped values to be replaced by the pragmatism of political expediency and the veneer of patriotism and moderation.

The term anti-Semitism was coined by a German journalist, Wilhelm Marr, in his work published in eighteen seventy–three, 'The Victory of the Jew over the German' and within six years was republished a further eleven times!

Within thirty years the notorious calumny and plagiarism, 'The Protocols of the Learned Elders of Zion' would emerge in Tsarist Russia.

It is not the purpose of this work to investigate the origins of anti-Semitism which have their roots(most likely based on Roman Catholic teachings) in the accusation that the Jews were responsible for the death of Jesus-Deicide; or the fact that the Jewish communities were deliberately incarcerated within confined, defined areas of towns and cities known as Ghettoes during the Medieval period and Middle Ages when wild, preposterous allegations such as the Blood Libel (which was regularly raised around Easter and Passover) was readily believed, as was the fact that the Jews engaged in usury because, of course, they were permitted few other occupations to pursue one of which was the profession of medicine.

John Tyndall had developed two unique intellectual arguments, the former which would be embraced by the leaders of the New Order, the latter pragmatically discarded (originally only temporarily) in the face of economic and financial pressure from the very community (that is United States Jewry) that would have been accused of utilising such pressure as part of the 'International Jewish Conspiracy'.

Of the former, which will be discussed later [Please see' Political Control By The Totalitarian State In The Former Great Britain'-author], it is sufficient to state that it concerns a warped interpretation of the epic work on population growth and its relationship to the supply and the increase in the production of food-*An Essay On The Principle Of Population* - by Thomas Malthus and Tyndall's perverted analysis which would become the foundation of the New Order's domestic economic policy.

What is of primary interest is his belief in the philosophy of anti-Semitism, this time based on a perverted interpretation of history. It is focused around events during Oliver Cromwell's period of Republican leadership, the Protectorate and Commonwealth, when an Amsterdam based Rabbi, Menasseh Ben Israel, visited London with a delegation and petitioned Cromwell for the readmission of the Jews after their expulsion in twelve ninety. The pragmatic reason for Cromwell's interest in the matter was that the Dutch Jewish community was actively involved in international trade especially in the East and West

Indies and the New World. Their presence in England would be beneficial. Thus Tyndall saw the hand and the tentacles of International Jewry but his paranoia was even more twisted for in sixteen sixty–five England was ravaged by perhaps the last wave of Bubonic Plague and for Tyndall this was evidence that the Jews had brought the Plague over from the European Mainland and were intentionally killing Christians and with the Great Fire of London the following year were cheaply buying land!

On that Monday morning the identity, existence and philosophies of John Tyndall were completely unknown to the Prime Minister who had more immediate problems to wrestle with and resolve.

The first official, as distinct from anecdotal reports, were rapidly arriving from the Police, Fire and Ambulance services which when read together were no more than a desperate appeal for massive additional support.

Wilson conjectured that if two bombs could cause such chaos then a concerted attack would not only overwhelm the country's infrastructure but make the United Kingdom ungovernable!

The anecdotal reports relayed to him via his civil servants and emanating from the news desks of Fleet Street were a litany of horror. Initially it reminded him of the firestorms created by 'Bomber' Harris and R.A.F. Bomber Command on Hamburg and Dresden; the weak, emaciated, semi naked concentration camp inmates wandering aimlessly about after their liberation by the Allies or the devastation of Berlin in May nineteen forty-five.

But above all the reports confirmed that the victims, the survivors, were utterly, yes utterly disorientated and mentally decimated by the shock of the event.

"Will the Survivors Envy the Dead?"

He pondered over that profound question raised as a chapter heading in Herman Kahn`s nineteen sixty work on the nature and theory of war in the modern age 'On Thermonuclear War' and concluded that Denis Healey`s remark and assessment the previous evening was the only realistic way forward but time was running out and Humphrey would soon be returning to Washington empty handed. Then, suddenly, he was brought back from his musing as he heard a knock on the door and in answer to his command, James Griffiths, the Minister of Transport entered.

The offer of a cup of tea was declined and Wilson was inundated by further depressing news.

Griffiths had been at his desk since six a.m. (before it was even light) and had been in conference with his senior civil servants since seven thirty a.m. since which time they had been in continuous communication with their associates in other ministries, endeavouring to coordinate a plan to rescue the survivors under the overall control of the civil defence, an organisation which had been pared down, since the war, by successive governments. The Emergency Services were in constant contact but the situation was on a knife edge. He had also spoken to Konni Zilliacus and it was imperative that a dialogue begin, without delay, to end the industrial action. Finally, Harold should think the unthinkable for a Labour politician and additionally call in the Army to assist the civilian services cope with what was a national disaster.

"The Cabinet or the special committee which comprises the bulk of the Cabinet will shortly meet and must make some major decisions - however unpalatable."

The two men went downstairs to the basement and were then guided by a receptionist through a maze of well lit tunnels to a secure nuclear bomb proof complex of rooms and additional facilities before they begun their meeting promptly at eleven a.m.

FORTY-THREE

The room and the atmosphere exuded an eeriness which transcended any emotions of foreboding or even claustrophobia. This was a war room and the nation appeared again to be moving to the edge of an abyss. Wilson requested that the lighting be raised and he was then able to clearly see before him a large rectangular table, covered in green baize, surrounded by most members of the Cabinet and behind them some senior civil servants, some of whom he did not recognise and six, no seven of the most senior officers of Her Majesty's armed forces. The wall to his right was partially covered by two maps, the first of the United Kingdom and the second, somewhat larger, of Western Europe, terminating on its right hand edge with the Ural Mountains.

Wilson suddenly realised how vast was the Soviet Union and how small and insignificant the U.K.

A line of clocks on the wall directly opposite him were labelled with the identity of various world cities or capitals, the hour hands showing different times but the longer minute hands the same time as London, however it was the blackboard beneath which caught his attention and immediately caused a fleeting void in his stomach.

He had to ask one of the civil servants to briefly move as he was obscuring part of the blackboard which Wilson was then able to view in its entirety and comprehend the display. Covered by parallel white lines, at the top neatly chalked, one under the other were the names of

Chelmsford and Harlow New Town followed by two sets of six figure numbers which he very quickly assumed, because they were similar, were the geographical coordinates, then, obviously the dates and times of the 'strikes' and finally a three digit number which later that day he was to be informed were the estimated kilotonnage of the weapons used.

Before he was able to speak one of the civil servants stood up, apologised, and confirmed, without gravitas or emotion, that:

"When, and if, it was determined that war were imminent, arrangements were already in hand to transport those present to three different sites outside of London (known as Regional Seats of Government), each equipped with various high technology means of communication in order primarily to maintain power and authority and secondly to prosecute the war.

At each location a facility was also available to communicate with 'Washington' and by Telex with the British Embassy in Moscow, who undoubtedly could contact 'The Kremlin' and the Soviet government."

Harold Wilson, the last legally empowered Prime Minister of the United Kingdom asked, for him, the only important question...

"Her Majesty and the Royal Family. What arrangements have been made for their immediate security and long term protection?"

Westminster Hall was being made ready to receive, on the following day Tuesday, the bier of Sir Winston Churchill which would be visited by Her Majesty, The Queen and other members of a grieving Royal Family and also preparations were being put in hand to erect barriers to control the crowds that would undoubtedly throng to the great historical building to pay their own humble and personal final respects and unbeknownst to everyone to the demise of democracy and freedom.

At around the same time Manny Gold exited Leicester Square tube station along with a seething mass of passengers and he mused over the unusually subdued nature of his fellow passengers, whose normal nature of taciturn silence seemed to be dominated by a sense of, he couldn't quite place the emotion, or put his finger on their attitude...

"Of despondency, no, fear, err...an ominous foreboding, perhaps that was the common denominator that obsessed those around him and also the whole nation."

As if affected by mass hysteria he noticed that everyone was suddenly looking skywards, South towards Trafalgar Square and beyond to the Houses of Parliament. A noise grew in intensity and like a Wagnerian Opera, like mythical Valkyries, five Vulcan Bombers were seen to deliberately fly over the site of the memorial to one of its country's greatest naval commanders and then veer off, passing over the symbol of democratic freedom and finally turn to fly West above a defiant River Thames. For a brief few moments an aura of hope seemed to bathe everyone and unite the people.

He collected his thoughts, waited for a set of lights to turn red and deftly, diagonally crossed over the road to the other tube exit before intending to walk towards Trafalgar Square. Eight or nine men were proudly holding up Union Jacks on long poles and he caught their cry of...

"Britain: stand up and fight union tyranny!"

A few yards away a police officer stood silently and apparently oblivious to the demonstration, more concerned to shelter in the doorway of the adjacent theatre and to remain dry as the first signs of rain appeared. Gold noticed that some pedestrians were actually going up to the demonstrators and handing them money, change or even fistfuls of coins or in one case he clearly saw a well dressed and elegant gentleman hand over a pound note and for an instance, a fleeting moment, he thought that the man was familiar but he passed off the conjecture to an error of judgement. Then strangely he remembered the incident at Piccadilly Circus when his sixth sense alerted him to the fact that he was being watched, but this time he also felt that he was being scrutinised. He looked round then suddenly saw one of the demonstrators clearly focussing upon him. There was something uniquely special about him which generated a jigsaw puzzle of confused memories hidden behind a mist of conflicting ideas and thoughts and that strong but indefinable sense that he had previously set sight of the man but he was unable to convert his thoughts into a single tangible memory.

The man was John Tyndall, the group were members of his organisation, the Greater Britain Movement, operating at that time from an upper room in a pub named 'The Silver Sword' in Petty France, S.W.1, not far from the Houses of Parliament or an address in Holborn evidence for which the official records or records have been conveniently hidden or lost if such formal documentation ever existed.

As a Jew, Gold (or Goldburgh) would have been especially interested and disturbed to learn that the man, whose attention he had caught, was the author of a vicious and morally corrupt anti Semitic and virulently Anti Democratic tract, 'The Authoritarian State' (published in nineteen sixty-two at a price of two and six pence). Not only that but the previous year (nineteen sixty-four) he had been released from prison following a successful prosecution and conviction under the nineteen thirty–six Public Order Act for attempting to set up a paramilitary force (called 'Spearhead') along with a fellow National Socialist, Colin Jordan, who having been released from prison prior to Tyndall, had married Tyndall`s fiancée, Francoise Dior, creating a schism between the two men.

Not only had the personal betrayal angered and rankled him but Jordan had 'stolen' a valuable item of memorabilia that had given him hope for the future and strength in the righteousness of his cause. It was an expensively framed press cutting dated Monday January 15 1934 of The Daily Mail (edition number11,770) and the page number (ten) was all but obliterated by the passage of time through the bleaching of the Sun.

The article was written by Viscount Rothermere and was entitled:

Hurrah for the Blackshirts

Adjacent to a photograph captioned...

BRITISH BLACKSHIRTS

MARCHING IN LONDON,

the article ended with a note confirming that:

Young men may join the British Union of Fascists by writing to the Headquarters, King`s Road, Chelsea, S.W.[sic]

Adjacent to the article an Editorial comment was headed...

THE GREAT ALTERNATIVE

and included the interesting observation that:

"We may regard it as certain that the Blackshirt leader, Sir Oswald Mosley, could do more in a conference at Berlin to straighten out the kinks in Anglo–German relations than any half-dozen of the elderly politicians whom the Cabinet persists in sending on fruitless missions to Geneva and elsewhere."

The contents of the article were certainly provocative and new in concept including an exhortation directed at the youth of the nation to support this new venture.

The following day and up to and including at least Monday January 22 1934 the letters column (TODAY'S LETTERS) received correspondence of support including on Thursday January 18 1934 under the general heading of...

TOWARDS A GREATER BRITAIN

correspondence from a Mr. Henry Welsh of 3 Hungerford -Road, Holloway, N...

"In helping to remove some of the fallacies and misconceptions concerning the Blackshirts` policy, Lord Rothermere has done his country a really good turn, for, whether we happen to like it or not, they have come to stay. What is more, it may well prove the modern solution to our modern problems."

On Saturday January 20 1934, the Editorial column, for the first time in any of the articles or letters mentioned anti- Semitism:

"Its enemies accuse it of Anti- Semitic tendencies. This is absurd. It has never attacked anyone on account of his race or creed."

On Monday January 22 1934 page eleven included extensive coverage of a rally held in Birmingham...

STIRRING RALLY OF THE BLACKSHIRTS

SIR O. MOSLEY`S CALL TO YOUTH

STOP NATIONAL SURRENDER

BUILDING A NEW BRITAIN

"WE MUST HAVE ACTION"

8,000 ENTHUSIASTIC LISTENERS

BY G. WARD, BIRMINGHAM SUNDAY

Adjacent was a caption...

A STRIKING DAILY MAIL PICTURE OF SIR OSWALD MOSLEY, FACING LAST NIGHT'S GREAT AUDIENCE FROM A ROSTRUM MARKED ONLY BY THE DISPLAY OF A UNION JACK.

The police officer interrupted Gold's train of thought as he turned to his right and walked up to the protestors and in an authoritative, quiet voice announced that:

"This is the second and last warning that I'm giving you. Begging is not allowed and if you continue soliciting donations without a permit I will have to arrest you."

John Tyndall turned to the officer and with a mixture of fact, courtesy and sarcasm responded that:

"Unlike the police force who were given a salary increase by the Prime Minister, as one of his first acts on becoming the P.M., we are demonstrating for the protection and rights of the majority of the nation suffering during these current harsh, economic times and who are being held to ransom by the Bolshevik trade unionists."

For Tyndall the political description Bolshevik, since many of the original 'conspirators' and revolutionaries had been Jewish, was an euphemism for the despised sub humans, the Yids, hook noses, usurers, Moses, carriers of disease such as Bubonic Plague or the other rat derived fatal disease,'Weil's' (Leptospirosis).

189

The word Bolshevik that he had used only yesterday, in error, instantaneously reminded him when and where he had seen the man. It was at the dock in Gravesend. His curiosity satisfied, he turned South towards Trafalgar Square and Whitehall.

Suddenly he felt the pressure of fingers and a thumb clutching and pressing into his right shoulder. Turning, he was confronted at a tactful distance by the leader of the demonstrators. In hindsight he should never have involved himself in a conversation with the stranger but the man was insistent and his reasons compelling.

"Yes, he and his associates had been at Gravesend yesterday in a fruitless attempt to draw attention to the trade union conspiracy to bring the country to its knees and to undermine the government and therefore the nation in a time of great danger. It was naked blackmail and did Mr Wilson really believe that 'they', the Bolsheviks, were really the country's enemy?"

Gold realised that he should extricate himself before again making a provocative statement and meekly stated with a candour that clearly impressed the man that:

"He appreciated the man's interest and his motives but that his position precluded him from making further public statements or comments."

He was such a fool. He should have denied his identity and responded that the man was confusing him with someone else of similar appearance.

"Could they meet again to discuss this and other important matters?"

This time with a firmness that even surprised himself he answered the man with one word and walked off.

"No."

The next time they would meet he would be the messenger and then the unofficial negotiator on behalf of a cowed and desperate government.

FORTY-FOUR

The United States ambassador to the Court of St. James, David Bruce, pondered not on his next instructions, but the manner in which he would not only communicate his President's wishes but more importantly how ruthlessly he should convey the new demands in a changing, fluid situation.

Hubert Humphrey was no longer in the country, having left under the tightest and maximum of secrecy and above all, security. The previous day, Sunday, he had made an impromptu and certainly unscheduled visit to East Anglia and a hurried, whistle stop tour of a number of U.S. air force bases. His unexpected and surprise visit had meteorically raised the servicemen and women's morale and was a coup for Washington. His last visit was to Mildenhall ending at the Base's ten pin bowling alley when they (he was uncertain who 'they' were) confirmed the two nuclear strikes and within minutes the Vice President had unceremoniously been bundled (but not literally) by secret service agents onto a military Boeing 707 jet and (Bruce estimated no more than nine minutes from the first notification of the two nuclear explosions to the moment when the wheels left the ground) accompanied by a wing of 'fighters'. Such was the haste that he had not been able to convey his best wishes to the President or ceremoniously end his joint visit with the V.P.

The new demands, sent by enciphered Teletype, were even more ruthless and uncompromising than the previous original demand. Johnson or his advisors, clearly recognised the British government's absolute inability to respond to the Soviet's arrogant display of measured force. The new demands made the United Kingdom no more than a vassal state, an island converted into a mighty and vast fortress, not to defend herself and her people, but to keep the Communist hordes at bay, encircled by powerful military bases of which the United Kingdom was only one part of a chain. This time a new condition was imposed that would destroy any pretence of the client nation's independence. For any external financial transactions these would have to be based on the U.S. Dollar, finally ending the country's independent economic power and the 'Sterling area'. Furthermore Britain would have to pay, in Dollars, a contribution towards its defence in order to support the cost of the new 'Monroe' Doctrine.

He would contact Harold Wilson late in the afternoon, suggest an urgent meeting, and would also notify him, in the absence of his reply to the first and original set of demands, that possibly Johnson, who would arrive on Friday for the State Funeral, would be prepared to have a 'face to face' meeting to discuss and finalise any agreement.

The former French naval dockyard at Le Havre was the scene and site of frenzied activity, for since the arrival of the two cruisers late the previous night, Sunday, under cover of darkness and tarpaulin strategically placed to hide work on the two cruisers, the vessels were each supplied with a replacement sea to land missile. The small flotilla was going to make a dash home, before their enemies might reap their revenge, but this time with an increased umbrella of fighters with instructions to engage the enemy, if attacked, and to support the two vessels in a pre planned assault as they left the English Channel for the North Sea, home and glory.

For the Soviet planners, this action, this foray into waters previously dominated by the British Navy, was not solely a military adventure but to check on the response of the British government (and their American masters, a description which lucidly showed their contempt for the so called 'Alliance') and their resolve, especially as Soviet Intelligence was absolutely certain that the R.A.F. was virtually naked and that they only had a mere handful of strategic bombers. The other question was to test the United States' strength of will to implement their new and much vaunted 'Monroe' Doctrine.

The final target or targets had still not yet been determined but currently there was an embargo on any U.S. bases or the use of thermonuclear weapons.

The catalyst that increased trade union militancy which had been sown earlier that morning and was still being maliciously spread by Jack Jones had incited the petulant and extremist Bill Martin who had all but 'high jacked' and wrestled power and influence from the elected leadership of the National Union of Miners and he was frantically visiting as many pits as possible, both stiffening the resolve of the strikers, cajoling the waverers and shaming a substantial minority that wanted to work but were effectively restrained from entering the pits.

Nationwide, his almost fanatical supporters, in contradiction to the union's instructions, deliberately pursued Martin's actions, virtually ending the production of one of the country's life bloods.

The body of the main union leaders, aware of Jones's information, were more pragmatic and definitely not phlegmatic about the direction and purpose of the national industrial action which could backfire and put back the movement and its aims by forty years to the time of the National Strike in nineteen twenty-six. There could and must be a better way forward.

When Gold arrived at 10 Downing Street he was informed that the P.M. was both unavailable and that he had an urgent task that required his discreet and immediate attention. The instructions were in a sealed envelope, hand written, scrawled and barely legible. He sat in the P.M.'s chair, in his private office and took the precaution and arrogance to instruct a senior civil servant to stand outside the room to secure *HIS* privacy. He was beginning to make enemies, both because of his arrogance and because of his rapid rise to power.

He spoke directly to the two Archbishops of Canterbury and York and the Bishop of Durham, thanking them, on behalf of the P.M., for their assistance concerning a confidential matter whilst not admitting his ignorance of the actual subject, and confirmed that Mr. Wilson wanted them again to contact the same people and to convey the P.M.'s great appreciation which he intended to make public on Tuesday night when he also would make a conciliatory gesture but he required confirmation that they would make arrangements to settle the matter. Gold was understandably fascinated by the intimate levers of power and realised how both close and far he was from the actual seat of power and began to wonder how, and if, in a fleeting moment, he could ever usurp his master and mentor.

"It was agreed ,some years ago, and only confirmed by your predecessor, Alec Douglas Home with Her Majesty, as the final act of his prime ministership, that in the event of, but prior to the outbreak of nuclear war, that Her Majesty, and members of the Royal Family, with the promise and agreement of the government of Southern Ireland, in a dramatic show of reconciliation and support for Great Britain, would be given temporary haven and refuge in the Republic and that if this arrangement became untenable then the family would leave for Canada and reign in the seat of the Capital, Ottawa. Logistically, to avoid a catastrophe, the family and their entourages would be transported by different civilian or military flights or even by submarine. It was recognised that the involvement of the Republic, which for many might prove politically embarrassing or intolerable, could, in the future, become the grounds for reconciliation."

For Harold Wilson and the other members of the Cabinet the information and its necessary secrecy surprised them and sensibly led them independently to wonder and conjecture what other secrets had been suppressed and had yet to be disclosed to them.

FORTY-FIVE

By five-thirty p.m. the demonstrators had dispersed, leaving John Tyndall and one acolyte not only to assess the day's events but to tally the donations and review the offers of support. Excluding the one pound note tendered by the well dressed gentleman they had accumulated a total of thirty seven pounds, eleven shillings and nine pence. Unsolicited, they had collected eighteen telephone numbers and twelve business cards from members of the public whose mounting anger against the use of the strike weapon was consistently described as undermining the nation and would be used by the country's enemies to destroy everything that that the nation stood for. Furthermore the government said and did nothing, the unelected Prime Minister and his Cabinet were Labour in majority and should put the national interest before their trade union masters, citing as a specific example, the delay calling a General Election. Firm, fair and resolute leadership was demanded, especially as the storm clouds of war appeared to be gathering again.

Then Tyndall, in one of those moments when inspiration (or even serendipity) apparently creates a masterpiece from a host of random thoughts, uttered a phrase that would become, in the weeks to come, the clarion call which would draw tens of thousands to the Union Jack banners that 'The First of the Few' patriotically waved in their confrontation with union tyranny and the menace of political and military action by enemies that threatened both from abroad and more sinisterly, at home, the latter like a fifth column.

Temporarily they would discard and deny their extreme right wing philosophy and policies and project an image of national patriotism. The Yids, the corruptors of every decent value that the British people held dear, would be dealt with when the time was suitable.

"Defend British Free Speech and Freedom from Bolshevik Terrorism."

"Yes, they would come out on Tuesday, proudly raise the Union Jack and support a movement that had the nation's best interests as its core value."

That was the general reply to the many telephone calls the two men made that evening. There was no formal plan but arrangements were made for demonstrations to be held outside of three Piccadilly Line tube stations, each within walking distance, and such was the support that there would be adequate reserves to relieve the first group of demonstrators. Thus Leicester Square, Piccadilly Circus and Green Park were to be the roots of the movement that the naive and those who would be manipulated, believed would sweep away the 'Ancien Regime' and restore national pride and British values in the face of overwhelming odds and hardships.

Had John Tyndall and his second in command tarried at the dockside in Gravesend the previous day, they would have seen the tragic and horrendous consequences of 'Bolshevik' perfidiousness and treachery that would have immediately created a propaganda weapon of immense emotion and influence. However the decision to moor the hospital ship across the Thames at Gravesend and not Tilbury was made with the intention to transfer the many victims to a nearby specialist hospital but the unexpected and catastrophic nuclear attack immediately altered the situation.

The crews of the two Soviet cruisers, still ecstatic following their recent action against the British targets, were due to return from shore leave in Le Havre by eighteen hundred hours, unaware that their vessels would depart the following morning at first light and assault, again, their enemy who (allegedly because of their own statements and propaganda) had colluded and attacked with nuclear weapons the Republics of Russia and the Ukraine. Revenge would be sweet.

The enciphered message, authorised and carefully considered by the Defence Council which included members of the Politburo including the First Secretary of the Communist Party, Leonid Brezhnev, gave only the coordinates of the two new targets, again with the reminder and implied threat of court martial proceedings if any U.S. bases were accidentally hit. The identity of the chosen targets would have meant nothing to the officers and crew of the two vessels but for many if not most of the residents of Ipswich and Bury St. Edmunds that night was to be their final night of life and those that survived would face the terrible suffering and lingering deaths that were now beginning to take place in Chelmsford and Harlow New Town, so reminiscent of the agonies of Hiroshima and Nagasaki.

By six-thirty p.m. that evening Wilson, established in the redoubt that was his private office, with only Gerald Kaufman and a secretary in attendance, had constructed the first draft of a statement that would be nationally broadcast the following evening. He made no reference, and did not confide in his assistant and admit to him the events of the four hour meeting that had taken place deep in the bowels of Whitehall.

Such was its current insignificance that no mention was made at the meeting concerning the fate of some of the returning troops and when Gold met the P.M. and informed him of the events at Gravesend it only added a further burden and an additional dimension. Gold was summarily despatched, along with a senior civil servant, and instructed first to locate the injured troops and then to prepare a report for the P.M.

The four hour meeting intended to prepare the government for imminent war, escalated from an initial confrontation between the military hierarchy and the government, or more specifically those members of the Cabinet who were present, and then the military hierarchy and the 'Inner Cabinet', en masse, in OPPOSITION to the P.M. Even the civil servants present at the meeting who were expected and should have remained impartial, only to offer advice, were undiplomatically scathing of Wilson's unilateral surrender to Soviet blackmail. The P.M., who was consistently reminded, on all fronts, by various groups and 'cliques' that his ally, Johnson, had announced a new 'Monroe' Doctrine, was unable to mount a credible argument and defend himself, based on the grounds that the declaration had been made AFTER his agreement and that he had not received PRIOR notice from Washington of the President's intended statement.

Wilson, isolated and embattled, did not want to further undermine his situation and the country's dire position by admitting the parlous state of the nation's relationship with the United States and he was, of course, unaware of the further demands that were about to be made.

The chiefs of the armed forces summarised the situation thus:

"Quite bluntly the nation was virtually naked and could not mount an assault on the Soviet Union, or Eastern Europe, and the potential of a Soviet counter strike was unimaginable."

Turning to his 'Inner Cabinet', Wilson saw in their eyes contempt and dread for the future.

The first use of the emotional and inflammatory word' betrayal' was not recorded, but both Ted Heath and Denis Healey both used the word in a comparison with Neville Chamberlain in nineteen thirty-eight after 'Munich' but no one in the War Room was prepared to ask the P.M. to resign and neither was anyone prepared to take on the mantle of leadership. For all intent and purpose the government was paralysed.

It was left to a cabal of senior civil servants to suggest the obvious and they essentially repeated Denis Healey`s earlier suggestion:

"That Wilson approach the U.S. President and negotiate an 'umbrella' that would protect the nation."

Wilson quietly realised that events and circumstances, completely out of his hands and control, were creating a situation whereby it was becoming unnecessary, indeed irrelevant, to disclose his secret negotiations with the Americans and he would allow those around him to propel him into a course that he was already following. He acquiesced to the suggestion and recommended that adequate time be found when, as he suspected, the President would be in London for the State Funeral. Taking the initiative he referred to the expanding industrial action and then going on the offensive he told a half truth (which was received with great relief) that he was in contact with the Union bosses-he really meant indirect communication through intermediaries - to end the dispute.

Wilson would use the evening to contact the major power brokers in the trade union movement, outline to them the relevant contents of his intended broadcast and endeavour to extricate from them a firm promise to bring the striking workers back to the factories, the transport system outside of London, and the various and diverse areas of trade and commerce including the semi paralysed civil service and even the sacrosanct National Health Service where the service was, in any event, deteriorating.

That evening he began to consider his relationship with the Cabinet and the absolute urgent necessity to continue and conclude negotiations through the United States ambassador and, in parallel, end the industrial dispute. The former was essential but he had little to offer in return so a deal or any deal at any price was important to satisfy the Cabinet and he could delay conceding certain unpalatable concessions to the unions until after the General Election which he wished to hold in the spring, using an interim settlement based on the 'National Interest'.

Of course he might even lose the election in which case his opponents would have to clear up the mess or possibly he could be returned with a big majority in which case he could, as he always wanted, and he wished that Barbara Castle was still there, so that they, no, he meant he, could effectively 'screw the unions'. Later, or at a more propitious time, he would thank such stalwarts as 'Ted' Heath and Denis Healey, before dropping them, or easing them out to be replaced with more loyal and pliant members.

He spent a profitable evening speaking to various trade union functionaries, outlining briefly pertinent details of his intended speech and listened attentively to their demands and visions of a Socialist economic utopia which they could not comprehend was currently, and in the foreseeable future, beyond anyone's grasp but his most profitable call was to the Lord Chancellor, Sir Reginald Manningham-Buller who...

"Would be more than pleased to be present at seven forty–five the next morning to discuss what Harold had called 'a most discreet matter' and that Harold was well informed as the lure of Scottish smoked kippers and lightly toasted, heavily buttered, thin slices of a cottage loaf for breakfast was both beguiling and enticing.

"

FORTY-SIX

Sir Reginald arrived prematurely but the P.M. was already prepared and had deliberately arranged for two senior civil servants to be present and to record the meeting which unknown to him would ultimately be used against him as evidence during his trial for High Treason and which would be recorded on a grainy sixteen millimetre black and white film.

"He had two, no three, major concerns. The ongoing industrial dispute was sapping the nation's strength but both he and his representatives (who he did not identify) had been in contact with the upper echelons of the T.U.C. and he believed that there could be an interim resolution by as early as the weekend and negotiations could result in a long term partnership between the government and the unions (Sir Reginald might superficially appear ethereal, but his mind, like that of the now dead Sir Ivone Kirkpatrick, was razor sharp and had a clarity of thought which led him immediately to note the omission and exclusion of 'the employers').

For some time I have been in secret negotiations with representatives of Lyndon Johnson including a meeting with his deputy, Vice President Hubert Humphrey, to arrange an agreement that would protect the security and independence of the nation and I can also reveal to you that as a major concession, *AT THE REQUEST OF THE PRESIDENT* [author's emphasis], and as a sign of this country's trust in the good faith of our greatest ally, I and I alone agreed to move the main bulk of our' V' bomber fleet to South Africa to bolster the overseas commitments of The United States in the Western Pacific and Indian Ocean.

It is my intention, as part of the arrangement, to obtain early delivery of our new Polaris fleet and its revolutionary missile system to defend our shores but also to take an active role in the protection and defence of our interests in the North Atlantic and to operate in the Baltic. Only you now know and are part of this country's greatest secret and I truly believe that you can now understand how humiliated and betrayed I felt when the military hierarchy, my own Inner Cabinet and above all the senior civil servants, turned on me yesterday.

Until such time as we can hold a General Election, over five hundred constituencies are effectively disenfranchised and the nation is administered by what was called under Churchill's stewardship a National Government but what we have called a Coalition. I am therefore enquiring if there is any legal objection expanding the Cabinet by the inclusion of the nation's best businessmen and administrators until a new government is elected?"

The Lord Chancellor would be able to give a considered opinion by the following day, Wednesday.

The two Soviet cruisers departed from Le Havre and begun their return journey to a new home base East of Hamburg, but the officers had been unable to quell the conjecture and gossip of the crew members that a second assault, en route home, would be made against further targets in the United Kingdom and their task was made more difficult by the secret cargo hidden beneath heavily secured tarpaulin sheets.

He had had great difficulty locating John Tyndall. The group of demonstrators outside of Leicester Square underground station waving their Union Jacks had only been instructed how to deal with objectors and those, like them, who wished to offer support, both financial or in person and their section leader had just left to deliver the latest collection of donations to their associates at Piccadilly Circus and would not return for twenty minutes. Andrew Duggan patiently persisted with a description of the man he wished to meet until a woman recognised his word painting and suggested he go to Green Park where the man he sought was to be found addressing passersby with a megaphone. As Duggan turned to walk to Leicester Square on his way to Piccadilly Circus, then along Piccadilly and thence to his final destination, he absentmindedly walked into another gentleman and as they courteously apologised to each other both immediately sensed that the other was known to them, a thought that was to play on each other's mind throughout the day.

Manny Gold was on his way from Leicester Square underground station to collect some documents including a special identification card before he left with his civil service assistant to resolve the location, condition and fate of the returning troops.

Harold Wilson feasted regally on the breakfast that had been especially prepared for his Lord Chancellor, or should it be Her Majesty's Lord Chancellor?, as Sir Reginald had urgently left the meeting, such was his attention to his responsibilities, and Harold understood that the Lord Chancellor had gone straight into a meeting with his assistants to resolve the question that had been posed. His first subsequent act was to contact his old and trusted friend, Jack Jones, a conduit to the T.U.C. leadership but also a source of priceless information, some of which was tittle tattle and salacious gossip but overall a powerful tool in any difficult negotiations. Jones was the type of man who he could see in a truly National Government, dedicated, efficient, patriotic and above all, loyal.

His response only confirmed Harold's astute analysis of the man and his earlier trust in his initial involvement...

"The major figures in the T.U.C. movement saw no future or reason to continue the ever escalating strikes and felt a moral duty to tell their members to return to work, indeed every day that the factories stood idle meant that there was less profit from which the employers could pay increased wages. But more important, was that ever increasing groups of workers were unnecessarily suffering hardship, symbolised by the terrible ordeal of the people of Chelmsford and Harlow who could not be moved because of the industrial dispute and the acute shortage of transport. If the government contemplated bringing in troops to help with the transportation of the injured it would be unwise to directly mention this option, only that any or every available option would be considered. All that was required in his forthcoming speech was a minor but specific public concession and since he had already told them the substance of his speech, this could be used to persuade the strikers to return to work. It was imperative to return a SOCIALIST [again the author's emphasis] Labour government in the imminent election and the funds of the unions would be totally committed to the campaign."

Jack Jones actually spent the rest of the morning speaking to his many connections but what he conveyed to them was not exactly what Harold thought he was going to tell them.

"Harold can only be judged by his actions and not his promises. What he might promise might not be what he was able or even intended to deliver. During my conversation, mention was made of bringing in troops! We have a unique opportunity to democratically negotiate with this government to protect the right to withdraw our labour, equitably share in the profits both of those nationalised bodies and private firms whose profits end up in the pockets of the shareholders whose only contribution is to look at the rising price of the shares that they own and to create the foundations of a fair and just society and not the illusion projected by the plutocrats and the selfish.

This was a confrontation that had to be won."

To finance his work, Jones, by the tried and usual method, collected on the Friday further funds from his Soviet handler, this time mainly in bundles of soiled, sordid, squalid used five pound notes.

His mundane duties completed, the P.M. focused on his diary and his visit that afternoon to Westminster Hall and his official duty as Prime Minister to represent the government and the nation visiting the coffin of Sir Winston but also to pay his own personal respects to the' old bugger' and his now anachronistic values of Empire and British Imperial power, but he would actually miss him.

Gold called in and confirmed that a preliminary telephonic report on the hospitalised soldiers would follow as soon as possible and that the task had been simplified by the recently acquired knowledge that, following some administrative chaos-there was no other phrase to correctly define the circumstances- the men, and a few unfortunate women, had been transferred to the Kent and Canterbury Hospital in Canterbury and had the twin nuclear attacks occurred earlier they might have been pushed aside in the tragic, frightening competition for bed space. Harold responded that:

"The duty of the nation to their fighting forces was paramount and the first act of his Premiership, and he would remind the country when the time was suitable, had been to recognise their brave contribution to the country's defence and security and that was why, in response, he had arranged for the salaries of all the armed forces to be increased, especially for the lower ranks, and at the same time increase the salaries of all the serving ranks in the many regional police forces."

As Gold left in a chauffeur driven ministerial vehicle, Wilson remembered Harold Macmillan`s oft quoted adage...

"Events, events my dear boy."

John Tyndall had purchased, with the one pound note donated by the anonymous gentleman, a megaphone, and his voice, or more specifically his message, attracted the attention and interest of a growing throng. The message and patriotic slogans were what they wanted, needed to hear, not the silence of the government or the selfish and thoughtless rants of the strikers whilst their fellow countrymen suffered. Their wallets and purses were readily opened without considering the origins and motives of the orator, whilst pledges of support were rapidly inundating the group of demonstrators.

"Britain stand up and fight union tyranny!"

Tyndall`s words magnified by the megaphone directed Duggan to his quarry. He, they, the ever expanding group were outside of Green Park underground station facing North, the Arcade of the Ritz Hotel to their right and behind them, the park. There was no necessity for him to walk up to Tyndall for the excited orator had instantly recognised him and the quarry temporarily neglected his duty and walked over to Duggan who put out his hand more through courtesy than acquaintance. The ensuing conversation was brief and to the point:

"It would be to our mutual benefit if you could join me and a dear colleague for lunch tomorrow to discuss matters of mutual interest. Mr. Keith Wagstaffe, a far more interesting lunch companion, needs your views and opinion on certain current issues and has already taken the impertinent opportunity to book a table at his favourite haunt, which I am confident you will enjoy as much as the possible suggestions he will undoubtedly make."

Andrew Duggan formally introduced and identified himself and then, in the most general terms, alluded to his place of work, turning one hundred and eighty degrees and pointing, with his furled umbrella, South East in the general direction of Whitehall but had he been truthful he would have pointed South and South West and the headquarters of M.I.6 and he should also have mentioned that having` served his apprenticeship' in intelligence work, beginning during the war in Cairo, was an officer in the more secretive M.I.6.

Tyndall was seduced both by the invitation and the reference to his interests. A time and location was promptly agreed and Duggan disappeared into the park whilst, coincidentally, and unknown to both men, Francoise Dior, having just left New Bond Street, observed her former fiancée but more importantly the enthusiasm and support of the large throng surrounding him. She would remember to mention the event to her husband, who might, in turn, go to the one man in England who could profit from such enthusiasm but who had previously been thwarted by the reactionary brigade of British pre-war conservatism, including his nemesis, the now dead Churchill.

FORTY-SEVEN

The hospital was efficiently managed and capable and competent to handle most medical contingencies but not the massive influx of severely injured patients who should have been sent to a specialist hospital unit with the experienced staff, equipment and abundance of drugs to give the patients the quality and standard of treatment that they required. The unexpected avalanche had resulted in more than half being temporarily accommodated in a hall, laid out on stretchers, constantly monitored by caring nurses who, unfortunately, did not have the expertise to help them, other than to offer palliative care.

Gold commandeered an office, grabbed the telephone and demanded that the staff vacate the room as he dialled the direct, ex directory number to Ten Downing Street. His attitude was a combination of the excess of power over tact and a reaction to the gruesome scene that had confronted him. A senior doctor, a Mr. John Wrighton, stood his ground and refused to leave and therefore heard one side of the conversation.

What he heard or his reaction is not important, but Gold managed to immediately speak to the P.M. and his comments and observations were emotionally charged and lacked the objectiveness that was paramount. His words spoke of betrayal, of men left virtually unattended to die on stretchers in a cold and poorly lit hall, as nurses made cursory, circulatory walks around the cavernous room administering words of sympathy but not treatment. And the condition of the men was frightening: some continuously vomited, some of which were of abnormal colours and others screamed of internal pain or even of blindness. It was horrible and reminded him of the vision of Dante`s Inferno.

He then made a comment, that like a knife sank deep into the ego of the P.M. but not into his conscience.

"If and when the press become aware of this tragedy and expose not only the condition of the troops but the lack of care and attention, then the government's apparent neglect of their responsibilities, will be a stain on your reputation and could affect your election campaign."

Wilson did not ignore the emotionally charged warning but he would await the more clinical, objective and considered report of his civil servant. He deliberately did not include the adverb trusted because of the attack on his actions by the civil servants in the War Room the previous day. He retired to his private residence in Ten Downing Street where he changed into a suitable lounge suit and chose from a rack of ties the most appropriate when common sense and protocol would have determined only black as being correct and suitable.

His thoughts were interrupted by the office telephone, which by convention and his insistence could only be utilised in the most urgent of situations. He heard the voice of David Bruce, his now hurried sprint through the usual courtesies and the nub of his message:

"Vice President Humphrey is due to arrive at three p.m. London time tomorrow and both he and the Vice-President were under orders to finalise an agreement by Thursday afternoon, when the President was due to arrive from Washington. Johnson intended to make a joint announcement with the P.M. no later than Friday evening before the State Funeral on the Saturday, for the benefit of the British people and to warn the Soviet Union and the Warsaw Pact that the United States (he forgot to mention and clearly the omission was indicative of his evaluation of...and Allies) would not tolerate any act or aggression in accordance with the terms of the new 'Monroe' Doctrine. We suggest a meeting at 'Number Ten' where, as before, we can gain an unobserved, discreet access by the usual entrance which is well away from the gaze of the general public and the prying eyes of the press. A third representative will also attend, to give Hubert certain political and diplomatic advice and may I ask, to facilitate a prompt resolution that your group of advisors comprises no more than six or seven in total? As a friend can I inform you that there is little room for negotiation and failure could result in the British Isles being denuded of our presence which would be relocated nearby."

The queue of mourners was far greater than the organisers had ever imagined and their attitude was subdued, passive and dignified. These were the 'ordinary' folk, many of whom had lived through the summer of nineteen forty and had seen the flame of Freedom and Democracy flicker and dim but it had not been extinguished because of the one man to whom they were paying their final respects, who had been the symbol of everything that they valued and treasured.

Within a very few days they would all be betrayed and the shadow of darkness would begin to cover the nation.

The arrival of the Prime Minister was acknowledged with the absolute minimum of appreciation by the general public, indeed had he tarried and listened to their thoughts and mumbled comments he would have realised that there was a growing, swelling tide of dissatisfaction and resentment of his government, of union power and the denial of an election which allowed so many people to be disenfranchised.

Inside Westminster Hall ,Wilson noted two former holders of his office, Clement Attlee and Winston's deputy in the tumultuous years of the war and Anthony Eden, Winston's successor as a peace time Prime Minister, however he was shocked at his appearance for he looked and acted prematurely old and exhausted and Wilson suddenly confronted himself with the realisation that it had been Eden's great ally, the United States, under the former military leader Dwight Eisenhower who had undermined the Pact between Eden , the French and Israel and forced them to withdraw from the Suez Canal zone, starkly compelling the two European nations to confront the reality that they were no longer global superpowers .

Despite the venue and the solemnity of the occasion Harold's thoughts focused and concentrated on the terms that he was to be confronted with or could squeeze from his great friends and allies.

He performed his duties and responsibilities in an almost robotic fashion and only realised he was on his way back to 'Number Ten' when he was in the chauffeur driven vehicle, driving around Parliament Square.

FORTY-EIGHT

Almost simultaneously, the sailors on the two cruisers peeled back the tarpaulin, exposing the now instantaneously recognisable shape of the SS-N-3b. The excitement of both crews could not be dimmed or thwarted by the bitterly cold Northerly wind which propelled the rain onto the deck like bullets. Once again the dead of the Ukraine and Mother Russia would be avenged.

The inquisitive crowd, outside of Ten Downing Street, instinctively peeled open to allow the Prime Minister's vehicle to pass through the hurriedly opened wrought iron gates but the chauffeur was confronted by a fleet of vans, lorries and trailers, most sign written with the logo, 'B.B.C. Outside Broadcasting' and both the street lighting and strategically placed and stunningly powerful arc lights illuminated the *cul de sac* and lengths of cable that inefficiently meandered around the entrance, then through the open front door and on subsequent inspection, up the stairs, like strings of spaghetti, into one of the reception rooms on the first floor, which was currently and apparently, with organised chaos, being transformed into a television studio.

He very nearly tripped on the cables as he tried to navigate the stairs then set about the urgent tasks which now confronted him.

The 'Inner Cabinet' including, most importantly, the Lord Chancellor would meet at five- thirty, first to agree the final version of his speech and then to discuss the conditions of the agreement which David Bruce had finally promised to have delivered, by special courier, no later than six- thirty. The meeting could continue, without interruption, whilst he left the room to deliver the speech, and would seamlessly continue on his return.

Her Majesty was due back the following day and a full meeting of the Cabinet would be held on Wednesday morning, to prepare and finalize their negotiating position and to delegate a group of ministers to assist the P.M. Gold might be a useful special advisor but he was becoming too arrogant and might overreach himself. Kaufman was reliable and steady but lacked the flame of inspiration that Gold possessed and was his strength. Instructions were given to the B.B.C. engineers and the unusually large number of their staff who were milling about and who appeared to have no gainful employment, other than to be either 'on call' or available, to respect the purpose of the building which primarily was an office and, surprisingly, the hub and focus of government.

The 'Number Ten' reception staff were charged to maintain both order and decorum outside of the office which was gradually filling up with the elite members of the Cabinet.

By six-fifteen the speech, with slight but insignificant alterations, had unanimously been approved, save at the suggestion of the Home Secretary, after the P.M.'s preamble, to include a binding promise to hold a General Election..."to enfranchise those currently not represented, no later than Thursday, May the twentieth."

Which in reality meant that campaigning would begin nearly a month before, since Easter fell in the middle of April.

As if the agenda was being organised with clockwork efficiency, the Cabinet Secretary entered, holding an envelope of unusual dimensions which implied its provenance and confirmed the promise and good faith of the United States ambassador.

The three page content was a copy of an original, impressively headed on the first page by its origin...'The White House'.

Although impeccably produced, it included a number of hand written corrections in ink, some grammatical, others to clarify certain paragraphs which initially would give its limited and privileged readers the unanimous view that the document had gone through, and was still going through, constant revision and amendment. The document was divided into nineteen sections of various lengths and was temporarily handed back to the Cabinet Secretary to be photocopied thus to enable each member to work on their own copy.

The room had been bathed in tranquillity and virtual silence for some thirty-five minutes whilst everyone present read and reread their copy of the document, each making notes with a pencil or fountain pen. A common, but as yet unstated opinion had developed; the various sections had no logical structure or order, indeed appeared to have been prepared as a preliminary draft. At about seven-twenty, Harold suggested that everyone present, briefly give their overall impression of the terms, which incidentally he found tolerable excluding...

When their attention was drawn to the Cabinet Secretary's unannounced entrance, but more significantly, his pallid and distressed appearance which like a Shakespearean tragedy clearly heralded news of immense importance and not to the advantage of those present.

John Tyndall quietly allowed himself to bask in the aura of his limited achievement and the possibility of real influence on the national stage. He was, of course, buoyed by the luncheon invitation and the hint dropped by Duggan, but it was the reality of actual events that boosted his ego and confidence. Outside, for the first time ever, he was being helped by volunteer supporters. Under supervision they were counting the donations collected at the three locations and he was optimistically hoping to have garnered over four hundred pounds. Early the next morning he could visit a local bank and set up an account with a sizeable deposit, in the name of his new organisation which he would have to register and gave a title which in itself should describe the purpose of his crusade.

He was in two minds whether or not to watch the P.M.'s statement in some forty minutes but, like so many others, believed that it would be, as evidence of his cynicism, just empty words. His growing support, they had had nearly one hundred and ten offers of active support that day alone, together with four offers of assistance in kind, including the free printing of leaflets and even more useful, free advertising space in a chain of local newspapers which could be used to confirm not only their philosophy but to attract support.

He was confident that his host would honour the bill tomorrow, but at the suggestion of his 'number two 'he would take sufficient funds to host the lunch. Again, at his 'number two's' suggestion, six protests would take place tomorrow, three at the previous locations and three new sites, all at central London railway stations, Victoria, Paddington and King's Cross, under his deputy's supervision and once again emphasising the message ...

"Britain: stand up and fight union tyranny!"

He would call his organisation 'The New Order' and its fundamental principles would be primarily to restore national dignity, respect for the State, the inalienable rights of the individual, an end to union anarchy and tyranny and security from hostile enemy action (both military and political).

"Two further nuclear strikes had taken place in the last forty minutes and what was absolutely certain was that they had again taken place in East Anglia, one possibly at, or close to a U.S. air force base."

Wilson instantaneously remembered the words of one of his recent predecessors as First Lord of the Treasury...

"Events, events my dear boy."

Denis Healey was the first to voice his opinion and suggested that:

"The P.M. should urgently consider either abandoning or postponing his speech until they had a clearer picture of the situation and until any agreement with their allies was resolved."

The Foreign Secretary then suggested, but his observation was promptly rejected by all those around him, that consideration be given to postponing the State Funeral on the spurious grounds of the present industrial crisis but the Lord Chancellor argued with an intellect and emotional passion that immediately guaranteed his success that:

"Winston would not have cravenly submitted to the threats and intimidation of his enemies and that the national mood might be irreparably damaged."

At seven forty-three p.m. when the P.M. would have expected to be made up for the television cameras (a procedure which he openly described as effeminate and intolerable) a message was passed to the producer that the speech was to be postponed and that an excuse had to be found cancelling the broadcast. At seven fifty–five an announcement was made both on radio and television stating that there would be a delay transmitting the broadcast and at eight minutes past eight a B.B.C. announcer, Richard Baker, appeared on both the B.B.C. and I.T.V. channels to announce, with both gravity and embarrassment that workmen in Whitehall had severed a major B.B.C. electrical cable and it would be impossible to transmit the scheduled speech that evening.

David Bruce spent that Tuesday evening reviewing the latest version of the proposed agreement that had just been sent, enciphered, by teletype and noted that the earlier version, which he had, as promised, sent to the P.M. was scheduled in an ascending order of importance whilst the latest version now had a logical order and sequence.

Johnson had no intention of honouring and implementing the December nineteen sixty-two agreement between his predecessor, Kennedy, and Harold Macmillan. Attached to the teletype was an aide memoire indicating his thoughts – leaving its reader to infer the President's distrust of the Prime Minister, his contempt for the 'British system' and his fear that union anarchy could result in an...

'Extreme left wing regime that would make U.S. interests untenable.'

Any demand to include a reference to the 'Polaris' deal in the agreement was to be deflected but if the matter was pursued, his special representative, who would also accompany the Vice–President to the meeting would, as a distraction, offer to lease to the British government up to one hundred (older model) B52 bombers and up to seventy–five bomb loads of mixed nuclear and thermonuclear weapons for a period of up to twenty–five years. A reminder was also specifically included that the Vice-President could and might make an oblique reference to...'Negotiations with the government of Southern Ireland' His animosity and vindictiveness was summarised by one phrase that appeared in his confidential aside. 'Screw them.'

The nature of the negotiating posture to be adopted by the Vice–President, H.H.H., was now self evident and that his help for Britain and her interests would be limited.

FORTY-NINE

The U.S.A.F. jet transporting the Vice- President was, not unexpectedly, diverted to an R.A.F. base, west of the capital, near the picturesque Cotswolds and landed, whilst it was still dark, at seven thirty-four a.m., and was met by the United States Ambassador to the Court of St. James who had been flown, by helicopter, from Regent`s Park to receive his very distinguished visitor.

They returned by the same helicopter to Regents Park and went immediately to the ambassador`s residence a few minutes before nine a.m. and in the exact words of H.H.H, before he went upstairs for a rest ...

"`Till at least three o`clock London Town [sic] time before embarking on preparations for what might be described as an extremely important meeting for all concerned", though Bruce noted his hastily added 'post script' that:

"Negotiations were not going to be that particularly tough, just one sided", which made him feel somewhat relieved, but morally ashamed.

The President`s special advisor was already in London, on a private visit, viewing and purchasing exquisite items of *objet d`art* for his collection, but he had been in constant communication with Washington and had been...

'Instrumental advising them on various aspects of the agreement but also analysing psychological evaluations both of the P.M. and the anticipated members of his team.'

The Cabinet meeting had been scheduled to begin promptly at nine a.m. but was put back an hour and began a very few minutes after ten a.m. to accommodate the Home Secretary, Harold Lever, who had been overseeing the rescue missions now in Ipswich and Bury St. Edmunds but also the unfolding catastrophe in Chelmsford and Harlow New Town.

Manny Gold, who had returned late from Canterbury the previous evening was now in possession of...

"His [sic] civil servant's report", and accosted the P.M., who was waiting patiently for the imminent arrival of the Home Secretary, and was thus able to give him some of his valuable, but limited, free time. He noted Gold's specific reference to the status of the civil servant but was more concerned with the report.

Its style, as was to be expected, was objective and bland, and its overall assessment of the situation almost dehumanised the suffering and the hospital's inability to cope with the deluge, indeed incidentally, the reader should note that such was the almost detached analysis that there was no direct reference to any of the female combatants, relegating them to an index with confirmation that of the six female soldiers who had survived the voyage, only two had survived the journey to, or the first night in the hospital.

Wilson 's inference was that any treatment that may have been given to the prisoners before their repatriation, however basic, had been more effective than the attention they were now receiving and he reluctantly realised that the laws of nature would supersede any assistance that he might be able to bring to bear and consequently he handed back the document, commenting that:

"In the present situation they would have to be left to their own inner strengths and the inadequate facilities of the hospital, but the National Health Service was the best in the world and he was confident that the majority would pull through."

Angry and frustrated that the paucity of his own real authority had been exposed and that he was unable to influence events (whether to enhance his reputation or status which was more likely than his ethical and moral obligation to help the wretched, abandoned troops), Gold made a verbatim note of the P.M.'s comment and, unnecessarily, the duration of the brief meeting.

The Home Secretary was invited to open the meeting with his report, but surprisingly ,and with Wilson's express consent, he began with a devastating statement concerning the contingency arrangements that were in place, and had apparently been developed over some fifteen years, in anticipation of the events that were now unfolding or to be more specific, in the event of a nuclear war and to avoid and cope with a possible breakdown not only of law and order but also the essential functions of an industrialised state.

His comments, noted by all those around the table was a bombshell, comparable only in magnitude to that of the weaponry whose use would trigger its introduction. Perhaps also their thoughts, in part, focused on the nuclear assault on Russia and the Ukraine and their spurious and fraudulent claims of involvement, issued for propaganda purposes.

He continued and confirmed that when he had completed his statement, that the Lord Chancellor should be called upon for his comments concerning the nineteen sixty-four Emergency Powers Act, a law that was ferocious and draconian and that its implementation was potentially the most dangerous challenge to democracy that the country had ever confronted.

"Within twelve hours, each of those present would receive a most Top Secret document outlining the implementation of the contingency plans, but in summary I would initially explain the background to the devastating report that you will read...

The new Act came into force on June tenth of last year and superseded the nineteen twenty Act .His enquiries confirmed that its origins lay in the potential threat to the Realm during and after the 'Suez' debacle (at which point certain of those present made noises of adverse comment) when Eden`s successor, Harold Macmillan, was recommended to implement new legislation but the matter received scant attention (at which moment those present who had just earlier made noises of adverse comment, repeated themselves and one Cabinet Minister was heard to make the partisan remark..."You`ve never had it so good", which made the Conservative members react in anger and force the P.M. to insist on decorum). His successor, Alec Douglas –Home, confronted by the November twenty-fifth massacre and the conflagration on the European mainland was rushed into putting through what must now be seen as drastic emergency legislation with little due diligence but it was in the implementation that he was about to disclose which would concern all those present.

In the period leading up to, then during the massive conflagration and in the aftermath (the post apocalyptic or post catastrophe world), the primary task and function of the government was not the continuation and urgent restoration of the infrastructure for the benefit and protection of the community but primarily to maintain the organs and continuity of government.

Civil defence was in fact an illusion created by previous administrations to placate and assure the nation as a whole not only that they would survive a nationwide attack but subsequently, as in the 'Blitz', that rescue would follow. The events of the last few days have exposed the reality.

The construction of a system of underground shelters to protect the population had not only been repudiated on the grounds of unaffordable cost, but on the military argument that their existence and locations could not be hidden and the inhabitants could, or would, be used by the enemy as hostages in a second strike scenario. With a logic that defied any unemotional response it was proposed that if the population, or chosen sections were to be ordered to enter the shelters then a nervous enemy might calculate that their opponent was about to launch a first strike, therefore forcing them to launch their own pre-emptive first strike.

He had been appalled to be informed by the senior civil servant responsible for the nation's 'civil defence' that evacuation was not considered a feasible option because (to quote his exact words)...

'They did not want a repetition of May nineteen forty, when in France the roads were clogged with evacuees. Roads must be kept clear for the military and the administrators.'

In the 'pre attack' phase before non nuclear or nuclear war began a greater emphasis was placed on the defence of so called strategic resources, such as reservoirs and power production sites, against potential 'fifth columnists' and saboteurs than the interests of the civilian community.

Thus, hospitals would be emptied of their patients who would be returned to the community for their care and the medical facility (including staff) would be turned over and guarded by the 'military' for their own benefit and exclusive use.

Martial law would be proclaimed and the country divided into, he understood, because the options were ambiguous and flexible, twelve regions, each under the control of an appointed Regional Commissioner, *WHO HAD TOTAL AND ABSOLUTE POWER LITERALLY OVER LIFE AND DEATH* [the author's own emphasis]. All assets, including property could be seized, presumably without compensation, for the benefit of the State, and control of food and water monitored so that only those who were healthy would be fed as it was uneconomic and wasteful to support those who would inevitably die.

'Special Rest Centres' would be set up to receive the ill, injured and those unable to be productive, especially the old, where, unknown to the general community, they would be allowed to expire (the word die implied a policy of euthanasia, when the reality was the pragmatic use of resources) and be disposed of.

Those fit to work, like the criminal inmates of a Soviet Gulag, would earn their sustenance by labour, the 'calorific daily allowance' being inadequate to sustain their weight and health.

Any illegal or criminal act(such as looting, food hoarding, possession of fuel such as petrol or coal, or even public objection to the withdrawal of the individual`s rights) would be subject to a cursory trial (because Martial law was in force) and immediate execution would take place since the concept of a prison system was economically wasteful, though arrangements were already in place, at the most inhospitable locations, to set up emergency prisons to house political dissidents and those seen as potentially dangerous or a threat to the State."

Harold Lever halted, noted the abject shock displayed by everyone in the room and after a brief break continued...

"The report that each of you will receive by ten p.m. tonight, is more comprehensive than my summary and, as I stated earlier, is Top Secret. Some of you may also be aware, by informed gossip or rumour that in the event of hostilities resuming, that the organs of government will be relocated to subterranean sites known as Regional Seats of Government and I therefore confirm, with the P.M.`s approval that following the latest attacks on Ipswich and Bury St. Edmunds, that my civil servants have set into motion the necessary contingency procedures, including, I am pleased to advise you all, the safety of Her Majesty and immediate members of her family, including her Heir, Charles."

At which point, the P.M. intervened and suggested a brief hiatus when tea, coffee and biscuits be served in order to give those present an opportunity to digest the information, but he did not allude to the grim air of morbid depression which hung over the room.

Refreshed, but visibly shaken, the P.M. and the Cabinet heard the Home Secretary continue...

"The epicentres of the two latest explosions, though in reality this information is superfluous, were, according to the Emergency Services, the Portman Road area of Ipswich and the old historic centre of Bury St. Edmunds but I have to report to you that on the admission of the Police and those from the Ambulance and Fire Services who have not joined the industrial dispute, that the situation is desperate.

Combined with the earlier attacks on Chelmsford and Harlow New Town, but above all the loss of hospital facilities and beds and the limited transport available, because of the effective strikes, I can now only recommend that the army be brought in and that the Prime Minister addresses the nation, as soon as possible, and makes an appeal, if necessary over the heads of the T.U.C., for a national return to work.

On a further matter, no doubt my associate, the Minister of Defence, Mr. Heath, in the context of my advices and suggestion, will inform the Cabinet what arrangements have been set in motion to help those repatriated troops suffering from chemical warfare injuries."

Edward Heath rose to make a statement, though his appearance and demeanour suggested he was unable to shed any light on the situation, however the P.M. gestured him to sit down and proceeded to explain that:

"Less than an hour ago a personal assistant presented me with a report that a senior civil servant had prepared following their visit to a civilian hospital in Kent where the repatriated troops had been sent. I am certain that they will receive the best care possible that the National Health Service and the hospital can provide but in view of the overall situation their plight must be considered in the perspective and context of the nation's trauma."

Thus Wilson had disposed of their fate but his statement would be used against him at his trial.

Sir Hendrie Oakshott, the Minister of Education and a quiet and rarely heard Cabinet member, rose and in a brief speech focused the Cabinet's thoughts on what he considered to be four outstanding matters: the urgency of a national address by the P.M., the strikes, Churchill's State Funeral and though he was unaware of the latest, imminent secret meeting, resolution and formulation of the Anglo–American relationship.

At ten twenty a.m. John Tyndall emerged from his bank, not only angry and frustrated, but still holding a carrier bag which contained, according to his calculations, the sum of seven hundred and eighty pounds. A desperate plea and reasonable request to temporarily 'bank', if only for safety, the monies into his own, currently overdrawn account, was (courteously) declined on the grounds that the money was not his own and that they, the Bank, were unable to open a new account for an unincorporated and unregistered political party and must have first the requisite documentation before they could not only set up the account but issue a 'paying in' book.

He resolved to contain and dissolve his anger by leisurely walking to Marble Arch where he was to be collected at eleven a.m. though he became irritated as he passed various banks and noted the activity of customers both entering and departing the premises.

As he passed Lancaster Gate on his left, he suddenly had, call it what you may, an inspired vision, a revelation or even a profound scientific insight, prompted perhaps by the sight of the Yid plutocrats in the banks acting as if they owned them. He realised why the Jews were forbidden to eat pork. The truth was self evident, simple, transparent and needed the obvious to be observed by only those who had not been corrupted or infected by racial impurities. The Jews, the chosen people, were clearly the human like descendants of pigs and apes and to eat pork would be a form of cannibalism.

He was in good time, went into a Lyons Corner House (he didn't realise it was owned by Jews) and ordered coffee and a 'round' of toast and spent the next ten minutes pondering the intentions of his hosts and the profound nature of his revelation.

He stood, as requested, at the junction of Edgware Road and Oxford Street, in his best suit, pitifully holding the carrier bag. At precisely eleven a.m. a blue Jaguar 3.4 with wire wheels and new tyres pulled up immediately at his side and the passenger in the front seat exited the vehicle and with great courtesy and respect enquired his identity, when on confirmation the man almost ceremoniously opened the rear passenger door and by a hand gesture indicated his desire to relieve him of his bag which was placed in the cavernous boot of the car. With reserves of power which exhilarated him, the vehicle accelerated away and the driver soon made a left hand turn before navigating around the roads of Marylebone before entering the Edgware Road and turning right. The driver's skill and expert handling of the vehicle almost matched his knowledge of the area.

Both the driver and his associate said very little, only confirming that they estimated that the destination would be reached...

"Around twelve –twenty", and that they envied his invitation because...

"The restaurant and the club had a reputation that put it at the pinnacle of the most superb dining in the South-East, let alone London."

Consequently he regretted having a late breakfast which caused him to temporarily fall asleep and when he awoke the area was unfamiliar. They had clearly left central London, either avoiding or passing through the suburbs into the countryside that made living in the great metropolis such a pleasure since most parts could be reached by the underground service. He relaxed, for he sensed that this journey was to be the beginning of a new future. At twelve twenty-three (he could see the time on the clock which formed part of the wooden, was it walnut?, dashboard), the vehicle entered a long drive flanked by mature trees bisecting a great open parkland leading to an imposing country house in immaculate condition.

The rear passenger door was again opened, for his personal benefit, and as he ascended the steps to the mansion's front door, he could see his new friend, Mr. Duggan waiting to greet him, yes him, Mr. John Tyndall.

By twelve twenty–three the Cabinet had resolved a number of separate but inter-related problems. The Cabinet Office had confirmed that all the funeral arrangements had not only been confirmed but additional contingency arrangements, already 'factored' into the proceedings, had been put in hand so that, excluding an outbreak of hostilities, the nation's tribute would proceed without problem. Critically an army engineering corps, historically trained to drive and operate steam trains would 'man' the locomotive that would transport the body and coffin on its final journey for private burial. With unexpected great pleasure they had just received an unsolicited approach from the crane operators in the Pool of London who...

"Would be proud and honoured to be involved, and they would temporarily suspend their strike action in order to lower their cranes in a final act of respect and homage."

To complete the arrangements, the Cabinet was reminded that on the following day, Thursday, it had been arranged for them to visit Westminster Hall, politically to display the unity of the Coalition and on behalf of the government and Parliament, represent the nation.

Despite the occasional volcanic eruptions of rancour and bitterness, with an unusual degree both of compromise and pragmatism, the various wings, factions and opposing political opinions in the Cabinet agreed that not only should the P.M. speak to the nation on the Thursday evening but that the contents of his speech would have to be drastically changed to reflect the developing and deteriorating situation. Furthermore, an approach had to be made, without delay, to the T U C, discreetly informing them that in view of the dramatic developments it would not be possible to publicly make any promises or within the imminent future to honour the original promises. The national interest, as in May nineteen forty, citing the 'miracle' of Dunkirk and the subsequent 'Dunkirk spirit' transcended the interests of any faction or group in the country.

Whether or not the mission was doomed from the outset will never be known, indeed the very circumstance of a group of Cabinet ministers, a deputation, actually approaching the T U C could only be interpreted as an act of weakness.

It was lead , according to hearsay reports, very ably by the Chancellor of the Exchequer, Denis Healey, accompanied by three other Cabinet members, the Ministers of Housing, Education and Transport, respectively, John Rankin, Sir Hendrie Oakshott and James Griffiths, the latter, an excellent choice because of his long association with the T U C hierarchy, and the only uncontested information known about the meeting was that on his arrival, amidst the fraternal back slapping, was a publicly stated greeting that:

"The government had come to deliver their promise", but by the end of the truncated meeting, apparently the atmosphere had descended into allegations of betrayal and of 'Judases'.

A reconstruction of the meeting, whether in summary or in exact detail, would, for the purposes of this work, serve no purpose since we are aware of the deputation`s message and the final response of the union leaders. Intransigence and an uncompromising posture by one side lubricated the ever quickening slide towards the end of democracy, whilst the government`s position had been dictated by events and the overriding, paramount national interest. Thus we will never know if mention was made, obliquely or directly that the army was now to be called in, though Denis Healey and the rest of the party, individually and as a group later denied any direct or indirect mention, consistently stating that the meeting was both brief and had rapidly descended into verbal conflict. George Woodcock, the General Secretary, not only telephoned Jack Jones immediately afterwards to acknowledge his wisdom and foresight but also to state that Wilson, his erstwhile friend, was a 'Judas' and now an implacable enemy of the working classes.

Denis Healey and his three downcast associates returned to Ten Downing Street at three fort –seven, navigated the line of cables that had caused and been the subject of much irritation to the many users of the stairs, and went to one of the rooms on the first floor and for those who are acquainted with the geography of what is now a derelict building used for storage, it is, or was, if you were facing the door to the Cabinet room, the one on its right hand side.

Inside the small room sat Wilson, flanking him were Gerald Kaufman and Manny Gold, whilst the remaining four places were taken by the 'Home' and 'Foreign' Secretaries, Harold Lever and Patrick Gordon Walker, the Minister of Defence and Lord Chancellor, Edward Heath and Sir Reginald Manningham–Buller.   Behind them sat, rather cramped, four senior civil servants. The four arrivals were unable to gain complete access to the room but they sensed the palpable tension of the meeting as the P.M. rose, managed to manoeuvre around the backs of the Home and Foreign Secretaries, very nearly tripping over the feet of two of the civil servants before he was able to exit the room.

Taking Healey aside and in the most hushed and secret tones he conveyed the news that:

"The meeting was scheduled for eight p.m. and that Bruce would bring with him the Vice–President and an advisor, by which time the meeting that he was 'chairing' would decide upon their negotiating position. Denis Healey tried to inform Wilson of the unsuccessful and acrimonious end to their meeting at the headquarters of the T U C but sensed, not unexpectedly, that the Prime Minister's thoughts were focused elsewhere.

On entering the Cabinet room they found Konni Zilliacus surrounded by a further five or six civil servants busily editing and butchering copies of the previous day`s unbroadcast statement whilst little thought or action was being given to a new version.

Ten Downing Street was a hive of great activity.

The almost leisurely meeting had ended at three forty-seven with total agreement by the three men in the room. H.H.H. would lead the delegation and would announce, with sincere regret, that the President was unable to attend the State funeral in view of the current uncertain security situation and that his staff had vetoed any scenario where the President and his Vice-President might jointly be at risk. In the present circumstances London was a potentially dangerous location, however to avoid causing any alarm or diplomatic discourtesy a carefully timed announcement would state that a minor re occurrence of a lung infection had caused his team of doctors to forbid him to travel, but to calm the nation and specially Wall Street, it was to be confirmed that he was still attending to matters of state in the Oval Office.

There would no 'beating around the bush', no reference to the now obsolete 'Special relationship' or compromises if, as expected, the British pleaded emotionally to the historical Anglo-American Alliance of the Second World War, symbolised by the arrival, on Thursday evening, of the former President, Dwight Eisenhower, and the Supreme Commander of the joint Allied forces that had beaten National Socialism and liberated Europe.

The so called 'Nassau' agreement was dead in the eyes of the President and he had no intentions of the Royal Navy and the British Prime Minister getting their hands on such a potent weapon as Polaris. Any reference by the British was to be deflected and the agreement would certainly not include any mention, directly or indirectly.

Indirect reference could however be made, in passing (by David Bruce), of negotiations with the government of Southern Ireland and the Vice- President might, when he thought that their victim [sic] was ready to agree a deal, offer control, on lease, of a number of (nearly obsolete) first generation B52 bombers together with a supply of nuclear and thermonuclear weapons which otherwise would, within a year or two, have to be recycled such was their antiquity. In any event the British government would be responsible to pay a substantial proportion of the United States' costs operating their military presence (at which stage, like a game of high stakes poker the annual figure was raised from $ Ninety five million, to $ One hundred and forty million per year).

President Lyndon Johnson's personal representative was due to fly back to Washington at eleven–thirty a.m., on Friday with the signed agreement when around the same time news of the President's health would be announced together with the publication of appropriate photographs taken in the White House confirming his attention to his many Presidential duties.

For nearly three decades the President's personal representative had experienced and been involved in the formulation and execution of power and diplomacy but his great expertise had been in the areas of intelligence and espionage. For Mr. David Lennox this assignment was unpalatable but absolutely necessary and imperative. The 'nouveau riche' would admiringly look up to him and jealously describe him as 'old money' but that description was totally inadequate and misleading. He immediately projected an image not only of probity but of excellent breeding, education and erudition; he had obviously been born into and raised in an environment and lifestyle of wealth, privilege and influence but above all, strangely, he always sensed that it had been for the purpose of national service. He was courteous and observed all the duties and obligations when in the presence of the Vice- President, even when, as at this time, the meeting was private. His appearance was impeccable, confident, assured and diplomatic. Immaculately dressed, from the cut of his suit, the elegant cuff links and shirt and tie, even down to his hand crafted shoes it showed his attention to detail as were his manicured nails and the slight hint of an 'Eau de Cologne'.

This was a triumvirate of power that the British would find unassailable.

Mr. Lennox intended to reread the reports on Wilson and the probable members of his team and would especially note the comments and observations but he knew, instinctively, that Wilson`s innate cunning and the hopelessness of the British position would ultimately be no match for the temptation of the beguiling American offer of military assistance and protection.

At three forty-seven, the front passenger seat door of the Jaguar was courteously opened on behalf of the important guest, but this time by the driver, as Keith Wagstaffe and Duggan acknowledged his departure whilst standing in front of the impressive front door. He had had a little too much, but not a copious amount to drink, and concentrating his thoughts through the euphoria of light headedness he realised that twice he had embarrassed himself, first when he had insisted on white wine to accompany a magnificent Chateaubriand which he had shared with Wagstaffe (actually that was not exactly factually correct because the head waiter had cut the two portions unevenly but his host was most adamant that he take the larger portion) however he knew instinctively that he would enjoy his preference over the normal accompaniment of Red. And as they shook hands on his departure he very nearly tripped over the feet of the two men.

He would balance his two errors against the substance of the bombshell offer made by his hosts or specially by Keith who seemed to dominate the lunch whilst Duggan (who for some peculiar reason did not appear to use or even have a first name) appeared to act in a supporting role.

He was' dropped off 'exactly at five o` seven outside of Notting Hill Gate underground station in a kaleidoscope of excitement and the anticipation of the potential fulfilment of his dreams and hopes. Once again he had fallen asleep during the journey and had therefore lost the thread of both the route and the location of the Golf Club and he had felt inclined not to ask for this information but during an informal interrogation of the driver he ascertained that the second man had stayed behind to chauffeur his two hosts back to London.

Fortunately for him his chauffeur remembered to open the boot and return to him the carrier bag, the contents of which had been a topic of conversation.

He would only tell his deputy enough to satisfy his curiosity and the rest would be prudently summarised especially...however at this time certain information would remain for his exclusive benefit.

They had been superb hosts and had made the most inspired of choices on his behalf and he hoped, with rational expectation, that he would receive a further invitation, when again he would finish the meal with bread and butter pudding and a side dish of profiteroles swamped in thick, sweet double cream. The choux pastry had been made that morning according to the restaurant manager who served them personally only leaving to welcome two famous actors but he couldn`t quite' put a handle' to their names and he did not intend to embarrass his hosts by being inquisitive, though he did recognise John Profumo, accompanied by a former politician whose name was on the 'tip of his tongue'.

"No problem" was Duggan`s laconic response to his tale of woe as he drew from his breast pocket a note pad on which he wrote, in block capitals, the name of an import/export company in the 'West End' who were" very substantial" but more importantly were intimately entwined with a private bank of impeccable discretion.

"If he were to visit them tomorrow after twelve and contact one of two men he would list, a very senior member would not only immediately set up an account but would steer him through all the laborious paperwork. Furthermore the General Manager of John Tyndall`s existing bank was a member of the golf club and he would arrange to speak to him as well tomorrow morning and no doubt he would smooth the path at his local branch."

He was elated.

"They had both served in the military (absolutely untrue in respect of Duggan but might, at some time, have been correct about Wagstaffe). They had many connections but preferred not, at this stage (which was why later he hoped would result in a second invitation), to elaborate though they had to be honest because ...

They were hoping not only for his cooperation and discretion, but if their proposition was accepted by him, his unwavering loyalty and resolve. They would not, because of their knowledge of his history, coerce or suborn him to agree but they hoped that the merits of their proposition would lead him to make a methodical and logical, positive decision. They would respect his negative decision but in view of what they had to say, their proposition, like a spy thriller, would be completely denied."

He was fascinated.

Wagstaffe 'took over the reins', finished his *hors d'oeuvre* of one dozen of the most mouth watering giant prawns that he had ever seen (unlike the miniscule ones served with a pink sauce that he had seen and eaten in local restaurants, which he sensed had been previously frozen), dipped his fingers clean in a bowl and then wiped them dry on a napkin. With an exhibition of subtle efficiency by the manager the dirty napkin was quickly removed and replaced by a fresh, clean one and with a flurry, placed on Wagstaffe`s lap.

"A number of leading and influential industrialists, politicians (though tragically some had been lost in the November twenty-fifth massacre), members of the judiciary and prominent business men saw the nation`s decline into oblivion as inevitable, not because of the catastrophic events which had begun with President Kennedy`s assassination, but because the Trade Unions were stifling growth and effectively strangling the country, possibly turning the nation into a Soviet style East European satellite of Moscow."

Tyndall almost jumped in shock when he heard...

"We also have likeminded friends in certain anonymous government departments who have wide ranging powers which are used quietly and unobserved by the Press and the general public, but in reality they are just men (and a few women) whose responsibility is to monitor and observe a vast disparate group whose loyalty to this country is suspect (it was at this very point that Tyndall almost jumped in shock). There is even a rumour that a file exists on the Prime Minister which includes both evidence of his true loyalties and unbelievably details of payments emanating from Eastern Europe through a leading trade unionist both to fund the Union movement and the Labour party!"

Wagstaffe stopped, caught the attention of the restaurant manager who came over and took an order for another bottle of red wine and he then continued.

"We cannot afford to let Labour win the forthcoming General Election. We believe that you can help by mobilising what is called 'the silent majority', first in an ever increasing public display of unity and support for British values and if possible by fielding your own candidates at the General Election though it may not be possible to organise yourselves in time, however there is a possibility that you could stand as an independent against a Labour opponent in a Tory stronghold. Indeed you would stand against a Tory candidate and once the nominations had closed he would withdraw (following a tragic diagnosis of cancer), recommending you to the Constituency thereby outflanking the Labour candidate."

Tyndall realised that there was a major impediment to this unexpected and life changing scenario and he did not know what to say.

"We understand that in your absence six demonstrations are currently being held and you will be pleased to learn, according to a telephone call that we received from our friends, that the support at all the locations has been even more enthusiastic than before, donations seem to be pouring in and, out of interest, we would like to know, in future, if you agree our offer, exactly how much you are collecting."

Duggan paused, watched Wagstaffe sample and appreciate a new bottle of wine, and on his approval, which was inevitable, three glasses were poured. The bottle had been recommended by the manager and more importantly Wagstaffe and Duggan had previously enjoyed this particular French vintage (which was still available by a circuitous route via neutral and profit minded entrepreneurs in Switzerland, Sweden and increasingly Portugal, who had ascertained that the occupying Warsaw Treaty forces, and their political masters, had recognised the benefit of trade and earning what was increasingly called 'hard currency').

Duggan then continued...

"We, our associates and friends are not *per se* anti trade unions, but pro commerce and trade which finances the welfare state and those for whom work is an anathema. We are offering you the opportunity to join us and promote our cause by creation of a great street movement of the people."

Wagstaffe surprisingly excused himself from the table and Tyndall made an erroneous assumption as to his reason but he very soon returned holding a thin green file which he placed on the table.

Suddenly and unexpectedly Duggan's tone changed, he was the inquisitor and Tyndall was the victim. Even when he had been arrested by the police or was it the Special Branch?, their interviews were conducted with respect and even dignity. There was something malevolent and sinister and his question was phrased as if he already knew the answer...

"Would you like to tell us something about yourself?"

He instantaneously knew that they had known all along about his conviction and probably his imprisonment, but he could not reconcile this knowledge with their offer. And if not, and this was unlikely, it would soon enter the public domain. He would make a full confession but would challenge them about the sincerity of their proposition.

"I think you already know that I was convicted under the nineteen thirty–slx Public Order Act and served time, but since I believe that you were already aware of this fact I am confused why you have made an offer that is fraught with danger."

For a few moments there was complete silence as if his hosts had never anticipated the final part of his response and then Wagstaffe and Duggan looked at each other, turned and smiled at him and said, in unison, as if they had a telepathic relationship...

"Welcome."

Wagstaffe slid the file across the table, narrowly avoiding Tyndall's glass of wine and then Duggan, in a different tone, friendly and helpful, commented...

"This is your M.I.5. summary file and, I understand, there are three thick files on your activities, including information on your friend Colin Jordan and background details of Francoise Dior. Our friends in M.I.5 have been watching you for some years but perhaps in this changing world and the realisation by many that politically the old ways are no longer effective, your time may well have arrived.

We have always been aware of your history and rabid anti- Semitic views which if you could moderate them, then you might have a political future [Tyndall knew at that moment not to share, or even mention, the profound 'vision' that had occurred earlier].

We have already considered your conviction, in anticipation of your honest reply, and more importantly spoken to solicitors who could arrange to apply to have the conviction set aside on grounds that are, at this moment, for the purposes of this conversation unimportant, but could be that certain members of the organisation that formed the paramilitary group enticed you into joining.

If our understanding is correct then once the legal application had been submitted, then the matter would become *'sub judice'* and the Press (which currently is cooperating with the government by self voluntary censorship so not to disturb the public) will not be able to publish details of your conviction."

Suddenly he grasped the nettle and put out his hand as a sign of his agreement, cooperation and above all, participation.

Although his star was in the ascendancy and in the future he would rise in status and power he did not realise that like a puppet, a marionette or a 'cat's paw', he was being and would be invisibly manipulated and controlled and finally, when he had served his purpose, destroyed by his new friends in cooperation with his successor. He had been bought for one magnificent meal.

The following week, Wagstaffe and Duggan hosted a further lunch and this time their guests were Colin Jordan and his fragrant wife, Francoise Dior. The format and events repeated their earlier lunch with John Tyndall even to the courteous flattery and then the confrontation, but the outcome was the same and they now had, in the parlance of the racing fraternity, an 'each way' bet.

The porter courteously opened the front door of Ten Downing Street at five o'seven and Manny Gold left what was still the centre of power though the meeting had ended with those present accepting the reality that they would have to, at best, temporarily relinquish the fundamental duty of the state, which was the defence of the Realm, and assign that duty and possibly by payment to what was known, in former times, as mercenaries. They naively believed, expected and hoped that their allies, who less than twenty years before had stood shoulder to shoulder with them in the defeat of democracy's greatest enemy, would act in accordance with that spirit.

He had been overlooked in favour of Gerald Kaufman though he would be on the periphery of an event unparalleled in British history but would not be amongst the party that would greet the Vice-President and his small team on their arrival.

Instead of taking a walk North towards Trafalgar Square, he exited the *Cul De Sac* and took a leisurely stroll South towards Parliament Square and the River Thames which would give him, after many years and periods of mental conflict, the definitive opportunity to finally and unequivocally define his loyalty.

The Soviet Union might produce his letter to the now dead (and discredited) Lavrenti Beria, but in view of the circumstances he could argue that it had been written under duress and since the British government and indeed the nation was about to become a colony of the American industrial–military complex he would have no qualms informing his American handler of the meeting's conclusions and incoherent negotiating position which would make little difference to the outcome but would enhance his reputation.

This would not be a betrayal of his duty to the Prime Minister or to his adopted country but evidence to the United States of his loyalty to them. He turned left onto the Embankment and walked towards the 'City' until he found a telephone kiosk. Inside there was a fetid smell of urine which made him retch but he manoeuvred himself to keep the door open as he dialled a new special number. It was five twenty–nine p.m. according to 'Big Ben' and even if the message was received by his 'handler' early that evening it was most unlikely that it would actually seep through to the Vice-President and therefore would not influence the inevitable outcome.

His true and exclusive loyalty was to himself.

He had made a faulty connection and hurriedly sank his hand deep into his pocket to seek further coins whilst at the same time managing to keep the door open and the smell at a tolerable level. His foot touched something firm on the floor and looking down he realised that someone had defecated on the concrete floor. He made the connection, left an urgent, brief but damning message for his 'handler', betrayed the country that had willingly adopted him, and cursed the person who had no decency and had made such a disgusting mess.

FIFTY

The procession of five anonymous, inconspicuous vehicles bearing innocuous registration numbers arrived late, having entered, via Horse Guards' Parade, the rear of the government buildings in Whitehall at eight twenty–seven and were personally received by Harold Wilson at a discreet entrance close to, but not immediately behind Ten Downing Street. He made no comment, not wishing to offend his three guests, and incorrectly assumed that their delay was a negotiating tactic though he did notice that David Bruce was unusually tense and the Vice-President, in contrast, was most effervescent and jovial, which he was to find to his cost was not because the Americans had relented on their negotiating position.

Indeed the reason was more prosaic and the result of human error, almost ludicrous and in hindsight more akin to a Mack Sennett Keystone Kops farce. The convoy was led and followed at the rear by secret service agents dedicated to the protection of the Vice-President, sandwiching in between them three vehicles each occupied by one member of the negotiating trio.

The route, for security purposes, had meandered from the ambassador's residence to the junction of Marylebone Road and Lisson Grove with the intention of joining the Edgware Road and going south to Marble Arch and then Park Lane, however the last three vehicles had been caught by the amber and then the red traffic lights and had flagrantly continued and been observed by a lurking police patrol car and had been stopped in the Marylebone Road. Two groups, each of two men, had immediately and automatically exited from the two vehicles 'sandwiching' the convoy and moved to the fourth car in which sat H.H.H., whilst a lone policeman walked to the third car which contained the unflappable, tactful and diplomatic special advisor who followed protocol and respect for any police force with meticulous attention. On learning of the alleged offence he apologised profusely on behalf of the errant drivers and offered his card and a special telephone number...

"Where the telephonist could confirm his bona–fides as we have a now overdue appointment at Ten Downing Street where also, no doubt, they will also verify our identities."

At which moment two further men, one from each of the front and rear vehicles, arrived but did not interrupt the police officer who was unable to observe them cautiously but confidently reach for their hand guns. It was then that the officer asked a further question and the answer created a dramatic escalation of an otherwise minor incident.

"Who are in the other vehicles?"

And the confidential and special advisor to the President of the United States of America could only respond with the truth...

"The Ambassador to the Court of St. James, Mr. David Bruce, and in the vehicle immediately behind him, the Vice–President of the United States of America, Mr. Hubert Humphrey."

He was promptly interrupted by the police officer with the phrase that shortly afterwards would give Humphrey such cause to laugh...

"Right, you 're nicked!", and the man, unused to the common parlance of the English, stared quizzically at the police officer who continued...

"You`re under arrest for wasting police time and an hour or two in a cell should teach you some respect and honesty."

When, like a poorly constructed, implausible plot by an aspiring and third rate author, two large American manufactured left hand drive automobiles bearing on their side the logo "United States Navy" roared up, having been hastily summonsed by radio, and six men, each heavily armed, jumped out and surrounded the entourage.

At that time of the evening and at that time of the year there were no pedestrians of any volume around though passing traffic alerted to a possible incident by the number of vehicles abnormally parked and the presence of men in uniform, slowed down to observe the incident which had reached an *impasse.*

A passing patrol car alerted to the event for the same reasons, made a deft U turn, parked deliberately to block the path of the leading vehicle and entered what under different circumstances could have been a major diplomatic incident, and ascertained the story. A call to Scotland Yard and a flurry of conversations with the American Embassy confirmed that indeed a large number of men had been called out to protect the ambassador but if, and it was stressed if, there were any other important people involved they were not aware and they were unable to comment further. The ambassador had to be protected and given every assistance.

Two police patrol cars, their sirens blaring, escorted the convoy to Hyde Park Corner before leaving them to continue their journey along Constitution Hill with Buckingham Palace on their right hand side and then into The Mall. The four police officers in the two vehicles never saw the occupants of the two other vehicles and were told not to discuss the incident, though no one would have believed them.

At eight twenty-seven John Tyndall watched the three volunteers counting the day`s collection and with that sum he calculated that he would have a total amount of fifteen hundred pounds to make an initial deposit with his new bank. More importantly he was forming a short term plan to amalgamate the nine separate demonstrations organised for the next day into a single silent march that would end at Westminster Hall. Certain remarks made earlier over lunch compelled him to consider the future of his deputy, a man also with a criminal record; he was expendable and if handled well the act would enhance his new reputation as a reformed, patriotic right winger.

The meeting was held in the Cabinet Room, the Prime Minister in his designated chair, flanked by Harold Lever, Edward Heath, Patrick Gordon Walker and Sir Reginald Manningham–Buller. Behind them sat Gerald Kaufman and the Cabinet Secretary, whilst opposite them were the three representatives of their most loyal ally whose ultimate intention was to emasculate their international influence and effectively control the independence of what would essentially become a colony of the United States. Before each of the British delegates, on the table, were heavily annotated copies of what was to be an obsolete version of the agreement.

Outside in the hall a cluster of senior civil servants stood around and Manny Gold, once again frustrated in his pursuit of power and influence.

Harold had hoped and intended to draw out the Americans in order to clarify their definitive terms but was cleverly thwarted by Johnson's advisor who had been introduced as such by David Bruce. Their as yet undeclared position was to ascertain the British reaction to the preliminary [sic] terms and to clarify what was required of their American allies.

The prepared response, in contrast to the coherent tactics of their American allies, agreed earlier that day in an adjacent room, almost immediately began to fray and tear apart; the Lord Chancellor introduced himself and stated that any agreement would have to receive the full Cabinet's approval the next day (immediately alerting the Americans and especially the Vice-President that their 'prey' could be caught that evening) and that the Prime Minister who was due to meet Her Majesty the following day, at Buckingham Palace, would then seek her tacit agreement.

Some fifteen months later, interviewed in the United States by representatives of the 'New Order', including Sir Hugh Stephenson, David Bruce, surrounded by legal advisors and State Department officials, and aware that Wilson was in custody awaiting trial for High Treason, confirmed that Vice-President Humphrey had led the negotiations but specifically did not mention the Vice-President's comment that the negotiations would be ...'just one sided'. He personally thought that the British team, who had little to offer other than their miniscule 'V' bomber force, meekly conceded on every point, which was defeatist.

Edward Heath, the Minister of Defence, as predicted in the psychological evaluation, wandered around the fundamental elements of Britain's military requirements until Patrick Gordon Walker, in a moment of frustration, requested his Cabinet colleague to exactly specify the nation's needs consequently clearly exposing the country's and the government's naked defence and retaliatory capabilities.

It was, de *facto,* an admission of the country's inability to adequately defend itself, or to launch a viable counter–attack, a retaliatory counter first strike, therefore giving the Soviet Union and the Warsaw Pact an overwhelming advantage. The ultimate defence of Mutual Assured Destruction was not an option. Until such time as the Polaris deterrent was operational or in the interim period they could retrieve their 'V' bomber force from South Africa they were highly vulnerable compelling them to look to their ally for protection beneath their 'umbrella'.

Humphrey had no intention of letting his quarry escape but permitted himself the pleasure of the *coup de grace* wrapped in a false declaration of friendship.

"Because of the current, uncertain military situation, Lyndon has been stopped from attending this Saturday 's State funeral and to avoid any embarrassment or concern in the financial area of New York, a press announcement has just been released in Washington, confirming the reoccurrence of a minor infection and to quench any worries on Wall Street and the Stock Market, it has been accompanied by photographs showing him continuing Federal business.

His personal advisor has virtual *Carte Blanche* to negotiate, without delay, because of our mutual interests and shared values, an arrangement that should, I feel certain, satisfy you but I must add, comes with terms that the President has stated are non negotiable. The draft agreement which you have in front of you has been revised and I believe David has now available copies of an agreement approved by the President in the last eighteen hours.

Primarily he will make an announcement, globally, and through the United Nations in New York, reaffirming the new' Monroe' Doctrine and confirming that the people of the United States are determined to defend freedom and especially the independence and freedom of their greatest ally, the United Kingdom, and that any attack on Great Britain will be considered an attack on the Continental United States and could result in the use of unlimited military force.

(Humphrey would have also stated that the United Nations, like their pre war predecessor the League of Nations, was no longer a credible forum and body but he realised that the British were now solely concerned with their own interests and survival).

The pace of military technology was accelerating and historical definitions of strategy and tactics were becoming anachronistic, however the British Isles, or if their fair offer was rejected, adjacent territories which had already been earmarked (at which moment Bruce noted that Wilson had suddenly become attentive) would become part of a string of fortresses that would contain the expansion of Communism and maintain the freedom of the Oceans and the Mediterranean.

(If the quarry became elusive, more specific details of the nonexistent negotiations with the government of Southern Ireland could be hinted at later or even an indirect reference to the regimes in the Iberian Peninsula).

The United States government required one hundred year leases on a number of locations in the British Isles, primarily for the Strategic Air Command to maintain part of their B 52 bomber fleet and as yet an unspecified number of naval bases including Faslane on the Clyde and possibly even the deep water facility at Scapa Flow."

It was then that the President's confidential advisor made his presence and interest known.

"I believe that we have now reached the stage in our discussions when we must confront ourselves with the financial reality of the situation. The Vice-President was about to inform you that to mount a long term defence of the United Kingdom would involve a financial burden upon our taxpayers and it is not necessary to explain to you, as politicians, the difficulty of justifying any tax increase. Furthermore, he was also about to inform you that it would be his personal responsibility to steer approval and legislation for such tax increases through Congress and we must now ask if not for a substantial contribution, or if indeed you will underwrite our costs?

I had hoped, and expected, that your Chancellor of the Exchequer, Denis Healey, a man well respected by his counterpart in Washington would have been present, to contribute towards an early resolution and settlement of this discussion and to give his imprimatur concerning the cost of this cooperation. May I request that, if possible, he be called and perhaps we could have a brief interruption of these proceedings?"

The Cabinet Secretary instinctively rose and went to the door beckoning the surprised Gold, now reduced to the status of a messenger, to enter, when the P.M. asked him to contact and bring Denis Healey, without delay.

As Gold turned to leave the room his eyes set on a man that he had last seen over twenty years before; they had both aged, or more courteously, matured, but there was no doubt in his mind as to his identity.

In turn, the man also instantaneously recognised Mandel Goldburgh (not being aware of his change of name) and was momentarily gripped by surprise and, dare he admit it to himself, shock, quickly regaining his composure and confronted by the success of his investment made all those years ago, realised that Goldburgh was the source of the intelligence that had been passed to the ambassador shortly before they had left Regent's Park.

Denis Healey was immediately located in his official residence at Eleven Downing Street, waiting for news of the meeting, where he had taken the opportunity to draft a proposal for the P.M. which he saw as an opportunity to satisfy the warring trade unions, their belligerent leaders and above all the general public and would involve an adjustment to his forthcoming budget by an ingenious use of creative accounting.

FIFTY-ONE

They were all very nearly exhausted. The meeting had ended shortly before eleven p.m. and immediately after the departure of the three Americans, Wilson insisted that, with the assistance of their civil servants, they prepare for the crucial Cabinet meeting which was set for nine forty-five a.m. and the further and final meeting at one p.m. scheduled at Regent's Park.

Edward Heath, Sir Reginald Manningham-Buller and Patrick Gordon Walker, assisted and supported by senior civil servants from the Ministry of Defence and the Cabinet Office were delegated to review the new and revised agreement. An ever mounting list of queries were logged but two matters above all concentrated their attention and raised the concerns of everyone, without exception, in the room.

There was no reference to the 'Polaris' missile system and then there was the cost of the agreement, however the whole problem was succinctly summarised by one of the civil servants when he observed that:

"The document of just three typewritten pages, on expensively produced notepaper, headed with the impressive statement ...Office Of The President of the United States Of America, was only worth the good faith and integrity of the incumbent President or his successors and that they were not currently in a position to dispute the terms and conditions, however they had no alternative but to inform the P.M. and recommend him not to sign the document on behalf of the British government until 'The Nassau Agreement' of December nineteen sixty-two was specifically included."

In the presence of his fellow Cabinet members and the group of civil servants, Edward Heath openly blamed and vehemently criticised the Prime Minister for his fatal error of judgement and his craven submission to Soviet blackmail, surprisingly raising agreement from the Wilson loyalist, Patrick Gordon Walker, who stated that:

"Whilst he had strong views concerning nuclear weapons that had been reinforced by the American assault on the Soviet Union, in view of the recent attacks on Essex and then Suffolk, he now, if somewhat reluctantly, realised that possession of a viable and flexible deterrent was crucial. "

Denis Healey, Harold Lever and Harold Wilson along with civil servants from the Cabinet Office and with Healey's senior staff, were in the Cabinet room discussing that morning's Cabinet meeting, the crucial and pivotal meeting with the Vice–President and the absolute necessity of a national broadcast to calm the country and it was agreed that it should be made on the eve of the State funeral after an improved agreement had been signed and once the P.M.'s audience, later that day, at Buckingham Palace, had concluded.

They had swiftly come to the same or a similar conclusion as had their associates in a nearby room, expressed again by another senior civil servant, permitted to speak freely without the fetters of his neutral impartial status, but this time going further on the 'Special relationship', commenting that whilst their political masters had to make the final decision they should view their allies as little more than avaricious mercenaries exploiting an impotent and ill close relative.

The Prime Minister should emphasise the few concessions rung from the Americans and he should promise and endeavour to reduce the cost of the 'Umbrella 'in order to secure, at least by a majority, the Cabinet's support and backing.

The meeting ended at three fifteen a.m., an hour and a quarter after the other meeting had finished and furtively Harold pulled aside Denis Healey, and asked him...

"To wait, since there was a matter he did not wish to discuss in front of witnesses."

At eight o'clock precisely, a surprised barber at a leading and well known emporium in the 'West End' was called, shortly thereafter arriving with his shaving equipment, and was escorted up to the private residence of the Prime Minister, unsuccessfully trying to navigate the spaghetti like lines of electrical cables still waiting to be used, where he twice tripped. At nine-eighteen he had completed his task and accompanied his client to the kitchen where not only was he remunerated, but he joined his client for a 'slap up' old fashioned English breakfast. In the next fifteen minutes the P.M. learned more of the national mood and the voters' fears and hopes than if he had sought this information from any of his advisors.

Refreshed, but still suffering from a shortage of sleep, Wilson determined and resolved not to mention or even, however obliquely, allude to the subject that he had discussed with Denis Healey, and if the matter was raised in Cabinet he intended to dismiss the possibility or economic necessity, with absolute conviction, as ludicrous.

He intended to devalue the pound and he had found an ally in the Chancellor who considered the economic outlook, at best, bleak. Wilson, as President of the Board of Trade, had been a member of the Labour government who, in nineteen forty–nine, had devalued the Pound from $four point zero three to its current level of $two-eighty. A fraction over thirty percent.

Literally, on the back of an envelope, in the presence of the Prime Minister, Healey had calculated alternative devaluations of just under fifteen and again thirty percent lowering the pound's value to $two-forty or $two exactly.

The envelope was prudently torn up and on a sheet of notepaper he made some approximate calculations that related to the annual cost of the "Umbrella".

Devaluation would promote the sale of British goods, especially the highly sought after range of sports cars (including the new Jaguar E-type and the M.G.B), alcoholic beverages (Whisky and Gin) and iconic clothing but there was a fundamental disadvantage. It would put up the cost of the American military 'umbrella' and in anticipation of an insufficient harvest (because substantial areas of agricultural land had been lost in Essex and East Anglia), the cost of imported wheat. Healey would arrange for a team of economists and actuaries armed with their slide rules to consider the various parameters and options and in due course, report back to him.

The Prime Minister entered the Cabinet room at exactly nine forty-five a.m. The mood was sombre and despondent. He announced that even though the Industrial situation was further deteriorating, certain discreet suggestions had been put to the T.U.C. leadership and that he was confident of an early resolution but that there was inadequate time to discuss the subject that morning, likewise the situation in Essex and Suffolk, following the nuclear attacks, would have to left till the next Cabinet meeting, which in view of the statement that he was about to give should be fixed for the following Monday, at an earlier time of eight thirty a.m. That said, following a subtle prompt from the Cabinet Secretary, he reminded those present that they were due to attend Westminster Hall that afternoon, as members of the Coalition government, to pay their respects to Sir Winston.

He had decided to inform the Cabinet of the previous evening's events in two parts: the first up to the arrival, at the request of the President's special and confidential advisor, of the Chancellor, which would allow him the opportunity to gauge their response and then tell them of the concessions and deal that had been negotiated. He would emphasise that he would put forward a proposal to the Vice-President that should, if accepted, reduce their annual expenditure.

When he had finished giving details of the first part of the meeting and copies of the agreement were handed out (without details of the cost to the Exchequer) he was greeted by a palpable chill of numb resignation as the Cabinet was confronted by the consequences and reality of the nation's plight and military impotency.

Sir John MacLeod, the Minister for Agriculture, Fisheries and Food who had been chosen not solely for his availability but his reputation for pliability, caught the attention of the P.M., rose and made a brief but devastating statement that pierced the chillness and enflamed the atmosphere.

"This agreement is a squalid and sordid betrayal of the nation, undermining every sacrifice that had been made by the country in two World wars, Korea and now, most recently, the heinous loss of life in the European debacle (then deviating from an argument that might have fatally wounded Harold Wilson, he asked...) and since the nation's sacrifice is at the heart of my brief statement may I also ask, what is the current condition of those troops that have been repatriated in the most sorry state of health since my senior civil servants' enquiries have been thwarted by a wall of silence, those involved claiming the ethical right of the patients to confidentiality?"

Wilson chose to ignore the remarks and requested the Minister of Defence, Edward Heath, to answer the query, but also to report to the Cabinet details of his meeting, thus permitting him also to confront the P.M.

"With sincere regret I must inform Sir John and those present that I have not received, from my civil servants, a further report within the last twenty–four hours, but details will be provided when we reconvene.

He, and his two fellow Cabinet associates, had been charged to review and examine the agreement and they and their advisors had identified a large number of inconsistencies, contradictions and uncertainties that under normal circumstances would oblige him to forcibly urge the P.M. not to sign the document, however there were two matters that had to be urgently resolved. The absence of any mention of the 'Nassau Agreement' and secondly a schedule of charges that they were entitled to make for the various leases and the cost of the leases for the fleet of B52 bombers and their weapons."

He concluded his comments and observations with the defeatist remark...

"We understand that the government is not in a strong position to bargain and therefore we have to trust our allies."

A morbid silence descended which was broken by Sir John MacLeod who suddenly threw a lighted fuse into the tense meeting as if he wished to add to his earlier comments...

"Personally, I hold the P.M. responsible for this disaster, the abrogation of our sovereign duty and the jeopardy that he has placed on the nation."

Konni Zilliacus and Patrick Gordon Walker could, and should, have supported the two speakers and emphasised their feelings, however when confronted by their duty they exposed themselves as weak and spineless, and the latent, simmering dissatisfaction which could have erupted and compelled Wilson to heed the comments of a disillusioned and partisan Cabinet dissolved, though in truth there was no rational alternative.

Wilson, with a hint of sarcasm and pugnacity, thanked the two previous speakers for their honest opinions but reminded the Cabinet that *THEIR* [author's emphasis] fundamental duty was the defence of the Realm and that by supporting him, the agreement would protect the nation.

Sir John MacLeod and Edward Heath had been both courageous and foolish, the latter now exposing himself to a vulgar, vindictive, vicious vendetta to be orchestrated by the Prime Minister, for his statement had not only confirmed Wilson's assessment of his Minister of Defence but more importantly accelerated his intention, when the time and circumstances were ripe, to expel him from the Cabinet along with the Chancellor of the Exchequer if and when the Pound was devalued, since he could be sacrificed to appease public opinion and any trade union anger. And within days he would learn that his Labour allies, Konni Zilliacus and Patrick Gordon Walker had indiscreetly voiced certain doubts and therefore their absolute loyalty was now in question.

The vendetta and Heath's gallant but futile response would continue even up to Wilson's trial for High Treason, when, including the whole Cabinet, Sir John MacLeod and Heath would also pay the ultimate price.

"I am shortly going to ask you for a unanimous vote in favour, and support, of the agreement that has been presented to you but I promise that I intend, tooth and nail, to fight both to reduce the annual charge requested by the Vice-President and to resolve any difficulties that might arise in connection with the 'Nassau Agreement' .Edward has mentioned certain minor problems with the agreement and I feel confident that since our interests are consistent with our equal American partner, then they will be resolved.

The cost that has been stipulated for the first five years has been set at $two hundred and sixty-five million per annum but excludes certain capital expenditures especially the construction of new facilities and this will reduce and this is not an error, to $two hundred and fifteen million for the second five years. This will partially be offset by an annual charge for the leases of £twenty-five million per annum reducing to £twenty million for the second five period. Denis and the Lord Chancellor will accompany me and I intend to endeavour to reduce these charges by negotiation and by offering leases on our naval bases in Gibraltar and Malta for a period of twenty years to further tighten the noose around the neck of Communism and its pernicious expansion which must be halted.

Maintenance work on our fleet of 'V' bombers in South Africa is proceeding satisfactorily (essentially untrue but since Heath was isolated and emasculated, Wilson did not expect to receive any questions requiring elaboration of his statement) though, unfortunately, some of the core elements of the nuclear devices have deteriorated to such an extent as to make them unusable, however as part of the agreement their American allies and partners would supply weapons from their own arsenals (not realising or even thinking that the American bombs might not be compatible with the design and carrying facilities of the Vulcan bomber). Perhaps Edward and his chaps could urgently investigate the feasibility of moving the fleet of 'V' bombers to bases in Northern Australia and Japan or Formosa to protect their joint interests and those of their allies in the Western Pacific and confront China if she began to expand in South East Asia.

With immediate effect the United States would lease fifty front line B 52 bombers to the United Kingdom which would be livered with R.A.F. colours and be crewed by R.A.F. officers and men though they would be supported by trained U.S.A.F. personnel (again what Wilson had not realised was that the American personnel would be responsible to control and arm the bombs since they and they alone would have access to the arming codes)."

The mood was certainly not euphoric but the Prime Minister had raised the spirits of nearly everyone present who then proceeded to accept the agreement in its current form but to charge Wilson to negotiate, if possible, certain amendments, though Sir John MacLeod and the Minister of Defence abstained, any potential support from Zilliacus and

Walker having finally been eroded by the plausible eloquence of their political ally and master, Harold Wilson.

At eleven fifty- three a.m. the Cabinet room emptied and everyone who had been present, without exception, was unaware that in less than two years they would all be dead as if they had signed their own death warrants.

FIFTY-TWO

At eleven fifty-three a.m. John Tyndall left his dingy rented flat dressed in the same best suit that he had worn the previous day (despite a small stain that he had managed to partially dissolve and hide), half aware that he had forged both the foundations of his destiny and ultimate downfall, holding the same tattered bag containing, in ten shilling, one pound and a few five pound notes, the sum of one thousand five hundred and seventy five pounds.

He hailed a taxi cab, inwardly smiling for *HE* [author's emphasis] was wearing underneath his shirt and vest a genuine Blackshirt that he had bought from an old supporter of Oswald Mosley who had stood 'shoulder to shoulder' with his idol during that epic meeting in Birmingham thirty years before. He would remain loyal to his principles even though others might think that he had compromised or even abandoned his values.

The taxi stopped outside of a nondescript terraced building in a road that indirectly, by a circuitous route, ran between Charing Cross Road and Bloomsbury Street, bounded on the North by New Oxford Street and he remembered that he had previously used this particular route as a 'short cut' but had not and would never have given the building or others in the same road a 'second glance' such was their anonymity and run down appearance.

He preferred the atmosphere of the streets and the clubs around Brewer Street and those fascinating alley ways in Soho, but none had those displays of little... (he stopped himself almost salivating, composed himself and noted the business plaque on the aged, front door whose black paint was rapidly flaking). It was not what he had expected but the plaque agreed with Duggan's specific advices and he rang the doorbell expecting it to malfunction but the door was promptly opened by a man in his early thirties, dressed in a lounge suit of a finer quality and cut than his own and strangely, eerily and too coincidentally, appeared almost like a clone of his chauffeur of the previous day.

The lift worked efficiently and rapidly took them to the second floor where he was received by a well dressed man of military bearing who was clearly forewarned of both his visit and immediate arrival. He was shown into an office that was in total contrast to the exterior appearance of the building, as if the building had been specially aged or allowed to deteriorate to avoid the public's interest. The walls were wood panelled to imitate the smoking room of a gentleman's club and behind a desk, built from a wood which he could not identify but which was of superb quality, was a painting of a country house as it might have appeared some two hundred years ago for he could identify the period by the costumes of the people in the foreground. There was something very reminiscent about the building but he had more important matters to discuss and resolve.

"As Major Duggan has told you we are an old established Import and Export Company with close associations with a discreet Merchant Bank that we have used since the formation of the firm during the rapid expansion of trade during the Victorian era. As a favour to him and to assist you I have arranged for a Solicitor to arrive at one p.m.to help you formally establish your political party and more importantly, we are empowered to set up your new bank account though it will take a week or so for a cheque book to be issued. You must have impressed the Major for this morning the Chief General Manager of your existing bank rang to confirm that he would personally arrange for your local branch to give you every possible help and where you can make deposits and withdrawals. I gather that you went to his favourite watering hole yesterday to eat and where he plays bridge with the Chief General Manager. I am certain that you must have some questions to ask me which I will try to answer until the Solicitor arrives."

Tyndall was anxious to arrange the bank account and requested that they commence completion of the documentation forthwith which the man, who then introduced himself as Colonel Lock-Wood, but now retired, was pleased to attend, producing a file containing some pre printed documents bearing the title of a bank that Tyndall had never heard of.

Having determined the title of the organisation ...'The New Order', he busily, with a fountain pen that appeared both unique and exquisite, completed the documentation and then requested Tyndall, both as a formality and as a prudent business procedure to check but (foolishly) and with short sightedness he hurriedly signed, being more interested in asking about the provenance of the pen.

"Only those cognizant of my life story or who are drawn to beautiful objects would ask such a question and the answer is both tragic and true. When we entered Nuremberg in May nineteen forty-five I was personally charged to locate, arrest and interrogate Julius Streicher and to seize as much documentation from his archives which I did, liberating at the same time from his desk, a personal fountain pen which you are currently holding and which I believe was part of *HIS* nefarious plunder. As you may know I was beaten to him by the Americans for he was captured on the twenty-third in the Austrian town of Waidring though I later did get to interview him-forming the opinion that he was criminally insane - and later his second wife and former secretary, Adele Tappe."

For Tyndall, whose values and standards were so perverted, the very act of holding a former personal possession of such a man was indeed an ecstatic or pseudo religious experience and which was only interrupted by the arrival of the Solicitor, who having formally introduced himself, proceeded to clarify and verify the nature of 'The New Order', then suggested that since Tyndall intended the organisation to promote a political philosophy and, at this time, he was the sole leader, then he felt that he should operate as a sole trader and that any income be controlled by two trustees that he could name in the near future. He would investigate the nineteen sixteen Registration of Business Names Act and would then write to Tyndall at his home address and keep Mr. Lock-Wood informed, who immediately realised that the forms that he had only just completed were inappropriate and would have to be completed again which was soon achieved however once more Tyndall did not, as he should have done, check them.

Tyndall was impatient to get back to the demonstrations and to supervise the march to Westminster Hall, though he thoughtfully asked for the contact number of Major Duggan which he took and later that day courteously telephoned the Major to thank him for his help and introduction. The meeting ended with the three men going their separate ways as Colonel Lock-Wood walked to Bloomsbury Street and proceeded north to Gower Street where he hailed a taxi which took him to Curzon Street, Mayfair where his 'firm' had their 'Head Office'.

The Prime Minister, Denis Healey and the Lord Chancellor nearly, but not quite, simultaneously arrived in three separate cars, having, for security purposes travelled by different routes, to the residence of the

United States Ambassador to the Court of St. James, five minutes or so before their scheduled meeting was due to commence.

In a gesture of friendship the P.M. suggested, requested and if the truth be known almost begged the Vice-President to accompany him to Westminster Hall later that afternoon to pay their joint respects to the memory of Sir Winston and whilst he appreciated the security implications...

"It would not only be a welcome fillip for the British people but would emphasise the strong bonds between the two nations, prior to the President making his promised, landmark speech.

The conditions of the agreement were acceptable, though in all honesty the more pedantic members of his government had noted some inconsistencies and contradictions, but he felt that to pursue each and every item would exhaust and extinguish any good faith and that each and every point could, and undoubtedly would, be settled when the problems arose.

He had however two matters to raise. The 'Nassau Agreement' which was not mentioned in the agreement and, like any businessman, the cost of the operation which they were effectively underwriting. Denis had been going over the figures which would put an enormous strain on the economy and could create considerable unrest and..."

At which point Humphrey slightly raised his hand to draw the Prime Minister's attention and interjected...

"We had anticipated such a response and in answer to your request is there anything that you could put on the table that I can justify to Lyndon?"

Wilson was slightly flustered not knowing whether only to mention Gibraltar or to make the offer more attractive by including 'Malta'.

"Edward Heath, my Minister of Defence, has recommended that our strategic base in Gibraltar be expanded and strengthened, thereby further dominating access to and from the Mediterranean and also facilitating control of a vast swath of the Eastern Atlantic. Your joint cooperation would be much welcomed especially if you could recognise this concession by reducing your charge over the next ten years."

Humphrey clearly looked to the President's personal representative for guidance, whilst Bruce sensed that Wilson was desperate for a 'life line'.

This was the exact moment that the destiny of Great Britain was sealed and symbolically the adjective great ceased to apply.

"Only the President can make a decision on Polaris, though he has entrusted me to assist Vice-President Humphrey to resolve the strategic relationship between our two nations. Both Gibraltar and especially the island of Cyprus, but not Malta, are of great interest to us as bases for our naval fleets whilst I am also able to offer an immediate compromise over what you call 'charges' but which the President simply views as your contribution to our costs .The best that I could possibly offer without incurring the wrath of the President, which could be economically justified to him as commensurate with the nation's commitment ,would have to be $two hundred and fifty million per annum for each of the next five years, reducing to $two hundred and ten million for the second five year period, however the leases would have to be reduced to £twenty million for the first five years and £seventeen million for the second five year period. If this offer was acceptable I could have the document promptly amended and ready for you to sign on behalf of the British government and for Vice-President Humphrey to countersign. (He paused, then continued) If you would like to point out the 'inconsistencies' and 'contradictions' I feel certain that Mr. Bruce could either answer your concerns or arrange for a further revised draft to be prepared."

By three thirty-five most, but not all, of the inconsistencies and contradictions, had been discussed and resolved by the Lord Chancellor, Denis Healey and David Bruce, whilst the Prime Minister had separately discussed certain political matters with the Vice-President and finally persuaded him to join him at Westminster Hall where, despite the solemnity of the occasion, he intended to use the opportunity to enhance his reputation and further his authority over the Cabinet and the British political scene.

As for the President's confidential advisor, he had resolved to exploit the infiltration of Wilson's government by Goldburgh, excusing himself and returning to the Embassy where he assembled the local intelligence heads including Gold's handler, first congratulating them on the success of their penetration, then giving general instructions that whatever was Gold(burgh)'s emolument (a word they had to look up in a dictionary after the departure of their superior) it was to be doubled, that he was to be protected in every sense of the word and that finally he would have delivered, to be stored in the Embassy, unknown even to Goldburgh, a United States diplomatic passport (which was dated from the time that he was first recruited) and would include a photograph taken whilst he was at university.

Such was the Prime Minister's determination to finalize the agreement and, in truth, parade the Vice-President before the British people, even though some queries had still not yet been resolved, or even discussed, that he arranged for a revised and updated agreement to be signed (by the three representatives of the British government, the Vice-President and the Ambassador to the Court of St. James) after which the Lord Chancellor returned to Ten Downing Street with the document whilst the four other participants, in an enormous limousine, were transported to Westminster Hall where they arrived shortly after four-fifteen.

Unfortunately his reception ranged from muted applause to disdain in stark contradiction to the rapturous reception that he had anticipated, substantially due to his current reputation and the national crises whilst the assembled crowds did not even recognise their important visitor, however after having completed their duty and on the way out, Wilson was very conveniently waylaid by a B.B.C. television journalist and made an impromptu statement...

"Today and now is not the time or especially the place to make political capital, however I intend to speak to the nation tomorrow evening with the most exciting good news that this country has heard for some time and, may I dare say, will be in recognition and reward for the many years and sacrifices that our nation and especially the people have made in the cause of freedom."

The journalist, ignoring protocol, turned to the surprised Vice-President and courteously requested him to ...

"Add a few words following his welcome but surprise and unexpected visit."

The Vice-President was not prepared for this situation and expressed in the most diplomatic of terms what he believed the British people would want to hear...

"The cause of freedom is a fundamental common bond shared by our two nations and I am proud to be here to pay my nation's genuine respects to a man who a quarter of a century ago, defiantly held aloft and defended the sacred flame of liberty. And now you should all be proud that your government has continued this duty."

The Prime Minister had achieved his wildest dreams in that impromptu and brief statement.

For Edward Heath, the bitterness of his treatment and the cynical betrayal of the government's sovereign duty consumed him so that, in his capacity as Minister of Defence, he should have pursued, as promised, enquiries to ascertain the fate of the repatriated British forces languishing in hospital, but he forgot until, the next day, he entered the Cabinet room, but in the excitement and consequent events, the subject was forgotten and their ultimate fate became a postscript to what is called history and any interest pursued by their families and friends fell on fallow ground because there were no M.Ps. to whom they could complain and then, soon afterwards, with the breakdown of the recognised systems of administration, it became impossible.

Shortly after four fifteen, Jack Jones received a telephone call from Bill Martin, but he was unable to transmit the contents to his handler for a few days, thus blunting the impact of Martin's intentions. In essence, to the intense satisfaction of Jones, Martin had proposed, without delay, and without even seeking the approval both of his union and the T.U.C., who he perceived as weak and ineffectual, to organise a demonstration and rally in London the following Friday, the fifth, against the Government's anti unionist policies and to facilitate the movement of his fellow members and supporters he had already secured the cooperation and support of various railway unions in order that sufficient numbers could be moved. He hoped and believed that the resultant crowd would force the almost Tory–fascist government to recognise their intense anger but above all the validity of their case.

Revolutions thrive on the chaos of anarchy.

Shortly after four fifteen, as dusk was descending, John Tyndall located the tail of the march, attached himself to the band of demonstrators who had circumnavigated Trafalgar Square and were slowly marching along Whitehall just before Downing Street, parading their placards, some crudely handmade but the majority professionally manufactured. The group surrounding him clearly had no idea as to his identity, or even the origins of the organisers and when engaged in conversation confirmed their approval for the motives of the march, reciting slogans in lieu of any intellectual argument.

Tyndall had not seen any of the manufactured placards which reiterated the organisation's original theme...

"Britain: stand up and fight union tyranny!", and...

"End union anarchy and tyranny."

Buoyed by the support, he temporarily left the column and approached a solitary police officer who was quietly observing the proceedings and who remarked to Tyndall, before he could ask his crucial question...

"It`s a pleasure to watch such a well behaved band of demonstrators, especially one with such an important message, unlike some of those C.N.D. marchers who were ill behaved, chanting their message without understanding the consequences."

"Officer, can you guess or estimate how many people are on the march?"

"Difficult, for people were joining all the time and their helpers are continually walking around and up and down the procession collecting donations from the general public and at the same time marshalling the supporters. It`s very well organised but I would think that there were, oh, some five to six thousand."

He rushed down the ever lengthening column, rejoining half way along and encountering a group of adults in their early twenties. He listened to their animated conversation before requesting their attention to ask a question. The response was a deluge of comments that cascaded down like a waterfall and nearly drowned him with the fervour and passion of their opinions, comments and finally a devastating question.

"Our university and college education has been interrupted and curtailed by lecturers who are solely interested in their idealist left wing politics and an unachievable Socialist utopia."

"It`s impossible to get to work in under two hours and getting home takes even longer and when we get to work the heating and lighting doesn`t always work because of the strikers."

"We are the future and the trade unions are dinosaurs from the past."

But it was the fourth person who asked a simple question which summarised the emotion and feelings of the marchers.

"Have you seen the placard at the head of the demonstration? The trade union movement is a fifth column in our midst and an ally of those who destroyed democracy in France, Western Germany and Belgium."

Elated at the success, not only of the turnout but of the sentiments of the marchers, he again left the body of the demonstration and, his age permitting, ran down the road and endeavoured to join the head of the demonstration which was led by his deputy and others of the original band. A firm and emphatic hand gripped his shoulder and a man in his thirties halted his entry and courteously informed him that as an official steward he had been instructed to stop the leaders of the march being overwhelmed and their presence being diluted by supporters.

"Would he please therefore join the main body of the march but his support was really appreciated."

As a tactic he again ran, his lungs nearly bursting with the effort, till he was ahead of the vanguard and as he turned he saw the motto triumphantly emblazoned on a banner that like an awning decked the leaders...

"Defend British free speech and freedom from Bolshevik terrorism."

At that moment, the Prime Minister's car swept past as Harold Wilson was being driven to an audience with Her Majesty.

Breathing heavily, he walked towards the front of the column where his deputy and supporters- the first of the few - who had stood beside him on the edge of the River Thames a few days before, which he now saw as the beginning of their journey, welcomed him and acknowledged his achievement.

His speech, before an estimated crowd of nine thousand supporters, increased by curious members of the general public who were dispersing from Westminster Hall, was deliberately brief and was preceded, on his specific instructions, by an introduction which described him as the inspiration, organiser and head of a new movement for change...

'The New Order.'

Before he began he noticed that his deputy, who in reality had efficiently organised the event, appeared sullen and despondent in the absence of any recognition. He remembered an old maxim and realised that he must be careful about his ally's intentions and his own desire to rid himself of the man who now might be a potential threat to his authority...

'Keep your enemies close to you and your allies even closer.'

"Friends, your response and support for our new crusade is greatly appreciated. I am not a great orator but I hope that my brief message will strengthen your support for our cause. We intend to hold a major rally next Friday, February fifth which will again be organised by my deputy, loyal ally and friend (a deafening roar of approval drowned his name), the venue has yet to be confirmed however by publicity and word of mouth you will be informed.

Please bring your friends and anyone who believes in our core values: especially freedom of speech, the democratic right to elect a government of your choice, a right that appears to have been stealthily taken from us, freedom from fear as this same government appears to intend to take no action in retaliation against those who, with apparent impunity, attack these shores and cause immense destruction, but above all our desire is to curb the arrogance and contempt of the trade unions who in the nation's hour of peril have cynically withdrawn their labour thereby effectively stabbing the country in the back."

At that moment, the final part of his speech was received by a roar of support that by the standard of the crowd's earlier response was of even greater magnitude.

The Times of Friday, January twenty-ninth reported in the Court Circular issued by Buckingham Palace on January twenty-eighth that:

'The Right Hon. Harold Wilson M.P. (Prime Minister and First Lord of the Treasury) had an audience of Her Majesty this evening.'

By convention the audience is private and confidential without any staff present.

Undoubtedly Harold Wilson gave details of the agreement signed by representatives of the British government and the Vice-President of the United States of America a few hours before, though we will never exactly know the truth, for at his trial for High Treason he claimed that he had only given an outline of the terms.

A personal diary left by the Queen prior to her departure for Canada on a hastily arranged State visit, ostensibly to offer her personal sympathy following a mining disaster, but viewed later as a flight from arrest by the New Order, and read in court, clearly and beyond dispute mentions that she enquired why the 'V' bomber force had been sent to South Africa LEAVING THE COUNTRY DEFENCELESS [author's emphasis] and also queried what action was being taken to assist in the rescue operation following the two nuclear attacks. There were two additional notes or abbreviations which were indecipherable but followed by triple exclamation marks which do not appear in any of her other diaries and clearly show great concern.

A private journal, also produced in court, the property of one of the Queen's retinue of trusted servants makes a specific reference to the duration of the meeting which was only nineteen minutes, and under questioning another member of her retinue stated that meetings usually lasted a minimum of forty minutes!

FIFTY-THREE

Even before he entered the Cabinet room he was confident that the amended agreement would not only be acceptable to the Cabinet but that he would receive a ringing endorsement of *HIS* handling of the negotiations. Anything less than a total vote of approval would expose the objectors to the deal but above all their disloyalty which he would not countenance. His audience with the Queen had not gone well, indeed her questions had been both too incisive and clearly based on intelligence and wise counsel. Hopefully no one in the Cabinet would be as inquisitive but the arrangement had now been signed.

At precisely nine forty-five a.m. he entered the room, refreshed by a deep night's sleep which boosted both his confidence and desire to impress the Cabinet with his report on the crucial meeting with the Vice-President. Above all he would look both for loyalty and acquiescence, virtues (or weaknesses) that would form part of his criteria when he formed a new, more malleable Cabinet, for he had no qualms replacing disloyal ministers by members drawn from outside of 'Westminster', including Jack Jones.

He had already drafted a speech to be broadcast that evening which only required their formal agreement but would need 'tidying up' and he would propose that the Lord Chancellor and the Cabinet Secretary be delegated to assist him.

A statement was made which summarised the main problems which confronted the nation including the ever increasingly effective industrial dispute (which was literally beginning to throttle the nation) but he deviously postponed any discussion on the matter by stating that:

"A solution was on the horizon.

He shrewdly demolished any potential opposition with his news concerning a potential agreement and concentrated on the financial concession 'wrung' from their ally, deluding himself and everyone present that the Americans had buckled under pressure. He intended to fly to America within the next two to three months to finalise (he should have said resolve) the outstanding 'Nassau Agreement' once the General Election had been held and he had the mandate of the people, whilst his audience, the previous day, was only briefly mentioned in passing, relying on confidentiality to avoid any questioning.

No reference was made and therefore Edward Heath was not called upon to report on the state of the hospitalised prisoners of war though the Home Secretary was requested to give an up to date report on recovery work following the nuclear attacks in Essex and Suffolk. Harold would include in his broadcast, details of the latest situation but it was agreed unanimously that the casualty figures be understated to diminish any panic or concern, justifying the lower figures by 'expert' opinion that the more substantial construction of the residents` homes had given far greater protection than had the flimsy wooden homes of the Japanese in Hiroshima and Nagasaki.

Cabinet records and later comments verify that no one voted against the amended conditions of the agreement but both Heath and Sir John MacLeod abstained and were joined by a third Conservative, Sir Hendrie Oakshott, who spoke on behalf of the three abstainers, informing both the P.M. and their colleagues that:

"Whilst there was no feasible alternative, he anticipated great danger in the abrogation by the executive of their prime duty to defend the Realm and to place their trust in what others had described as mercenaries, but which he personally defined as a questionable ally (especially after the Suez debacle) and which now led him to register his disapproval but he wished to stress that his personal decision was not based on insular party politics."

Wilson, having achieved his victory, concluded the meeting by formally requesting the Cabinet`s agreement that the Lord Chancellor (who had remained surprisingly loyal) and the Cabinet Secretary assist him finalise his speech.

The heated disagreement had been tempered by discretion, for in an adjacent room a small team of volunteers, under supervision, had been counting the donations collected on the march, whilst another team had based themselves in the home of one of the many new volunteers and were creating lists of volunteers together with details of any special skills. Independently, one of John Tyndall`s 'lieutenants' was compiling a list of suitable volunteers who would serves as stewards.

Tyndall`s deputy had expressed his dissatisfaction that he, and his associates, had not been consulted about the new march which was planned for the following Friday and Tyndall did not wish to admit that his announcement had been made on' the spur of the moment' in response to the unexpected display of support. They were both pacified, when, at around one twenty–five in the morning, a volunteer conveniently interrupted them by handing Tyndall a piece of paper which confirmed that donations had amounted to one thousand, eight hundred and nine pounds, six shillings and three pence together with miscellaneous foreign coins including $three and ninety one cents and...

"What should she do with the foreign coins?"

Which ultimately found their way into the pockets of John Tyndall.

He arrived at his local bank around a quarter past twelve and realised that he had no documentation with him and that this time, solely for security purposes, he would claim that the large amount was his own funds and when he reached the cashier`s till he was ready to make his opening statement when the cashier greeted him and surprisingly stated ...

"That the Branch Manager wished to personally attend to him and would be here in a few moments."

And within a minute or so he had been ushered into a private office (which in no way measured up to the superb accommodation of Major Lock-Wood) by an obsequious and fawning man who normally, by his insignificant appearance, would not warrant a second glance. He was offered tea, which he declined, but took advantage of a small plate of biscuits which would suffice as his breakfast.

"I was unaware of your connection to our Chief General Manager and this morning was the first time that I had the pleasure to talk to him. May I ask if that bag contains funds for your new account? In which case I can make immediate arrangements for the deposit to be credited to an account that I can set up. If in future you have to wait in a queue or have any queries please make yourself known so that someone can give you priority attention because I wouldn`t want any complaints from my Head Office."

Major Duggan was clearly a man of influence.

He had ascertained from his deputy, despite his meticulous attention to detail, that he had not approached the Police for any authority (formal or otherwise) to hold the previous day`s march and that omission had angered Tyndall but he was not inclined, at that particular time, to raise the subject, deciding to fend off the objection that he had announced a further rally without reference to his supporters.

By bus, then 'tube' and finally 'shank`s pony' he travelled to West End Central Police Station in Savile Row where he intended to apply for permission to hold a public demonstration. He was somewhat proud, for as he turned off Regent`s Street, unexpectedly and without warning, a member of the public walked up to him, enquired if he was the gentleman who had made such a profound speech the previous day, shook his hand and passed over a crisp, unused five pound note.

A very young police constable who attended to his enquiry admitted, rather forlornly, that this was only his second day on the job and that:

"He had no idea whatsoever how to deal with the application, but he would get his 'sarg' who would know 'the ropes'.

Some fifteen to twenty minutes later the more experienced officer had completed some obscure documentation which he...

 "promised to forward to the relevant office and that he should call in on Monday to obtain a decision."

His sixth sense detected a problem for when he gave his personal details, as organiser, and his estimate of the number of anticipated participants ("was ten to twelve thousand accurate, or a fanciful exaggeration?") he felt that the officer was somewhat cynical and had also recognised his name. He stressed that there would be an adequate number of stewards which did not impress the police officer and as he left, thanking the man for his assistance, he crossed his fingers in the hope of divine intervention.

FIFTY-FOUR

"I am speaking to you from the Cabinet room at Ten Downing Street. Tomorrow the nation will unite both in prayer and homage to remember and celebrate the life, deeds and service of a man who transcended party politics and led, with conviction and bravery, his country in its most darkest and dire hour.

Your freedom, your right to freely express your opinions and to practice your religious beliefs, are for some, who did not live through those titanic events, rights that might now, very nearly two decades after the end of the war, be taken for granted but for the majority, those rights are appreciated for they were earned at a great cost.

When I was asked by Her Majesty to form a government, my first and immediate intention was to secure the defence of the Realm and earlier this week after extensive negotiations with our friend and ally, an agreement was signed that guarantees our mutual defence and protection. I hope that you will all realise that, for strategic purposes, it is not possible to disclose specific details of the arrangement, however what I am able, at this stage, to tell you is that any act of aggression could be dealt with by the use of force whose power was, until the few years ago, unimaginable and would defy comprehension.

In a few days our great friend and ally, President Lyndon Johnson, will not only speak to his fellow Americans but also to the free world and we both hope that the people of occupied Europe will learn of his, no our, great crusade that will one day soon result in a liberated Europe.

The weapons now at our disposal are so powerful that their use must be carefully controlled and supervised. Their use some time ago by a joint British and American force demonstrated both their immense power and our prudent use of their destructive force.

I am pleased to report that the rescue programme by our emergency services in Essex and Suffolk is going well. The nuclear attacks on Harlow, Chelmsford, Bury St. Edmunds and Ipswich will not be forgotten and the perpetrators will one day suffer for their transgressions. In the mean time our hospitals and volunteer organisations are coping with the injured, who I intend to visit shortly and I must add that the level of casualties was much lighter than originally feared because of the standard and quality of the construction of much of the property which shielded the occupants, in comparison with, for example, the flimsy wooden buildings that housed the populations of Hiroshima and Nagasaki.

Whilst our emergency services have worked tirelessly, aided by various voluntary groups, the sum total of their efforts has been diminished by the consequences of the strike that has not only cast a shadow over the whole nation but has effected the efficiency of the rescue operation. When I personally vividly remember how we all pulled together during the Blitz and then the rocket attacks I cannot but think that there is something missing in our nation.

The Coalition government, formed following the heinous attack on Parliament, symbolises our national unity and it will not come as a surprise to many of you if I confirm that over the last week or so approaches have been made to the leadership of the T U C to resolve the industrial dispute. Tonight I appeal directly to those who have withdrawn their labour to return to work on Monday whilst we continue to negotiate. I must add that this is not a political manoeuvre to isolate you from your negotiators and my old friend and the General Secretary of the T U C, George Woodcock, but to get the country moving again and to win the battle against our enemy.

I reaffirm my sincere promise that by the spring you will have the opportunity to elect a new government in a General Election which, for me, will symbolise the freedom that Winston Churchill so valiantly fought for. Thank you."

"That was the Right Honourable Harold Wilson M.P., Prime Minister and First Lord of the Treasury who has just spoken on B.B.C. radio and all B.B.C. and Independent Television Channels.

"

FIFTY-FIVE

No! The negative answer was absolutely emphatic in its denial of his application and John Tyndall stopped himself from asking on what grounds had his application been refused, but he suspected, from the moment of his application on the previous Friday, that his reputation and record would influence the decision. He suppressed any hint of sarcasm when he thanked the officer for his advices (for he had not made the decision) and nearly bit his tongue to stop any reflex ill tempered reply and walked away to consider his options.

He located a vacant telephone box, opened the door and was confronted by the nauseous stench of urine and rang Major Duggan who belatedly answered.

"You were right to contact me for I may be able to help you. Please ring in an hour's time when I may have an answer."

Major Duggan already knew that the application had been refused, for on his specific request his opposite number, Keith Wagstaffe at M.I.5, had blocked the approval and Tyndall's desperate plea would indebt him to the Major who deviously intended to manipulate and operate him as would a puppeteer who dextrously controlled the movements of his puppet.

Tyndall enthusiastically, with almost infantile animation, explained the theme of the demonstration and was most effusive and appreciative when Duggan suggested ideas for some of the banner headlines. He had access to some of the most important people in the land and quickly persuaded the office of Sir Joseph Simpson, Commissioner of Police of the Metropolis to sanction and authorise the demonstration albeit subject to the march being overseen by one hundred and twenty five police officers who the organisers would have to pay for, but their coffers were full and Tyndall would have to personally deliver to 'Scotland Yard ' by the following day, Tuesday, a bank draft.

For the ever increasing number of volunteers, Tuesday and Wednesday were busy days visiting every underground 'tube' station in the London network where they distributed and put up posters but they were less successful obtaining the cooperation of the bus services and in some cases they witnessed the notices being rapidly torn down.

The bank draft was promptly issued with the minimum of inconvenience, best wishes conveyed to the absent branch manager and the cheque delivered within the hour to 'Scotland Yard' where a most helpful officer suggested that Tyndall return on Thursday morning to liaise with the officer in charge of the police supervision and to go through the timetable, route and any other incidental matters.

"You were right, he can't be trusted."

Jack Jones could have said...

"I told you so."

But it was convenient for him to bide his time and that afternoon both report to his 'handler' and collect further funds to support some of the strikers, but specially the miners. Officially, on the Monday morning, the T U C had no comment to make about Wilson's statement but most union leaders were furious at what they saw as a calculated and deliberate attempt to undermine both their authority and their bargaining power. Inter union communication became urgent as they discussed a coordinated response and a common policy but a pattern was emerging, both prudent and wise: they would await anecdotal and empiric information in the next day or so which would confirm their members' response to the P.M.'s request and they would strongly consider official support for Bill Martin's unofficial and wild cat demonstration on the Friday.

The cynical analysis (or what he wanted the unions to believe) of Jack Jones had been proved correct and had enhanced both his reputation and status within the movement to the extent that the General Secretary, George Woodcock, unilaterally determining Congress policy, had authorised Jones, as an unofficial emissary, to approach the Prime Minister and convey a message that stressed the unions' determination to defend its rights and to make the strike not only official but general!

Jones realised that the stakes were increasing rapidly and that he would have to seek instructions from his ultimate masters in Moscow and passed his thoughts via his' handler' who suggested that he tell Wilson the truth, or part of the truth. Thus on the Tuesday, Wilson was elated to learn that his old and trusted friend was now acting on behalf of the T.U.C and that, as a conduit, he could confide in the P.M. that the unions might soon be ready to negotiate, but a sign of good faith might accelerate matters.

Mr. Tyndall left 'Scotland Yard' satisfactorily prepared for the following day's demonstration. The Police had been most helpful and not only gave constructive advice but unofficially approved the official banners and their slogans. It was unlikely that the march would attract more than twenty thousand supporters but in the event that additional officers were required then they would be called upon by the officer in charge and the organisers would be invoiced.

Unofficially and off the record, they had intelligence that a march had been organised by dissident members of one of the coal mining unions who had not applied for permission. It was critical that in the event that the two marches met that his stewards maintain discipline as violence, even provoked, would not be tolerated.

The telephone call was both unexpected and welcome. An exuberant Harold walked out of his private office, his face beaming with pleasure and satisfaction. He urgently requested the presence both of the Chancellor and the Minister of Defence to be informed that the latter was making an official visit and that the Chancellor was temporarily unavailable on a call of nature. Gold and Kaufman were, as substitutes, called in and informed that:

"David Bruce had just telephoned and confirmed that the President would make his broadcast the following week, most likely on the Wednesday, that Vice-President Humphrey had completed a draft speech and as a sign of their friendship he had authorised the draft to be submitted (Harold's voice became louder) for approval by the British government and he would welcome their comments."

He had been proved correct and his strategy right, not only that but it appeared that the trade unions` noose around the nation was beginning to loosen as reports were coming in confirming that the transport system was beginning to function again, at least for the next day, Friday, and that a number of industrialists were hoping to resume production on the following Monday. The T U C were still silent and he awaited some intelligence from Jack Jones.

In the skies above the North Sea, United States reconnaissance planes were hunting their unsuspecting prey.

FIFTY-SIX

One tragic and dramatic photograph shocked the nation even more than the horrific pictures taken less than fifteen months before, moments after the American President had been shot in Dallas, Texas, or some months later when the government belatedly released heavily censored photographs of the atrocity in the House of Commons. The nation was far less sympathetic, though still emotionally distressed, to view stunning colour photographs shot from the still secret maximum altitude that a U 2 spy plane could reach, showing a vast panorama of the Soviet Ukraine covered by gigantic mushroom clouds in the aftermath of the joint Anglo-American retaliatory attack.

Of all the British national newspapers, on Saturday February sixth, only the Daily Worker failed to publish a report of the previous day`s events, preferring to give coverage and support to...

SAVE LOPEZ DEMAND

A deputation from the Appeal for Amnesty in Spain yesterday at the Foreign Office saw Mr. George Thomson, Minister of State, about the pending trial by a Spanish military court of Justo Lopez (a former Republican commander during the Spanish civil war-author`s note).

The Daily Telegraph banner headline on page one encapsulated the sentiments of most of the nation which was repeated, with variations, by most other national newspapers...

A GRIM DAY FOR ALL WHO VALUE FREEDOM

The photograph was *prima facie* evidence to substantiate the result of the uncontrolled, unofficial union protest. The real truth was less partisan and an insight into the callous, brutal and vicious sub culture and underclass that existed, for the perpetrators had nothing to do with the social and political ideals of the two marches, indeed intellectually they were most likely unable either to comprehend the motives of either party or were unable to articulate their own motives.

They had attached themselves to the body of striking coal miners who undoubtedly were never intent on violence but were frustrated and starved of common sense and wise leadership, either by their renegade leader, or the union`s weak leadership and finally the T. U. C.`s myopic vision. In any event, despite this analysis, the truth was that a small minority, intent on mayhem acted unilaterally, without thought and it became convenient when the truth was exposed for it to be ignored because it was no longer in the interests of the prevailing political opinion to publicise the truth.

Thus the event very quickly became the myth and then the legend and finally the' truth'.

The photograph showed a dying woman strewn across the steps of St. Martin in the Fields, her right arm and hand appearing to point to the entrance of the church, the drizzle diluting the blood which was still exuding from her body and, standing over her, holding a child who was still too young to walk or to understand that her mother would never caress her again, a devastated man. Later identified as the woman`s husband, he was also unable to comprehend the brutal nature of the assault, its viciousness and the complete futility of the act which had been caused by the use of a 'knuckle duster' and worse still an eight inch hunting knife, its handle protruding from her spine at an angle clearly showing that she had been stabbed with a violent downwards motion.

John Tyndall and his cohorts had arrived early, at around nine a.m., in Trafalgar Square, and were met by dozens of volunteers who had already set up the rented public address system which they were also testing, whilst they were surrounded by a swelling crowd already estimated to be several hundred strong and when the vanguard of fifty police officers arrived at nine forty-five, their commanding officer estimated that the attendance had swelled to some eight to nine thousand. By ten–thirty that figure had risen to between twenty and twenty–five thousand as the balance of a further seventy–five officers arrived and Tyndall was informed, for the safety of the general public, that in the opinion of the commanding officer, that the march along Whitehall and then around Parliament Square, returning along Whitehall, passing Downing Street ,be curtailed so that when the head of the demonstration reached Parliament Square, only about two thousand demonstrators be allowed to continue and the vast bulk, guided by their stewards and some of the police, be turned back to reassemble in Trafalgar Square, awaiting the organisers and the small symbolic demonstration, to return.

At ten fifty –five, with the crowd overflowing into every adjoining street in the area and now estimated to be anything up to fifty thousand men, women and children in number, an announcement was made welcoming everyone present, then giving details which were repeated as to the route and the requirements of the police and importantly a request not only for patience, but to obey the stewards' instructions. Tyndall, flanked by his deputy and 'the first of the few', were escorted through the mass of applauding supporters as hundreds of banners suddenly rose into the air and they slowly moved off, their motion compared by a watching journalist to a sleeping giant being awakened.

The march would have received scant coverage, especially with the ongoing restriction on newsprint, but the dramatic, violent end ensured that the national newspapers, television and radio gave extensive coverage. Overall, journalistic opinion agreed that the march had not only been peaceful but well organised, and at one stage certain journalists had reduced their objective observations to wagering how much was being collected in donations which were rapidly filling buckets, very efficiently being hawked around the marchers by attractive young women volunteers.

Such was the vast support, that as the head of the march entered Trafalgar Square on its return, those at the rear were only just beginning their rotation and had not yet passed Great Scotland Yard on their left.

For the first time in his life, or in his political career, Tyndall was being mobbed and applauded, so it took him some time to reach the plinth and the public address system. He then announced, to the cheers of those already assembled, that he would delay his brief speech until, with consideration for all those still marching, their return but he would venture off the plinth and talk to some of those nearby to listen to their thoughts and opinions.

He would speak *extempore*, his themes plucked from the fears and aspirations of the many people who he had just been speaking to, which coincided with the tail of the demonstration entering the Square just as...

Major Duggan and his co conspirator Wagstaffe, extricated themselves from the heaving mass, satisfied that their investment was beginning to bear fruit, and slowly weaving their way around the gradually thinning crowd on the perimeter of the congregation, made their way to the tranquillity of the R.A.C. Club in Pall Mall.

Activation of the railways, mentioned by the Prime Minister, was in fact only for the convenience and benefit of the striking miners and their supporters as they used the railway system to converge on central London. Their assembly point was Hyde Park Corner and their route, which could have been and was actually drafted from a tourist map of London, was along Piccadilly to Piccadilly Circus, thence to Leicester Square and finally along Charing Cross Road, past St. Martin in the Fields and finally to the Square where Bill Martin would speak to his supporters and then deliver to 'Number Ten' a letter demanding that the government immediately resolve their grievances.

Tyndall's original speech, which was literally consigned to a rubbish bin and never retrieved, and his actual *extempore* speech, which was never completed, was intentionally short because he had always been of the opinion that the masses had a short attention span and anyway were more satisfied by slogans and emotions than intellectual argument and persuasion.

Martin's march, consisting of no more than six to eight thousand supporters, unauthorised and without police supervision, coincidentally also began at eleven a.m. and like a juggernaut, marched along Piccadilly ignoring the traffic that was piling up behind them and the civilised derogatory remarks of the group they would call the plutocrats as they passed the bastions of Capitalism, the Ritz hotel, New Bond Street and the discreet and elegant Burlington Arcade.

Oswald Mosley, elegant and immaculately dressed, stood outside the entrance to Fortnum & Mason, contemptuous and angry, not realising that the demonstrating, striking miners and the events that would shortly unfold would change his destiny and end his lonely vigil as the defender of true British values against the tide of insidious and pernicious socialism and the malevolent, cruel, cunning, clinically calculating force of Jewish Zio Bolshevism.

"Friends (Tyndall briefly paused), in your presence I feel humble, both because of the massive numbers that have turned out today but more importantly, the personal messages of support and of the hope and trust that you have placed in our cause.

I am no Winston Churchill or Horatio Nelson (the next few words were drowned in a spontaneous roar) and therefore will not insult your commonsense by invoking Churchill's great clarion call...

'I have nothing to offer but blood, toil, tears and sweat,'

however I promise you that I, we, will try our best (there was a visible pause, perhaps for effect but more likely for him to craft his next words). We are a great nation but we must be realistic for in this new world and whilst we have the power of an unimaginably mighty weapon and the means to deliver a deadly blow to our enemies, we are also vulnerable and our small country is open to the terrible potential of an all out enemy attack.

Our reputation as the bastion of freedom, democracy and diplomatic fairness can still play a large part in forging peace, perhaps not the ideal peace of a utopian world but one where at least you and your children will be safe. The responsibility of our leaders to maintain democracy and the rights of the individual are fundamental and therefore I must emphatically tell you all, having spoken to so many of you in the last few minutes, that my resolve has been enormously strengthened to pursue your lawful right to express your will (Tyndall was able to dramatically emphasise those two crucial words) through the ballot box, the right that the so called Coalition has appeared to deny us (At that moment a deafening roar went up and it took some moments for the sign of approval to subside).

In conclusion, I hope and ..." (His words were drowned by an altercation outside of the National Gallery).

As if ordered, with almost military precision, the great mass turned one hundred and eighty degrees and faced North to observe and hear the banners and slogans of the miners and their supporters as they collided with the official demonstration. For an instance there was an ideological melding of their two contradictory arguments, Tyndall's allegation against the Coalition and the miners' accusation of the government's and the Coalition's betrayal. Banners vied with each other including one that had not been submitted for approval and which bore the provocative statement...

"The Bolsheviks will hang you one day."

It was anathema to the miners and only a few, a very few, less than a handful knew that these were the final words uttered by Tyndall's idol, Julius Streicher, as a hood was placed on his head early on the Morning of October sixteenth, nineteen forty-six as the final act before his execution.

This was the catalyst, the lighted fuse, the progenitor of violence. Although outnumbered, the miners were far physically stronger if far shorter in self control and discipline, leading to an attack on the holders of the banner and those around them who were caught up in the *melee*, as were many desperately attempting to flee who were drawn into the fray. The police, inadequate in number and isolated from the focus of the event, were delayed in their attempts to reach the erupting fighting by the sheer mass that obstructed their path and when they did arrive, in sufficient numbers, the damage had been done and the course, and tide, of history set.

In the skies above the North Sea, United States reconnaissance planes continued to hunt for their unsuspecting and apparently elusive prey.

FIFTY-SEVEN

The lawful demonstration broke up amidst panic and whilst he was buoyed by the praises and appreciations of the vast throng that still surrounded him, Tyndall felt dissatisfied and unfulfilled by its outcome. It took some time to navigate through the crowds that continued to heap their congratulations on him and they formed a buffer between him and the events which had just taken place no more than seventy-five yards away, for they could have taken place on the other side of the moon.

Eventually he managed to hail and accost a taxi which soon took him to his small and squalid flat. In the tranquillity and quiet of the early afternoon, for he had not turned on his radio or television, he wondered where his destiny lay as he considered the curtailment of his speech as an abject failure.

He was woken from his sleep by the sound of the telephone ringing and the caller's statement, though at first their request did not register with him, or did he comprehend the ramifications of their statement?

They had obtained his telephone number-which was unlisted- from certain sources and wanted to interview him that evening on B.B.C. Television about the movement and above all *HIS* thoughts on the tragic events which marred what was otherwise a well organised and peaceful demonstration. He must have said something, he couldn`t remember what, but he clearly recognised the despondent response...

"Has the other Channel contacted you first? We can arrange for a car to collect you, when convenient, but we would like a statement for the early evening news, on the tragic death of one of the demonstrators."

He suddenly realised that the immediate consequence of the demonstration was a dimension that he had never conceived, then he hurriedly seized control of any emotions that might compel him to make an injudicious, impetuous response and held his counsel, did not admit his ignorance of the tragedy and requested that:

"The journalist provides him with the latest information before he made an appropriate comment on the awful event."

The response and the information provided, inspired him to make a wise and prudent decision. He would seek the advice of Major Duggan before he made any public statement. The hospitalisation of eight supporters, two of whom were in a critical condition, the death of a twenty seven year old housewife and the arrest of three members of the unofficial miners` march were events that he had never believed could ever happen in Britain. His first duty above any other act was to visit, without delay, those in hospital.

"I will make a formal statement early this evening, but in the meantime I intend to visit, if possible, those in hospital, to offer what little support or comfort that I can provide (and in an additional unintended remark which would raise his personal stature and the status of the New Order, when he continued). I would prefer and request that my imminent visit was not publicised in order to avoid pressure on any of the unfortunate victims or being accused of making any political capital."

"Major Duggan was not available and not expected to return to his desk until tomorrow morning."

An urgent approach to his mentor had not been successful.

Within twenty-five minutes he had arrived at St. Thomas` Hospital, which was surrounded by a swarm of journalists and photographers who belatedly recognised him, followed him inside oblivious to the inconvenience caused to the staff and many patients waiting to be treated, and only extricated himself with the assistance of the staff who guided him to another department and his injured supporters.

A second supporter had just died of stab wounds and he was left to console a grieving parent who had accompanied his twelve year old son on what was, and would be, his first and only demonstration in the cause of freedom and democracy. Tyndall was visibly shaken, an emotion that was caught by an errant photographer who must have evaded the sparse, or nonexistent security, and sneaked his way in and the resultant photograph received prominence on the inside of most of the national dailies.

Permitted to use an official telephone he unsuccessfully tried again to speak to Duggan, but was rebuffed by the same response though he was additionally informed, to his relief, that the Major was aware of his earlier call, had tried to contact him, without success, but would speak to him shortly, on the number which the operator would take and that:

"He should not, at this time, make any statement."

The Major, as promised, did telephone back, actually within ten minutes or so, the longest ten minutes up to that time in his whole life. He did not mention that he was in the exclusive R.A.C. Club, or that he had witnessed the tumultuous support (which had exceeded even his own expectations) or that, more importantly, he was aware of the events which had been reported, by 'news flashes', on both the B.B.C. and Independent Television channels.

"You are not yet ready to appear on television and might prejudice your future in politics by an ill advised remark. Announce to the press that your thoughts are now with the families of the two victims and with those who were hospitalised, though you understand that their injuries, thank God, - remember to use that phrase, it is most important -are not critical. Then conclude your very brief statement with an appreciation of the Police, emphasising that in the highest traditions they conducted their duties in the most difficult of circumstances. Do not answer any questions and Keith Wagstaffe will contact you, at home, and arrange a meeting at a safe and secure location."

In quick succession he received three important telephone calls; At five forty-five from the B.B.C.to whom he gave a succinct statement in accordance with Duggan`s instructions, at five past six, when his second in command called to confirm that four or five volunteers were currently counting the donations and would not finish until ,at least, nine p.m. and that he awaited instructions as to what to do with the money that was estimated to total anything up to twelve thousand pounds, and then within a further ten minutes, as promised, Keith Wagstaffe rang...

"The same Jaguar and driver who originally collected you at Marble Arch will arrive in fifteen minutes and you should be ready with an overnight bag and a suit."

Harold Wilson almost greedily, like an undisciplined child seizing a birthday present, grabbed the envelope, delivered by a special courier accompanied by a security officer, which he knew contained the draft of the President's speech and which was provisionally due to be delivered on the following Wednesday evening (local U.S.A. time), after midnight, early Thursday morning, London time and in his hurry to open the envelope he also slightly tore across the folded four page document.

He would arrange for both Kaufman and Gold to read the transcript on Saturday morning and submit a report which he would review in the afternoon. At seven twenty-five p.m. on a Friday evening very little could be done and he would watch the television news to learn more about the tragic deaths that had occurred during the demonstration, though in the meantime he would have a bite to eat and consider his options concerning the Industrial dispute.

In the skies above the North Sea, United States reconnaissance planes continued, with relentless, dogged persistence, the hunt for their unsuspecting and elusive prey though the air crews conjectured that the two vessels were hiding from retribution.

FIFTY-EIGHT

The journey was conducted in virtual, almost morbid silence and in the dark, though he recognised some landmarks and significantly certain locations en route, which led him to hope that he was returning to the exclusive golf club where only recently he had been so lavishly entertained. Keith Wagstaffe met him at the top of the surprisingly unlit steps that in daylight so elegantly welcomed the visitor to an exquisite example of the best in British hospitality and tradition.

He had never stayed in a hotel or accommodation that reached such standards, unless sarcastically, residence in one of Her Majesty's prisons was deemed a *de-luxe* hotel. His room expressed superb taste combined with the very best of facilities.

There was a separate shower room, the walls tiled up to the ceiling, entered by a glass door, adequate space so that he could actually sit down on a ledge whilst showering and cleverly located, to be viewed from the shower, on a raised shelf and on a decline, a fifteen inch television! The manager had personally supervised his arrival and delivered to him a menu so that he could dine in the privacy of his room, after which Wagstaffe promised to call in to discuss 'tomorrow' and his plans; all he lacked, and he started drooling, was a little...

He took the opportunity to phone his second in command who confirmed that they had raised the sum of nearly thirteen thousand pounds. Tyndall instantly had a brainwave but he would speak again, as soon as possible, and confirm to him what action should be taken about the enormous amount that was assembled before him.

He chose a menu commensurate with the best of British cuisine; wild Scottish smoked salmon, medium rare Angus roast beef with roast potatoes and bread and butter pudding topped with cream. He was pleasantly sated and sober for he wished to be in full control of his faculties when Wagstaffe arrived.

"The B.B.C., in the last fifteen minutes, have announced that a third person has died of their wounds and the Prime Minister has just been quoted as saying that union anarchy cannot and will not be tolerated. All in all you've done well, far better than we had hoped or expected. Your statement was most impressive and has definitely raised not only your reputation but also the profile of the New Order, however sooner than we expected your past history has been uncovered.

Tomorrow morning we are arranging for a T.V. producer and director to come here and spend all day and if necessary all night developing and polishing your communication skills, making certain that you can survive a news conference, otherwise you will be 'dead in the water' and your potential career will be thoroughly over. With some assistance, your members will organise a news conference for Sunday which will be orchestrated by your tutor because Major Duggan and myself cannot be directly or even indirectly linked to you.

Major Duggan has suggested that you read from a prepared speech and have a list of pre prepared stock answers which will be drafted tomorrow and refined before the conference. I will also be helping you tomorrow. We do not wish to alter your natural style of oratory which is superficially honest and sincere but in the cauldron of a studio where you may be subject to what is effectively an inquisition, the consequences of an ill conceived reply might have terminal consequences.

We confined you to this room not to imprison you but because there are downstairs a lot of very important people, industrialists, financiers, T.V. and newspaper proprietors, many of whom, if they were aware of your presence, would like to shake your hand and offer their support, but the press and photographers are also in attendance, which was also why you may have noted that the lighting when you arrived was purposely turned off and you were rushed up to your room, *incognito*.

I want you to think about the following ideas and thoughts and how you would explain your position:

The ultimate goal is the attainment of influence and power but before this objective is reached we have to construct a viable and above all plausible facade that will withstand and defy the intelligent investigation of those who are determined to halt your meteoric rise.

You, no we, are not concerned with ethical or moral judgements of your past activities but to convey a philosophy, an ideology and policies that resonate with the general public and you will have the added burden that the conference may be broadcast live. The stakes are enormous.

We think that your statement should not be dramatic, but an honest confession using your own words, which will already have been prepared. Openly admit that you went to prison for membership of a paramilitary organisation and that the experience and shock - which you should emphasise-enabled you to examine your values and philosophy. You can go on to explain that whilst 'inside' you met a few (don`t say 'a lot of') Jewish prisoners and learned of their arguments against extreme right–wing philosophies, exposing your own misconceptions and values, allowing you to change yourself.

There will be two very astute left wing journalists from the Daily Worker who are well respected and you will have to contend with them, we will give you their details tomorrow but you will be coached in how to neutralise them. As well, some sympathetic journalists will plant some questions which they know will interest their readers and give you the opportunity to shine."

In response, Tyndall had only one question to ask and it was his brainwave and inspiration...

"The unexpected, unfortunate, tragic death of three innocent people could be used to everyone's advantage and I suggest, not for political capital, that we could announce, since our fund raising was so successful, that we intend to make a donation of three thousand pounds to each family and, if it were also possible, to announce that it was our intention to hold three rallies in one day, in London, Birmingham and Manchester. If I had a fast car it could be possible and any monies raised would again be donated to the bereaved families."

"Brilliant and ingenious..

"

FIFTY-NINE

Their names, faces and reputations were known and recognised nationally and internationally and Tyndall was most confused and surprised when Wagstaffe called into his room, the following morning, and in contradiction to his comments of the previous evening absolutely insisted that he come down for breakfast "to meet a few influential guests", who were most interested to meet him.

The press and their attendant photographers had long gone and there was no one (provided that you did not include the newspaper proprietors) to trouble him.

"Get the country working again, persuade the unions to act responsibly, end the hypocrisy that was symbolised by John Profumo and whilst we may no longer be the most powerful military nation on earth, show the people that, at least, we can defend ourselves and punish those who attack us."

"Fine words, but how are you going to do it? It sounds like an aspiring candidate's election speech."

Tyndall looked round and instantly recognised the speaker. He was the proprietor of one of the country's leading national newspapers. Without preparation, or thought, he rushed into an explanation.

"First, by persuading you and the other newspaper proprietors to support me and the New Order. Start a crusade that would democratically sweep away the existing moribund order. The nation and especially the electorate are looking for a banner to follow, a cause and above all a national purpose and identity. There may still be time before Wilson calls an election to create that purpose, but however large are the rallies, it will count for nothing if I do not have a voice in Parliament and even then there may not be enough time to find likeminded people and constituencies for them to stand and represent.

If I were a lone voice it would be as if I was speaking in the wilderness and it would only have force if it were supported by other M.Ps. If we begin now and do not delay, do not find reasons why we can`t succeed but just one reason why we can, perhaps then the voters will be inspired by a purpose and will reject the parties that have failed us.

Next weekend, I plan three rallies, in a single day, in London, Birmingham and Manchester; it may well be the foundation and spring board for a truly national movement.

Without the oxygen of your publicity and support, the New Order will wither away and union anarchy will rapidly destroy us as the fifth columnists did to Madrid in the Spanish Civil War.

I would appeal directly to the strikers to return to work, warning them that the financial consequences both to them and the country in general would be disastrous if they continued, that in the long term their actions would be futile and perhaps their loss of wages could never be recovered. I would reasonably expect that the response would enable many factories, offices and the transport system to begin functioning again.

The country`s finances must now be in a parlous state and, without delay, I would decimate every and I mean every, unemployment benefit that is draining the nation`s coffers. "

The same man asked another, even more probing question.

"And if the remaining strikers dug their heels in what would you do then?"

"I hope that everyone in this room believes in a compassionate society where the weak and those who are unable to look after themselves have at least the security of a safety net, but for those who intentionally do not contribute to the prosperity and wellbeing of the nation, then they would automatically exclude themselves both from the benefits and their rights and responsibilities to and from the state."

Originally there had been some five or six men clustered round John Tyndall but by the time he had finished the number had risen to about a dozen or so and one of the new arrivals bluntly asked a question that had already been partially answered...

"What do you want from us and is there a *quid pro quo*?"

"I`ve already answered the first part and as for a return you might have an elected House of Commons that really represented the country and not a Coalition that apparently does nothing."

Had he succeeded? The men drifted away, though at least half of them courteously shook his hand and two actually went further and stated that:

"If he needed further assistance he should contact them direct."

One of whom deftly pulled from his wallet a personal visiting card which he placed in Tyndall`s hand.

He forlornly sat alone outside of the restaurant, as the inviting smell of kedgeree wafted in the air trying to seduce him. The future was in doubt and in the balance as he wondered if he had accomplished his task and persuaded those who might be his most powerful and influential supporters to back him. A voice interrupted his thoughts.

"A passable performance but in the lions` den you could have been savaged and torn to pieces. We have much work to do today and I hope that first you will join me and enjoy breakfast; fortify yourself for once we begin there will be no respite."

The man introduced himself both by name and his purpose though Tyndall soon forgot the name however he focused on the man's purpose which was to train him in the art of public speaking and diplomacy. And time was short.

Duggan arrived just as Wagstaffe, Tyndall and the T.V. producer finished their coffee and the four men retired to a small conference room where two powerful arc lights had been strategically located, specifically oriented to light one seat whilst two other seats were placed opposite, and a fourth, its back to the other three, was adjacent to a large table which, at a stretch, could accommodate twelve, perhaps fourteen people.

"My people are contacting your number two about now and are arranging for him to book a conference room in a leading West End hotel, to notify the press, radio and television and to confirm that you intend to make a major statement."

Duggan might have continued and added to his statement but was interrupted by a curt knock on the door which he acknowledged and a smartly dressed porter entered, carrying in one hand what appeared to be a heavy attaché case and in the other, two or three felt pads which he placed carefully on the opulent, highly polished oak table, leaving the case on the floor. Shortly after he left the room Wagstaffe's attention was drawn to a second knock and a woman, in her early sixties entered, a cigarette clumsily drooping from the corner of her mouth.

Her impeccable diction belied her appearance.

"Mr. Wagstaffe? I have been sent by the Major and brought along paper and carbon paper; have you any special instructions?"

He spoke briefly to the woman who then prepared for her duties by pouring herself a cup of coffee without requesting if any of those present required a beverage for themselves.

"Arrive early, prepare both your place and yourself and make certain that you will be comfortable. I will be the only other person on the dais- Duggan and Wagstaffe will not even be in the hotel - and I will act as the chairman. After you have read the prepared speech, either verbatim or paraphrased, I intend to ask for any questions specifically in response to the statement and we should be able to anticipate the general nature of those questions. I will allow Peter Zinkin and George Sinfield, both from the *Daily Worker* to ask the first questions and as we know they have uncovered details of your history. They are both highly respected -and probably Soviet Agents - but don't even allude to that, they will undoubtedly refer to your previous political activities and might attempt, no most certainly, draw you out to make a statement or statements that you would regret.

Tell them that you covered the question in your statement and then lower the temperature by skilfully changing the subject, if it is Zinkin very courteously call him by his first name, Peter, remind him that profound changes in one's political philosophy can take place and that, at the height of the general strike, he left the ILP (Independent Labour Party) to join the Communist Party, then flatter him, complimenting him on his subsequent involvement with the National Unemployed Workers Union. He's clever, very clever, and I will then invite his associate George Sinfield, a football fanatic and also a *Daily Worker* journalist to raise a question. It will disorientate him by mentioning your respect for him and the work that he has done in the field of amateur football, but be brief, there will be a crib for you, the more that you might say will give him a greater opportunity to question and examine you.

Journalists from the "*Mail*" and "*Express*" always have some kite to fly but have agreed to plant a question which I will of course forewarn you of and give you a draft answer. Not unexpectedly I will allow them at least one further question each, think carefully about your answers. We will go through how to handle questions later, but begin to learn to immediately think about your answer and any consequences. I hope Harry Boyne of the *Daily Telegraph* will attend and ask at least one question. He is dour, dignified, polite and extremely skilful, also a genuine gentleman. Remember to address him as Major-it may surprise him- but he could be as pleased as punch.

You will commence your opening statement with confirmation of your conviction but then emphasise your change in political direction, caused by your experiences in prison where you met some Jewish prisoners – don`t mention any names - if pressed use your common sense. Explain that their anonymity should be respected, subtly changing course by mentioning, for example, that even Winston Churchill 'crossed the floor' but don't even think of mentioning Oswald Mosley who more than once in his career changed his allegiance, that will open up a route for those who wish to halt your career and they will mercilessly crucify you and it will be all over. Wagstaffe has mentioned about the donations. We will incorporate that and also, I suggest a donation to a Jewish Holocaust fund of say, can you afford it, two thousand, five hundred pounds? It will disarm a lot of waverers and most certainly raise your reputation. Remember, think before you speak even if your answer appears obvious!"

Tyndall was prepared and indoctrinated for four or five relentless, unremitting hours, taught tricks, some of which were obvious and others unrecognisable. During this period they revised, improved, refined, and altered both his statement and a number of responses to questions that they anticipated would be raised and also considered replies that would stop or stall any unexpected probing questions. Tyndall was warned, in no uncertain terms that he should not, under no circumstances whatsoever, state or imply any course of action that in any way hinted of political extremism, and should emphasise throughout, the rule of law and the pre eminence of Parliament.

During all this time the secretary tirelessly transformed their oral instructions into typed print though they were deafened by the sound of the archaic typewriter in her capable hands, or should it be finger tips? Tyndall succumbed first to exhaustion as Wagstaffe argued that the actual meeting would take no more than an hour and a half, two, if the chairman allowed the inquisitors a free rein, which, of course he wouldn`t, and that the room would only have been booked for a period of three hours.

She presented them, in triplicate and double spaced, so that notes could be inserted, the latest version of the completed statement and draft replies together with, where applicable, supplementary notes and cribs. She had been well trained and requested their further instructions but in the meantime she incinerated the used carbon paper which was ignited by one of her cigarettes and the ashes crushed. The earlier typed copies had been placed in a waste paper bin and again burned and disposed of. She had learned that procedure many years before and had last seen that method used when she had worked, nearly two years before, for a very special, extremely discreet job in South Kensington during the bitter depths of winter...

"There will be no official record of my instructions to you and if I had involved my civil servants then I would have expected, with their training and attention to detail, that a file would be created, generating a record. You were asked to review the draft Presidential speech which was forwarded by our dear friend, David Bruce."

Manny Gold and Gerald Kaufman, despite their ongoing rivalry, later agreed that the P.M.'s remarks characterised his dark, even Machiavellian approach both to his responsibilities as a Prime Minister and also, more realistically, his actions as a leader. They handed back the original, slightly torn document, together with the copies that they had taken and their typed report. They anticipated and expected a less than happy response to their candid and critical analysis of the speech which formed part of a delayed 'State of the Union' message. They would argue that Bruce could be used as a conduit to Humphrey and perhaps the focus and emphasis could be modified and altered.

As he reviewed the notes he became less buoyant and more morose as the reality of the situation became more obvious. The statement formed only part of the speech and specifically related to the future overseas policy of the United States. Primarily it was an exhortation of confidence in the people, the strength that they would draw from the roots of their pioneering origins and their ability to confront and surmount the insurmountable.

The nation was to be defended by a trident of weapon systems, missiles fired from submerged nuclear submarines, upgraded B52 bombers of the Strategic Air Command and Inter Continental, land based, Ballistic missiles, fired either from hardened subterranean silos or on movable railway platforms but every device would be constantly upgraded and their power amplified. Such was the awesome magnitude and volume of the available weaponry that a Soviet First Strike against the Continental United States was both inconceivable and mad because an American counter strike by its sheer volume and destructive power would utterly destroy their enemy.

A new generation of weapons were currently under development and looking further ahead their replacements were being considered and 'on the drawing board', but above all there would never be, under the watch of this President or his successors, a thermonuclear Pearl Harbour.

Wilson understood that this was both a statement of fact and a call to strengthen the resolve of the nation but what disturbed him was the second part and the absence of any reference to the 'Atlantic Alliance ' or 'Special relationship.

America was also to be defended by an outer layer of military bases on the Pacific Rim in Japan and Taiwan and in the Southern Pacific by Australia; in the Eastern Atlantic by facilities in Norway, Southern Ireland, Britain [had the adjective Great been accidentally omitted? - author's comment] and Spain, indeed great emphasis was placed on the involvement of Spain, ignoring the fact that the nation was ruled by a Fascist government whose leader, Franco, had usurped power from the legitimately elected Socialist government just over a quarter of a century before and that great importance was placed on their pivotal role both in the Eastern Atlantic and as the 'cork' that controlled entry and exit to the Mediterranean, ignoring the existence and strategic location of Gibraltar.

The United Kingdom had been reduced to the status of an insignificant colony.

As a matter of national pride, as evidence that the 'deal' he personally negotiated with Humphrey and Bruce meant something more than a military agreement, and finally so that the British people, as he had promised, could learn of the great arrangement that had been negotiated, it was desperately essential that the President publicly refers to the Special relationship.

All attempts to contact the United States ambassador proved fruitless and Wilson was impotent and unable to resolve the problem until the earliest Monday, though by late Saturday afternoon the three men had drafted a confidential letter to Bruce, which if necessary could be reviewed on the Sunday before being passed to the ambassador the following day.

Tyndall was the subject of an almost cruel, incessant and vindictive indoctrination which continued after a brief hiatus when sandwiches, coffee and soft drinks - but not alcohol-were consumed in the conference room and even during this respite his tutor constantly, *ad nauseum*, reminded him that it was imperative to learn his cribs, because constant reference to them during the meeting would indicate to the journalists present that his presentation had been carefully choreographed and that his answers were all pre prepared.

He would be chauffeured in the Jaguar direct from the club to the hotel in the morning, leaving no later than eight- fifteen and would arrive in the Strand at nine–thirty, giving him an hour and a half to prepare himself and to take into account any unforeseen delays. Either, with an attention to detail or vanity, Wagstaffe arranged for a barber to attend Tyndall at exactly seven a.m. to shave him, before permitting him to have a leisurely breakfast and to compose himself. He would, no doubt, suffer 'first night' nerves but his mentor was confident of his ability to shield Tyndall in the event of a major *faux-pas* though he was expected to show well.

In the skies above the North Sea, United States reconnaissance planes again completed, with relentless, dogged persistence, another fruitless and futile sortie in the hunt for their unsuspecting and elusive prey. On return to their bases they were informed that the search had been called off but not, for security reasons, advised that the two vessels had been located and identified in a Baltic sea port some six hours before, following analysis and interpretation of film taken by a U 2 'spy-plane'.

SIXTY

The Jaguar sped towards London along the old A3 road, protected by two paramilitary security vehicles, identified by their unique registration plates, one ahead and the other behind the Jaguar, and four motorcycle outriders dressed in their distinctive all black uniforms.

The rear side windows of the Jaguar were tinted allowing the sole passenger to look out but not for prying eyes to look in, though they could observe a burly security officer in the front passenger seat. The journey was uneventful and quick since the level of private vehicle traffic had been dramatically cut because of a deliberate, intentional shortage of fuel which was not planned to be increased in the foreseeable future, if ever.

That Monday, February fifteenth, John Tyndall was concluding an extended weekend vacation at his estate outside of Winchester, before returning to his duties based in a large suite of offices which completely occupied one floor of an exclusive Knightsbridge hotel and which included his private, personal accommodation, discreetly separated from his obsequious but highly efficient staff though he also had access to other residential accommodation, if he so desired.

February fifteenth marked an important landmark in his career and the implementation of his most brilliant idea, well actually it had been the brainwave of one of his staff, but since he had proposed the key concept in council and the cunning, devious reasoning behind the action, which had been unanimously agreed amidst sounds of great raucous laughter, he professed that it had been the result of much intellectual thought.

With effect from Monday, February fifteenth, Sterling as an internal, domestic currency would cease to have any legal validity, indeed it would be an offence, punishable by imprisonment to be in possession of any Sterling currency, notes or coins. All the previous week, and even yesterday, Sunday the fourteenth, every Post Office was the sole location for the conversion of currency to the British Dollar, which was not convertible, that is it could not be exchanged in the United Kingdom by British residents for the United States Dollar or any other currency, indeed this regulated the control of the money supply since, by decree, it was already a capital offence to be in possession of any foreign currency.

With great finesse, as an inducement to the British people to give up their heritage, the shops were suddenly full of various foodstuffs and clothing, which had previously inexorably disappeared over the last five years and could only be purchased with the new currency.

Once the stocks had been exhausted the economic policy of deliberate shortages would not only return but become the norm with the intention of grinding down the population using food shortages combined with unsatisfactory educational facilities and inadequate medical services.

So much had changed since that Sunday six years ago and he could never have believed that on this Monday, February fifteenth nineteen seventy-one, he would have reached the pinnacle of power, literally over the dead bodies of the last British Cabinet and many others, dispatched by the legitimate process of Martial Law, which the final

British Prime Minister, Wilson, had reluctantly brought in, at the beginning of what he had been advised were clear and unequivocal signs that the nation was being sucked into the outbreak of the Third World War.

He personally traced the 'End of Democracy' to that pivotal Sunday morning, February seventh nineteen sixty–five.

That day had begun badly for him, when on arrival at the hotel, he had been confronted by his deputy who, without tact or discretion, and in a tone and volume that could be heard everywhere, complained that he had not been given instructions to secure the donations collected on the previous Friday, even to the exact penny, vociferously confirming the total sum. It was unfortunately Tyndall's own mistake as he had forgotten to telephone either late on the Friday evening or on the Saturday, however his deputy's outburst, though justified, confirmed his recent opinion that the man, for various reasons-but specifically his criminal conviction and his intransigent, vociferous, and uncontrollable ultra right wing views - was now a liability, perhaps as were 'the few' who had stood by his side from the beginning, but now he should concern himself with the future, *HIS* future.

He still vividly remembered the news conference (well actually, his most latest biased, even corrupted memory), how he was confronted by sixty or so journalists, some of whom were clearly baying for his blood and who would be satisfied to savage both him and his plans. Strategically placed, recording his every move, were television cameras from both the B.B.C. and Independent Television News. Suddenly, just as he began his opening statement, his mouth and tongue became dry and he had to sip a glass of water which strangely not only lubricated him but gave him the strength to speak. He opened the statement by confirming that donations to the three bereaved families of the innocent demonstrators would be made immediately together with the same sum of three thousand pounds to the Jewish community with the request that they allocate the payment to an appropriate holocaust fund.

He paced himself by introducing a brief hiatus, which allowed the journalists to absorb his unexpected benevolence, but then he took the 'bull by the horns' announcing, with compelling solemnity, details of his conviction, imprisonment and above all his genuine contrition. With apparent great humility, he took the opportunity to confirm that these events had changed him irrevocably and that his political philosophy was now firmly guided by the principles of democracy and patriotism, but not nationalism.

He ended his brief – and well rehearsed – address with confirmation that he intended next Sunday, February fourteenth, to hold three rallies in London, Birmingham and Manchester where he proposed to amplify and confirm further details of his political policies as it was his intention to stand in the forthcoming general election and he hoped to find like-minded people to stand in as many constituencies as possible on his platform of 'my country, not self'.

Correctly sensing that his audience were in the 'palm of his hand' - other than the more cynical and politically left-wing journalists - his final remark was to confirm that if future donations were adequate he would match the original payments that he had promised at the commencement of his address.

There was, as he was informed later, a most unusual silence that permeated the room and allowed him to focus on the reactions of the assembled journalists and television crews.

Later, much later, when he had become an accomplished orator or a demagogue, depending on one`s interpretation of the contradictions between his promises and newly embraced philosophy and the reality of his use of power, he boasted of his effective performance at the news conference but the real truth which, in confidence, he admitted at the time, was that the questions and his answers, were received and dealt with in an euphoric rush of excitement as if he had been drugged and the only definite memory were the words of congratulations from his mentor when the event had ended. He had survived the ordeal but more importantly, in the words of his mentor, coach and the chairman of the conference...

"He had not detected any gaffes or had to rescue him from any *faux-pas*."

The litmus test of his performance was its reception by the press, radio and television that evening and the following day. Sunday evening`s B B C radio news broadcast at six p.m. on the Home Service confirmed that the Metropolitan Police Commissioner, Joseph Simpson, had been summonsed to meet the Home Secretary, Harold Lever, to discuss the ramifications of the death of three demonstrators and that there was a still unconfirmed report that the P.M. had demanded, in the most categorical terms, an explanation from George Woodcock, but this would further complicate any delicate negotiations regarding the ongoing industrial dispute. Indeed, in a subsequent article, the B B C`s industrial correspondent hinted that the government was becoming increasingly worried that the economy could survive the ongoing industrial dispute.

But the very best stimulus for Tyndall was a brief reference to the news conference and at the end of the report mention of the donations to the three families and the Jewish community.

The following morning he woke late, no doubt the delayed reaction to the concentrated labours of Saturday and the hormone charged experience of Sunday morning. He washed and dressed but did not eat as his sole concern was to read and digest the morning's papers and to ponder their reports. He was genuinely surprised that his local newsagent stocked the *Daily Worker* and even more surprised when the man, who spoke with a definite Liverpudlian accent addressed him as Mr. Tyndall, especially as his visits to the shop could be counted on one hand and there was no reason for him to know his identity.

As was to be expected the report and comments in the *Daily Worker* were both unfavourable and uncomplimentary. The columns of Peter Zinkin and George Sinfield reflected the high standards of their journalism but their comments inevitably reflected the political orientation of the authors and more importantly, their readers. He even was mentioned in their front page editorial column, as expected most unflatteringly, but perhaps it was true...

'A man with a dangerous past and reputation who should not be trusted by his followers and the electorate if he stood at the forthcoming general election.'

The Guardian, certainly left of centre and most incisive both in the quality of their reporting and analysis actually congratulated him on his honesty and the sincerity of his intention to make amends to the Jewish community and generosity to the bereaved families but warned that his motives, combined with his record, should be carefully weighed before he was given their readers' support.

His photograph appeared on the front of the down market, but highly influential *Sun*, but more important was the attached caption. It was worth its weight in gold and could not have been secured by the most effective record plugger in the music business...

'This politician has the guts to tell the truth, even if it is to his disadvantage, and is prepared to spend his [sic] money on those who deserve financial assistance.'

The editorial, on page two, expressed his own ideas in a similar down to earth style...

'If John Tyndall can expand on his policies and raise constructive ideas to resolve the ongoing and crippling industrial dispute he will not only have this paper's gratitude and support but our endorsement of his, and his supporters, at the overdue forthcoming General Election.'

The Times and Daily Telegraph were, as to be expected, more objective, less emotional and more thoughtful in their analysis. Whilst they both congratulated him on his philanthropic donation to the Jewish community and his magnificent gesture to the three families, they believed that he should and would have to further prove his rehabilitation.

The Daily Mirror was cautious and even, and it was an honour, afforded him a Franklin cartoon on page seven showing him looking both ways whilst shrouded in a mist. A caption succinctly enquired...

"What are his real intentions?"

The observant reader would, and should, notice that he was standing in front of a flag incorporating a Swastika.

Both the Daily Mail and Express stated, but did not dwell on or emphasise his confession and contrition, concentrating on both his benevolence and forthcoming 'barnstorming 'rallies on the following Sunday, the Express even included a special report from their motoring correspondent who took it upon himself to calculate the best route to be followed but concluded that the speed limit would have to be broken.

Early that afternoon, to clear his head, he went for a long stroll and to collect a copy of the Evening News, a fruitful decision, but he missed two telephone calls of ascending importance. The first, from the Major, to congratulate him and to suggest a meeting to review future progress, and the second, from the editor of a national newspaper, which would be a most spectacular fillip, and was undoubtedly instigated by the owner who had handed his business card to Tyndall on the Saturday morning.

The Evening News banner headline read ...

HAROLD, WATCH OUT!

The ensuing article warned the Prime Minister that he had to resolve the industrial dispute without delay and that if he did not settle the matter then there was a new, young politician waiting for his chance who might be able to represent the nation and give it the leadership that it craved.

As he walked home the first threads and ideas for his speech were beginning to form and grow in his thoughts. Mere slogans would be inadequate and would immediately be exposed under scrutiny whilst at the other end of the spectrum, in depth details of his programme would permit his detractors, and there were many, the opportunity to dismember and discredit his plans. He had to strike a balance that was not too shallow in depth and did not have the paucity of information that would render him open to the accusation of having no coherent or viable programme.

Early that afternoon a sullen Harold Wilson was instantly transformed by a single telephone call from the office of David Bruce which confirmed receipt of his urgent transmission that morning, but more importantly asked for a meeting to discuss certain developments that had occurred in the last twelve hours and it was arranged that the two men meet, the following evening, in the privacy of the Embassy.

For Bill Martin, that afternoon saw him leave, with a National Union of Mineworkers' solicitor, West End Central Police Station, on bail, to return on Tuesday April twentieth, after the Easter weekend. It was to the credit of the solicitor that yet again, painstakingly, he explained to Martin that potentially he could face charges of organising an unauthorised march and assembly, riot and affray but above all the more serious charge of incitement to murder. He was presently free but he could not accept that such a combination of outrageous charges could be fabricated against him, indeed it was now indisputable and persuasive evidence to him that the authorities, or in his own words...

"The Establishment Down South",

were deliberately conniving against him and that the ever increasingly effective strike which he intended, 'by hook or by crook', to make both official and general, was succeeding in its purpose.

SIXTY-ONE

John Tyndall was confronted both by his own inadequacies and the magnitude of the task before him. He could find no inspiration or articulate any concrete ideas on which to base a statement of his political policies that would be either meaningful or withstand intense scrutiny. They were just ethereal concepts locked in his mind and he needed, desperately, to unlock them and to convert them into a persuasive argument that would catch the imagination of his audiences and then, even more importantly, the general public, whose votes would propel him first to Westminster and then...

But he was capable of creating his own good fortune or luck, call it what you may, and he took the initiative to telephone his mentor and coach of the previous weekend for his advice and assistance. The telephone rang interminably but as he was about to end the call and admit defeat he recognised the voice which answered.

The response to his request for someone...

"To tidy up his notes and preliminary draft and perhaps assist him structure his speech, with hopefully, some inspiration",

...was received with a positive reply and later that day he received confirmation that on...

"Wednesday, two experienced television and film scriptwriters would arrive and (verbatim), rescue him."

Perhaps the following day, Tuesday, represented the nadir of his career as an orator, since he failed miserably to convert his thoughts and concepts into a clear or lucid oral argument that even the most gullible, no!, he must never, ever, express his disdain for the electorate as an admittance of his arrogance and true nature which would certainly repel his potential supporters.

It was late on Tuesday afternoon, as depression began to sap his will and the commitment to put 'pen to paper', that he received a telephone call that was to propel him to the forefront of national politics and gave him the impetus not only to write but to create some, actually a few, ideas that would inspire his three audiences.

It was the editor of the 'down market' tabloid, but highly influential *Sun* newspaper whose circulation and resonance with its large readership could guarantee massive support if...

The offer was as powerful as a blacksmith's hammer blow.

"At the request of the owner of this newspaper and with my wholehearted agreement we would not only like to support your platform but give you tangible help in the next few days either in the form of the free use of a private aircraft seating up to seven passengers or possibly even a helicopter seating three passengers but in exchange and I am being absolutely up front and open, we would insist, in return, for exclusive access to you, behind the scenes, before and during your journey and to the following Monday."

He couldn't even remember immediately saying yes to the offer, only writing down two important names and telephone numbers of those people who would organise his itinerary from Saturday lunchtime onwards until he returned home on the Sunday or Monday.

Earls Court, as a venue for the London gathering was discounted because of its pre-war associations, and unusually for this type of event and time of year three football grounds had been hired, Craven Cottage, in West London, Molineux, the home of Wolverhampton Wanderers, in the Midlands, and finally, Maine Road, the base of Manchester City, each one enticed both by the uniqueness of the event and the generous fee (Tyndall's number two and his ever increasing army of supporters were able to scrape together the costs and gambled that donations would cover the balance and Tyndall's promise to make further charitable donations).

Invigorated, Tyndall suddenly found the inspiration that had temporarily deserted him and that symbolic key to unlock and release those thoughts and ideas that he had conceived and glimpsed and was now able to quantify and he made ready, for the following day, a list of his key ideas but also drafts of part of his speech incorporating those ideas.

Downing Street and the many government buildings in the area are honeycombed by passages and interconnecting doors, together with subterranean tunnels, one of which is underneath Whitehall, some containing telephone cables which help facilitate at least two secret telephone exchanges including the ultra secret "Federal" exchange which would be available to the government in the event of a national emergency.

Much of the work and facilities date back to frenetic building during the Second World War and in Marsham Street, Victoria, for example there is a 'siege suite' and nationwide, in the event of war and prior widespread public unrest there are the 'Regional Seats of Government'. Furthermore to maintain the infrastructure, authority and above all power of government -especially in the event of war- are...

THE PUBLISHER REGRETS TO CONFIRM THAT THREE SENTENCES COMPRISING APPROXIMATELY SIXTY-SEVEN WORDS AND THREE HUNDRED AND TWENTY-SEVEN LETTERS AND DIGITS HAVE BEEN EXPUNGED FOR LEGAL REASONS AND TO PROTECT THE AUTHOR.

...the urgent evacuation of the Royal Family and the Cabinet.

Thus the Prime Minister was, and is able to leave, and return, to Ten Downing Street unobserved.

He was ushered into the embassy after dark on the Tuesday around five fifty p.m. and found himself alone with the ambassador in his private apartment. Throughout the informal meeting, David Bruce was clearly intent in demonstrating his personal feelings for the United Kingdom-putting those above his opinion of Harold Wilson and his analysis of Humphrey's 'appreciation' of the 'Special relationship' - but unfortunately these matters were subject to the President's whim and *HIS* final veto and decision.

In accordance with the joint agreement that had recently been signed, within the next few hours details would be supplied to the British government confirming the location of the two Soviet vessels, now berthed somewhere in the Baltic, that had fired the nuclear armed missiles and more importantly, details of planning, which was at an advanced stage, to launch a joint non nuclear strike to take out both vessels as a warning both to the Soviet Union and the Warsaw Pact that Britain and her ally, the United States would not tolerate an attack on sovereign British territory .

The United States would seek the approval of their ally who they wished to lead the assault with fighter bombers in a joint demonstration of force and political resolve.

"The reason why this meeting is being held in my private apartment is primarily because I am certain that these rooms aren`t bugged and that, for once, I could speak openly and candidly, unfettered by diplomatic protocol. The fundamental problem, which currently is insurmountable, is the President, who has blamed the previous Conservative government for the intelligence debacle which led to the humiliating defeat and tragic suffering of United States forces on the European mainland and the expansion of Communist influence and control of many of our N A T O allies and the subsequent loss of valuable trading areas.

The immediate political consequence was that L.B.J. could have lost the November Presidential election but above all it was your ill advised, almost insane and disastrous decision to withdraw the 'V' bomber force leaving the British Isles virtually defenceless and exposing American forces, on land, at sea and in the air. Johnson has refused to deal with you face to face, which was why he delegated negotiations to his Vice-President and you must now accept that the Polaris agreement is dead and buried. As a friend of Britain, my only suggestion is to wait patiently until Johnson`s successor is inaugurated and brings in fresh, new ideas by which time the second generation Poseidon system, which was announced last month, would be launched and perhaps, maybe, then the tested Polaris system might be offered to you. The B52s are only being supplied to increase the cordon that surrounds and contains the menace of Communism."

Now Harold could understand what difficulties he and Hubert (Humphrey) had had with part of the delayed 'State of the Union' message which was due to be delivered the next day, Wednesday.

"Humphrey intends to suggest that Lyndon includes an illusion to the 'Special relationship' including a reference which emphasises the President`s commitment to...

'Our special friend and ally, Great Britain',

but there is no guarantee, indeed I have just read a further extract of the complete draft speech which emphasises the President`s commitment to freedom ...

'We will pay any price to make certain that freedom shall not perish from this earth', however, and I must say this rather cynically, he might make this statement solely in relation to the Continental United States and for the consumption of the nation."

Harold now realised why the subject of the Polaris system had been deliberately marginalised and avoided at their previous meeting and that, in reality, the British government would be little more than a cipher when it came to the matter of a joint military policy.

But he would have the B52 bombers, T.S.R.2 and American supplied nuclear and thermonuclear weapons provided that the British had the keys. Attlee's secret post war decision to develop the atomic bomb was absolutely correct and succeeding P.Ms. right to expand research and development of an independent thermonuclear device. In his eyes Britain was still a major military force.

They were worth their weight in gold. What had seemed to him insurmountable obstacles were for the two young scriptwriters mere irrelevancies that could be by- passed or easily surmounted. From the outset there was agreement that the speech-which would be recycled at the second and third venues, with slight local adaptations - had to be brief, no longer than fifteen minutes or so and would, of course, include his various themes together with, if possible, memorable phrases which the audiences would specially associate with him and the New Order. Their suggestion, to return on the Friday, would give him the opportunity, on the Thursday, to learn and rehearse the speech which they could fine tune and check, and very importantly, that he was delivering the speech with apparent sincerity, confidence, but above all conviction, was readily accepted.

Time flew by as the two scriptwriters raised new ideas, especially phrases that expressed his philosophy and plans in a manner that would connect and resonate with his audiences, as their fingertips deftly danced across and around the typewriter key boards. Slowly, he could see emerging, coalescing, *HIS* speech that had been locked away in the depths of his mind and had been released and formed by him. He looked forward to the challenge that confronted him.

It was during that same day he made a profound decision to embark on a journey of duty and discovery, not unlike Siegfried or Parsifal, a symbolic affirmation and dedication of his true motives but he was astute enough not to compromise his newly acquired position, for behind the public image that was being crafted was the private face and his intentions were dark and malevolent.

He would send a messenger, an emissary, one of *HIS* original supporters who had been in Earls Court some thirty years before and could actually, and honestly boast, that he had stood beside *THE* leader when the people were calling out both for leadership and direction.

SIXTY-TWO

For the Prime Minister, Harold Wilson, the renegade union official Bill Martin and the aspiring politician, John Tyndall, the pace of events both accelerated and encroached upon the plans and actions of the other two, their destinies becoming more and more entwined and interlinked.

Manny Gold was a silent witness, observing events unfurl from the sidelines, unaware that ultimately both he and Tyndall, first by circumstances and finally by cunning and deceit would profit from the others' failure to achieve their goals.

Harold Wilson placed too much emphasis on the content of the President's much delayed 'State of the Union' message and his concern and hope that Johnson would specifically refer to the - if indeed it ever had any real meaning in the White House or on Capitol Hill and the Pentagon - so called 'Special relationship', but Wilson was clutching at a straw that he could garner public confidence and support with a favourable quotation and reference from the speech.

Because of the time difference and the fact that the speech was being made late on the Wednesday, he did not expect the text to be made available until the Thursday morning and on arrival, at his desk, on that day, was a summary of the speech that had been routinely sent 'in clear' by telex from the embassy in Washington and in response to a subsequent enquiry the embassy confirmed that no special reference had been made, however within the hour his deflated spirits were raised as he received a top secret message. *HIS* political authority had been requested in accordance with the new secret agreement.

The phraseology permitted him, for the first time in a long while, to manifest his own self importance and influence and to approve a joint Anglo-American attack on the two vessels, now lying off of the island of Rugen, clearly visible from the resort of Thiessow, that had been the launch pads of the two devastating nuclear strikes.

His inflated ego was already calculating the political capital that would accumulate and the nature of the broadcast that would precede the dramatic announcement.

A stark and candid assessment of British capabilities, suppressed from their allies, was a scathing and sombre analysis of the R.A.F. compiled by the 'Pentagon' as an adjunct to their plans. In essence the report concluded that the R.A.F. did not possess a fighter-bomber suitable for the type of operation then in preparation though reference was made, in glowing tones, to the T.S.R.2 and how it favourably compared to the TFX (a revolutionary, but untested 'swing wing' fighter–bomber). The observation was of interest to some in the White House or to those who had the ear of President Johnson.

The intended political and military message to the members of the Warsaw Pact and the Soviet Union was that no assault on either ally would be permitted to go unanswered and that by the use of non nuclear weapons they wished to demonstrate that they did not want to embark on the slippery and potentially fatal pathway which might lead first to the use of nuclear weapons and then to the catastrophic escalation of all out thermonuclear war.

Perhaps also it was a moral admission of guilt that the Americans had used the nuclear weapon of destruction in response to the unprovoked and deadly attack by the Warsaw Pact on Western Europe, or fear that their enemy might themselves use the nuclear weapon (remembering the dramatic and potentially dangerous attempt by the Soviet Union to attack the coast of the United States which had been thwarted by their brave pilots and their fighters) though its earlier use appeared to have stemmed further military action until the unexpected, unprovoked and unwarranted attacks on the United Kingdom. Both sides might now be more temperate in the confrontation between the two ideologies and spheres of influence.

The attack was designed as a surgical strike of great precision, intended to cause as little collateral damage as possible, indeed the high altitude pictures showed no other vessels in the area as they lay 'at anchor' in the open bay – known locally, geographically as Wieken.

The British could utilise the few Vulcan bombers now based in the U.K. but they were unsuitable for the mission and were probably now vulnerable to the local air defence comprised of the latest generation M.I.G 21s, Sukhoi 9Us (historical N A T O designation 'Maiden') believed to be now fitted with four AA-I, Alkali air to air missiles or possibly the Tupolev TU 28P'Fiddler' armed with a mix of infra-red homing and radar homing 'Ash'air to air guided missiles. The British front line fighter, the English Electric Lightning, which was produced to a high specification (it could climb to thirty eight thousand feet in under two and a half minutes and reach just under sixty thousand feet) was designed to defend the British Isles against incoming bombers and was just not suitable for the role of a fighter -bomber which meant that the United States would have to mount the mission and the British would, in reality, take a back seat and peripheral role.

Without hesitation or consultation with any of his many civilian or military advisors, Wilson gave his imprimatur to the mission and begun to plan his dramatic announcement, whilst leaving the R.A.F. to offer their cooperation and limited support.

The mission was scheduled to take place on the Sunday, permitting a U2 'spy plane' to make a final reconnaissance flight on the Saturday afternoon and for the intelligence services to confirm their targets. The attack would be overseen by a Douglas R.B. 66 electronic surveillance aircraft and R.A.F. reconnaissance planes (not actually ideal for the mission), thereby cementing the joint action. The U2 report indicated that the vessels remained apparently idle in the open bay basking in the false confidence of their undetected location.

Thirty one U.S. McDonnell Douglas Phantom F4C fighter- bombers already armed with a combination of air to sea and air to air missiles were dispatched to their N A T O ally, Norway, and based in aerodromes on the Southern tip awaiting flight orders. Their flight paths would violate neutral Swedish air space, both to reduce flight times and to confuse their enemy's radar, and the consequent diplomatic complaints would have to be resolved, weighed against the emphatic message of the strike and destruction of the two vessels.

It will serve no purpose to compare, or even contrast, the personalities of the two political adversaries, Bill Martin and John Hutchyns Tyndall, since ultimately they should be judged less by their rhetoric, statements and exhortations and more by their deeds. The paradox is that despite his final denigration, Martin truly believed in his actions that were intended primarily to raise the quality of life for his fellow members and supporters whilst Tyndall, cynical, malevolent and manipulative only espoused policies that would help him secure power and influence, based on a credible platform of rational democratic values and policies but crucially finely tuned to the opinions and aspirations of his audience.

When later his actions exposed his true intentions and flagrant contempt for the spirit of democracy, many of his supporters justified and supported his actions on the rational and spurious grounds that they were only temporary measures and would be revoked once the crises had been overcome and because they were not of his making, indeed he had warned the nation of the impending storm. Neither men were accomplished orators with the skills of Adolf Hitler or Winston Churchill, but both men, Tyndall more so, were convincingly sincere.

It was public knowledge that Martin had been bailed and to various degrees the press, still restricted by the ongoing shortage of raw paper, conjectured about the potential nature of the possible alleged offences that he might have personally committed, or more likely incited, and the charges that could follow. This treacherous and pernicious atmosphere did not constrain him on his return to Yorkshire and the many coal pits in the area which were the bedrock of his support.

None of those who were in the vanguard of the bitter, violent confrontations that very soon followed are alive, and whilst press coverage ranged from crystal clear, concise objectivity to biased patriotic support for the coal miners' opponents, the National government (led deviously by Wilson, a coalition riven between responsibility and duty, tribal political loyalties and finally short term political expediency) was exposed as incapable of resolving the underlying industrial problems of the nation.

Clearly Martin intended, if possible and as soon as possible, to make the strike both official and nationwide which would require the support of the T U C and more importantly the work force, colloquially 'at the coal face', both literally and symbolically.

The labour movement and the leadership of the unions were split, more in favour of rapprochement with the government than those who wanted a final showdown, though initially it was the violent tactics of the extremists that prevailed until moderate union counter action and the support of Tyndall's...

...and the response of the Warsaw Pact and the Soviet Union which precipitated the creation of what is now called, originally with great affection but soon with regret and fear, the New Order.

John Tyndall had spent the Thursday intensely learning his speech and honing its contents though he had remained faithful to the vast majority of its contents which *HE* had conceived and which the two scriptwriters had, like a mason's apprentices chiselled the finishing touches to their master's creation. On the Friday, as promised, the two men returned and dutifully listened and approved his oration then made one or two minor improvements - presumably to inflate their egos and contribution - before finally reminding him to deliver the speech with conviction but above all without haste.

They would be used again, and again.

"Shut down the mines, close the factories, strangle and throttle the businesses and offices that organise the nation's commerce and administration. Flying pickets were to be the spearhead against the government - the symbol of injustice and intolerance; undermine the police and the army, let them desert their ranks and support their blood brothers, and from the ashes create a new, fairer, equitable society."

Monday, February fifteenth would see the militant miners begin their crusade.

SIXTY-THREE

His humble, battered suitcase, devoid of any ostentatious labels identifying earlier journeys to exotic locations, contained the majority, if not the sum of his clothing and footwear, totally unnecessary for one night's stay in one of Manchester's leading 'five star' country hotels but John Tyndall was preparing himself for most eventualities.

The national newspaper had been exceedingly generous with its financial support, not solely for him, but to the movement and he was to travel, by train, of course first class, accompanied by his deputy and at least two journalists from the paper together with a photographer.

His chosen supporters (they were soon to usurp and replace 'the few') had been taken by coach to Manchester and Birmingham earlier that morning, supplied with more than adequate funds to cover their accommodation and expenses, and the fifty or so workers would begin preparing the venues once the football matches had ended. 'The few' would remain in London and supervise (and be supervised) preparations at Craven Cottage. The organisers, the new elite chosen members of the movement and the two representatives supplied by the newspaper's editor had made special arrangements for a large number of attractive young ladies (and some especially chosen for their voluptuousness) to be available at each venue to collect donations and presumably to be photographed by, and for, the paper with the intention to increase circulation.

This was a new type of politics and mass communication.

When the doorbell rang, Tyndall not unexpectedly thought it was the driver to collect him and his battered suitcase but it was his emissary, bristling with excitement and news. He was one of the 'few', now 'foot soldiers' that soon, but not too soon, would find themselves on the rubbish heap of the expendables. John Hutchyns Tyndall was preparing to sever all his connections with the past and even he did not know that there were no ends that he would go to hide his future intentions and previous history.

"He had met Oswald Mosley", and...

"Our leader actually remembered me and how we had stood side by side."

A meeting in Central London was not suitable at this time for either man...

"He had reason to believe that both M.I.5 and the 'Special Branch' were both watching and 'tailing' him for reasons best known to themselves and that whilst he had been avidly following the sudden emerging career of John Tyndall, he thought it unwise that they meet in public lest it be exposed by the national newspapers, prompted by the plague infected, mentally deficient and avaricious Yid owners [sic] who still had a violent hatred for him and his policies, which he believed were now being proved correct, less than twenty years after the last war, when Adolf Hitler had fought to repel the Bolsheviks beyond the Urals and so save Europe, its culture and above all its racial purity from the virulent infection of Judeo-Slavic interbreeding.

They could however meet outside of Central London and he knew of a country house that would give them the privacy and freedom to exchange views and ideas."

Tyndall made both a mental and physical note of an innocuous, innocent and naive intermediary to whom he could pass messages for his 'friend' which would then be forwarded to an anonymous party who had a direct connection with Mosley which the authorities would not query (he was, and he had no connection with the events that are being recounted, his gardener). Messages addressed to Tyndall would follow a different route and he set up a line of communication ending with his newsagent who dutifully followed a code of absolute discretion believing that the messages had emanated from a secret girl friend that his customer wanted kept secret from publicity.

Oswald Mosley`s 'sixth sense' and observations were correct that he was being watched, but it was not M.I.5 or the 'Special Branch'. They were a group of former Jewish servicemen who, as part of the vanguard that had liberated some of the 'Death Camps', had witnessed the gruesome and macabre horrors of the Concentration Camps and had vowed that such deeds would never be allowed to reoccur.

Their surveillance was not as complete and comprehensive as a professional organisation but they had detected a clandestine meeting, in Curzon Street, Mayfair between their quarry, Colin Jordan and his wife, Francoise Dior. It was a coup in itself but they were unaware that the visit was not an act of homage and reverence but the first steps of a speculative attempt to profit from his bitter rival`s apparent rapid rise towards power and influence.

He could not remember when, or if ever, he had travelled in a first class compartment but he was concerned that his deputy might destroy all his good work and the investment in his new image which, that very day, had been satirised in one of the 'left leaning' national newspapers, caricaturing him as if he was a commercial product of Madison Avenue, New York. He was totally concerned that his deputy, not in a moment of foolishness or even stupidity, might suddenly espouse a litany of his extremist policies which he felt certain would shock the two journalists who were accompanying them. He recognised that the journalists would use a very liberal and flexible licence when reporting the events of the weekend and he was at pains to present himself – and his number two – in the most benevolent and positive of terms.

Thirty one Phantom F4Cs were scattered around the aerodromes, some in hardened hangars but the majority widely separated so that they would make more difficult targets if there was an unexpected attack, but in any case they were cleverly and meticulously camouflaged.

They were armed to fit their specific roles; some with air to sea missiles for the attack itself, most others with air to air missiles to defend themselves and their comrades whilst five other planes also had fitted the latest and most sophisticated electronic counter measures to thwart any incoming defence fighters. Two waves of planes, each fitted with disposable external fuel tanks (to extend their range), would attack their quarry from three different directions supervised by the lone Douglas R.B. 66 electronic surveillance aircraft, surrounded by three R.A.F. reconnaissance planes which sarcastically the planners had described as irrelevant appendages.

Bill Martin had also disposed of every irrelevant appendage that could interfere with his plans and he was surrounded by a hard core of likeminded, almost fanatical and ruthless miners who shared his vision and final goal.

He had been buoyed up by a most unexpected and unsolicited telephone call from one, if not his greatest hero, Arthur Horner. A *protégé* of an earlier trade union militant, Noah Ablett, following a spectacular and chequered life he had been from nineteen forty–six to nineteen fifty–nine the General Secretary of the National Union of Mineworkers and during his period of leadership had promoted and put in place the twelve points of the 1946 Miners` Charter. Martin also knew and greatly respected the integrity of the now seventy year old for in nineteen thirty one he had the strength of character to travel to Moscow and appear before, and appeal to the Comintern, successfully arguing his political case and genuinely admitting some faults for his behaviour. What Horner and Martin did not know and would never learn was that both the Comintern and Horner had been manipulated by the Jew Joel Ben Yitzhak.

The plan and the planning was simple: reliable transportation facilities (but almost like the German Blitzkrieg of May nineteen-forty) and above all men who could live 'off the land', succoured by local supporters. Opposition would be crushed by their resolve as intellectual argument and negotiations had failed because their enemy was blind to the rights of the workers.

SIXTY-FOUR

Whilst he had become the centre and focus of attention of the other guests in the hotel lounge, John Tyndall quietly spent the Saturday evening discreetly discussing his speech with the two journalists (and their photographer, who had already taken some benign and unexciting pictures) and was gratified to receive their seal of approval but he had also taken note of their constructive comments and he recorded, verbatim, their suggestions which he would incorporate in his speech and then, most importantly, further practice in the tranquillity and privacy of his room.

The two representatives appointed by the newspaper editor were extremely efficient and had organised his itinerary with the maximum of thought for his convenience but above all, the promotion of the New Order. The first meeting at Maine Road would commence at ten thirty, followed by the second at Molineux approximately two and a half hours later and the final rally at three thirty (or thereabouts) at the home of Fulham Football Club, Craven Cottage.

He slept deeply and soundly, waking refreshed even before the requested 'wake up' telephone call or the promised knock on the door by one of the journalists. He had time to enjoy and appreciate a lazy bath and to shave himself before dressing, packing his suitcase which he deliberately placed just inside the main entrance door and which would accompany him back to London.

He enjoyed a second bowl of delicious 'homemade' porridge, liberally sprinkled with brown sugar and indulged himself by immersing the contents of the bowl with double cream. He felt no embarrassment indulging in such a luxurious pleasure and certainly no guilt, for guilt was an emotion of the weak and those who had a conscience. In truth, if he felt any emotion it was when, unexpectedly, a hotel guest came to his table, apologised for the interruption and requested his autograph across a photo of him displayed in one of the day's national Sunday newspapers. Standing next to her was, presumably her son, angelic, androgynous, attractive and pure, his skin was as magnificent as porcelain. He had a penchant for small, but now was not the time or place.

Suddenly the attention of the whole room was captured by the noise of something that he, and most likely all the other guests had never, ever encountered. It was at the same time deafening, rhythmically harmonious and mesmeric. The little boy smiled at him and he reciprocated the emotion suppressing his true carnal emotions before the child rushed off towards the bay window to catch sight of the object some one hundred yards from the room, hovering above the lawn outside. A helicopter descended, a magnificent metallic bird that was to be his chariot.

The arrival of the Bell204B was both dramatic and spectacular and when repeated at the three venues created such an impression that the crowds were silenced in amazement. The helicopter's rotors wound down and tranquillity returned though a number of excited and brave guests opened the bay window, allowing the cold damp February air to rush into the room as they ran towards the object of their interest.

John Tyndall was as excited as the other guests, possibly even more so, but with a Herculean effort returned to his lightly buttered, underdone toast, liberally spread with Orange marmalade and pretended that the dramatic arrival of the helicopter was a natural part of his life style.

The helicopter could adequately cope with the seven passengers and their luggage but before their departure and the many good wishes of his fellow guests he forgot to collect his suitcase, but this item was only a symbolic metaphor as he cast aside his former life and prepared himself for an as yet unknown future, but later when he realised what had happened he resolved, on his return to London, to purchase a complete new wardrobe to enhance his new image and growing status.

He had never seen, in full, the remarkable but fatally flawed documentary, Triumph of the Will, by Leni Riefenstahl recording the nineteen thirty-four Nuremberg Rally and was unprepared for the unfair comparisons made in certain newspapers the next day when they compared his arrival at the three venues to Adolf Hitler's almost Wagnerian appearance over the city of Nuremberg but such comparisons were swamped by the reception of his audiences.

Each meeting was similarly choreographed. A simple dais was positioned outside of the centre circle in one half of the pitch over which flew the Union Jack, whilst equidistant in the other half was laid matting the purpose of which intrigued the crowds until the arrival of the helicopter which, without doubt, transfixed everyone who witnessed the dramatic arrival.

In order to keep the audiences' attention, Tyndall first asked for a period of one minute's silence to remember both the recent loss of loved ones and their duty towards the state and above all their loyalty to Her Majesty and the Royal family. The National anthem was then played, Tyndall deliberately and lustily leading the crowds.

He began his speech by apologising for the seasonal cold weather explaining, to great laughter, that no British politician could control the weather despite assurances to the contrary and that he had no intentions ever to make any promises that he could not keep or honour.

At each venue he made a reference to the performance of the host club (Manchester City had drawn away the previous day 0-0 to Rotherham in the Second Division, whilst in the First Division Wolverhampton Wanderers had lost 2-1 at Anfield against Liverpool and Fulham, to enormous cheers, had 'thumped' their North London rivals, Tottenham,4-1). Continuing the theme and now becoming more and more self confident, as was usual at football matches, he announced the attendances, 'rounding them up' and slightly exaggerating them which were incidentally 31,000, 28500 and at Craven Cottage 29750.

Financially, like the reception to his speeches, the event was a resounding success and at the end of his final speech he made a surprise statement.

With almost slavish attention to his coaches' instructions, each speech was evenly, almost leisurely paced, clearly audible and delivered with the sincerity and integrity of an honourable man.

"I thank you all for coming here this morning (altered to this afternoon for the speeches at Molineux and Craven Cottage) in such unexpectedly large numbers, braving bitter weather conditions that should have deterred many of you.

I want to repeat and remind you all of the promise that I made last Sunday at a news conference, that your donations will be promptly forwarded to the three families who were so cruelly deprived of their loved ones and also the Jewish community as proof my party's commitment and your generosity to those who suffered under the yoke of National Socialism."

An intended pause was rendered unnecessary by loud cheering and shouts of approval.

"A house divided by internal strife and jealousy can never be at peace with itself and is doomed to maintain an endless cycle of struggle and enmity. Thus, we clearly see a continuous battle between the Trade Unions and the owners and operators of trade, commerce and industry, even those organisations that are owned by the state for the benefit of all and which, even at this very moment, are being torn apart. The motto of the New Order could be 'My country, not self'. By your very presence, you have shown that Britain means more to you than your own interests."

Tyndall had not intended to stop at this point but his voice was drowned in a deluge of patriotic cheers.

"For some years, I had hoped that the cumulative efforts of successive post war governments would have banished the terrible spectre of poverty but there are still isolated pockets and lingering remnants of the tragic inter- war years. I truly believe that a unified nation, at peace with itself, with a single objective could provide for every family a standard of living and quality of life that would make us all proud.

Do you want to see your children raised in an unjust and selfish society, where the wealthy or influential eat bread made of fine flour, and the many, because they do not have the financial resources, or influence, eat bread baked with coarse flour adulterated by sawdust, or the mince meat in a traditional cottage pie that you would serve to your family, unknown to you, dishonestly corrupted by horsemeat or if the milk that you poured for your growing children or the beer that your husband enjoyed after a day of labour and toil was watered down, or the money in your pocket was debased by the scourge of inflation because some greedy members of the community demanded increased wages but were not prepared to work harder to produce more?

Look at the coins in your pocket. Have they been milled around the edges?   There are still twelve pennies to the shilling and twenty shillings to the pound but at this very moment Great Britain is being adulterated, debased and watered down by most of the unions and what I will describe as a minority of employers. My vision, the purpose of the New Order and my profound intention, is to try, and I cannot make an absolute promise, to forge a new, fairer society that we can all be proud of."

He deliberately stopped, as instructed, to gauge the audience's reaction.   At first there was an ominous silence as if they did not understand him but then a groundswell of approval and above all, of support, rose as they realised and understood the orator's new and unusual description of their nation's plight.

"If I was asked to summarise my vision in one word, that word, without hesitation, would be compassion. A society that cared and cared for the weak and those who were unable to fend for themselves. Everyone here today, myself included, resents and regrets having to pay those abominable taxes that governments impose and then sometimes squander. I cannot promise, but if I reach a position where I can influence those who gather in the vast amounts of revenue and those who dispense the income, I will do my best to impose a regime where those who spend the money act as if it were their own, that is with prudence and common sense.

I want you to be proud of Great Britain but at the same time to be realistic about our place in the world and the military and political influence that we can bring to bear on allies and foes alike. I truly believe that we are in a unique position to give wise counsel to friend and foe alike, for we were and still are the bastion of democracy and freedom because we, no you and your parents' generation, stood literally alone in June nineteen forty against a tyrant, an ideology and a terror that never in the history of civilisation had been encountered before. And you, my fellow citizens, won, by strength of character and sacrifice."

He had planned to stop and catch his breath but such was the amazing response that he had no alternative but to stop.

"A former ally has recently and cruelly displayed their true intentions and even today, brothers, sons, husbands and friends lie incarcerated and deprived of freedom. Ask yourselves what has this government done to repatriate your loved ones?

We are defended by our fleet of 'V' bombers that perhaps again may, God forbid, be called upon to attack our enemies and many millions of innocent civilians will be destroyed, that were not led, but misled, by leaders whose philosophy and motives are immoral.

Whilst we are supported by an ally who shares a common tongue and much of our history, heritage and above all common values, we have to recognise that militarily their power greatly exceeds our capabilities but we have a right to sit at the same table as the two global super powers and voice our wise counsel and to influence the well being and destiny of the world."

It was only at Craven Cottage, the final venue, that he added an unexpected additional comment:

"I had planned to end my brief speech at this point but I have only just been informed of some exciting news. I said earlier that unlike other politicians I would not make any promises that I could not honour. Well I'm going to join them! It's only a preliminary calculation, but I am reliably informed that your generous donations mean that the further donations will be swelled over and above that originally promised and will be directed to the three families and the Jewish community. Thank you."

He did not return to his dingy flat in West London, or even ever again expected to see his battered suitcase and its contents, but to a suite of rooms, in a five star Knightsbridge hotel, ultimately paid for by wealthy businessmen and leaders of industry keen to be associated with the rising star of British politics and also, surprisingly, but not so by as a substantial amount, by long sighted Trade Union leaders who recognised in which direction the wind was blowing. Perhaps the common, venal consideration amongst his new benefactors was that ultimately their largesse would be reciprocated and that he would willingly succumb to their demands.

He would infrequently, then rarely return to his old home, the only reason, which he would shroud in secrecy and subterfuge was to furtively receive, and deliver, messages to and from Oswald Mosley until, though he did not then know the circumstances, his accession to power and after a period of 'consolidation', the ruthless use of totalitarian authority.

SIXTY-FIVE

Independently, the two men had come to the same inevitable, logical analysis and decision. It was pure chance, or fate, that their hastily organised flights arrived at the same military airbase outside of Moscow and within minutes of each other, and conveniently they decided to share both the same Zil limousine and their deepest, most guarded thoughts. They were also able to compare their preliminary reports of the attack on the island of Rugen, that their staff had hurriedly prepared, following the not unexpected summons from the Defence Council which answered only to the Politburo and the First Secretary, Leonid Brezhnev.

They also allowed themselves to reminisce and conjecture. Nearly twenty-five years before, a similar summons from a previous First Secretary, Stalin, would undoubtedly have resulted in their immediate execution, but they were now living in more enlightened and, dare they say the word, democratic times. At least this Council would eagerly give them the chance to review both the event and their observations, for they were A.A. Grechko, Commander in Chief of the Joint Warsaw Pact Armed Forces and Marshall of the Soviet Union and I.I. Yakubovsky, Commander in Chief, Group of Soviet Forces, Germany and Army General.

The vehicle was fitted with a permanently scrambled telephone, for as yet unsubstantiated rumours that had permeated through to Moscow alleged that the new generation of American spy satellites were already or would soon be able to eavesdrop on the most confidential telephonic communications of the Soviet Union`s highest echelons.

A telex message had just been received and a special courier, escorted by a peleton and outriders of motorcyclists would meet them on arrival at the Kremlin to deliver a comprehensive report and an up to date intelligence assessment.

Moscow, on the morning of Monday, February fifteenth, was still gripped by the vicious Siberian winter made more unbearable by a rampant easterly wind that relentlessly pierced every exposed nook and cranny or orifice despite everyone's attempt to thwart the invisible assailant.

They passed legions of labourers, mainly old men and women, busily shovelling snow from the streets and paths unaware that the passing limousine was pleasantly warm and comfortable.

The two men decided to briefly circle Moscow and jointly read, review and analyse the report that they had just collected, for if they had entered the Kremlin, they would have been immediately rushed to a secure subterranean conference room and be expected to present their reports and then be aggressively cross examined.

The intelligence assessment supported their original joint, but independently derived analysis of the action. It was, in the candid opinion of those who had compiled the report, a measured and calculated response against the two vessels that had mounted the nuclear attacks specifically ordered by the Kremlin, despite misgivings voiced by military planners, to test the resolve of the Americans and their emasculated canine ally. It was significant and most important that they had not resorted to the use of any tactical nuclear devices but had risked so many of their latest front line fighter –bombers to hammer home their message.

Intelligence had been received late on the Friday confirming the unexpected arrival of a number of Phantom jets at the Rygge and Torp Airbases (the former some thirty seven miles from Oslo and the latter about seventy-five miles South of the same city) but their deployment and the purpose of disposition had originally remained a mystery and the subject of conjecture, especially as the Torp base was the location of a subterranean arsenal, built into the bedrock and reinforced with concrete, to store , in the event of war, nuclear weapons.

The first wave had been identified crossing neutral Swedish territory shortly after daybreak, before they made a supersonic dash towards the island of Rugen. Defence fighters were immediately called up and were airborne within three minutes and twenty–five seconds, justifying the policy of eternal vigilance, both in costs of Roubles and operational commitment, for never again would the Soviet Air Force be caught asleep as they had been on that morning of Sunday, June twenty-second, nineteen forty-one.

Grechko spoke on behalf of his fellow officer to the assembled elite of the elite, for the Defence Council was only answerable to the Politburo and was composed of the First Secretary, members of the Politburo, the Secretariat of the Central Committee, Minister of Defence, Chief of the General Staff and representatives of the Ministry of Defence. His statement was deliberately directed at the First Secretary and the members of the Politburo for they had ultimate power over the military hierarchy. Any further military investigation of the event would be conducted with, or by, his fellow officers in terms and language that their training had taught them.

"Our calculations and knowledge of our enemy's capabilities lead us to believe that the first wave was at the absolute limit of its combat range which explains why, immediately after the attacks on the Alexander Nevsky and Potemkin, which were both sunk after taking some fourteen missile hits, they turned for home, protected by a wall of electronic counter measures which temporarily affected the air to air missiles on the six M.I.G. 21s but not on the twelve Sukhoi 9Us who were able to dispatch three or possibly four of the American Phantoms, but with the loss of six of our defence fighters to the accompanying fighter escort.

It is now clear to us that the capabilities of the Phantom, as a combat weapon, combined with its electronic countermeasures must not be underestimated.

Our remaining fighters, under orders, were joined by sixteen further Sukhoi 9Us which then proceeded to chase the aggressors but were then confronted by a second wave of Phantoms, lying in wait, who attacked our fighters head on. We inflicted substantial damage against our enemy but with the loss of eight further fighters and three damaged planes to air to air missiles known in the West as 'Sparrow' and 'Sidewinder', however during their return flight to bases on the Baltic coast they unexpectedly caught an American electronic surveillance plane which was monitoring the attack, and we believe, beaming back, in real time, the pilots' battle reports which were recorded at our surveillance base on Rugen, and three obsolete British reconnaissance aircraft which were little better than fodder for our pilots and the four aeroplanes were quickly downed by our missiles.

You may also already be aware that three damaged Phantom jets have been observed at the end of the runways at Torp and Rygge having failed to successfully complete their take offs."

Marshall of the Soviet Union, A.A. Grechko, sat down and awaited both the whirlwind and the retribution of the political elite. The first question, from a Politburo member, left him more surprised than confused.

"Do you regard the loss of two vessels, planes and pilots, balanced against the losses of our enemy as a victory, a defeat or a salutary and beneficial lesson?"

His reputation had been founded on decisive, almost reckless leadership on the battlefields during the Great Patriotic War, though his respect and concern for his forces never once permitted him to waste their lives, relying on an innate sixth sense, whilst his post war rise in the military hierarchy had been based on his proven military record and his canny ability to recognise his political masters' requirements and with prescient foresight, their future demands.

He prudently considered his response before embarking on a course that would not conflict with the political objectives of the Politburo members in the room or above all, the First Secretary.

"A victory for American bravery and initiative, proof of their current technological superiority combined with their absolute ruthlessness as evidenced by their earlier devastating attack on Russia and the Ukraine. But above all it is a beneficial lesson for our cause, as I have argued, direct confrontation with the United States will be, in the future, based on tactical and unimportant minor territorial skirmishes at the edges of our spheres of influence, like tectonic plates colliding or scraping past each other and where victory, or defeat, is of little importance since the only important fact is the potential threat not of all out thermonuclear war where ultimately there will be no winner in the accepted phraseology but if our enemy could develop a weapons system, which I am assured could be decades away, which would give a first strike advantage of such magnitude that we would suffer the effective loss of a viable counter first strike system. Therefore, it is now absolutely essential and our paramount duty is to concentrate on research, development, even theft from our enemy of their expensively acquired knowledge, and constant improvement of new weapon systems.

Perhaps my thoughts and analysis will hasten the demise of my career and the premature retirement of my fellow officers but the planning of vast military actions, is now, I believe, an historical anachronism and in conclusion I would like to think that planning for the future, whether military or political, recognises the joint opinion of myself and Army General Yakubovsky."

First Secretary Leonid Brezhnev who had previously remained silent, contemplative and even morose, stood up, was clearly heard to confide to some of the other Politburo members the words...

"I heard enough, my mind is made up,"

and he left the room where the Politburo had clearly rejected the observations that had just been presented.

Grechko and Yakubovsky were in a minority of two confronted by their peers, the Minister of Defence together with representatives of the Ministry of Defence and above all the Chief of the General Staff.

SIXTY-SIX

On Tuesday, February sixteenth, two stories vied for priority in every national newspaper even including the *Daily Worker*, but their coverage reflected, if anything, both their political orientation and opinion of the two main figures at the eye of each event.

Shortly after three a.m. on the Monday, miners loyal to Bill Martin, began to assemble at various pits in Yorkshire, solely illuminated by the lights on their headgear and were addressed by Martin at Cortonwood colliery at Brampton Bierlow and by his inner core of followers at other pits including Bullcliffe Wood colliery near Ossett, Ackton Hall colliery, Featherstone and the vast Manvers complex. Speakers at the various pitheads explained that their very existence and the survival of their communities was now imminently under threat and that they could no longer rely on the support of the T U C, but only on their fellow workers who were also on strike. Like them, they had realised that only united and concerted action, in solidarity with other workers in different industries and commerce would compel the government to recognise the rights of the workers. It was therefore absolutely essential, by argument and example, to persuade miners and then other industries throughout the country that were not already on strike, to join them in solidarity and in the cause of the workers' fundamental rights.

This would not be an easy struggle or a symbolic action, for they anticipated confrontations with scabs and strike breakers, assisted and supported by the police, and they further expected that the government would deviously bring in police from other parts of the country and rotate local forces elsewhere in order to undermine any local sympathies. They had to be strong both in physical strength and spirit for the authorities, in order to break their resolve and morale, intended and would , no doubt, circulate lies not only about their behaviour and actions but relentlessly emphasise the failure of their movement, creating false reports about strikers returning to work in the coal and other industries and growing anger by what was currently a sympathetic nation who more than the politicians, realised the difficult circumstances of the miners' work but, above all, their contribution to the community.

They would have to live 'off the land', supported by sympathetic local communities whilst their families, for the next few weeks, would be helped by their meagre funds, but to put off this action because of their concerns regarding their families' welfare was only putting off the inevitable confrontation which would become steadily more difficult as the government inexorably destroyed the coal mining industry and its traditions in the name of 'Economic Modernisation'.

Martin had not confided to his inner core of supporters that secretly he had been in communication with Jack Jones who had intimated that certain anonymous 'friends', sympathetic to the cause of workers' rights, were prepared to contribute towards the cost of supporting miners' families which would supplement their welfare benefits.

Despite his almost vitriolic hatred of the 'Establishment', his genuine desire to raise the quality of life for his fellow workers and the labour movement, he recognised that the strike, if it were to succeed, had to be swift and ruthless for if it was protracted, then the government would wear down support by attrition.

At this time it could not be reasonably argued that the looming confrontation was the first stage in the 'class struggle' that Socialist intellectuals believed would precede revolution but it is most likely that Martin hoped that a dramatic escalation of pressure would cause a major change in industrial and political relations.

Miners, emboldened by the rhetoric of their leader, flooded in their thousands across Yorkshire, mainly in coaches, swamping existing collieries that were either already on strike or teetering on the brink and by argument tightened their grip on the means of production. By midday, the same coaches, perhaps fuelled by almost evangelical fervour were carrying some of the original 'flying pickets' north and north east, supplemented by additional supporters from other Yorkshire pits to Scotland and the counties of Northumberland and Durham.

On the Tuesday, one national daily newspaper, erroneously compared the previous day`s events to the embers that blazed into the Russian Revolution whilst, with infinitely superior prose, the atheist *Daily Worker*, with almost Christian zeal, compared the day`s events to the First Crusade.

At that very early stage ,the procedures to maintain the initial impetus were forgotten, for the strikers and their leaders were all flushed with the euphoria of victory and by nightfall the' bloodless liberation' of the Scottish and North East pits had begun and news was telephoned back to Yorkshire where Martin and his acolytes breathed a great sigh of relief at the exciting news, whilst one leader actually described the 'flying pickets' as their 'shock troops', who were then currently receiving the hospitality (and warmth) of local mineworkers and...unofficially the facilities of a few, supportive, local councils.

Harold Wilson had no qualms whatsoever using the military adventure for his own political advantage. Swedish radio had initially reported the incursion into their airspace and later in the morning relayed unconfirmed reports of the attack on Rugen.

In neutral Switzerland rumours surfaced of the attack which was unofficially verified by Soviet diplomats. It was only, by early evening following a U 2 reconnaissance flight, that an official statement was prematurely and erroneously released to the press and media in London; however Wilson, with an eye to the forthcoming election and his own success had an immediate embargo placed on the news, the Ministry of Defence citing, as yet, secret-but actually spurious-possible, other coordinated military actions.

In truth, Wilson would cynically portray the action as an equal, joint venture. He had hoped to broadcast a dramatic and spectacular announcement on the Sunday evening, which would have coincidentally obliterated any coverage of John Tyndall`s successful meetings and effectively severely hampered his meteoric rise, but the B.B.C. was riven by fermenting union unrest and 'wild cat' actions (engineering and manual staff demanded an increased overtime payment, over and above the agreed weekend rate, because of the late notification and possibly because of their desire to show solidarity with the national strikers) and the obsessive necessity of the channels to maintain their schedules and therefore they could not accommodate his last minute demand.

The delayed statement, and television coverage, was set for eight p.m. on the Monday evening and Wilson unethically connived with the television organisations not to announce the broadcast in a revised evening schedule so that he could convey a sense of dramatic urgency and importance and then he would permit the Press to publish brief details along with the exciting announcement that the British offensive capability was being increased by the supply of American B52 bombers, though no mention would be made of the transfer of the bulk of the 'V' bomber force to the Pacific rim.

Much of Monday was spent placating the editors of the two London evening newspapers and persuading them not to break the embargo – 'For the security of our military forces'- and preparations for the 'emergency' statement both in terms of its content as well as the style of its presentation and delivery. Wilson was both intransigent and adamant that he wanted, no demanded, to deliver the announcement as if the attack had very recently taken place, even to give the impression that the statement had been hurriedly prepared. He rejected the wise and honourable counsel of those around him, including Gerald Kaufman, yet again exposing his almost arrogant contempt for the opinions and ethics of others and his unilateral action in terms of policy decisions, though Manny Gold, not unexpectedly, brazenly supported him and his original and novel concept which would herald a new modern style of communication, finally ending the now clichéd fireside chat.

SIXTY-SEVEN

At approximately seven forty-eight p.m., television screens displaying either the B B C or I T V channels inexplicably and without warning went dead, surprising and irritating their many viewers who were watching on B B C 1, The Rare Ones, a programme about wildlife in danger, or on B B C 2, Pick the Winner (a panel game), whilst on I T V (Rediffusion, Channel 9, for Londoners), the latest episode of Coronation Street was cut short (The next episode was preceded by an *UNPRECEDENTED* -author's emphasis- announcement apologising for any disappointment and then briefly summarised the unseen scenes).

Some viewers must have turned to their radios where existing listeners were enjoying Ring Up The Curtain on the Home Service, or The Clitheroe Kid on the Light Programme and finally Man and His Environment on the Third Network or Birth of an Opera: Turandot on the Third Programme but at nearly three minutes to eight the stations also suddenly went dead.

Viewers and listeners were undoubtedly becoming concerned but at about one minute to eight the television and radio stations burst back into life.

On the two B B C television channels the reassuring sight of Robert Dougall appeared, though ominously he seemed grave in demeanour whilst on the I T V channel, unexpectedly appeared a photograph of Big Ben and after a few seconds the anonymous and unknown voice of Gordon Honeycombe, who had recently joined Independent Television News, was heard.

The four B B C radio programmes also relayed Robert Dougall's announcement.

Their brief statements were similar, but for some of the older viewers and listeners who were watching and listening to the B B C, the voice of Robert Dougall revived memories of Sunday, September third, nineteen thirty-nine for he had been the broadcaster on the old Empire Service who had announced Britain's declaration of war on Germany.

"All television and radio services are to jointly broadcast a statement by the Prime Minister, the Right Honourable Harold Wilson who will speak from the Cabinet room."

There then followed a period of almost funereal silence and on the three television channels the 'snow' of static before the P.M. appeared, sitting in the Cabinet room, his face clearly etched with stress and lack of sleep and what hair he also had was unkempt, as was his suit, which under the poor lighting mirrored his features, creased and ill fitting, as if he had been sleeping in his clothing.

"The prime duty and responsibility of Her Majesty's government is the defence of the Realm and the protection of her citizens. The National Coalition government of which I am the leader is absolutely committed to their duty on behalf of the nation and the continuity of Parliamentary democracy and I am pleased to announce that, within the next twenty-one days, the statutory procedures will be enacted to call a General Election when you will be able to decide who will govern the nation for the next five years.

Two events currently cast a dark shadow over all of us. The ongoing and pernicious unofficial industrial action, which now appears to be weakening, indeed like a storm, it seems to be wearing itself out, as workers who may have genuine grievances, return to their factories, the mines, offices or the transportation system knowing that the common sense approach of their leaders, the T U C and business leaders or the operators of the nationalised industries will try to resolve the many problems that confront them.

I am pleased to report that life is getting back to normal in those areas directly and indirectly affected by the unprovoked and heinous nuclear attacks but, I regret to state, that because of the selfish industrial action which still continues, there was both a delay and inadequate resources to begin the rescue of the injured and those who had been traumatised by the attacks. The government would like to thank the three emergency services, together with detachments from the army along with the flood of civilian volunteers who saved many lives and began the task of rebuilding the fabric of the stricken communities."

Harold Wilson stopped and appeared to be gathering his thoughts before making a dramatic and important announcement. Some viewers may have noticed that he did not raise his famous pipe and publically take a relaxing puff though many must have sensed that he was about to impart the most ominous and calamitous news.

"After much thought, consultation and deliberation, I personally sanctioned and authorised, in partnership with our friend and ally, the United States, a pre emptive non nuclear strike against a single target in the Baltic sea. Its sole purpose was not the base motive of revenge but a measured warning that we are not prepared to suffer aggression against our island or our interests. I am pleased to tell you that the two vessels responsible for the nuclear assaults, identified as the Alexander Nevsky and Potemkin have been sunk but that we lost three planes and their valiant crews, though the enemy also lost about ten of their high performance fighters.

[Readers will note that no reference was made to the losses suffered by the United States or the types of British aircraft that were lost].

I am now also able to inform you, for up to this evening our actions have been shrouded in secrecy, that our military capability has been massively increased and you will realise that for security purposes the government is not able to disclose numbers, however deliveries have been ongoing for some time from the United States of a large number of B52 bombers and their very presence will deter any foolhardy act of military adventurism or opportunism by our enemies.

The last fifteen months have been a period both of uncertainty and traumatic events. I believe that we are now entering a period of stability and above all, peace and tranquillity which is now why we intend to call a long overdue General Election. On behalf of the government I hope that our news will give you all confidence in the future and I personally thank you for sharing these last few minutes with me."

But life is not predictable and you, the reader, are aware that events took an unexpected and different course and that within three weeks Martial Law was declared and the promise of a General Election was broken, never to be honoured. Soon, by the misjudgement and foolishness of those in power, John Tyndall would begin his ascent to the heights of power though the catalysts would be Bill Martin and Leonid Brezhnev.

The television and radio services resumed, their schedules only slightly distorted by the ministerial broadcast, whilst the country reverted (for a few weeks more) back to its false sense of freedom and security.

SIXTY-EIGHT

By early evening on the Tuesday, the Scottish and Northumberland and Durham mines had been secured because, in the main, the miners had already withdrawn their labour and were in sympathy with the militant Yorkshire miners, and within a further twenty four hours the flying pickets, who had been 'bussed' overnight in two convoys had shut down the 'Kent' mines whilst in South Wales they had been welcomed, as 'comrades in arms' by the already striking miners.

All the pits in the South Wales area (over thirty) were paralysed including the ninety year old Tymawr-Lewis Merthyr colliery near Pontypridd in Mid Glamorgan which symbolised both the Welsh miners' struggle and the dilemma and economic paradox at the very heart of the confrontation between the miners and the mine's operator. It was recognised that the mine, and others, were reaching the end of their productive lives as the coal seams were becoming exhausted and were also becoming more expensive to mine, but its closure would wreak havoc amongst the close knit community and therefore the dilemma was whether the workforce should accept the economic reality or put pressure on the mine operator and the government to financially support, like the props in the mine tunnels, an ailing body.

Pitmen at the militant Betteshanger and Snowdown pits in Kent welcomed the arrival of miners from as far away as Kinneil and Polkemmet in Scotland whilst the larger convoy which had dispersed on arrival in South Wales had been filled with Yorkshire miners from the Grimethorpe and Hatfield colliery, near Doncaster, and also the Kiverton Park and Kinsley pits.

It was imperative that the remorseless momentum continue and the miners' enthusiasm be maintained for whilst the continuing news of successful shutdowns was received in Martin's makeshift 'war room' with great satisfaction, he knew that success had been achieved in those areas where support was already strong, however the pits in North Wales and especially Nottinghamshire, Derbyshire and Lancashire would, most likely, strongly reject and stand firm against his supporters.

By the Wednesday evening all the mines which were 'locked down' (though essential maintenance work and protection of the coal faces against any geological activity carried on) were also 'quarantined', thus thwarting any existing stocks of coal being transported to the power stations and disabling any contact with the railway depots.

Durham miners from the small inland pits such as Herrington and Hordern and the big coastal pits at Wearmouth and Westoe were directed, along with militant (and potentially violent) Scottish pitmen, to the Nottinghamshire, Staffordshire and Derbyshire mines and their less militant workers.

SIXTY-NINE

They were abruptly and rudely woken by the noise of muffled shouting and violent banging on the front door of their apartment and they automatically looked at each other, but of course, in the winter darkness, neither could discern the appearance of the other. He turned round, his fingers searching for the box of matches which he knew were on the table, located them and ignited the wick of the ornamental lamp which burst into flame illuminating them both. Her face displayed the fear which for months, if not years had obsessed her thoughts. The night time knock on the door.

This was the second time that he had been arrested and seared by the previous brutal experience, she had ingeniously and methodically prepared for this moment and without thinking, automatically went to the clothes rail and selected his old Patriotic War grey coat which she laid out on the bed. In the meantime he had slipped on his service trousers and loosely tucked in a shirt.

"I`m coming.  Don`t wake up the neighbours!"

He hurriedly opened the door to be confronted by two stereotype K G B thugs, a remnant of the Stalinist and Beria era and not to be taken lightly.

"Yes", he answered in response to their enquiry as to his identity. There was no point misleading them, since the consequences would be dire. Uninvited, they entered the apartment and made immediately for the bedroom acting like sniffer dogs hunting and tracking their prey even though they had located him already.

"Am I under arrest and on what charge. Where is your Arrest Warrant?"

Their response was immediate and evasive...

"Our orders are to collect and take you to our superior officer to whom you should address any questions. You have no more than five minutes both to dress and take a small suitcase. Wrap up warmly for the harsh Siberian wind is extremely bitter tonight. We see your wife has been sensible and already provided you with a winter military coat."

The reply to his next question immediately further distressed his wife and instantaneously created an ominous, gruesome and frightening perception of his imminent future.

"No, you may not be allowed any privacy to say farewell to your wife and neither may you kiss her on her lips. A kiss on her cheeks is all that we can permit."

They looked at each other for a final time and as he turned around and descended the concrete staircase his old military grey coat distorted his silhouette. For the second time in their lives he was a prisoner but they had prepared for this moment.

When he returned from Moscow, early in nineteen sixty four, and been quickly posted to an isolated and barren secret Soviet military outpost, they agreed that he should learn from the experience of his predecessors and she had carefully and meticulously removed one of the shoulder pads and sewn an additional layer of cloth and inserted a cyanide pill wrapped in a sheet of paper on which she had written, in Cyrillic and Yiddish, a language which her husband did not understand, the Twenty Third and Fifty First Psalms and of her undying love for him and to disguise her handy work the other shoulder pad was suitably tailored.

He was confused, for one of the men, with great respect, actually opened the car door for him, permitting him to slide into the rear seat, whilst his suitcase was deposited, with care and not thrown, into the boot of the car which was driven by a third man.

They passed the well lit railway terminal which was busy at, he estimated, four fifteen in the morning, and he observed heavy industrial boring parts being unloaded, for this was the railhead servicing the expanding subterranean centre of Mezhgorye in the Yamantau Gory (mountains) in the Urals. He was aware that a vast subterranean complex, for military purposes, was being constructed with labour from the Gulags but his moral objections had been dismissed in favour of his desire for self survival. The same road on which they were travelling led directly to the military aerodrome for there was no other destination.

He examined his recent behaviour and actions, searching for a reason to justify his forthcoming confrontation with the K G B. His work had been commissioned by the highest possible authority in the Soviet Union and whilst he had been given 'carte blanche', delegating as little as possible and not even permitting his nearest fellow officers access to the American and British books and publications that had been at his disposal, and especially not the 'analysis reports' that had been supplied monthly from 'Moscow', he had been absolutely discreet about his mentor`s identity and the purpose of his work.

The first draft of his plan had originally been sent to his mentor some six months before, and was continually being updated and revised though, in principle, the thrust of his recommendations remained constant.

He had also been permitted to attend a screening of the satirical anti war film, Doctor Strangelove, which he had viewed as recently as late January in the company of two senior Army Officers and a lone projectionist, however the fundamental premise had been dismissed by him and had not inclined him to alter his plan.

Life, and events, had taken a most unexpected turn since his first arrest in December nineteen sixty-two, when Military Security officers had burst into a scheduled planning meeting where he and a fellow officer were analysing his new and original potential first strike scenario against N A T O and the United States, and the two of them were arrested. They were falsely accused of organising a coup d`etat, soon after which they were handed over to an elite K G B unit who immediately begun to' soften them up 'before delivering them to Moscow. Life had become like an incomprehensible, convoluted and labyrinthine dream – or nightmare-for shortly before reaching their destination they had been diverted to a dacha, just outside of Moscow, where most unexpectedly they were confronted by the First Secretary, Nikita Khrushchev, interrogated by him, and then he was released, to continue with the embryonic plans. Suddenly he wondered about the fate of his comrade.

He had been sent as a secret emissary to Paris, because of his knowledge of English, returning to his work, culminating in the successful liberation of the occupied West European States and the expulsion of the American Colonists and their British lap dog. But life, influence, security and power are, as he was soon to discover, transient, and when Leonid Brezhnev and his supporters overthrew his mentor he was most surprised that the new First Secretary did not discard him but took him to his bosom and promoted him, albeit to the anonymous, God forsaken wilderness that was the secret complex in the Yamantau mountains.

With the procedures and accompanying paper work normally associated with the nation's legion of lowly administrators, he was delivered to a K G B officer, along with his suitcase, on the apron of the tarmac and instructed to follow the man to a waiting four engined propeller powered plane, passing a number of K G B troops and from their thinly disguised mutterings he gathered that their departure had been delayed for his arrival.

They were seated at the front of the aircraft, separated from the disgruntled troops, and, even taking into account the spartan nature of the internal fittings, in the choicest part.

"We will be met in Moscow where I am to hand you over. Please do not cause me any problems for I expect that at your reception will be at least one General and any difficulties could affect my career."

The Sun's rays which were streaming through the porthole, warming the side of his face, roused him from his interrupted deep sleep and his first thoughts were of the pangs of hunger which strangely subsided a few minutes later when he actually felt the plane descending and shortly afterwards, the undercarriage being lowered.

A macabre, black 'Zil' limousine immediately drew up on the tarmac adjacent to the taxiing aircraft and the two men were given priority to descend down the hastily positioned stairs and he was greeted, with open arms, by, as he had been earlier informed, a lavishly decorated general, and within moments he was sitting in the rear of the pleasantly warm vehicle while his former guard stood ignored and alone as the vehicle sped off.

The general appeared as excited as Kashkarov was confused, and after having identified himself seemed to be in awe both of his presence and his achievements, but more importantly he confided there was a strong rumour that his presence had, in some way, to do with possible military action in revenge ...but he stopped and surprisingly stated that...

"It is extremely unusual that an officer of your rank would receive a personal summons from the First Secretary but no doubt there are State secrets that you cannot confide in me and you must be, with great interest, anticipating receipt of your instructions. Perhaps you could confirm that the unprovoked attack on the Island of Rugen is but a prelude to war?"

They passed a sprawling complex of anonymous, featureless, high rise blocks of apartments, a legacy of the Stalinist era, but it revived memories of an earlier, simpler and happier time for they occupied the area where he had lived, immediately after his marriage. He felt inclined to test or assert his presumed status and request, no order, a detour but he could not keep the First Secretary waiting.

SEVENTY

The dacha was situated in its own private estate with, and he couldn't believe his eyes, a heated indoor swimming pool which was clearly visible, since its outer walls were formed by vast panes of glass which he discovered later, on closer inspection, were in fact perspex. He estimated that it would take no longer than twenty to thirty minutes to reach the Kremlin by car but first he had to attend to the tantalising contents of a safe that sat in front of the two men, abutting a wall opposite an open and empty fire place but the room was pleasantly warm. As an officer entered the room, four guards ceremoniously turned and marched to the room's perimeter in order that they were unable to observe the proceedings.

"This officer is my personal adjutant who is now at your disposal and available twenty–four hours a day. The guards and staff are all K G B military personnel responsible to me and with instructions to protect you and the documentation which I will personally transfer to you in a few minutes. The combination of the safe will only be known to us two and the First Secretary. The facilities of the dacha, especially the swimming pool are at your disposal and should you require anything you only have to make your demands known.

The documentation will be guarded at all times especially if you wish to take some time off to visit Moscow, however since you must be already aware, you may be summonsed by Comrade Brezhnev at any time. I envy you and the power and destiny which is in your hands."

He chose an easily memorable combination for the large floor safe, the anniversary of the Great Patriotic War (22061941), followed by his wife's maiden name, but with the letters randomly transposed and one letter added-her initial (NRLPKEIS).

It was nearly eleven-twenty, about half an hour after his arrival and immediately after the general had made his exit. He opened the safe more out of duty than curiosity, in the presence of the adjutant, but requested the four guards, for their safety, and without the stern authority of a person above his status, to turn their backs.

There were three packets deposited on two shelves and without a second thought he extracted the smallest, as the adjutant, with discretion, informed him that he would be outside and always immediately available.

A desk and its contents had been prepared and arranged in anticipation of his requirements. There was a bounteous supply of lined paper, pens, pencils, slide rules and even a number of biros, in a rainbow of colours, which he had never seen before and which he and his fellow officers had believed were the creation and propaganda of Western myth and legend.

He began his journey of discovery at about eleven- thirty five.

In front of him was a copy of the latest version of his plan but not only had it been retyped, it was triple spaced and between each line, typed in red, were its reader's comments and occasionally a further hand written remark was inserted. He read, then reread both his plan and the reader's typed and hand written comments and observations. He would need to justify, to the most powerful men in the nation, the feasibility of the plan but above all the potential statistical risk of failure. Confidence was insufficient, his plans had not been dismissed by its reader and neither had the First Secretary exposed any flaws or raised questions that he was unable to answer and most importantly, justify. However the plan was devised by a human being and a single human error could cripple the whole project. Above all the Politburo (or was it still called the Presidium?) had to demonstrate to the Americans their unwavering, ruthless resolve, for the plan had already taken into account a display of force which should cower the American people. 'Spheres of Influence' and a new 'Monroe' Doctrine were impressive political slogans but would Johnson sacrifice Los Angeles or New York for one of his potential secondary targets - Manchester or Southampton? When it was time for him to appear before the leadership he would appeal to their determination and ruthlessness.

He looked at his wrist and realised that in the commotion and upheaval he had forgotten to fully dress himself. Automatically he called out the name of the adjutant who, like a released compressed spring, sprung from his location and almost instantaneously appeared.

It was shortly after three-thirty p.m., dusk was fast approaching and the guards had not been relieved. The adjutant resolved the matter whilst Kashkarov conscientiously covered both the plans and the voluminous folio of notes that he had produced and pondered the adjutant`s question.

"His attention to duty was paramount, and no, even though he had not eaten or drunk since about eight p.m. the previous evening- in what was now a different world – he did not have the time, or desire, to eat."

He was consumed by a passion, and whilst an atheist, his zeal was almost Messianic in fervour and which drove him on relentlessly. Such intensity and urgency had only ever once before occurred, when his force of T 38 tanks remorselessly attacked and then counter attacked the German Panzers in a life and death confrontation and now he sensed that the Union of Soviet Socialist Republics was on the brink of an even mightier, titanic struggle.

The two remaining packages yielded two identical ring binder files. Both covers were blank, therefore neither identifying its owner`s identity or the nature of its contents.

The only feature to differentiate the two files was that one was far bulkier than the other and as he turned to the first page of the larger file he noted an index which he intimately examined and grasped the full nature of the contents. The 'analysis reports' which 'Moscow' had each month forwarded to him were but a resume and a highly abridged, sanitised version of the document that lay open before him. It was obviously maintained with a compelling attention to detail and clearly, frequently, parts and possibly whole sections were regularly updated or revised.

It was a treasure trove of information that listed and scheduled the complete deployment and inventory of the nation's forces but more important of all, itemised the military capability of the Union from tanks to ballistic missiles. It was, and would be an impossible Herculean task to read, let alone absorb the cornucopia of information, but since the index led him to the highest security level of information, he was now able to verify if his plan was technically feasible or if it had been built on a foundation of speculative thought and the dissemination of propaganda to raise the spirits of the nation or cower their enemy, the United States, into passive and meek submission.

The second ring binder file was identical in format, the first page was again an index which he closely perused and realised that it was an assessment of the United States' global military capability together with details of their allies' forces including Great Britain.

Both files had been created and prepared for the benefit of a member of the Politburo, if not the First Secretary, and in a format and non technical language which he found not only easy to grasp but would made his calculations far quicker to compute.

Other than the First Secretary's positive comments, there was no reference or documentation concerning the first part of his four part plan which was solely and purely a political manoeuvre with effectively no military overtones whilst the second and third parts relied on both military strength and political will. Of the final part, he would have no control over. A confrontation between the two major powers, both able to deliver a devastating and gruesome thermonuclear blow against the other.

Thus the resolve and credibility of the Politburo, that in nineteen sixty-two had wilted over Cuba, would be tested again and this time, at stake, would be the *de facto*, if not formal acceptance of Soviet hegemony and control over the liberated European nations of the former West Germany, France, Belgium, Holland and Denmark for he was not aware of the punitive agreement that had been imposed upon the United States President that he had acquiesced to in order to 'bring his boys' home.

There was an additional prize: the possible neutralisation of the British Isles as an American 'aircraft carrier'.

At the core of his plan were the performance capabilities of the R-36 and UR-100 land based missile systems which had recently been deployed (U S Department of Defence and N A T O designations SS-9 Scarp and SS -11 Sego respectively) and their locations.

He soon realised that the existing first generation of Soviet missile systems had become highly vulnerable and their combat readiness was slow for they were sited on open launch pads in clusters, each separated by only a few dozen metres and all of them could be wiped out by a single nuclear warhead following a first strike and their vulnerability was compounded by a long launch procedure which could be anything up to several hours.

The RVSN (Strategic Rocket Forces) and the Central RVSN Command Station had recognised these inadequacies and the R-36 and UR-100 silo based missiles were the subsequent result and had come in time to counter the United States Minuteman system.

He began his journey of discovery to ascertain each missile's true performance capabilities, their 'throw weights', range and accuracy.

Suddenly he was interrupted by the adjutant and advised that ...

"It was nearly ten and did he require dinner?"

Such was his concentration, that time and events had passed without him noticing; he looked up and realised that night had arrived and that the room had been illuminated by lighting that was soft and gentle and not strong and intense. He also saw that the four guards, staring out into the black void, were visibly tiring and he instinctively ordered that they be relieved.

"No!, he would have a leisurely swim which would allow him to clear his mind and then he would have a small snack. In the meantime the room could be left empty with the lights switched on, provided that the entry was guarded and that troops were stationed outside, meticulously guarding the room and its priceless contents."

Steam rose from the pool which was obviously maintained regardless of cost and he was assured measured exactly one hundred metres for three lengths. There were two lifeguards and four guards charged to protect him. It was magnificent and wonderful. It must have been four, no five years since he had last swum and that had been in a military leisure complex in the German Democratic Republic in a pool that had seen better days, the concrete was flaking away and the tiles were wearing thin and loose. He remembered being told that the complex was a pre war Nazi Germany centre for elite S.S. troops. But this was something different, an experience to be savoured and cherished. That one word, cherished, was a catalyst, for it prompted a series of logical thoughts culminating in the realisation that his wife must be frantic with fear. He had to get a message to her that he was 'all right', but he couldn't disclose to her the reason for his absence.

He swam leisurely for about fifty five minutes and ceased exercising when he completed about eighteen lengths just as the adjutant entered the poolside, bent down and asked what he wanted to eat. He seemed both surprised at the athlete's specific demand and the frugality of his palate.

It had been magnificent and wonderful, indeed it was an experience that he would never forget and he looked forward to recounting the event to his wife and then he wondered if they would ever meet again. His thoughts turned to the imminent meeting with the Politburo which would certainly decide his fate and perhaps the destiny of the Union of Socialist Soviet Republics, or was this all a drug induced dream perpetrated by the K G B that was a prelude to his own destruction and for what purpose?

He showered, dried himself in a special cubicle constructed possibly even for the First Secretary, for his girth was dwarfed by the circumference of the unit which blew hot air all around and from above, necessitating only a gentle rub of his body with a towel so soft it reminded him of his beloved wife's gentleness and kindness.

He dressed in the same clothes that he had donned some twenty hours before when his life had taken an unforeseen and dramatic new course.

The lifeguard tactfully entered the room and with consummate discretion enquired if ...

"He would like a short massage that would take some ten or fifteen minutes?"

He thought of every logical negative reason why he should refuse the offer but the novelty and bourgeois or aristocratic luxury was a temptation that he could not resist. He undressed, relaxed, and less than fifteen minutes later his mind and body were freed of any superfluous, irrelevant distractions and he was strong and confident, possessed now with an incisive clarity of thought. He could persuade the Politburo that his plan and their strength of purpose could not only outwit the Americans but could secure mainland Europe and possibly even neutralise the British.

The kitchen was vast and appeared to be constructed of gleaming stainless steel and pinewood, with cupboards coloured in soft brown. Sitting at a long pinewood table were twelve or fourteen troops and at the head of the table was the adjutant who immediately sprung to attention, saluting him, whilst the soldiers stood to attention, heralding a clatter which shook the room as a number of chairs fell over. No one in the room, including the new arrival knew that just over two years before a very similar event had taken place no more than a hundred kilometres away in a series of events that had still not yet reached its climax.

He could smell the rustic rye bread and when he held the loaf with the intention of tearing off a chunk, his hand automatically let go, such was the heat of the loaf which must have just come out of the oven.

The chef, with both hands, brought out a massive jug of cold borscht from a fridge, itself gargantuan in size, and then produced a large bowl of sour cream and a similarly sized dish of cold boiled potatoes. With almost military precision he finally produced a one litre glass and proceeded to combine the three ingredients whilst the troops remained at attention not knowing what was expected of them.

He was also uncertain how he was expected to handle this matter of military protocol and decided to both sit down and instruct the adjutant to put the men 'at ease'.

He ate and relished both the food and the experience, remaining silent whilst he noted that the intensity and content of the men's conversations were both muted and cautious.

It must have been close to midnight when he signalled to the adjutant that he needed to speak of matters that were best discussed in the solitude and tranquillity outside of the dacha.

A soldier collected his old military coat which he put on and joined the adjutant outside of the indoor swimming pool.

He felt embarrassed and even ashamed. He had no other clothing or shoes, for in her haste, his wife had only packed three pairs of winter socks and a number of thick woollen vests and underpants, as he assumed that she must have anticipated the worst outcome of his early morning departure.

He then summonsed up the courage to ask two pressing favours from the adjutant...

"He had no clothing suitable for his meeting in the Kremlin but just as important he wanted to contact his wife and assure her he was well. They had no telephone at home and was it possible that she could taken to a local public office and be connected to him?"

He smiled, the first time that the guest recognised the emotion of compassion and friendship in the usually cold and efficient officer.

He returned to the room around twelve twenty a.m. intent on working for another two hours or so when he was soon to learn the absolute truth of the nation's current capabilities, making copious notes of his discoveries. The Cuban crisis and then the war of nineteen sixty-three and four had hastened and accelerated the research and development stages of both the R-36 and UR-100 missiles and their flight tests, which on the orders of the RVSN had been truncated, no doubt at the behest of the Supreme High Command which was but a branch responsible to the Politburo of the CPSU Central Committee.

Both systems had been accepted for service and combat duty over one year early and the Chief Designer of the R-36, M.K. Yangel had personally written to Leonid Brezhnev, from the Omsk Aviation Plant, number OKB 586 at Dnepropetrovsk warning him that...

"...further testing was absolutely essential...the fuel system was new and inadequately tested ...and the gyroscopes of the guidance system were prone to jamming.'

The question was how could he confront the Politburo with these doubts or should he suppress this knowledge but use the demonstration of the nation's capabilities and strength of will as a test for their own benefit?

Currently there were deployed thirty six R-36s and one hundred and thirty -four UR-100s. A demonstration and test of five of these missiles within a short space of time would not dent the nation's capability.

He became more confident that his plan could succeed, provided that the missiles could perform to their specifications and not be proved defective.

The new 'second generation' of missiles were a quantum leap in comparison with the now archaic 'first generation'. They were permanently fuelled ('ampulised' or sealed and kept fully ready for launch), each in a hardened single-silo launcher which were scattered over a large area, significantly improving their survivability. The throw weight' of the 'light' UR-100 meant a 1.1 megaton warhead could be carried with a range of twelve thousand kilometres and the 'heavy'R-36 could carry a device with a yield of up to ten megatons (That is ten million tons!) making up for poorer accuracy.

He selected three sites that currently were the homes for the widely scattered silos and their missiles at:

BRODY	50 06N	025 12E,	
KANSK	56 23N	095 29E	and
DROVYANAYA	51 26N	113 03E .	

Their 'target' would be a defined area in the Pacific and central to this show of force would be prior notification, via neutral intermediaries, to the United States President of this vital 'test programme', for if their enemy was to detect an unannounced flight of five or so missiles it would undoubtedly assume the launch of a pre–emptive first strike triggering a counter strike (or launch-on-warning strike) with only one outcome.

He pondered why no information had been made available concerning the first part of his plan and then he continued his work, collating the information and setting out the format of a possible statement he might have to make.

SEVENTY-ONE

He was woken by a knock on the door and the rays of the Sun which was low in the winter sky. The chef brought in a tray which he placed beside the bed. The aroma of strong coffee began to permeate through the room as did the smell of a variety of small loaves of bread including the distinctive fragrance of rye bread.

The chef took it upon himself to point out a plate of soft runny, creamy butter and confirmed, with a suppressed smile, that the bread was cool enough to be held.

"It was two ten in the afternoon. He had come on duty at four thirty five and seen him limp wearily to his room, utterly exhausted. The adjutant had news and was available at anytime."

He ate sparingly but with great pleasure, showered and dressed himself.

The adjutant stood to attention as Kashkarov entered the room and he immediately noticed that the room was devoid of guards who were patrolling outside and that the adjutant was in full ceremonial dress. As he sat down he did not notice a telephone which had been installed earlier that morning and which sat almost forlornly in the far corner of his desk, thus avoiding any of his paperwork and the two files which dominated his desk, sprawled almost carelessly and without any regard to their top secret contents.

"I have news of the greatest importance. You will be summonsed to the Kremlin no earlier than twenty three hundred hours and must be available from twenty–two hundred hours to be urgently driven to the Kremlin. I will accompany you to Moscow and, of course, carry any documents and papers that you need. A tailor has been waiting to see you since nine a.m. and will urgently attend to your needs. You can also speak to your wife at any time from now on."

And then, because life and events are sometimes unpredictable, he suddenly spoke in halting and poor English.

"I understand that you speak good English and I wondered if, for a brief minute or so, I could practice?"

And then he did something most unexpected for he cupped his left hand to his ear and with the other hand began tapping his fingers slowly but methodically on the table.

"I enjoy, so much, the pleasure of playing the works of Chopin or some of our Russian composers whose pieces have been transcribed for the piano but have so little time for my passion that sometimes I practice as I am doing now."

Kashkarov was then instinctively drawn to the man`s drumming fingers and then a pattern emerged. He had signalled, in English, the Morse code for three words, 'Be very careful'. And as he finished, his cupped hand moved from his ear and changed shape pointing to the telephone.

He reverted to his birth language and said...

"You have a direct line to your wife. I will leave the room until you call me."

SEVENTY-TWO

Confrontation! The struggle between two factions of miners, each believing that their diametrically opposed assessment of the coal industry was right. Thursday, February twenty-fifth, nineteen sixty-five.

No reliable documentation or records now exists but estimates and calculations made at the time, by local journalists, are consistent with the numbers given to the national press, radio and television by the police and there was very little possibility that any of the pickets had been 'doubly' counted.

Some one hundred and fifty to one hundred and seventy coaches, carrying about six and a half thousand pickets, had been mustered on the Wednesday and then flooded south overnight to 'liberate' the Midland pits.

Martin and his closest supporters had supplied his 'shock troops' with two weapons to further their task. Obsolete, but still effective, World War Two military wireless transmitters, which had been loaned by enthusiasts, and for every group in the great crusade a stirring speech that had been hastily printed on a Roneo.

With foresight, and in anticipation of the potential chaos that could ensue, Jack Jones had dispatched a trusted and anonymous ally - a cadre in the language of his true masters - laden with money to be distributed to the leaders of the pickets at each pit which would cover their sustenance and raise their morale.

Peter Zinkin and George Sinfield, writing in that morning's (Thursday) *Daily Worker*, had requested donations be made to the miners' cause, without specifying to whom or where such donations should be sent, resulting in Jones being able to funnel further and larger amounts via the paper in 'anonymous' collections that nearly became an embarrassment.

Some miners, possibly from the Scottish pits, brought with them used Gillette razor blades whilst most, because of the weather, had Balaclavas which, like a uniform, unofficially identified their loyalty but also hid their identities.

How many of them actually read or were inspired by Bill Martin's statement, no one will ever know, but it was cited later as the order to cause violence, mayhem and wanton destruction.

They concentrated on some nine pits in the Nottinghamshire and Staffordshire regions, sending only some twenty to forty men to each of the other pits. Scabs would be asphyxiated by the sheer weight of numbers, about six hundred would be allocated to each of the nine pits.

"The tremendous solidarity that you have already displayed, and the support and single mindedness of your fellow workers will compel the National Coal Board to capitulate and reward you all with a wage increase and improved conditions that are a recognition of your hard work and contribution to the national wealth...the savage butchery of our industry will stop and be reversed... their hit list of pit closures will be terminated ...the gloves are now off. This will be your victory!"

Thus by three or four o'clock in the morning, 'liberators', as they were to be described by Martin's associates, began to assemble at the collieries of Harwood, Harworth, Hucknal, Bevercotes, Ollerton, Thoresby and Bilsthorpe in Nottinghamshire and Lea Hall, near Rugeley and Littleton near Cannock, both in Staffordshire.

The same press release describing the pickets as 'liberators' also, in the most emphatic terms, confirmed that...

"Responsible and peaceful picketing has always been our Union's policy."

This press release, including an inflammatory statement that...

"...in consequence, law and order in the form of police supervision would be respected, however belligerent, or even worse, violent supervision could not be tolerated",

would also be cited at the trial of David William Martin.

In reality, picketing began both amicably and unbelievably, in good humour, as the morning shifts began to arrive to replace the night shifts. Local journalists had not yet arrived to independently observe the events so we can only rely on the many statements that were made by the local miners and the pickets, editing out some of their more colourful language which at that time had not become inflamed.

By the time the journalists started to arrive, a pattern had emerged at the nine major mines and the thirty or so other less heavily picketed collieries. About twenty per cent of the incoming miners had, for various reasons, agreed to withdraw their labour and some, a nominal minority, had even agreed to join the picket lines, but the vast majority, again for various reasons, had crossed the lines, which by all accounts were still peaceful and not aggressive, to begin their shifts.

It is believed, and unfortunately this author was unable to verify the facts, that at this early stage in the confrontation, some of the night shift miners were followed home, their addresses identified and particulars of their families obtained.

Policing, at this stage of the 'confrontation', was light and cursory, even at those nine pits where picketing was intense and no doubt the constables on duty conveyed messages that they were able to maintain law and order without further support.

At the risk of contradiction, and the only extant evidence was a newspaper report in a local regional paper which no longer exists, it was commonly believed that the initial spark, or catalyst ,which ignited any simmering tensions that were festering beneath the superficial good humour of the pickets, took place at the Ollerton colliery when the wives of the local miners unexpectedly arrived with urns of tea and even some biscuits which first they handed out to their own kith and kin who were guarding the pit head and then they offered the same to the few policemen who were on duty. It was then that the flame of confrontation and the clash of two opposite forces was ignited.

There was a local newspaper journalist present at the time, but at the moment the fire was ignited, he was, as he claimed afterwards...

"A few yards away, but more importantly, his back was turned, and to compound the situation he was making notes for an article that he was about to 'file'."

Truth or its interpretation is, like time, elastic and even flexible.

The pickets' leader later stated categorically that a remark by one of his pickets was made as a light hearted jest...

"Darling, we're thirsty. Bring the urn over here."

Whilst the husband of the woman immediately responded by claiming that...

"His wife had been insulted, that she had, as a Church going Christian woman, every intention of giving sustenance, even to an enemy, but he would not permit his wife to be insulted and treated disrespectfully."

Thus this minor and innocuous misunderstanding, though not the first link in a chain of events, would end in the execution of Bill Martin in what would be the first trial for treason by the New Order under martial law.

The pickets, *en masse*, surged forward, overwhelming the three police officers who stood between the two groups, and closed in on the very heavily outnumbered local miners, whilst their wives fled in terror, their tea urns being trampled underfoot.

Victory and territorial advantage was swift. Bloodied and bruised the beaten locals slunk away as the victors cheered and raised a symbolic flag around the access to the mine shaft which they now controlled.

Within minutes, news had been transmitted to all the other wireless operators and by various means to those locations not on the net, by car, motorcycle and even bicycles. However because no verbatim note was ever taken, the contents and phraseology are still in dispute, but again, at the trial of Bill Martin, it was claimed that the contents were so inflammatory and a distortion of the truth that this was the key moment when his long term plans came into operation.

At nearly forty pits the pickets, in a loosely coordinated and even for them a surprise act and without just cause attacked the local miners and by, in every case, the end of the morning shift, had gained control of the pit heads and the winches which would bring the shift workers to the surface.

At Harworth and Lea Hall the first fatalities were recorded. At Harworth, a miner with less than four months service remaining before retirement was crushed to death, therefore fulfilling the wishes of those who had inspired the pickets, and at Lea Hall at the very other end of the spectrum, a young miner who had only worked underground for less than three weeks, was found dead in a foetal position, two domestic knives buried deep, one in his heart and the other in his abdomen. An unofficial remark from the police surgeon, who conducted an interim post mortem, which was quickly relayed to the local miners, was the starting pistol that began a vicious, violent counterattack.

The remark also received great prominence on the national news that evening and in the national and regional newspapers the following day,

Friday, and formed the banner headline in the *Daily Mail*, *Express* and even the *Mirror*...

"He died in unnecessary and excruciating pain and was treated with the inhumanity and callousness that only a beast would exhibit."

How the news was received in Yorkshire by the leaders of the striking miners or even by strikers in other industries or commerce will never be truly known though government officials claimed a week later that there had been a marked increase in the number of strikers returning to work and facilitating an increase in industrial and commercial production, however these comments were repudiated by Bill Martin and the leaders of other striking unions as propaganda.

SEVENTY-THREE

They were both crying, as if the telephone call had physically united two young lovers, forcibly separated by the terrors of war, which in the circumstances was not exactly untrue. He allowed her to speak, unrestrained by the thought that others might be monitoring every word or emotion but, by necessity, he would be both specific and vague.

She had hardly slept for two nights, fearful for his predicament, but at seven that second morning she had been woken from a light sleep by heavy knocking on the door, which immediately she thought was the prelude to her own arrest, transportation to the camps and then, finally, death by exhaustion or starvation - or both. Four men had brusquely entered and informed her that they had been instructed to install a telephone which would only receive incoming calls. Such had been the commotion that her neighbours from the adjacent apartments and from the next floor had gathered, *en masse*, outside of her front door to ascertain, for the second consecutive night, the reason for the disturbance.

She had tried to make an outgoing call to the only number that she knew, the military establishment where he had worked, but was unsuccessful.

"I'm not in any danger. Now listen very carefully. I cannot tell you where I am, or what I am doing, or even how long we will be separated. I do not need my military grey coat. Do you understand what I mean? In a few minutes I am going to make arrangements to return the coat to you with a gift. In the meantime please could you have ready my watch which I left in the confusion of my departure but also, and only, the medal that I was honoured to receive after the Kursk campaign. None of the other medals mean as much to me as that one honours and you, my Darling.

I will try to contact you again but you must not speak to anyone, including my colleagues, of my call or requests. I love you."

It was so pathetic, she ended the call by asking if they were treating him well, if he had eaten or if there were adequate washing facilities. But he could not, dare not, explain his circumstances.

The adjutant would arrange collection of his watch and medal immediately and saw no reason why they would not be in his possession by twenty–two hundred hours.

"He would take the old army grey coat which his wife would have within twenty-four hours and the gift that he wanted to send? He would arrange for a food parcel from the K G B Officers` establishment weighing some fifteen to twenty kilos and did his wife have any special demands?"

He thought of requesting Kosher food but stopped short, suggesting that his wife, for dietary reasons, did not eat pork but enjoyed the rare delight and pleasure of beef and lamb.

The stoic tailor was summonsed and never alluded to his enforced wait. A bespoke uniform could not be crafted in time but he had available a selection of dress uniforms which could be quickly tailored to his requirements and measurements which were swiftly gathered. The uniform would be delivered later that day but in good time for his meeting, together with a selection of clothes suitable for his rank and the winter climate. He unexpectedly remarked, perhaps with knowledge that should not have been revealed that:

"Comrade Brezhnev has a distinct dislike of military personnel appearing before him, festooned in medals or opulent uniforms since he could not believe that any soldier had been so brave during the four years of the Great Patriotic war."

His preparations were all but complete and now he had time to contemplate his situation, and doubts began to coalesce: perhaps there was an Achilles heel which would expose a weakness in his plan? Yesterday, time had flown, but now inexplicably, it moved with the pace of an old man and not the swiftness of youth. He had an idea and it would take only a few calculations to verify.

It was so obvious and self evident. Fatigue and tiredness had dulled his senses. The dual testing and demonstration could be both in the Pacific *AND* the Atlantic with the launches from bases in Central Asia, therefore hiding the locations of the many launch sites scattered in Russia and the Ukraine. But then a doubt seeped in; what if the missiles fell short in Western Europe even though their thermonuclear payloads had been substituted by dummy payloads of equivalent weight? He would have to be careful, very careful.

Time suddenly flew by as would, he hoped, the R-36 and UR-100 missiles, the culmination and result of Soviet technological and scientific expertise.

His mind projected to the forthcoming meeting and slowly his confidence ebbed away.

He was brought back to the realty of the here and now by the return of the tailor, this time accompanied by two assistants, wheeling in three rails overloaded with uniforms, trousers and jackets and other clothing that he had only seen in photographs on either elite troops or officers.

He felt distinctively uncomfortable whilst surrounded by, and pampered by, the three men and he became irritated wasting time changing from one pair of trousers to another but ultimately they were satisfied that their mannequin was correctly attired and they departed wheeling away three depleted rails and leaving piles of clothes together with packets of underwear and socks. The adjutant removed the piles and confirmed that the housekeeper would put away the clothing and, with foresight, confirmed that he would have delivered a valise, suitable to his rank.

It was dark and time moved inexorably onwards. A messenger arrived at about eight- thirty p.m. and delivered a small package which contained his watch and treasured medal.

The adjutant had procured two briefcases and Kashkarov used the small one to hold his notes whilst the other, held by the adjutant, which was much larger, managed to contain the ultra secret briefing files, but so much was ingrained in his mind that he felt sure he could avoid referring to his notes or the files.

He waited and waited.

SEVENTY-FOUR

He instinctively looked at his watch which read six-nineteen as he and the adjutant, led by the general who had originally met him on his arrival in Moscow, marched up to a double door guarded by two elite K G B soldiers resplendent in their full ceremonial uniforms, however as the three men advanced to the door, the hand of one of the two guards suddenly was projected towards the adjutant and general, palm outward, clearly denying them access.

Suddenly he was alone. When the doors opened he would be, without doubt, in the Inner Sanctum of the Politburo and he expected, what? He knew that his plans and ideas would be robustly questioned and minutely investigated, but what else?

And then, just as the doors began to open from the inside, accompanied by the screech of unoiled hinges his thoughts turned back to the last two hours or so and the strange confrontation that had revived half forgotten memories of the most pleasant kind.

He had been woken at about quarter past four and told that he, at long last, had been summonsed to the Kremlin and had to be available from five forty-five a.m. and no later. He showered, shaved and dressed himself, unencumbered by his wife's supervision, absolutely making certain that he put on both his watch and his treasured medal.

He had no time for a hurried breakfast which included fresh and inviting kovbasa - his favourite, which his wife would not let into the apartment because it could contain pork, "God bless her "- but the chef supplied him with a piping hot piece of black bread torn from a freshly baked loaf and wrapped in a napkin which would be shared with the adjutant en route to Moscow.

The driver of the Zil limousine, which formed the central focus of a small convoy, was clearly knowledgeable of the unlit roads which led first to the suburbs of Moscow and then the poorly lit area close to the Kremlin complex. The convoy was comprised of two other vehicles, one ahead and the other following, and six motor cycle outriders. They remained silent throughout the journey, enjoying the bread and both undoubtedly conjecturing on the events that were to unfold.

But it was only after they had entered the Kremlin and been ushered, with fawning courtesy, by a government official into an ante room that the surprise, unscheduled, but clearly carefully engineered meeting took place.

They were invited to eat from a sumptuous buffet, but the dishes were too rich and opulent so they requested and were provided with coffee, which was both strong and with a delicious flavour.

It must have been between about five– forty to ten to six when another man entered the room. He was clearly Semitic in appearance but without the extreme features crudely caricatured in one of the pre war Nazi Germany propaganda films. Neither was he from one of the isolated villages in the Pale, or, as they called them in Yiddish, as his university educated wife might do, without intending to be superior, the shtetls, for he was immaculately dressed, indeed the only time that Kashkarov had ever actually observed such elegance was when he had travelled to Finland to meet his dear old friend.

The man silently drew two glasses of borscht, placed in each a lump of sour cream and walked up to Kashkarov, offered him a glass and in perfect English welcomed him to the Kremlin...

"After a long journey that had begun at Kursk...," digressing, for a fleeting moment, to acknowledge and admire his medal, then continuing obliquely to refer, almost with absolute certainty to...

"...his sojourn in the Ukrainian forest...,"

and more recently, without identifying the former First Secretary by name, as if his identity and reputation was as besmirched as Leon Trotsky, to...

"... his elegant and extremely successful plan."

It was evident that this man possessed certain esoteric knowledge but it was his next remark that immediately confirmed his knowledge of recent events...

"Your visits to Finland to meet your old friend Mandel Goldburgh were ill advised and only permitted to gauge your loyalty and whilst I had the necessity to meet him recently, I am absolutely sure he would have offered his best wishes had he and I known of this fortuitous, chance meeting, though in truth it was engineered in the best interests of both the Party and my own priorities."

He reverted to Russian and announced the dramatic news that in the next hour or so the destiny of the Motherland could be in his hands, for the Politburo was deadlocked and that his expertise and foresight, combined with his imaginative skills could persuade the doubters and waverers. It was then that Kashkarov delved into memories long since intentionally hidden in the deepest recesses of his mind and he decided to ask the fate of the young female K G B officer (he had deliberately, after more than twenty years, forgotten Natalia's name) but the man was suddenly called away, though he shook the hand of Kashkarov, who in the rush also forgot to ask Joel Ben Yitzhak his name.

SEVENTY-FIVE

He was immediately drawn to a single photograph which occupied a large, prominent space on the wall adjacent to the double doors. It was the ubiquitous portrait of the founder of the USSR, Vladimir Lenin. The room itself was austere and much cooler than the ambient temperature that he was normally used to; he had expected there to be a map of the Republics or even Europe or the World but the walls were bare. A haze of tobacco smoke hung over the table which occupied much of the room around which sat men in grey suits, most of whom he recognised from their official photographs, but in the cauldron of power, suddenly had become nameless and anonymous.

He became aware that a heavily built man was standing to his right and glancing furtively, he recognised the unmistakeable face of the First Secretary who signalled him to sit down beside him.

The two briefcases were nowhere to be seen and he didn't even have time to draw a deep breath.

"Comrade Mazurov [Kirill Mazurov would be ousted from the Politburo on March twenty-sixth and was Brezhnev's most implacable political opponent]. You have expressed a most cynical objection to the complete plan, essentially that the Americans would never acquiesce to our demands. No doubt your interrogation of this man will either confirm your opinion or persuade you and others in the room that we must now urgently act to confirm our absolute authority and hegemony in the liberated Western States of Europe."

This was now the test that he had prepared for but he did not expect the question that was put to him.

"Young man, why should we supply to our enemies, via the International Red Cross in Switzerland, a comprehensive list of the many thousands of political prisoners and enemies of the State who have been rounded up and arrested since our victory in Western Europe, even specifying the nature of the crimes that they have been charged with and finally identifying the location of their internment, which in most instances are military locations, thus supplying their military intelligence services with precious information. Furthermore, following exhaustive enquiries, it now appears, in some cases, that the information is both obsolete and inaccurate. What type of web are you trying to weave and for what purpose?"

Before he could answer the unexpected question and was given an opportunity to formulate his answer, the man sitting next to Mazurov rose, put down his cigarette and demanded to know ...

"What qualifications could you bring to this most crucial of meetings which would affect the future of the Party and the destiny of the nation?"

Leonid Efremov sat down. He had been a member of the Politburo since November twenty-third nineteen sixty-two and would survive till March nineteen sixty-six when a triumphant Brezhnev would have him replaced by the loyal, nearly senile and pliant Arvids Pelse.

Perhaps, at that very moment, both Kashkarov and the First Secretary realised that their futures were intertwined.

"Our enemies must be aware that we have turned Westwards and that the many military bases in the liberated West that formerly faced towards the East have been turned round and now face the Atlantic. This is not a game of chess with rules or various complex strategies. These people are effectively hostages against an attack on the many bases where they are held or purported to be located, as comrade Mazurov's investigations have revealed and I personally thank him for bringing this information to those who are assembled here this morning.

This does not mean that the bases are inviolate but will, in general, remain unscathed until we have secured an advantage and a negotiating superiority when some could suffer attack and destruction.

As a servant of the Party I am only able to present to you my conclusions and reasonings. It is up to you to implement my recommendations but they must be carried through with ruthless determination as did Marshall Stalin in the crisis years of the Great Patriotic war."

For a moment a dark silence reigned as if he had raised a forbidden spectre, but Viktor Grishin, who had turned on his former mentor, Nikita Khrushchev and transferred his loyalty to Brezhnev and precipitated the former's fall, recognised that the man in front of him was slowly persuading the doubters. He then questioned him about the intended demonstration of strength.

"Never before in history has a nation demonstrated such strength to its enemy. The Germans, even to the best of my knowledge, ever test fired or launched more than one A4/V2 rocket simultaneously and the Americans have never attempted a multiple launch of any of their sea or land based missiles."

Kashkarov's response was devastating.

"The coordinated, almost simultaneous launch of ten to twelve R-36 and UR-100 Inter Continental Ballistic missiles and their successful flights (each carrying a dummy pay load) would be a propaganda coup that would surpass the launch of Sputnik. It was crucial that the United States was given adequate prior warning of the intended launch, without initially disclosing the number of rockets, because if their defence systems detected a multiple launch they would have no alternative but to assume that a First Strike had been launched and they would order an immediate Counter First Strike (launch-on warning) and when the incoming 'attack' failed to materialise the Americans *MIGHT* [author's emphasis] then launch an unbelievably massive Retaliatory First Strike using their fleet of B-52 bombers under the command of the madmen in the Strategic Air Command, the ever growing numbers of Minutemen silo based missiles and their fleet of Polaris nuclear submarines.

This must be a propaganda exercise unparalleled in the history of the Soviet Union. The prime purpose was to frighten and intimidate the American civilian population who initially would view previously censored graphic film and television of the suffering of the people of the Ukraine and Russia and then would learn that if the fair demands of the Soviet people were not met then the cities of the West coast, San Diego, Los Angeles, San Francisco and Seattle and on the East coast, New York, Philadelphia and Miami would be primary targets in a first strike.

Great Britain, who had boasted of their complicity in the nuclear attacks on Russia and the Ukraine and the assault on the island of

Rugen would be attacked, without warning, by fighter bombers based where prominent prisoners were kept.

Their targets would be civilian city centres only, and any pilot who attacked an American base or plane would be summarily court marshalled and shot and his family immediately sent into exile, without remission. Therefore if they were engaged by any U.S. plane they must not return fire but return to their base, without disgrace.

High yield nuclear weapons would be used and their targets would be London (five devices), Bristol and Birmingham (two devices each), Manchester (again two devices), Liverpool and Edinburgh. Glasgow would be spared, not because it was a centre for militant communists but because they did not want to hit the complex at Faslane on the Clyde.

Once Britain had been attacked it would be up to the Politburo to secure a political victory because the shock of the attack on Britain would frighten the American people into forcing their politicians, including McNamara, Bobby Kennedy and President Johnson into a humiliating compromise and with the potential added probability that support for an independent British nuclear weapons system would collapse and a policy of disarmament and neutrality, promoted by left wing organisations and front groups such as the Campaign for Nuclear Disarmament (C.N.D.) might prevail."

He did not see a broad smile spread across the face of the First Secretary.

A number of other questions were raised and answered, but Andrei Kirilenko and Alexei Kosygin obtained confirmation that the target sites for the multi launch would be predetermined areas in the Pacific and Atlantic which would be only identified some twenty-four hours before impact giving their enemy little time to place observers but giving them the opportunity to monitor and measure the flights.

He first looked down at his watch; it was twelve–eleven p.m. and as he looked up a beaming First Secretary walked towards him thrusting a glass of ice cold vodka into his hand.

"But I don't drink this early in the morning and not when I am on duty."

"When the First Secretary orders you to drink a toast, you will, without question, obey. To victory."

You, the reader, would expect that he would become the focus of the Politburo's interest, and shine in the appreciation and congratulations of its members, but power has its own priorities. He was ignored, for he had served his purpose; he finished his drink and found the adjutant outside still holding the two briefcases.

SEVENTY-SIX

At his trial before a military tribunal, Bill Martin was painted by the prosecutor as a single minded, obsessive, almost demonic megalomaniac, who nonetheless organised his supporters like soldiers with the same meticulous precision, ruthlessness and barbarity that Hitler and his generals had planned the blitzkrieg in the spring of nineteen -forty and the invasion of the Soviet Union in June nineteen forty-one.

By dawn on Friday, February twenty-sixth, a further estimated three and a half thousand miners in approximately one hundred and ten coaches had arrived at the pivotal Nottinghamshire and Staffordshire mines to buttress support for their comrades(indeed the prosecutor relished in the word comrades, with its Socialist overtones)and on the Saturday, Martin would himself make the journey and fatally, in a speech at Ollerton colliery, which was recorded by the B B C, advocate the use of unrestrained violence in the pursuit of their democratic demands.

Yet again, relying on estimates calculated independently by the police and 'pooled' by local and national journalists at the various collieries, some two thousand strikers were allocated to the smaller pits whilst about fifteen hundred men were sent to the remaining nine pits which would be the focus and epicentre of their actions.

Any possibility of compromise or reconciliation had ceased by late Thursday afternoon, when Martin's 'forces' had refused to allow the day shift to return to the surface and had, at first, refused to send down any sustenance, however a parish priest close to the pit at Lea Hall in Staffordshire, acting independently of the local community and without seeking guidance from his religious superiors, had crossed the symbolic dividing line between the two factions and requested...

"In the name of God and Jesus Christ, that food and water be sent down the mineshaft at regular intervals until a resolution of the dispute could be found at all the local pits."

The tense situation was taking on the appearance of an invasion and occupation, such was the atmosphere and the vehement language of the local residents, but surprisingly an arrangement was hammered out on the understanding that the local community would, for health and safety purposes, allow the troops, for that was the description that the locals had given the invaders, access to the local public toilet which strategically was sited in an area controlled by the local miners.

Within hours and by evening on the Thursday, the arrangement, or similar arrangements suited to each of the pits, was in force, though feelings and emotions were further rapidly hardening and festering especially when the news, which was broadcast on the national radio and television, of the death at Lea Hall of the young miner, officially confirmed an unofficial rumour. The subterranean incarceration of their kith and kin combined with rumours emanating from the 'barricades' of the 'invaders' that further support was expected and even anticipated, further raised the temperature of the confrontation.

Whilst they were financially bolstered by the unexpected donations that had anonymously been provided by supporters of their cause, money became locally worthless in the tight knit communities which were the backbone of the mining complexes of Nottinghamshire and Staffordshire and the strikers were literally forced to forage afar to locate markets and shops that would supply them. A diet of that great British staple, fish and chips, was provided, but in many cases it was literally a dish eaten cold such were the distances that had to be travelled to locate shops that were prepared to supply them and in amounts to meet their enormous demands and they became the victims of economic forces suddenly finding that prices increased because of the pressure on supplies.

Violence again erupted on the Friday afternoon when almost simultaneously, but independently, local miners at three pits endeavoured to reclaim control and to secure the release of their friends and neighbours trapped deep below the surface. Only at one small pit did they succeed but more importantly, like defeated and exhausted troops, the beaten and ousted strikers left the village and dejectedly marched off unable even to muster any semblance of defiance.

However, at the other two pits the attempts to dislodge the strikers failed but the cost to both sides was massive in terms of casualties and the political consequences. In all, it was estimated that thirty-nine strikers required hospital treatment (three of whom were seriously injured) and twenty-seven local miners, two of whom died that Friday evening. Local emergency services were called but with an irony that symbolised the chaos that was descending, it was found that the ambulance services were on strike in support of the miners and that they had stated emphatically that they were not prepared to cross any picket lines or to give sustenance to "Scabs" or anti unionist activists.

For the strikers, perhaps they had been 'hoisted on their own petard'.

Local doctors accompanied by nurses were the only source of medical assistance, organising priority attention to their own locals and arranging for cars and even a local butcher's van to transport the injured to the nearest cottage or regional hospitals. But such service did not extend to the suffering of the injured invaders. They were subsequently attended to, with great professionalism, by the doctors and nurses, but with a not unexpected vindictiveness and anger they were refused transport facilities on the grounds that fuel was scarce because the nearest depots supplying the area's petrol stations had recently gone out on strike not so much in support of the miners but to bolster their demands for an increase in their hourly pay.

The fundamental reason for Bill Martin's urgent journey from his Yorkshire headquarters to the Midlands on the Saturday, was not solely in response to the news of violence (on both sides) and the hardening of opposition both amongst the local miners and their communities, but to evaluate the logistical problems that were being encountered by the striking miners, who numbered around ten thousand, obtaining the fundamental essential of food and water that literally could starve them out.

Thus the support that his miners had received in Yorkshire, the North East and Scotland was clearly being reversed in the first area where he had anticipated opposition, but not on this unexpected scale.

On his arrival, at Ollerton, he was booed and the target of pieces of coal thrown with venom and luck by his enemies (one of which brutally caught him on his cheek opening a wound that observers calculated should have taken at least ten stitches to repair, thus permitting him, in his speech, to join the ranks of the injured) and to the repeated chant of ...

"Murderer", whilst his supporters responded, but without the conviction of their opponents...

"Traitors and scabs."

His speech was brief and specifically directed at his own supporters, both exhorting and haranguing them, the highlight being not the contents but his refusal to seek any form of medical aid thus a large patch of congealed blood was clearly visible on his left cheek and would be publicised in the following day`s national and regional Sunday newspapers, though the news coverage and editorial content was overwhelmingly unfavourable.

His brief speech, recorded by B.B.C. sound engineers, was unmemorable, urging his supporters to remain strong and resolute but above all defiant and that they could, and should, use any means including violent force to secure their cause against the forces of oppression that now confronted them in the form of the police and communities that had cravenly submitted to the false promises and implied threats of the National Coal Board.

Sunday was to become the bloodiest day ('Bloody Sunday') in the confrontation and the number of deaths and severe injuries would shock the nation and have unexpected results.

SEVENTY-SEVEN

On Friday evening, February twenty-sixth, nineteen sixty-five, in Curzon Street, Mayfair, London, a secret and unrecorded event, that was afterwards to be the subject of much speculation took place, the consequences of which had a profound effect on the British people.

At the meeting hosted by Sir Oswald Mosley, at which both John Tyndall, whose star was rapidly ascending, and his nemesis and rival Colin Jordan, whose career and reputation had reached its nadir, were invited, though neither would have probably attended had they known that their arch rival and former friend would be present. At the root of their enmity was that they blamed each other for a period of imprisonment under the Nineteen Thirty Six Public Order Act and the fact that Colin Jordan had used a later opportunity to seduce Tyndall`s fiancée, Francoise Dior, and marry her.

Neither man trusted the other and it was self evident, because of future events, that both parties saw the agreement, or understanding, as a temporary measure.

Briefly, historically, Tyndall's National Labour Party (which the mainstream Labour Party had prevented him from using the name) merged, in nineteen sixty, with Colin Jordan's White Defence League to form the British National Party and later, with others, they formed a paramilitary private army, which was illegal under the Act, called Spearhead.

In August nineteen sixty-two (in fact on the sixteenth) along with others, they were arrested and subsequently charged, convicted and imprisoned. Jordan was released first and possibly to assist Dior, who was Tyndall's fiancée, avoid deportation, they were married thus creating a schism.

Before the Second World War, following the death of his first wife, Oswald Mosley was secretly remarried in the Berlin home of Joseph Goebbels where Adolf Hitler was an honoured guest. Mosley never forgot that on May twenty-third nineteen forty, as the French and British armies collapsed before the German blitzkrieg, that he and his wife were interned under Defence Regulation 18 B.

Central to the meeting was that Mosley persuaded the two men to swear an oath on his personal signed copy of 'My Struggle', given to him at his wedding, compelling the two men to abide by his judgement and wishes.

Sir Oswald Mosley was not naive, indeed he expressed his uncertainty about the future, but his analysis, perhaps partially based on erroneous biased reasons was correct. With great foresight he believed that current events and the dramatic rise of the New Order had never placed them in such a strong position to influence the nation's destiny. Chillingly, he announced that perhaps even a single major catastrophe could send democracy over the edge of a precipice and into an abyss creating a void where the national trauma and demand for security and stability would allow them to directly influence national policy.

Mosley then suggested that he could, at some later stage, represent the 'New Order' as a figurehead, the representative of stability and British values, though he conceded that power should and would be concentrated in an inner core, where even he might not have the final authority or veto.

Not surprisingly, exposing his obsession and paranoia, he referred to the 'Jewish Question' and it is clear that if anything his almost criminal and pathological hatred had not subsided, indeed it had, because of events over the last twenty years, hardened, and his comments and warnings specifically referred to the secret Jewish conspiracy culminating in the foundation of the State of Israel in nineteen forty-eight, "By the Zios" and the ongoing, almost continuous, confrontation with her neighbours and separately the emerging struggle of militant Islam which he believed would intensify, spread and engulf and destabilise the white Aryan nations of Christianity.

Zionism and the State of Israel (which in private he sneeringly referred to as occupied Palestine) was but the public face of a poison that had insidiously permeated white Christian civilisation and was a precursor of a bacillus that would destroy the values and traditions that had, from the time of Christ, been the strength of Western society.

But in a conclusion that further confirmed his position he argued that Britain's greatest ally and cultural partner, the United States, was infiltrated and dominated by Jews ('Yid vermin') and their supporters and it might be necessary not to publicise or promote their policies until such time as there was a more favourable attitude in North America.

Mosley proposed that Colin Jordan be allowed to found a new clandestine quasi military force to defend the community, independent of the police and of the New Order, whose existence could initially be hidden from the authorities and the application of the Nineteen Thirty-Six Public Order Act. Its prime purpose would be 'direct action' against enemies and opponents of the New Order whilst the New Order would continue as a purely political party espousing policies, and if it reached the seat of power, enacting policies that satisfied the demands of the people until such time as they could freely pursue their real agenda.

Tyndall remembered the lessons of history, both recent and ancient, and how plots and coups had been engineered against civilian governments by small military groups led by single minded and ruthless power seekers, but agreed to the arrangement, much to Colin Jordan's surprise, though he intended, when circumstances warranted, to have access to far stronger military power.

The three men had each achieved some benefit from the unexpected meeting, more so Mosley and Jordan but Tyndall realised that it was only a matter of time and place before, like Hitler's 'Night of the Long Knives, 'The Terror' of the French Revolution and Stalin's purges and 'Great Terror' he would have to ruthlessly annihilate and dispose of his enemies.

SEVENTY-EIGHT

Sunday, February twenty-eighth, was recognised both as the most violent day of the miners` confrontation but also when support began to erode from the unofficial strikers across the nation, in transportation, industry, commerce and public services. Indeed, there was a common thread amongst the editorials that readers read on the Monday morning...

'Enough is enough' and 'the rule of law must prevail'.

No one knew, not even the Prime Minister, that by the following Sunday, March seventh, Martial Law would be in force, but not publically evident, and that democracy would never return, despite the sincere promises of the few remnants of the decimated government.

In all, most likely, about twenty-seven people died that Sunday, definitely including three serving police officers and two nurses. No definitive figure can ever be confidently confirmed since there were various numbers estimated by the national newspapers on the Monday and during the ensuing week, though once Martial Law had been declared ,one of the first acts of the government and its representatives was to release a statement confirming that the total dead numbered forty-seven!, an amount that was generally received with doubt and was an indication of how truth was to be perverted, but in any case the situation was overtaken by an event that was completely unexpected and catastrophic. The seriously injured numbered in their hundreds (possibly as high as two hundred and fifty) where hospitalisation was necessary (many, mostly the insurgent strikers, had to return to the North East for treatment) and those suffering minor injuries, that could be treated on site, were well into four figures.

There was no formal plan, nor was each mine acting on its own initiative. Local journalists with access and sometimes intimate knowledge of the miners` intentions conjectured that, by telephone, a network had sprung up, loosely coordinated by the emotive desire to rid their pits of the invaders, 'once and for all ', and to secure the liberation of their friends, imprisoned in what might shortly be their tombs and quoting an age old adage...

'The sooner, the better'.

The apportionment of blame, for the vicious sectarian violence, is not the responsibility of this author, for his responsibility is to present to you, the reader, the facts as best as possible, taking into account the mayhem and biased observations of those who were actually involved in the confrontations or who were witnesses, but partial to one side or the other.

Film taken at the time is now very rare and all that can be verified is that the strikers could, but not conclusively, be identified by their balaclavas whilst many of the local miners wore their safety headgear in anticipation of the likely violence.

The following narrative is a mosaic that perhaps offers a distorted panorama of the various confrontations that occurred on the Sunday and possibly projects an unfair picture of the events because within the confines of this work it is not possible to tell the story of each of the forty or so pits.

The only and most consistent fact is that events began when, at what would have been about clocking on time for the morning weekday shift, local miners, many of whom intended to follow, as soon as possible, the observation of the Sabbath, began to mass at their local pits.

Most would not be able to attend Church later that morning and for three men from one small village, tragically, they would be driven to their local place of worship in funeral hearses such was the violence and unrestrained mayhem.

But by lunchtime, nearly all, over thirty of the smaller pits had been reclaimed and the local miners, who had been incarcerated since the Friday afternoon, had been winched to the surface and were able, once again, to experience and enjoy the pleasure of fresh, crisp, winter air.

Victory had been accomplished by sheer weight of numbers since the occupying strikers were vastly outnumbered by the local miners and their supporters, whose anger and vehemence meant that there was, or could be, no compromise, no informal or formal request for the usurpers to vacate and leave under a symbolic flag of truce. Indeed this was a classical case of one of the roots and causes of war: the recovery of lost territory justifying the use of force.

There was no common pattern to the confrontations at each mine, however the initial response to their opening salvoes was unexpected and cruelly vicious. The occupying strikers, who had barely eaten or drunk for some twenty hours, were subjected to a deluge of lumps of coal, thrown by the locals, which rained down on them, causing the small number of police on duty at each location to temporarily leave the field of battle, find shelter and to contact their superiors for additional support and instructions.

Much of the coal that had not shattered or was reusable was thrown back, causing more damage because of the greater and more concentrated number of locals.

The missiles were beginning to cause minor injuries on both sides, when, in an escalation, the occupying miners began to throw rotting potatoes, impregnated with protruding razor blades and at some sites, rusty nails or shards of glass were also used. The shock and damage that these weapons caused was out of all proportion to the number of missiles thrown.

Two extremely nasty devices were found at Harwood colliery: two steel catapults able to propel a stone up to seventy yards with great accuracy and power.

Revenge enflamed the locals, who began to dismantle rows of iron railings whilst others dismantled or wrecked their own bicycles, salvaging the chains which many then began to whirl around their heads as perhaps did David, brandishing his loaded sling before Goliath.

A few, remembering the almost semi comic efforts of their fathers and even grandfathers when they joined the Local Defence Volunteers (the embryonic Civil Defence) on the outbreak of war, quickly went to their allotments to retrieve their three or four pronged garden forks which, in close quarter combat, were most unwieldy, but as a weapon confronting the chaotic departure of the beaten foe was a formidable instrument of revenge.

No record exists if anyone contracted tetanus from the prongs of the garden forks.

Outnumbered, cold, hungry, deprived of fluid and alcohol to stimulate their confidence, the usurpers were confronted by a barrage of their own vicious weapons that had survived the initial delivery and then, again and again, further showers of pieces of coal.

The similarity between the assaults, later led to the accusation by Bill Martin that the events had been planned and coordinated, but the only justification is that most likely they were the simple, impromptu ideas of the locals whilst the use of razor blades was a deliberate and preconceived plan.

Wielding their iron bars, they recklessly bore down on their quarry, hitting out indiscriminately, and as the enemy broke rank and fled they were confronted by the flailing chains that were dextrously utilised and many of the injuries sustained were the nasty impressions moulded onto the faces and arms of the fleeing miners who were then finally confronted by an impenetrable wall of prongs which were used to cause further pain and injury.

The death of one human being is a tragedy, the death of three men from one small village, whose very existence evolved from five generations of miners is, and was, a disaster that created a bitter legacy that would last for years and decades, fermenting an internecine struggle between different regions of the nation's miners and was exploited by those who were to manage the production of coal, fuel and energy.

What took place at the nine larger pits is a more complicated and confusing story simply summarised by the tally, at the end of the day, as six pits being liberated and the other three being isolated and quarantined, though the incarcerated miners at the coal face were then deprived of food and water, a most terrible choice to be made by the local communities, which again was the foundation of years and decades of enmity between regions of coal mining production.

Possibly the invading miners, not by weight of numbers, but by better organisation, were able to defend some of the mines that they had 'liberated' only a few days before or perhaps they represented the more ruthless and determined elements of Martin's Yorkshire pits or those who had grown up in or had experienced the brutality of the Gorbals where the rules of pugilism were unknown or most probably ignored. Thus, when the fighting was face to face or hand to hand, the use of knuckledusters was initially a tactical advantage, but later was to be a mark that identified the users, for at the pits of Hucknal, Thoresby and Bilsthorpe, twelve of the dead, unusually laid out in rows beneath overhanging parapets, were found to be both wearing balaclavas and each, a knuckleduster. But it was the manner of their deaths which was grotesquely uniform and, even taking into account their heinous and atrocious acts, despicable. They had been beaten and kicked to death and at some stage, probably as the *coup de grace*, their heads had been crushed by large pieces of concrete dropped from the nearby parapets.

Many of the injuries, and three confirmed fatalities, were clearly identified by professionals as being caused either by the use of knuckledusters or similar devices including coshes simply constructed from leather sleeves and containing sand or in one case, ground glass.

The 'Order of Battle' was in many ways similar to that which occurred in the smaller pits, however they were marked by greater brutality and innovation.

The most successful manoeuvre, which ultimately broke the backbone of the usurpers at the six pits which were reclaimed, was the use of lorries as battering rams. In anticipation of the defenders' intention to attack the driver and a brave 'mate', they were locked inside and the windscreen and side windows were covered by a triple layer of mesh and then barbed wire, secured from local farmers and National Coal Board warehouses, which was weaved around the outside of the cabin to delay and deter their enemies from ripping off the layers of mesh.

At some locations up to three lorries would simultaneously, line abreast, 'rev up' and then rapidly accelerate into the body of the occupying miners with devastating effect (and then quickly reverse back to their own lines) though the method was rendered obsolete once the defenders began to recognise the impending attack, for they were to use, with the most horrible and tragic consequences, two nasty devices, for those who would suffer injury (and sometimes death). The first was a simple Molotov cocktail formed from milk bottles filled with petroleum and ignited by a simple fuse of a strip of clothing but much more cruel was an adaptation using possibly, as an additional ingredient, petroleum jelly, which made a rudimentary and crude, though highly effective, napalm bomb, which the defenders used both against the local miners and their lorries, for the petroleum or mixture would seep into the vehicle and the ignited jelly like matter would stick to the skin, burning through muscle and bone resulting in hideous injuries to the driver and passenger or even worse be ignited by the heat of the engine, exploding and wrecking the lorry as one did at Thoresby colliery.

The death of two nurses and three policemen took place at Bevercotes colliery when one of the police officers had vainly and bravely tried to intercede between the two opposing groups and had been knocked over by a lorry which then having successfully rammed (and possibly killed two or three of the less nimble or perhaps foolhardy and brave opposition), reversed into a group of two nurses and two policemen who had come to the aid of the fatally wounded officer. The driver, possibly unaware of the accident, automatically reversed back with disastrous results, hitting the four and killing them, possibly instantaneously.

Like the Tiber, in an earlier conflict, blood flowed indiscriminately, as chaos and mayhem triumphed over law and order.

Reports broadcast to a shocked nation beginning early that Sunday afternoon and the evening's news were viewed, or listened to with increasing disbelief and incredulity. Comparisons with the General Strike, nearly forty years before, were mentioned but no one who was interviewed or who was asked to comment on the events could, in any way, relate the violence and details of the casualties and rising number of dead to any known peace time occurrence

Ten Downing Street was unusually active for a Sunday evening, as the P.M. and Home Secretary were, by telephone, in constant communication with the local police, and the Cabinet Office, on their own initiative, had arrived 'en masse', in anticipation of urgent business and both Mandel Goldburgh and Gerald Kaufman could be seen, waiting for a summons. Wilson had lost patience with the Unions and the T U C. Law and order had to be restored, the nation had to return to work and he wanted the nation to present a credible, unified force in the eyes of her major ally and an enemy that dangerously lurked close by across the English Channel.

Martial Law would bring the nation to its senses and would give him the opportunity to control the Unions. The Cabinet Office was urgently charged to organise the necessary procedures.

SEVENTY-NINE

It was exactly twenty-nine hours since the First Secretary had pressed a glass of ice cold vodka into his hand and ordered him to join the Politburo in a toast.

He was still experiencing both the thrill and euphoria of that seminal moment and the earlier tension as he waited to enter the conference room, but from the instance he entered and stood at the side of Leonid Brezhnev and began his presentation, it was as if he was suffering from amnesia! He vaguely recollected, at some stage, that he must have made a strong impression, for he remembered the First Secretary raise a smile as if to support him.

More so, he vividly recollected leaving the room and being greeted by the adjutant who was holding the two briefcases which he never saw again and he felt certain that the contents would have been returned to its owner.

He was unable to confide in the adjutant and realised that any explanation he would give his wife might not be believable, especially when she saw his extensive new military clothing.

The Zil limousine, again accompanied by a team of motor cycle outriders and two cars, had swept out of the Kremlin and travelled along the road at the side of the mighty river though he was both too exhausted and elated to appreciate the importance of the moment.

He had been greeted at the entrance to the dacha by the adjutant's superior who had real tears in his eyes; the general hugged him and with sincere emotion stated that he had, in truth, been aware of his work and had just heard how the Politburo had been swayed by his convincing presentation.

The members and candidate members of the Politburo were, even as he spoke, being disbursed to pre determined hardened shelters in the Ukraine, Russia and in the vast, almost unending lands East of the Urals in preparation for Plan Kashkarov!

From now on he was in protective custody on the orders of the First Secretary!, which sounded more ominous than the reality. Their immediate task was to destroy any documentation that had been left on the desk, after which, with the tacit approval of the general, as a memento of his work, he retained two slide-rules, a number of pencils and as many biros, in a rainbow of colours, that he could hold, but a few minutes later he was presented with a box containing a great number and mixture of biros.

He was to be flown home early the following morning, reunited with his wife and then both of them were to be moved to the still unfinished and spartan subterranean complex of Mezhgorye in the Yamantau Gory where the adjutant and a dedicated team of troops would protect him. Two members of the Politburo had been allocated to the complex and his duty was to be available at all times and to offer them advice and assistance on any matter.

The general suggested in the short time left that they should visit the city and view the many magnificent sites including the tomb of Lenin but when Kashkarov suggested the G.U.M. department store, he burst into laughter and confirmed that his wish would be immediately granted.

It was to be now or perhaps never. As they entered the outskirts of the city he recognised the area where they had first lived, so happily, after their marriage; he gave the driver the address and the limousine, flanked by the motorcyclists and protected by the two cars, deviated from their route and began to explore the neighbourhood. The old area had been obliterated and razed and there was nothing left except his memories for all he could see was a symmetrical pattern of anonymous, soul-less, boring and dull tower blocks, a memorial to, and a symbol of Stalinism.

It was only a few minutes later that they reached the great and spectacular building, in the Kitai-gorod area of Moscow, facing Red Square, which as usual, was swamped by a massive, but organised queue, waiting patiently to be admitted.

He quietly resigned himself to a long wait but was surprised when the vehicle stopped immediately outside the main entrance and the general, without waiting, marched in with the obsequious assistance of the two burly doormen. Ignoring the many displays and counters, he continued to march to a lift, isolated from the other bank of lifts and with severe authority ordered the compliant staff to transport him to Section 100 on the top floor.

On arrival, Kashkarov was blinded by the rich and varied selection of goods that he had only once before seen when in Finland, but had also read about in Western newspapers and magazines that had been supplied to him for their contents on military matters.

The general laughed again, this time more discreetly, when he answered his guest's plea that:

"He had very little money, a few roubles", explaining that:

"This was to be a gift from the Party and the State for his service."

He was so embarrassed and the general could not again help laughing at him. He had no idea how much his wife weighed, or her height or shoe size or even the colour of her eyes. It took almost a parade of some ten or so assistants for him to sheepishly point out one who," he thought", was most similar to his wife.

With largesse the general permitted the man to accumulate a treasure trove of clothing, sometimes leaving the choice to a female member of staff. The cavernous boot of the limousine only just swallowed the mountain of gifts.

For the second and last ever time he swam in the indoor pool until overcome by sheer exhaustion, then permitting himself the hedonistic pleasure of a long massage and went to his room for a well earned and necessary sleep.

That evening, accompanied by the general, he returned to Moscow for the final time, where they were driven to an unimposing terraced building that, by its architecture, had been built before the Revolution and displayed nothing to suggest its purpose. But once inside he was overwhelmed, not by its dramatic grandeur, but by the opulence of the reception room and beyond that, the first of, he was informed, three elegantly furnished and decorated restaurants.

He had never experienced such luxury or superb service, even fleetingly remembering that train journey during the war, from Moscow to the Ukraine, but as the vodka loosened the tongue of his host, he was to learn so much that had been hidden from him including an answer to the almost bizarre encounter before his conference meeting.

He had been searching for the most suitable and appropriate words to describe his host; effusive and garrulous would have adequately applied, but he also noted that whilst the general obviously enjoyed the vodka that was being served to them, that his host was in total self control and would not allow the alcohol to control him or his tongue.

How they arrived at the subject, he did not remember, but his host informed him that he had joined the OGPU (Joint State Political Directorate) in nineteen thirty-one and in nineteen thirty-six the NKVD (Main Directorate for State Security) of the USSR, which had absorbed and superseded the OGPU; later the bureau had assigned him to the Inostrannyi Otdel (Intelligence and Overseas Special Operations) and sent him to Spain under cover as an representative of a Soviet government body supplying humanitarian aid and medical supplies, thus giving him the cover to visit hospitals and even prisons and it was at a secret prison that he was a witness to the execution, or murder, in June nineteen thirty-seven of (the author has deleted the vile expletives) Andres Nin, by garrotting, carried out by an extremely sadistic and cruel Soviet NKVD agent.

All that Kashkarov subsequently remembered of the man's life was that in nineteen fifty-seven he had been promoted to deputy head of personal security for members of the Politburo and other high ranking officials and in nineteen sixty-four had been assigned to the new First

Secretary, at his personal request or on his orders, following the 'retirement' of his predecessor.

The general seized Kashkarov's complete attention when, without an indication of his intentions, his voice became quieter and certainly more discreet and judicious. The First Secretary had been actively involved in Plan Kashkarov for some three months and his adjutant had passed secret instructions to the head of the RVSN thereby bypassing the Supreme High Command, authorising four missile launch complexes special training, where they had perfected both the urgent replacement of the missiles' thermonuclear warheads with non nuclear weapons that could be detonated by a highly advanced encoded trigger mechanism and frighteningly, multiple launches, which led the RVSN staff to believe that all total was imminent.

On January fifteenth, just over a month before, at Chagan (Kashkarov had never heard of the place),in the Semipalatinsk Test Area (he was well aware of the purpose of this isolated region), an underground nuclear test had taken place which complied with the Partial Nuclear Test Ban Treaty, but it was rumoured that not only had there been a leak of nuclear material in violation of the Treaty but more importantly it was believed that the nuclear test (incidentally with a yield equivalent to 140 kilotons of TNT) and ostensibly designed to produce a peaceful nuclear explosion for earth moving purposes, was a 'cover' in preparation of a far more crucial test using the nuclear device as a trigger for a new generation of missile warheads, thermonuclear devices in the fifteen megaton range that, if accurately targeted, could destroy any city on Earth.

The menu was international and comprehensive. He ordered a 650 gramme New York Strip Sirloin steak, a dish that he remembered eating, with relish at the camp, but of course he was unable to explain his reason and was disappointed when the waiter, with great regret, apologised, and explained that their last four portions had just been served but he could recommend the Nebraskan Prime Rib of Beef, seven hundred and fifty grammes, which would be cooked medium to well done and that he should not be daunted or intimidated by the size, but should enjoy the superb flavour, indeed earlier ,at lunch, a regular visitor from Europe had signalled his appreciation and enjoyment of what he had called 'a superb example of American beef'.

It was an excellent choice but a challenge that was not successfully completed.

The general was less than forthcoming when he summonsed up the courage to ask the one question that had played upon his mind and indeed confirmed his suspicion that the man was in complete control of his thoughts despite his continuous imbibing.

"I understand that from the time of Lenin, the First Secretary and his opposite number in the White House, the United States President, have found it convenient and expedient to sometimes bypass normal diplomatic channels so that certain matters could be explored and discussed."

"There are only two men capable of acting as intermediaries or messengers, one of whom was raised in the United States but both, from childhood, were brought up in households where Russian was their second natural tongue and both, coincidentally, also came from Jewish stock. Armand Hammer is an American industrialist and a true and genuine friend of the Soviet Union. There is even an aura surrounding him for his relationship with the Soviet Union goes back to the days of Lenin. I have heard from his own lips that after the civil war, during the period of famine and later a typhus epidemic, that for both philanthropic and commercial reasons, he was able to facilitate the urgent import of surplus American wheat and medical supplies, bartering a deal with Lenin himself for furs and caviar.

Despite what the world views as a confrontation between the Soviet Union and the United States, bilateral trade still exists and, I understand, that Mr. Hammer is rewarded in return by generous gifts of Impressionist and Post Impressionist paintings.

The other man, who is the subject of your interest, is more enigmatic and even his true identity and origins are confused and ambiguous. Whilst Armand Hammer`s primary residence is the United States, the other man`s sphere is mainly Europe and Israel which is seen as the only stable nation in the region and whilst our loyalties sometime lie with her enemies it is prudent to develop and expand our contact.

Of the two, Hammer is the more refined and predictable, the other is enigmatic and his motives more clandestine and unpredictable but his faults are outweighed by his cooperation and integrity."

He had become not only a little wiser but proud that his plans had reached fruition.

The plane landed with a bump and skidded slightly, bringing him back to reality.

EIGHTY

Joel Ben Yitzhak thoroughly enjoyed his gargantuan Nebraskan Prime Rib of Beef which defeated his best efforts, however the remainder was crafted into an appetising sandwich encased in rye bread with a layer of coleslaw which he would eat en route to Washington and before his meeting with the President. He flew to London via Stockholm and boarded a Pan Am flight, which was delayed for his exclusive convenience by some thirty minutes, much to the annoyance of the other passengers who had been waiting, strapped into their seats.

The appetising sandwich was devoured with relish and the trencherman`s appreciation of good wholesome food.

Both Armand Hammer and Joel Ben Yitzhak could precisely understand the nuances and subtle tones of the First Secretary`s messages but were also able to translate and communicate in English exactly the equivalent of the original Russian.

He had travelled through perhaps eight or even nine time zones and when the plane touched down he was initially unaware of the local time since he had drifted into, and out of, sleep and had missed any announcements that might have been made whilst his body clock was sending out contradictory and disorienting messages.

He was rushed through the formalities of immigration and customs and met by a Cadillac limousine which urgently transported him to an obscure rear entrance to the White House where he was ushered through subterranean tunnels that shielded his presence from prying eyes, including the ever vigilant and inquisitive press and entered the Oval office where Robert McNamara and Bobby Kennedy were seated each side of, and in earnest conversation, with the President.

Any formality was immediately swept aside when LBJ enquired if...

"That miserable bastard in the Kremlin had any good news for him and if he had smiled recently?"

He had brought an unexpected message, the final part of which was both chilling and menacing and...

"Yes, apparently the First Secretary had smiled once during the course of a rather tense meeting of the Politburo which had ended less than forty–eight hours before (he was not, at that precise moment, able to calculate exactly when) and the President and his closest advisors would be put under great pressure because of the time scale laid down in the message.

Present at the meeting had been the First Secretary, Politburo member Andrei Gromyko, an unnamed man who appeared to be a specialist in biological and chemical warfare and the head of the RVSN - The Strategic Rocket Forces - (The messenger noted that McNamara had, first of all, by his facial expression, exhibited concern when the presence of a 'specialist' in biological and chemical warfare was mentioned but then became extremely interested when the RVSN was raised as a subject and presumably, for intelligence purposes, had written down the man`s name, possibly his status and most likely the confirmed title of the organisation). His briefing must have started almost immediately after the end of the Politburo meeting and incidentally he had earlier fleetingly met the planning officer who had subsequently, as he understood, given a presentation to the Politburo which, he was reliably informed, had raised a rare smile from Brezhnev."

Robert McNamara briefly interrupted him to remind the President that Gromyko had signed, for the Soviet Union, along with Dean Rusk and Alec Douglas–Home (LBJ always thought of him as the cadaverous aristocrat), the Partial (or Limited) Test Ban Treaty only eighteen months before on August fifth nineteen sixty-three and in anticipation of an important message summonsed a secretary to record the statement.

"The Union of Soviet Socialist Republics would not, on moral, political or military grounds be the first to employ the use of thermonuclear weapons, indeed the fundamental principle of their military forces on land, sea and in the air was based on the defence of the nation and only afterwards to retaliate against aggression.

Reluctantly it had been found necessary, indeed there was no alternative, but to violate the terms of the Limited Test Ban Treaty and on Saturday February twenty-seventh, a surface test explosion of a fifteen megaton device, the latest generation in the RDS series of weapons, specially designed for their retaliatory Inter Continental Ballistic Missile force, would take place somewhere near Mityushikha Bay in the Novaya Zemlya Island complex located at approximately 73 degrees 45 minutes North and 60 degrees East. The estimated time of denotation would be approximately ten hundred hours G.M.T."

At that point Kennedy, who had been feverishly calculating the equivalent time on the Eastern seaboard confirmed that the detonation was some forty one hours ahead.

Clearly this test had been planned for some time and the information would give them the opportunity to monitor the explosion by seismic recordings, space satellites and possibly, but now very risky, by U2 spy planes operating outside of Soviet territory, one of which might be able to 'scoop up' debris from the blast, allowing their scientists to possibly calculate the structure of the device.

They were not prepared for the second part of the message which would be received with shock and perhaps even disbelief, whilst the third and final part was an unambiguous warning and portent of an ominous development in Soviet intentions.

"The RVSN had upgraded their capabilities and had requested permission to launch a multiple firing of the current generation of Intercontinental Ballistic missiles from bases in the Asiatic theatre, fitted with dummy, non nuclear warheads. It was imperative that their request be met and the launches, from one, or more likely two sites, would take place on the Tuesday morning again, but not exactly, at ten hundred hours G.M.T. In all anything up to nine missiles would be launched at two targets in the Pacific and North Atlantic."

He briefly stopped and produced a sheet of paper on which the head of the Strategic Rocket Forces had written two sets of coordinates and in Cyrillic had made some brief calculations that, as was later observed, could have been made by an above average grade sixteen year old High School student.

"It was recommended, for safety purposes, that an 'Exclusion Zone' of some twenty thousand square kilometres be observed but if for any reason, and the United States was an independent sovereign nation, they wished closer access to the 'Target Area', a shrunken inner exclusion zone of only five hundred and fifty square kilometres was suggested, such was their confidence in the accuracy of the rockets.

It was realised that an unannounced test firing of such magnitude would only be interpreted as a surprise first strike and the fragile peace which currently existed would be shattered and the world would be plunged into global war.

The 'Hot Line' should be activated without delay in order that the President could acknowledge the message and confirm his acceptance of the tests, though, for security and strategic purposes, the location of the launch sites could not be divulged.

It was further intended to publicly announce the missile tests on the preceding Sunday at twelve hundred hours G.M.T. simultaneously in Geneva and Stockholm and the statements were being drafted, possibly concurrently with the delivery of this message. The American people and especially those living in the coastal cities of San Diego, Los Angeles, San Francisco, Seattle (then rather peculiarly, Las Vegas), New York, Philadelphia, Norfolk and finally Miami had nothing to fear and should be assured of their safety."

Later, when the coordinates were checked, the significance of the target area in the Pacific was realised. It was North East of Midway and South of the Aleutian Islands exactly where, in June nineteen forty-two, an outnumbered American naval task force had made a victorious stand against a larger, invading Japanese task force that had intended, after wiping out first Midway and then Pearl Harbour, to destroy domination of the Pacific by the United States navy.

Perhaps the target point symbolised the Soviet Union's desire and intention to declare their undisputed influence and presence in that great Ocean?

The other site lay two hundred miles South of Iceland where ships plied between Scandinavia and the 'New World' and where Britain, whose primary purpose was secretly designated to act as an impregnable and unsinkable 'aircraft carrier 'containing Soviet expansion, also sent her merchant fleet to the 'bread basket' of Canada.

Joel Ben Yitzhak continued...

"The perfidious and belligerent British under the war monger Wilson had not accepted the *de facto* reality and moral right of the Soviet Union and her allies in the Warsaw Treaty Organisation to liberate the nations of Western Europe, a task which the Red Army had only partially completed twenty years before, but had been prematurely halted in the razed city of Berlin to accommodate the glory of general Dwight D. Eisenhower who had ignored the sacrifices of Mother Russia and stopped her forces liberating and freeing occupied France along with West Germany, Belgium and Holland..."

At which moment the President bluntly interrupted the ongoing statement and with barbed irony and rhetoric asked...

"If those present had the same view and understanding of twentieth century history?",

but then apologised for his interruption and requested that, hopefully, the message could be completed.

"Our Defence forces have irrefutable evidence that the attack on the Island of Rugen had been overseen by airborne British control centres that had been shot down, however the wreckage had been salvaged, recovered and pieced together. But the gangster Wilson, to his eternal shame, also had the blood of millions of innocent women and children on his hands for he had boasted to the British people how the Royal Air Force had actively participated in the attack on Russia and the Ukraine which was genocide by any other name.

Indisputable evidence had very recently been received that large consignments of the chemical sodium fluoride had been delivered to Porton Down, a location known to be a centre for the production of nerve gases and he was assured (at which point the messenger mentioned that the unnamed man had interrupted the First Secretary's comments and had unsuccessfully endeavoured to inform Brezhnev that the chemical, in conjunction with others ,was a 'precursor', but Brezhnev brushed aside his advices) and that the nerve gas Sarin could be manufactured in vast amounts. The tragedy of retribution would be that the innocent British people would suffer for his actions."

The President allowed him to finish and then asked, and probably expected confirmation of his opinion...

"What his assessment was of Brezhnev's statement?"

The answer was not evasive and clearly was in resonance with the President's opinion, for he nodded his head before asking McNamara and Kennedy for their comments which were in total agreement.

"My responsibility is only to convey to you the First Secretary's message and not act as an analyst or strategist, however from the tone of his statement and the words that he employed I can only assume that he intends to punish Britain and that can only mean military action."

He was thanked for his services and in response confirmed his willingness to again act as an intermediary.

EIGHTY-ONE

The 'Hot Line' was never originally intended to be a two way telephone system where spontaneous verbal communication might lead to misunderstandings and misconceptions, but a telegraph terminating in Moscow and Washington each with a teleprinter, the former location supplied by the United States with a Latin alphabet and the latter location supplied by the Russians, but manufactured by the West German company Siemens, with a Cyrillic alphabet.

Messages would be encrypted using an electronic system utilising the unbreakable one time pad method, details of which were supplied by each country to the other via their embassies.

There was almost immediate, unanimous agreement that, without delay, the message be acknowledged, but until they had carefully considered what was almost a veiled threat to the United Kingdom, and the ramifications of the two tests, that a comprehensive response be delayed. Thus within an hour a reply was sent via the telegraph which read (in clear)...

"The messenger has delivered the First Secretary`s statement and comments. We will reply, in detail, within approximately twelve hours."

Some members, but not all, of the National Security Council, were urgently summonsed whilst those who could not be present or were not invited to attend, were kept informed and were able to participate by scrambled telephone conference call. It was deemed imperative that the media was not made aware of a potential crisis and the nature of the problem.

Johnson had begun, less and less, to rely on the wisdom and advices of the N.S.C.`s members, more and more using them to 'rubber stamp' decisions made beforehand. Each of those present had a copy of the statement before them and the four members not present, including the Chairman of the Joint Chiefs of Staff, who was in the Pentagon, had their copies within a further ten minutes.

Secretary of State Dean Rusk could be relied upon to give an unbiased, objective and pragmatic analysis of the message and clearly his comments were received with grave concern.

"The shock, destruction and trauma suffered by the Soviet Union was immeasurable, but the intended tests showed their determination to confront the United States with a weapons system that would deter us from repeating the attack. The two tests were probably, on one level, just tests, but also a warning of their capabilities... Notification (to the American people) was no doubt a veiled threat that could cause widespread panic and had to be countered by a statement from the President... If this was a prelude to war (which was unlikely), the opening salvo, then the Soviet Union had lost the initiative.

Strategically, the United States' medium to long term policy was the containment of the Soviet Union and their potential expansion. Recovery and liberation of lost territory on the European mainland was no longer a feasible option and possibly their bellicose posturing was a prelude to a diplomatic offensive to legitimise, by treaty, sovereignty over the occupied territories.

He feared the worst. Brezhnev's diatribe was both dishonest and hypocritical for the same source of intelligence would have confirmed that the nuclear attack on Russia and the Ukraine was an American operation as was the attack on the two vessels moored off of the island of... (he had forgotten its name, such was its insignificance).

The most imminent threat was to the United Kingdom. If Brezhnev did plan an attack on their ally he felt morally, politically and militarily obligated to warn Wilson, if only for the sake of the British people who had gone through so much in the blitz in the defence of their freedom and to keep the light of..."

At which point LBJ interjected and caustically observed that:

"His Presidential Oath was to uphold the Constitution and defend the nation, not to look after the fate of the British people and her feckless government and its predecessor."

Dean Rusk, clearly directing his remarks to the President and not to those present at the meeting, sombrely reminded him of the declaration that he had made effectively 'modernising and updating' the famous 'Monroe' Doctrine which created a line, which if crossed would, or should, draw the United States into war to defend her interests, but before the President could even consider his response the disembodied voice of the Chairman of the Joint Chiefs of Staff was suddenly heard requesting that his observations and comments be urgently heard...

"The current level of military readiness- known as DEFCON - be immediately raised and as a precautionary measure, the Russians be made aware of their actions, furthermore the Strategic Air Command should be made ready to launch, in the event of the unthinkable, a counter as distinct from a retaliatory first strike."

At that time the S.A.C. was under the command of four star general Thomas Sarsfield Power (an ultra ruthless 'Hawk' who believed that the only effective policy was deterrence, more specifically known as Mutual Assured Destruction) who should have retired on the previous November thirtieth, but had been requested to continue for a further six months following an illness suffered by his successor, John Dale Ryan).

Displaying an unexpected degree of wisdom and rhetoric he confirmed the philosophy which was to form the backbone of the President's later speech to the nation...

"We are ready to defend the freedom of our nation and there would be no thermonuclear Pearl Harbour; the nation's forces were more than adequately armed and that their primary duty was to maintain peace and to deter aggression."

Perhaps inspired by the previous speaker, the Secretary of the Treasury, a non statutory member of the Council, boldly challenged the President's position on the transfer of intelligence to the British Government and suggested that:

"Whilst we are all aware of the President's injunction on the transfer of intelligence to our British friends, the potential of military action is so strong and possibly imminent that I would like to ask the President's permission that we convey, perhaps via the British ambassador, and possibly unofficially, a warning, without disclosing the source of our intelligence, of a possible imminent Soviet attack. It is in our own interests that Britain remains a viable base for our military to encircle and contain Soviet expansion and if Britain became a nuclear wasteland it could dramatically affect our plans. I believe that we cannot dissuade the Soviet Union from carrying out the tests though I also believe that it could give us the opportunity to open diplomatic channels on the grounds that the Partial Test Ban Treaty be reviewed and endeavour to diplomatically persuade the Soviet Union and her allies to withdraw from Western Europe but I for one consider their hold to be unbreakable (He briefly paused).

It is imperative that when the President addresses the nation on his regular Friday radio broadcast that his statement be also televised. If the American people were forewarned by the Kremlin of a multiple test launching and an earlier thermonuclear test explosion, the information might create panic and it is therefore paramount that before news was released on the Sunday that the President speak to the nation."

The members turned to the President for his response and after a few moments of contemplation he briefly conceded to the reality of the situation.

Dean Rusk would be permitted to speak unofficially to the British ambassador; DEFCON was to immediately raised, his speechwriters were to prepare a new statement for his broadcast, which would be also televised, and that, without delay, a message be send on the 'Hot Line'.

Significantly, no mention would be made of, or even alluded to, the consequences of the new 'Monroe' Doctrine.

That Friday evening, February twenty-sixth, the people of the United States were to be confronted with a peril even greater and ominous than the one just over two years before when the now slain, young President had shocked the country when he told an incredulous nation that missiles, aimed at their homeland, were at that moment being deployed in an already hostile Cuba.

Different time zones in Washington and Moscow meant that the message was sent only a few hours before the test explosion and especially when it was found that Bobby Kennedy`s calculations were in error.

Dean Rusk, displaying both the cunning of his office and his Anglophile leanings delivered the warning to a surprised British ambassador, but neither of them knew and would probably never know that the 'perfidious' British and more specifically their Intelligence Services had tapped into the 'Hot Line' somewhere between Copenhagen and Stockholm and were desperately, but vainly, endeavouring to decipher the original first brief message.

The second message, which was sent at nine forty a.m., E.S.T. was not vitriolic or even threatening but clearly expressed the concerns of the President and his Administration...

"The current situation has given us no alternative but to globally raise the readiness of our military forces and the Strategic Air Command and will only be lowered when considered prudent.

The imminent test explosion is a clear violation of the Partial Test Ban Treaty and unravels all the work and goodwill that resulted some eighteen months ago when your representative, Andrei Gromyko, was a joint signatory to the Treaty.

The multiple test firing scheduled for next Tuesday is, in our opinion, an act that could destabilise the existing, fragile peace. We would ask you if it is necessary to carry out such an immense launch and also why you indirectly intended to notify the American people?

Sabre rattling and your veiled threats against the United Kingdom are again viewed as actions which could unbalance the equilibrium of the world's current delicate status.

Confirmation that you have received this message is awaited and we would once again ask that you reconsider going ahead, in the interests of peace, with the proposed tests."

Three hours later, on the specific instructions of the President, in the absence of an acknowledgement or a reply, the message was again sent and this time a reply was promptly received but it was not the one that was either expected or desired.

"We have a responsibility and duty to our citizens to protect them. A credible defence and the will to use that defence in response to aggression is essential."

President Lyndon Baines Johnson addressed the American people from the ultimate seat of power, the Oval Office, and as the opening picture widened to show the office in greater detail, to his left was seen his wife, Lynda Bird, and opposite her the Secretary of State, Dean Rusk.

"My fellow Americans, this is not the first time that I have addressed you in a time of crisis, however I have to share with you certain facts that have accumulated in the last few days. We detected unusual activity in an area known as Novaya Zemlya, an inhospitable island complex North of the Siberian mainland which was, and still is, the site of the Soviet's main testing ground for nuclear weapons.

In August nineteen sixty-three, my predecessor, the slain John F. Kennedy, authorised the signature to, along with the United Kingdom and the Soviet Union, of an agreement known as the Partial (Nuclear) Test Ban Treaty which we believed would be the first step in creating a nuclear weapons free world. It was especially intended to ban the detonation of thermonuclear and nuclear weapons on land and in the atmosphere thereby beginning the process of ridding our world of the horrendous threat of global destruction.

Further investigation of the site, by satellite, convinced us that, in violation of the Treaty, a ground based test was in the process of being set up. I have to report to you that the First Secretary, Leonid Brezhnev, has confirmed that a ground based test is to take place in the next twenty –four hours and that he is not prepared to cancel the test.

I have found that in the mature democratic society that we live in it is best to present unpalatable information honestly and devoid of any superfluous facts that might distort the nature of the problem.

Three days ago our continuous surveillance of the Soviet Union, by methods that must remain secret, combined with human intelligence, led us to realise that a limited number of launch complexes in the Asiatic theatre were being brought up to combat readiness and that a number of Inter Continental Ballistic missiles were possibly being armed. I again discussed this matter with the First Secretary who assured both myself and the Secretary of Defence, Robert McNamara, that this was to be a unique, multiple test of their weaponry and we were also able to verify their intended targets in the Pacific and North Atlantic.

Earlier today, on my orders, our forces on land, at sea and in the air were placed on an increased state of readiness and to avoid any misunderstanding the Politburo was informed of our actions which will continue until we are certain that the crisis is over.

You will note that I have not used the word danger for I believe that the tactless and clumsy acts of the Russian leadership are nothing more than an attempt to make us cower in response to their sabre rattling, but we are not a nation to be intimidated.

Less than twenty–four hours ago in a meeting, shrouded in secrecy, the National Security Council was inspired by words spoken by the Chairman of the Joint Chiefs of Staff that I would like to share with you all...

"We are ready to defend the freedom of our nation and there would be no thermonuclear Pearl Harbour; that the nation's forces were more than adequately armed and their primary duty was to maintain peace and deter aggression."

With my beloved wife and family, we will remain in Washington and not cower, craven in a bunker, immune from the terror outside because I am certain that the Soviets do not want war, having already experienced the sword of our just cause.

Finally, remember the words of a great American and former President...

"The only thing we have to fear is fear itself."

The picture dissolved and the radio broadcast went silent.

EIGHTY-TWO

Friday morning E.S.T.

The British ambassador urgently sends an encyphered message to the Foreign Office in London, following his surprise meeting with the Secretary of State, which, combined with the intercepted and undeciphered messages sent between Washington and Moscow, alerts the British government to a potential new crisis. Their code breakers are currently unable to penetrate any of the messages.

Friday afternoon G.M.T.

Harold Wilson is informed by the Foreign Secretary of the ambassador's message and demands that their code breakers penetrate, crack and unbutton the intercepted messages without delay. He is currently embroiled in the miners' confrontation.

Friday evening E.S.T.

President Johnson speaks on the radio to, and is seen on television by, the American people.

Late Friday evening E.S.T.

"Straw" telephone polls conducted by the Washington Post and Los Angeles Times show overwhelming support for the President. The nation stands firm.

Friday evening, believed to about 2255 hours E.S.T.

The President is interrupted in his private apartment. Within the last fifteen minutes satellite reconnaissance and two independent seismic recordings confirm a thermonuclear detonation in the Novaya Zemlya region.

Saturday morning 0032 hours E.S.T.

In a subterranean bunker carved beneath the White House, the President, in the presence of Dean Rusk, Robert Kennedy, Robert McNamara and the Joint Chiefs of Staff agrees that DEFCON be raised again. The United States is now but two levels from total war. He confirms that if the Soviet Union carries out its threatened missile test he will raise the level of readiness by a further one stage.

Saturday morning 0234 hours E.S.T.

The Joint Chiefs of Staff in a hastily convened meeting begin to think the unthinkable and conjecture the possibility of the consequences if the Soviet Union attacks the United Kingdom. General Power is notified that war could be imminent and that he has authority to prepare for a massive launch of every available bomber

Saturday morning 0711 hours G.M.T.

Harold Wilson is interrupted, whilst shaving, by his private secretary, a most unusual procedure and is informed, by telephone, that the B.B.C.at Caversham have monitored a Moscow radio station broadcast which claims that within the last few hours their scientists and engineers have successfully detonated a thermonuclear device of 15.9 megatons, engineered to be accommodated inside their latest generation of Inter Continental Ballistic missiles.

Saturday evening 2257 hours local time.

Kashkarov is visited in his small cell like apartment, deep in the bowels of the Yamantau mountain complex, by his security guard and informed that Politburo members Nikolai Podgorny and Mikhail Suslov have scheduled a meeting for midnight. The general's adjutant orders his detail outside of the room and confides to Kashkarov and his shocked wife, who still knows nothing of recent events, that he has been instructed to inform him that he must be ready to assist the two men and he is advised of the successful test explosion of the new generation of thermonuclear weapons.

EIGHTY-THREE

By Sunday afternoon the Politburo, having been successfully and secretly dispersed across the Soviet Union, leaves only the aged

Nikolay Shvernik in Moscow, where he is to suffer a massive heart attack. The First Secretary, Leonid Brezhnev, together with a very small family entourage, has been flown South to the Ukraine and to an isolated bunker complex located as far from any military establishment as possible to avoid being hit by or caught in the tidal wave of a thermonuclear explosion aimed at a military target.

Politburo member Gennady Voronov, a long time Brezhnev loyalist, is sent to a bunker complex near to the naval base of Petropaviovsk-Kamchatsky on the North Pacific coast and will be responsible to oversee and verify the success of the missile test in the Pacific whilst candidate member to the Politburo, Dinmukhamed Konayev will supervise the 'Atlantic' test performance. They will report back to the First Secretary before the Supreme High Command are notified.

The Supreme High Command, who are responsible to the Communist Party of the Soviet Union and through them, the Defence Council, have been informed of the intentions of the Politburo and await orders to instruct the Strategic Rocket Forces to disarm their missiles and insert dummy payloads. So disciplined are the Supreme High Command that they do not question the fact that their political masters have not previously informed them that some of their forces have been in special training for some time.

The bases at Teykovo (56 52N 040 33E), Vyru (57 46N 026 47E), Chita (52 22N 113 17E) and one of the launch sites in the vast Drovyanaya complex at 51 53N 113 02E,'earmarked' by Kashkarov are to be assigned the 'honour' of the test.

Politburo members agree that there will be no benefit announcing through Geneva and Stockholm on the following day, Sunday, details of the tests however Kashkarov will make a brilliant, inspired, tactical suggestion.

Politburo member Sharof Rashidov, having secretly flown to France with two members of the Supreme High Command, informs the First Secretary that bases in France and Holland have been placed on high alert and on Tuesday morning will receive their tactical nuclear weapons and will be ready to attack on the Wednesday afternoon.

Brezhnev is further informed that the weapons will have a destructive force ranging from twenty to forty-five kilotons and insists that London be allocated four to five bombs.

Rashidov returns to Germany and to a hardened bunker just within the boundary of the old East Germany where he will finally authorise the action and oversee the attack.

The die has been cast.

EIGHTY-FOUR

By mid day on the Monday a clearer picture was emerging of the nation's situation. The moderate local miners had regained control of all but three of the mines in the Midland region, whilst the three, in the hands of the extremists from the North East and Scottish regions, were effectively under siege, denied food and water though their plight was also being experienced, but more so, by the still trapped miners deep underground.

In the North East and in Scotland the militants still continued to be stubbornly defiant and in those regions no coal was being mined at all.

The government would have to wait until the evening for any light to be shed on the general industrial situation, but the omens, or more honestly the optimistic hopes of Wilson and those around him, more strongly held by sycophantic civil servants, was that the drift back to work had swelled, since early signs indicated the nation's revulsion at the level of violence and a rejection of the strike as a weapon of negotiation.

The national newspapers excluding, not unexpectedly, the *Daily Worker* were uniform in their exhortations to the nation to return to work.

The two exclusive, scoop photographs in the *Daily Mirror*, which later drew glowing admiration and plaudits from her rivals was banner headlined by the brief statement...

BRITAIN 1965

The whole of the front page displayed the grim, gruesome, gory, graphic picture of a man, identified as a miner from Staffordshire, his face ripped to shreds as if a demon barber had gone berserk, and on page two was the evidence, in the hands of a police officer, who was widely praised for his bravery (though both his hands had been slashed in the *melee*, wrestling the item from its owner - a Scottish miner). It was a tartan tam-o'-shanter but sewn into the peak were rows of razor blades creating a formidable, vicious weapon that he had wielded without compassion.

Wilson had called an urgent meeting of his inner circle of ministers which took place in the Cabinet room. Facing him, from his left to right were the 'Home' and 'Foreign 'Secretaries, Harold Lever and Patrick Gordon Walker, the Minister of Defence, Edward Heath and the Lord Chancellor, Sir Reginald Manningham–Buller. This was the last time democratically elected Members of Parliament would ever sit in the Cabinet room together and by the end of the meeting underlying tensions would be exposed.

Wilson announced that:

"He considered that the nation's state was now critical. Although the extremist miners seemed to have been repulsed in the Midlands, no coal was being mined in the North East or Scotland and that the country was close to paralysis. He had now to report that the main reason for the meeting and the presence of especially the Minister of Defence, was that the Foreign Office had received an urgent communication from their ambassador in Washington which in summary stated that their American allies had information that the Soviet Union was about to attack the United Kingdom!"

Wilson looked across the table, deliberately avoiding the gaze of Patrick Gordon Walker, who knew that the message had been passed to Wilson some sixty hours before and should have been circulated immediately, whilst the faces of two of the other Ministers clearly expressed their shock and incredulity. Wilson continued...

"I immediately informed Edward (Heath) and understand he has a major statement to make. Last night, (he now lied) before I even had word from Patrick (Gordon Walker) I asked the Cabinet Office, who, on their own initiative had come into work in view of the dramatic events in the Midlands, to investigate the procedure to bring in Martial Law and, no doubt, Reginald (Manningham–Buller) you will advise us of the constitutional procedure."

Edward Heath, Minister of Defence rose, assuming that this was his cue to make what would be a broad statement of his actions and more importantly what action the Chiefs of the General Staff had taken, though it would terminate in a grim and dire analysis...

"Our forces on land, at sea and in the air have been placed on a raised state of readiness. Only a few, a very few of the most senior officers have been made aware of our intelligence and its source.

A contingency plan has been activated known as 'First Foot Fast Forward', which alerts our forces and defence infrastructure that a major exercise is imminent and cancelling all leave. A rumour, to substantiate the government's intended test of readiness, has been sown that officials have been sent to command and control bunkers (our secret Regional Seats of Government) to oversee the exercise and that if members of the government are seen to leave central London then that will indicate that the exercise is about to commence.

In anticipation of a worst case scenario an additional plan, code name 'Sabre Tooth Tiger' has, I understand, already been implemented and strategic reserves of equipment, fuel and above all weapons from arsenals and bunkers have been released and will be held in reserve close to, but not in the immediate vicinity of military bases to forestall any questions or, if war breaks out suddenly, to avoid being hit.

I am awaiting an inventory of our current stock of weapons, especially aircraft, but I have to report that without the assistance of our American allies we will not be able to mount a meaningful counter attack because of the few B52 and 'V' bombers that are available. We are very vulnerable.

You may ask, quite rightly, if our actions could incite the Soviet Union to launch a pre-emptive strike and I do not think that Harold's comments to the country after the attack on the island of Rugen have helped the situation but we can only deal with events as they now arise.

Since we must all be aware of the announcement of an illegal thermonuclear test and the President's speech on Friday evening, which was unusually also broadcast on television, we cannot be certain of the Soviet's intentions.

I have said that we are very vulnerable and I must, in the confidentiality of this room, comment that our position is dire and I doubt if we can hold out for more than a few days though in conclusion we may have to think the unthinkable and the use of nuclear and, God forbid, thermonuclear weapons, that is if the Americans allow us to use such devices, but the only delivery platform that we have, our few bombers, could be our enemy's first target.

I would, for once, concur with my former political foe and agree that Martial Law be brought in immediately or arrangements be made ready. God help us."

An unnatural silence pervaded the room and they might even have heard members of the public playing in the park not far away, oblivious to the potential imminent cataclysm.

Edward Heath had one other contribution to make, which in fact was a rather pertinent observation...

"My dear Harold, for over a year our allies (the tone of his voice expressed disdain and cynicism tinged with a hint of sarcasm) have deprived us of intelligence and now suddenly pass this news or conjecture without an apology or reason for their recent actions and you assume it is a priceless nugget of fact that must be accepted without question."

Wilson, obviously angry at the comments responded that:

"As Prime Minister he had the right, no the duty, to consider any reasonable possibility and that any other course would be a dereliction of his duty..."

At which moment the Lord Chancellor interjected and stated that:

"There were merits in both men's comments, more so the P.M.'s, but ultimately their duty was the defence of the Realm and the Chiefs of Staff were to be congratulated for not creating a panic by using the ruse of an exercise to possibly prepare the armed forces for an attack.

I recommend that a Royal proclamation be issued or prepared to bring into force the 1964 Emergency Powers Act, however the consequences of the Act and of Martial Law could be draconian and had to be controlled and supervised so that the underlying principle of British democracy could be protected.

Furthermore the Prime Minister should seek an urgent audience with Her Majesty not solely to obtain her approval, but to seek her support and wisdom."

At which point the previously silent Patrick Gordon Walker drew the others' attention by a loud cough as he intended to expose the P.M's. lie (according to his 'confession' that, in his absence, would be read out for him at Wilson's trial for High Treason).

He had been brooding and fervently resented that not only had the lie gone unchallenged but that Wilson based the image of his integrity on a foundation of deceit and misrepresentation.

But at the last moment, when the stakes were so high, weakness overcame him and he raised an enquiry that he should have realised that the P.M. would easily parry...

"Why Harold (Lever) and Sir Reginald had not been notified earlier of the ambassador`s report?"

Harold already had a stock response prepared which attributed the delay to the then overwhelming problem of violence in the Midlands and the uncertain industrial atmosphere which was adequate to satisfy the questioner though in reality he had avoided the real reason for his delay.

EIGHTY-FIVE

The answer was an unexpected, passionate and even dogmatic, "No!"

Harold Wilson was driven the relatively short distance from Downing Street to Buckingham Palace for a hastily arranged audience which commenced, spot on, at six p.m.

When he returned, pale and obviously disappointed, at six twenty-six p.m., the only comment that was forthcoming was the succinct observation ...

"That in the presence of the sixteen year old Prince Charles, the Queen had emphatically and adamantly refused and thwarted his request."

At his trial for High Treason, a servant, who had been standing outside of the chamber confirmed, without apparent duress and under oath, that the Heir Apparent was present at the meeting and he had heard, for the first time ever, the Queen raise her voice in anger.

Sometime later, as has previously been stated, her personal diaries, left in haste following her flight to Canada, also confirmed the presence of her eldest son and that, in handwriting which betrayed her anger, she had made the terse and candid comment that:

"I did not swear my Coronation Oath to see the nation under the cudgels of totalitarianism."

EIGHTY-SIX

For both Kashkarov and his wife, the only diversion to pass the time was the continuous broadcast of Radio Moscow and its boring, bland, sterile and predictable content matter which even his wife observed gave no hint of an impending crisis, though the news announced the successful test explosion, accompanied by symbolic fanfares of the usual proof of Socialist achievement but he could sense that his beloved wife realised that events of the greatest magnitude were unfolding.

She was an impotent spectator and he was unable to confide in her but she was now able to reconcile his new military outfits to his absence, somewhere, some days ago, though she still could not understand, on his pay, the unexpected, exciting gift of clothing, especially his exquisite taste and surprisingly, for a man, his accurate assessment of her size. He clearly had qualities that she had underestimated or had not given him credit for. The evening dragged on until they were interrupted by a knock on the door and the announcement that he was to prepare himself for the imminent meeting with the two Politburo members which shocked his wife.

Conveniently he had already showered in the impractical, confined space of a cubicle located in the corner of their room and had found the soap as coarse as in the officers' quarters of his barracks.

He sat on the bed in his impressive uniform for over an hour until a brisk knock on the door alerted him. He was allowed, this time, to kiss his wife, however now she knew, with confidence, his destination.

A map of the Soviet Union covered most of one wall and was being critically scrutinised by two men whose backs were facing him as he entered the room. Two other men in the uniform of the K G B were also in the room, one of whom opened a file and even from a distance he could see his photograph alongside a dossier which presumably was his personal file.

They both saluted him and requested that he adjourn to an adjacent room where he was asked to peruse a file which from the imperatives on the front cover clearly identified the contents to be of the highest grade of secret intelligence.

The first part confirmed the successful test detonation near Mityushikha Bay on the island of Novaya Zemlya of a fifteen point nine megaton thermonuclear device the previous morning and confirmation that thirty-seven further devices had already been manufactured and could be delivered, installed, become operational or held in reserve within twenty one days and would replace the existing five megaton devices currently being carried by the R 36 missiles.

The second part confirmed that Politburo candidate member Yuri Andropov and member Pyotr Demichev had been allocated the responsibility of overseeing the multi missile test launch and were on their way to Drovyanaya (3) where they were to authorise the nationwide virtual simultaneous firing of the R36 and UR100 missiles and that they would be in constant contact with Gennady Voronov and Dinmukhamed Konayev.

He noted with personal satisfaction that the four launch sites were the ones that he had recommended but realised that if the American surveillance facilities were as effective as the intelligence reports had suggested, then they could identify the vast Drovyanaya complex and target them in a pre emptive first strike. He would urgently report his thoughts to either Podgorny or Suslov since there could still be time to change the plan.

In all, as a show of strength they were prepared to launch from the four sites, virtually simultaneously, six R36s and twelve UR100s, in itself a potential feat of technology, a pyrotechnic spectacular and above all, fundamentally, a sign and warning of immense power.

The attack on Great Britain was virtually identical to the scenario that he had presented, but in scope was larger, though the planners had set a trap for the British R.A.F., which if successful might also destroy a substantial number of their fighter planes.

The statistics favoured the Soviet's plan of surprise: from the time that the first fighter /bomber was airborne till the last fighter landed, would be less than fifty minutes and for a second time in less than two years would emphatically change both the political landscape of Europe and also the physical landscape of Great Britain.

The SAA (Strategic Air Armies) had allocated fifteen Tupolev Tu-22 (N.A.T.O. Designation Blinder D) bombers with interceptor capability (carrying up to two tactical nuclear weapons, a mixture of free fall or parachute dropped) and up to sixty (!) Sukhoi Su-11s (Fishpot C) fitted with air to air missiles.   The fighter bombers would be launched on Wednesday at approximately 2.35p.m. (G.M.T.) from bases in France, Belgium and the Low Countries and ordered to attack the following targets:

London	Five bombs
Birmingham, Manchester and Liverpool	Three bombs each
Southampton, Bristol, Cardiff and Glasgow	Two bombs each
Newcastle, Hull and Nottingham	One bomb each.

Pilots and crews were warned, that under no circumstances whatsoever, were they to attack any American installations and *ONLY* attack United States` fighters in self defence. The R.A.F. was *NOT* subject to the prohibition.

The compilers of the document had plagiarised his paper, effectively copying his presentation, verbatim. The intention was clear. Do what the German Luftwaffe had failed to do in the blitz of 1940-41, destroy in an instant the morale of the British people and reap revenge for their heinous attacks on the soil of Mother Russia and their premeditated attack on the Island of Rugen.

Thirty of the fighters would provide some protection for the Tupolevs and would entice the R A F to chase them into 'friendly' territory where the thirty remaining fighters would pounce on them.

The most secret and intriguing part of the documentation was a briefing paper, again 'plundering' details of *HIS* (he savoured their use of his presentation and suggestions) recommendations and included an appendix in the original English and a Russian translation of the U.S. President`s speech the previous Friday. He inwardly laughed, for the speech had not been reported by the Press or Radio.

He read through the suggestions and options and realised that the most important option, the veiled threat, had been omitted or ignored. It was imperative, if the plan was to succeed, that he inform his superiors.

The door opened behind him, whilst he was scribbling legible and intelligible notes and he barked out a firm order for the visitor to wait whilst he completed his work, taking his time to properly draft his argument and his reasons.

As he turned round, Politburo member Mikhail Suslov, without sarcasm, quietly and humbly enquired if it was now convenient for him to talk.

His argument and reasons clearly resonated with the two Politburo members for they immediately set in motion a request that Andropov and Demichev be diverted to the launch site at Chita where they could supervise the operation and instruct the forces at Drovyanaya to stand down and rearm the missiles.

Suslov was clearly impressed with his argument and confirmed that by teleprinter he would urgently contact the First Secretary. An announcement by the Soviet Union of the successful multi missile test launch, combined with the United States admitting that they were unable to alter the inalienable right of the Soviet Union to defend itself, and the dramatic news that the United Kingdom had been attacked in retaliation for their assault on 'Rugen' would create such fear and panic in the U.S. that President Johnson would dare not sacrifice Los Angeles for London or Miami for Manchester (though they would be ,by then, incinerated and a vision of the Apocalypse).

Suslov had read the notes and suggested that the First Secretary`s speech, addressed to the people of the United States, should spell out the suffering of the people of Russia and the Ukraine where even now (a rare admission of the true situation), fifteen months or so after the nuclear attack, the hospitals were still overwhelmed with the injured and those who were still suffering from the radiation and would inevitably die. The Soviet Union would never inflict such an horrendous act on the American people who had been their allies in the Great Patriotic War, provided that they agreed not to attack in support of the British.

EIGHTY-SEVEN

Two mighty armadas of United States vessels converged on the 'inner' target zones in the North Atlantic and South of the Aleutian chain of islands and unofficial verification of their navigational skills was confirmed when reconnaissance planes observed an unusual concentration of two much smaller fleets mainly comprised of Soviet 'weather' ships brimming with aerials and other electronic devices, for they were known, in reality, to be 'spy' ships constantly monitoring the United States Pacific and Atlantic fleets.

Whilst the Americans had also deployed nuclear powered submarines in the two areas, the Soviet Union had, to protect their weather ships, in the North Pacific, two Kynda class CG guided missile cruisers (the 'Admirals' Fokin and Golovko) and in the North Atlantic, the Groznyy and Varyag.

Incidentally, some recent press speculation in the United States suggested that a seventeen thousand, two hundred tonne Sverdlov class CL guided missile light cruiser and command ship from the Northern Fleet had also been deployed in the North Atlantic but access to Soviet archive documentation has proved that the suggestion was based on erroneous information.

Within an eighty–five second period four R36s and ten UR 100 missiles were launched from three sites commencing one fifty seven p.m. (Greenwich Mean Time) but two UR100s fired from the Vyru site exploded as they exited their underground silos. They had been the first production line missiles that had been delivered and were proof of faults that had been predicted by their designer.

No doubt the explosions were observed by American surveillance satellites together with the heat plumes of the twelve successful launches and for the President, now well protected in a subterranean bunker outside of Washington (despite his promise), immediately, as he had promised, raised the DEFCON level again a notch. The United States was on the cusp, the edge of an abyss, of the unthinkable.

Tracked by radar it was all over in less than twenty- three minutes. For the Soviet Union it was an unparalleled success, even to the extent that the 'UR`s' designer had been proved correct, that their launch crews had performed beyond expectation, but above all none of the missiles had to be destroyed mid flight for technical reasons and that they had all 'peppered' the 'gold bull`s 'eye 'of their two targets.

I have been unable to verify a rumour that circulated in the Intelligence community that a U S reconnaissance plane, circling the North Pacific target zone, more by good fortune than planning, had caught in its high speed cameras a R36 and an UR100 missile actually crashing into the sea! In any event the exhibition of power shook the President, his administration, the military establishment and the intelligence community to its foundations.

Would the Soviet Union now respond to the nuclear attack fifteen months earlier?

Prime Minister Harold Wilson was informed of the Soviet tests at about four p.m. (G.M.T.) and his immediate reaction was to contact his Minister of Defence who correctly notified and instructed, through the normal chain of command, the armed forces to discreetly raise their level of readiness.

An answer to the question was imminent.

EIGHTY-EIGHT

Wednesday, March third, nineteen sixty-five.

Soviet planners had specified the epicentre of each target but recognised that in combat conditions error would cause deviation and wind conditions might affect the parachute assisted bombs, whilst the free fall bombs, delivered by 'lobbing', might go awry, though the crews had been relentlessly trained to use a parabolic manoeuvre including a new computer controlled release device.

It was again an unrivalled success of planning, technology and pilot skill, combined with an element of good fortune and to kind, prevailing winds.

But for the British people it was to be a catastrophic disaster, for all the preparations and planning of their government had not considered or conceived a scenario which was in contradiction to the logical action of a Soviet first strike which should target military, industrial and administrative locations therefore rendering the United Kingdom incapable of functioning as a coherent force.

The earlier Times weather forecast proved accurate...

"The severe early morning frost was (sic) followed by sun and later cloud and temperatures did (again sic) not exceed 37 degrees F (3 degrees C) until..."

The Tu-22s left exactly on time from eight bases scattered in a roughly crooked line near to the English Channel and North Sea, spreading out to vector in on their allocated targets. As planned, seventeen and a half minutes later, the thirty Su-11s left the same eight bases and cruised at thirty thousand feet awaiting the British interceptors.

The parachute assisted bombs were the more devastating and lethal, being programmed to detonate at a height of five hundred metres (one thousand, six hundred feet) in order that the blast was not absorbed by the ground whilst the 'free fall' bombs were more powerful, gouging craters in the targets that they devastated.

For the smaller, nuclear weapons used in this mission, accuracy was paramount, as distinct from the fifteen point nine megaton thermonuclear devices that within weeks would be installed in the R36s and could totally destroy any city in the United States even if they missed the epicentre.

The blast effect as it spreads out into the volume of air around the centre of the explosion reduces in power with the cube of the distance. The shockwave therefore becomes less potent the further away from of its origin but in non technical terms the pressure created will cause great and widespread damage and destruction.

The even more callous and vicious damage caused by radiation and heat blast will be mentioned later.

London had been targeted for five bombs:

A twenty kiloton device centred on the broadcasting tower of Alexandra Palace in North London overshot, hitting the Dollis Valley, Barnet (estimated forty-two thousand immediately killed).

A thirty five kiloton parachute assisted bomb aimed at the Crystal Palace radio aerials which was on target was estimated to have immediately killed one hundred and twenty thousand human beings.

A thirty kiloton weapon aimed at Northolt aerodrome overshot, hitting the prison at Ducane Road, West London and the adjacent Wormwood Scrubs. The blast and heat destroyed much of Harlesden and the White City estate (estimated dead WITHIN SEVENTY TWO HOURS, one hundred and forty-eight thousand people).

The largest weapon, a forty-five kiloton parachute assisted air-burst, latest generation bomb was targeted at Central London, with Nelson's Column as its distinctive epicentre, but the Tu-22 was intercepted by a

British Lightning fighter, and dropped its load late, exploding symbolically directly above the Imperial War Museum, coincidentally vaporising British military Imperial history, devastating (a description previously used but suitable for the catastrophic damage) and immediately killing an estimated two hundred and seventy-five thousand souls including members of the Coalition Cabinet (especially the Attorney- General) who were unfortunately caught in the open or were in residence in their homes. Nelson`s Column survived (but was structurally weakened), however the blast blew the eponymous, fragile statue from its plinth and it came crashing down, narrowly missing one of the ceremonial lions but smashing itself to smithereens.

The last attack was on East London and for no logical reason the target was the Ilford area. It was later estimated that one hundred and ten thousand people were killed outright within seconds.

The British government and the various organs of the civil and military authorities had been virtually caught naked and exposed.

Completed in nineteen sixty-four, the function of the massive radars at Fylingdales Moor, near Scarborough, Yorkshire, was to look across the far horizon and 'see' missiles as they passed the top of their 'boost' phase, whilst the more numerous air defence radars linked to "ADOC" (Air Defence Operations Centre) at R.A.F. Bentley Priory in Stanmore, North London performed satisfactorily but because the incoming fighter/bombers reached most of their targets within twelve to sixteen minutes and the defence radars were 'tuned' to a potential attack originating from sites three or four hundred miles further East, insufficient time was given for interceptor squadrons of mainly English Electric Lightnings based at Wattisham, Scampton, Waddington and Conningsby to scramble.

Buckingham Palace suffered both blast and heat damage, thus symbolically uniting the Queen and the Royal Family with the millions of others who were to be immediately killed or who would die, some relatively soon, others whose deaths would be lingering and without medical assistance. Tragically, the young Princes, Andrew, who had just turned five and Edward, who would have achieved his first birthday within a week, would be killed by falling masonry violently dislodged by the pressure waves of the blast as their nannies made a desperate attempt to reach the safety of the Palace having been playing close by in the gardens, whilst the rest of the family had fortunately been in residence, deep within the interior and were thus shielded.

For Harold Wilson fate bestowed good fortune upon him. Staff, with almost a sixth sense, recognised an imminent but unspecified danger and managed to rush him, Patrick Gordon Walker, Harold Lever and a frightened entourage to the maze of tunnels beneath Number Ten and the comparative safety of a nuclear bunker, fitted with a communications system and facilities to sustain the existence of its inmates for up to fourteen days.

By six p.m. information was being received by telephone on the exclusive, secret Federal exchange whose existence was discovered by this author, and a teleprinter was chattering, without interruption, delivering an ever increasing flood of gruesome news.

Reverting to almost primitive methods of communication, contact was made with Buckingham Palace by pedal cyclists and news of the tragic death of the two Royal Princes was delivered by courier, on foot, but the information was temporarily suppressed.

By nine- thirty it had become apparent that some of the Cabinet had most likely been slaughtered but there was definitive evidence that the Lord Chancellor had been killed when his home collapsed on him and that the Minister of Defence, Edward Heath, beyond reasonable doubt, had suffered the same fate.

It was at ten fifty-five that Manny Gold and Gerald Kaufman, who had been in deep conversation, approached Harold Wilson and with a rare display of agreement asked him to immediately arrange for an audience with the Queen and for her to sign a proclamation declaring a State of Emergency. Wilson was already traumatised by shock. Perhaps over a million people had been killed within seconds at the eleven targets and the ever chattering teleprinter was providing assessments that were being regularly updated, the latest one at ten thirty-five, which stated that within seven days the total death toll would reach two and a half million and that within six months that figure would at least double.

Utilising the original document that had been prepared under the auspices of the Lord Chancellor, the two men drafted, to the best of their limited ability and expertise, a simplified statement which was then checked, probably cursorily, by Gordon Walker and Lever though they had a duty not only to check the document but also to consider its consequences and ramifications.

It did not include, and actually omitted, one fundamentally important condition, that would have the most profound effect on the governance of Britain and its people. The state of emergency and the imposition of martial law were not subject to any time limitation and consequently were open ended in duration.

EIGHTY-NINE

Thursday, March fourth, nineteen sixty-five. One forty-six a.m.

It was a blend of both Heaven and Hell, for pure, pristine snow was falling but combined with tiny specks of grey radioactive particles that could have included miniscule portions of burnt human remains.

Harold Wilson was ushered from the safety of his subterranean bunker, accompanied by Manny Gold, who was holding a dispatch box which contained the flawed document. Under any other circumstances his demeanour would have been of triumphal success but as the two men emerged into the new real world, any earlier preconceptions or hopes were soon to be shattered by the reality of the apocalypse before them or during their short journey to Buckingham Palace.

Over a year before the P.M. had made one crucial mistake when he had succumbed to the dual pressure and wiles of the Soviet leadership who had both pressurised him and entreated him ,as a sign of his commitment to peace, that he now realised was an error of arrogant judgement, by denuding the country of its primary defence, the 'V' Bomber force, which had been sent, almost in disgrace to South Africa and Australia, as a sign to the Soviet Union of his determination to pursue a path of peace and reconciliation.

And this was the result.

The meeting was scheduled for two a.m.

They were to be spared the worst of the horror that confronted the traumatised and massively depleted emergency services who faced an appalling challenge which even if they had been fully manned and prepared, would have proved to be an impossible task. As they were led out into Horse Guards Parade at the rear of the government buildings, they were met, not as usual, for the world had been irreversibly changed, by uniformed police officers but by soldiers dressed in military fatigues, standing by three camouflaged cars, however they efficiently and courteously saluted him.

Their attention was drawn to the almost eerie scene that lit the sky and highlighted the falling snow and ash. There was no street lighting and the buildings that were normally lit at night were dark and the horizon through three hundred and sixty degrees, or as much that was not obscured by the buildings, was lit by great fires and they could just make out, unless they were deceiving themselves, the remnants of three mushroom clouds which seemed to climb infinitely into the sky and beyond.

Wilson momentarily stood transfixed and was only brought back to the hideous reality of the here and now when the silence was broken by the sound of an emergency vehicle that was driving along Whitehall.

'As the crow flies' the distance between the Imperial War Museum and Buckingham Palace is just under one and a half miles and for those pedestrians and motor vehicles caught in the open of The Mall, they reaped the diminishing force of the blast and the heat pulse. The P.M. could just discern the sight of many of the trees that had lined the important thoroughfare to the Palace, mostly lying across the pavement, whilst a few grander trees were just about still erect or inclined at an angle displaying the direction of the pressure wave. Coming from the opposite direction was a lone bulldozer that, without respect or investigation, was clearing the road of any vehicles that might, or might not be occupied by any living people but certainly by the corpses of the dead.

Dead, charred bodies had been dragged into piles and were waiting unceremoniously to be collected and burned unrecorded, without respect for their religious beliefs or final wishes, on pyres, for there was a new potential fear, the spread of disease, but on the lips of Harold Wilson was one unspoken word of inevitability, Gotterdamerung.

It was not until the party entered the Palace that Manny Gold realised that certain rooms and areas of the Royal household were lit, but his thoughts concentrated on the realisation that he was a participant on the verge of an historic meeting and that the knowledge he was soon to acquire could be passed, or traded, to his American friends and perhaps could secure benefits that at that instance in time were unquantifiable.

He was quickly introduced to a traumatised Queen, who was dressed in mourning black, and was accompanied by her husband, Philip, and eldest son Charles, who he recalled later said very little but that his contribution was pompous and bore no relation to the reality of the situation ("Call out more ambulances to deal with the injured") however it was the atmosphere of shock and helplessness that he later remembered as being most prominent.

He found himself ushered into a small annex along with an elegantly dressed man with impeccable bearing and a refined clipped accent who introduced himself, without pomposity, as the Queen's principal private secretary. For a fleeting moment the man reminded him of another elegant gentleman, but one who spoke with an American accent and who, and it was remarkable that he should identify him so strangely, had superbly manicured nails.

The document was produced from the dispatch box and minutely examined by the secretary who, with apparent great interest, enquired who had drafted the document and with obvious satisfaction, acknowledged that both Gold and Kaufman had produced the abbreviated proclamation, based on the Lord Chancellor's earlier document that the Queen had not seen but had rejected outright.

Suddenly the secretary announced that:

"The document was not correct",

disappointing and surprising Gold who witnessed the man leave the room, without apology. Some ten or even fifteen minutes later the man returned, profusely apologising both for his absence but above all his rudeness not excusing himself.

"The document has been retyped on the correct headed notepaper, that of Buckingham Palace and not Ten Downing Street and furthermore is dated today and not yesterday. We must be correct and especially punctilious."

Gold witnessed Her Majesty, with melancholic resignation and perhaps with a tear in her eye, sign the instrument that ended over seven hundred years of the democratic process which had begun at Runnymede with the signing of the Magna Carta.

Democracy, R.I.P.

NINETY

Events now began to take place with alarming rapidity, beginning overseas where the £Sterling collapsed on the financial markets and trading centres as diverse as Wall Street in New York and the back streets of Indian markets where the Hindu soucars plied their trade.

It was recorded, at one centre in New York, that the exchange rate had reached the almost preposterous level of seventy–nine cents to the £Sterling but as Thursday ended in different time zones the Pound had rallied to parity.

Parliaments in Canada, South Africa, New Zealand and Australia and the United States' Congress each independently held a two minute silence before ending their sessions prematurely giving the Executive a breathing space when they could gather further information and assess their future actions.

Harold Wilson was entrenched in his subterranean bunker some sixty to one hundred feet beneath Ten Downing Street and had become a virtual prisoner of the system and its administrators who now were enacting the result of years of planning but had not considered the nature of the enemy`s unexpected and unusual attack strategy.

Beginning at about four–thirty on the Thursday morning and initially necessitating the Prime Minister 'rubber stamping' decisions that had been made months and years earlier by committees that had been secretly formed to confront the consequences of the unthinkable, his first duty was to approve the wording of the document that would be printed within hours and distributed nationwide to both inform the population and to complete the legal formality of the proclamation.

The document read, including one error, as follows and would be publicly displayed on every public building even embracing damaged or destroyed structures, town halls, schools, libraries, health centres and above all hospitals, fire brigade and police stations:

STATE OF EMERGENCY-DECLARATION OF MARITAL (sic) LAW

On Thursday March the fifth in the year of our Lord, nineteen sixty-five, Her most Excellent Majesty, by the grace of God, Queen Elizabeth, the second of that name, signed an instrument and proclamation in accordance with the Emergency Powers Act of nineteen sixty-four, Chapter 38, to protect the nation which is threatened with interference to the supply of food, water, fuel or light, or with the means of locomotion.

It must be noted that when originally displayed, the proclamation was received by the British people with a sense of humour and resigned stoicism.

Twelve Regional Commissioners, directly responsible to a new National Council of the same number (together with the Prime Minister), were to be granted unlimited power over life and death and were composed of former Army officers of impeccable integrity, many of whom had been in occupied Germany after the Second World War where they administered the rebirth of the nation but more importantly had overseen the very matters which were at the heart of the proclamation.   Directly responsible to them were twelve deputy Commissioners and both groups had been secretly prepared and readied for their task over the last few months in anticipation of the 'unthinkable'.

Still suffering from shock and unable to make rational decisions, Wilson was being assailed and influenced by various contradictory advice tendered by different factions of civil servants who were based at other strategic locations and were connected by conference telephone. But it was the view supported by Gold and Kaufman which finally prevailed. The National Council, headed by the Prime Minister, would include members from outside of government with diverse qualities who could steer the country back to democratic Parliamentary rule.

But from the vast reservoir of different talents that were available, the first three chosen were the heads of the Army, Navy and Air force, then Patrick Gordon Walker and Harold Lever.

Two high ranking civil servants were also included and as a portent of the atmosphere of lies and deception that was soon to be a part of the operation of government, were given false names and even their biographies and identities were hidden, for they were, in fact, the heads of MI5 and MI6 and therefore responsible for both internal and external intelligence and security matters.

With shrewdness, Gerald Kaufman suggested the head of the T U C., George Woodcock, who the almost permanently dazed P.M. readily accepted, but the next two names, if they were still alive, raised vehement arguments from opposing factions, for they were two industrialists without any experience of government and unbeknownst to any of those involved in the discussion were two of the financial backers that had plucked John Tyndall from virtual obscurity and had helped to propel him and his career to that of a nationally recognised figure.

Despite the chaos that existed in the real world sixty to one hundred feet above the bunker and at great expense in manpower and equipment both men were contacted within three or four hours and patriotically agreed to serve the nation (and their own agendas) in roles that they did not really comprehend but clearly involved power and influence.

It was that power and influence that they both used cynically and with devious intent which would later form the foundation of a new, malevolent government.

If any minutes were taken of the proceedings then they certainly no longer exist or remain misfiled or forgotten in some obscure filing cabinet which perhaps has become so rusty that it is impossible even to forcibly open.

When it was too late and the organs of power had been prised and wrestled from the democrats and moderates and those who had supported the inclusion of John Tyndall and were incarcerated in prison, or even worse had been later sent to the Scottish penal colonies, then their protestations that they had opposed his inclusion were futile arguments and they did not understand that John Tyndall, together with his sponsors, had been underestimated and that he was personally ruthless, executing his path towards total power, lubricated by the finesse of playing various groups off against each other and always undermining their authority.

NINETY-ONE

Who first proposed that John Tyndall be invited to join the new National Council is now unimportant, though it was likely that one, or both of the co-opted industrialists made the suggestion. Perhaps what is more interesting and significant are the memories of one of those who had been present in the bunker. Gerald Kaufman emphatically stated that a body of opinion concurred that Tyndall could be used and then discarded when he had served his purpose and that, in response, another group remarked, with disbelief, that such an argument had been used over thirty years before during the death throes of the Weimar Republic about another charismatic politician who also had a large following, which then produced a further, third argument, that Tyndall's popular following and his inclusion in the new leadership would revive confidence in the country and its future direction.

He had been suffering from a debilitating cold for some days which had conveniently confined him to his luxury Knightsbridge hotel which had also become the base of his political power.   This inconvenient circumstance had favoured him for at the moment of the 'Imperial War Museum' nuclear detonation he had been incarcerated in the hotel's sauna, safely located in the basement, and had been shocked by the force of the shock wave but had also been protected from the searing heat blast.

The hotel and its superb staff responded well to the crisis, helped by the previous prudent installation of an in-house generator which alleviated the inconvenience of the breakdown of the electricity supply.

A delegation of supporters had been patiently waiting for him since just before the Soviet assault began and had avoided most, but not all of the blast. Although sitting some distance from the exterior windows, they had been showered by glass and one of the delegation had been quite badly cut.

Tyndall used the situation to his advantage and insisted that the man use his own apartment whilst he made arrangements, despite the chaos and uncertainty, through the hotel's staff, to accommodate the other members in less opulent surroundings.

The following day the delegation managed to return to the more luxurious surroundings, having braved the chaos and destruction that littered the streets and gardens of Mayfair.

They were all to be witnesses when the call from the Prime Minister arrived and their later recollections became part of the folklore of the New Order before most were purged and history was rewritten.

What is certain is that a convoy of three military Land Rovers, escorting the Prime Minister's personal limousine, arrived outside of the hotel and the officer in command was initially refused entry by two burly but well disciplined (for they were apparently former soldiers themselves) doormen but they soon acquiesced, with deferential tact, when a pistol was produced and entry emphatically demanded.

This whirlwind of activity must have caught Tyndall's attention for he, as witnesses reported, unexpectedly stood up, presumably to observe the commotion and must have been shocked when the officer, ignoring the other guests and his visitors, marched up to him, the pistol gripped in his left hand, halted and instead of, as most of the witnesses instantly thought assassinating him, stood to attention and courteously stated that, on the Prime Minister's personal instructions...

"He was to be escorted to a place of safety and offered a position in the new National Council that was being formed to deal with the crisis."

NINETY-TWO

The Prime Minister, with the help of medical treatment, was now more in control of himself and with a rare hint of charm, tentatively but amicably introduced himself, then offered his hand to Tyndall who, surprised and overwhelmed by the events of the last few minutes and indeed the catastrophic events of the last twenty–four hours or so, shook the P.M.'s hand and without thinking, mechanically and rhetorically asked, with apparent sincerity ...

"How he could help the nation in this time of dire emergency?"

He briefly noted the presence of the two industrialists who had been financially sponsoring him, but avoided any eye contact or act that could be interpreted as an acknowledgement of their association though he realised it was more than likely that the relationship was already known in certain quarters.

Only ten members of the new National Council and the P.M. initially sat round the table at four twenty-five that late afternoon. George Woodcock had been located in the 'North East' where he had been endeavouring to resolve the strike with an intransigent Bill Martin and was being driven back to London under armed guard and at breakneck speed.

The Prime Minister (the Council had yet to define a title for the chairman) agreed with those present that the heads of the three branches of the armed forces who were absent, busy attending to the nation's defence and a possible retaliatory first strike, could be, when necessary, temporarily replaced by designated senior officers and it was further agreed that this option could apply to the heads of MI5 and

MI6 and even for their temporary representatives to make decisions without reference.

In a most unexpected move that might have been made literally on the spur of the moment, and to the chagrin and surprise of Gerald Kaufman, the Prime Minister nominated Manny Gold as the twelfth member of the National Council, possibly viewing his appointment as a counterbalance to the membership of John Tyndall.

By ten-fifty that evening a succession of civil servants had delivered a number of top secret reports, some accompanied by hastily printed A4 sheets summarising their advices, most of which would be conveyed to each of the twelve Regional Commissioners who had already been provided with teams of dedicated civil servants who would be constantly available to give advice and administrative support.

Not unexpectedly, Tyndall and the two industrialists were shocked to learn some, if not most of the nation's most guarded secrets, especially the low level of the reserve food stocks, however the truth of the country's military weakness, if not total inability to independently launch a viable retaliatory first strike, was suppressed.

None of those present, the eleven (Manny Gold had taken his place) members of the new National Council, were to swear an oath of loyalty to the Queen, indeed the most important moment was when they were each presented with a leather bound document, sequentially numbered and marked 'Top Secret' and were requested to sign a brief statement primarily to acknowledge receipt of the document and secondly, as if it were a hastily added post script, to promise that they would carry out the requirements of the then unknown contents ...

"In the best interests of their Sovereign Lady, Queen Elizabeth and the nation."

A clearly despondent Gerald Kaufman sat immediately behind the Prime Minister and, in turn, was flanked by three civil servants solely responsible to Harold Wilson, whilst a delighted Manny Gold sat next to Patrick Gordon Walker. He had 'truly' arrived at the top table, both figuratively and literally.

Within a few minutes those present would begin to learn the immediate future destiny of the nation and how the Regional Commissioners were to impose law and order in accordance with instructions which it had inherited from government planners, indeed the face and emotions of Gerald Kaufman exposed his shock when he learned how the overwhelming majority of the British people would be betrayed and left helpless, hungry, cold, without shelter and medically neglected. In effect they would be abandoned.

The civil servant began:

"The document that you have in front of you summarises the unavoidable and necessary measures that need to be taken to protect the long term interests of this country and I can assure you all that whilst some, and many combined together appear draconian, there is no other viable alternative course than can be followed.

A representative of our armed forces will shortly present the latest military analysis but I trust that he will not object if I briefly explain what has been the thinking behind our military posture and our commitment to freedom.

The overriding military purpose of the nation, along with our N A T O co-members and led by the United States, is to act as a forward base to repel any Soviet or Warsaw Pact attack and to contain and repulse their aggression.

The prime duty of the National Council of which you now form a part, is to maintain the organs and levers of power globally, nationally, regionally and even down to the smallest hamlet.

The Declaration of a State of Emergency and the imposition of Martial Law means that the twelve Regional Commissioners are now personally responsible to maintain absolute power ,authority and public order, however the actual administration will be handled by their twelve deputy Regional Commissioners who are all also former British army officers and over the last few years, and with an increasing intensity over the last few months, because of the deteriorating and uncertain political situation, have been planning the actual transition to military rule.

Each deputy is answerable only to their immediate superior and the Regional Commissioners to the National Council and either rank may be dismissed, should no less than four of you deem their removal be in the best interests of the nation, and you then also have the power to appoint a replacement who must be approved by no less than four others of your fellow members of the National Council within seven days, thus giving a check against any form of favouritism or bias.

The police will become, no now are, a civilian arm of the military and are consequently answerable to them.

Since the late nineteen-fifties a secret building programme has been operating and subterranean Regional Seats of Government have been built across England, Scotland and Wales which we consider are sufficiently well protected to survive all but a direct thermonuclear strike. Your book lists their general locations which are also shown in the map on page four.

London, we believe, is indefensible and still remains a prime target of an all out Soviet attack so for some years we have been developing a vast subterranean site at Hawthorn, near Bath, a former Second World War munitions storage depot, where the P.M. will shortly be based.

If you refer to page five you will find listed the general location of the numbered Regional Seats of Government (RSGs.), some of which lie beneath military establishments:

RSG1	Catterick	Catterick Camp
RSG2	York	Imphal Barracks
RSG3	Nottingham	Chalfont Drive government buildings
RSG4	Cambridge	Brooklands Avenue government buildings
RSG5	(Author's note: On legal advice the location of RSG5 cannot be disclosed)	
RSG6	Reading	Warren Row
RSG7	Dartmouth	Bolt Head
RSG8	Brecon	The Barracks
RSG9	Kidderminster	Drakelow,Kinver
RSG10	Preston	Fulford Barracks
RSG 11	Edinburgh	Barnton Quarry
RSG12	Dover	Dover Castle

Additionally there is a chain of Sub-Regional Headquarters (SRHQs) including Kelvedon Hatch-which has been specially 'hardened'-near Brentwood in Essex where Mr. Tyndall will be temporarily based and incidentally where he will also be responsible for overseeing the

Regional Commissioner who has the responsibility for an area which includes the whole of East and North London and Essex.

On pages seven and eight are listed a broad outline of the responsibilities of our internal forces which I will shortly describe in greater detail."

The anonymous civil servant fell silent, presumably to allow those present to review the list of Regional Seats of Government and then to familiarise themselves with the responsibilities of the army, whilst some, if not all had noted the ominous title of 'internal forces'.

Control of movement and the maintenance and control of essential service routes

Controls to prevent the spread of disease

Control of the supply of food, water and all aspects normally associated with the sustenance of life, for example fuel (for heating)

Subjugation, arrest and, if necessary, the elimination of hostile individuals and groups

Execution of sentences

Guarding internment centres

Bomb disposal (but not of nuclear or thermonuclear weapons) and demolition

Control over the availability of weapons

Personal protection of V.I.Ps. and protection of convoys

Above all the maintenance of law and order including the support and protection of special courts ('Courts of Protection').

After some time, when most of those present had been seen to make notes, possibly, especially to clarify the purpose of the 'special courts', the civil servant continued:

"The consequences of a single thermonuclear (hydrogen bomb) strike or a massive all out ground or air burst assault with thermonuclear weapons is beyond imagination and the aftermath of such an attack would see the effective destruction of the nation's fabric to such an extent that the words of an American expert in this field succinctly describes what I have endeavoured to persuade you to recognise and accept...

"Will the survivors envy the dead?"

An all out attack would utterly destroy society, civilisation and the value of existence.

My associate will speak shortly to update you on the current situation concerning civil defence, the rescue of survivors and post attack recovery."

Suddenly and chillingly, as if his whole personality had ominously changed from Dr. Jekyll into Mr. Hyde, he calmly announced, without emotion, as if he was reciting a railway time table, that ...

"You must accept the indisputable reality that there is no defence against thermonuclear weapons and the great investment made over the last few years will only protect a few thousand people made up of the leaders of government, administrators, advisors and V.I.Ps.

There are contingency plans to send Her Majesty and other senior members of the Royal family to Canada in small, separate groups by R A F passenger jets or submarines but Her Majesty has consistently stated that her duty is to remain in this country alongside her people.

There is nowhere for the city and town dwellers to flee to, for the countryside would be polluted by radioactive ash and any available food supplies would be quickly exhausted. We have encouraged a policy of 'protect and survive'. As we have already anticipated, food supplies are being rapidly exhausted and will not be restocked whilst raw materials, the basis of building primitive shelters are likewise being ravenously consumed. This situation now permits me to explain the role of our 'internal forces'.

It is essential for the war effort, that the major trunk roads and railway lines are free to transport troops and military equipment and that injured troops can be moved to medical centres. The population will be instructed and exhorted to stand firm and to store necessary essentials including up to fourteen days supply of food and water. As stocks become increasingly short and are then exhausted the public will, no doubt, begin to panic and attempt to storm warehouses and any location where food and other necessities are stored.

In anticipation of this scenario, the Regional Commissioners and their deputies, as their first official act should have, and I understand have begun to order troops and the police under their authority, to begin to requisition petrol stations and the larger food retail outlets and their distribution centres, together with pharmacies in order to commandeer their supplies of drugs. Within twenty-four hours or so, the pharmaceutical manufacturers will also be placed under military control however all these sites will be guarded whenever possible by the civilian police but if the situation gets out of hand because of public disorder and dissent then armed forces will be called in with instructions to fire (and his voice expressed an inflexible, cold determination that signalled the new reality) into, not over the heads of the crowds to maintain authority.

City and urban areas will be isolated and travel absolutely curtailed outside of their perimeters; the new identification documentation will, from now onwards, be rigorously supervised.

I am now requesting my fellow civil servants to give you their reports."

Another civil servant, if on cue, rose and unemotionally delivered the latest available assessment of the potential European theatre of war.

"Latest reports from Rome and Madrid indicate that Warsaw Pact forces based in Southern France, using a massive pool of tanks, are poised to attack the Iberian Peninsula through Barcelona and the North Italian plain and the city of Milan.

British and United States bombers in joint partnership are being readied to launch a devastating assault to stop the attack, using nuclear weapons, but would stop short of employing thermonuclear devices unless the enemy maintained their aggressive posture or if their twin assaults were making substantial advances.

No doubt our adversaries are bracing themselves for a devastating attack by our bombers."

Questioned by one of the industrialists to clarify who was responsible to order any military instructions, the civil servant turned to Harold Wilson but also clearly stated that this would be a democratic decision of the Council members but in reality events might take place at such a pace that the Supreme Commander of N A T O might unilaterally have to give the final orders on his own judgement.

When the other industrialist asked for an inventory of the nation's forces and especially of her tanks, B52 and 'V' bombers, the civil servant was brusquely interrupted by the Prime Minister who brazenly and angrily confirmed that they had, at their disposal, sufficient forces to ...

"Not only contain Soviet aggression but also to reap revenge for the heinous attack of the previous day."

A third civil servant was then introduced and he gave a callous analysis of the consequences of the attack:

He first listed the eleven locations of the attack and the number of weapons used and whether they had been ground or air bursts but did not give an assessment of each bomb`s estimated power and also did not specify that they were all nuclear devices.

"A predetermined plan has already been put into force. First of all losses to the emergency services in terms of manpower and equipment had to be approximately determined and whilst the local populations are at best still dazed and disoriented and at worst incapable of providing for themselves, volunteers were being utilised to assist the fire brigades in *PRIORITY* [author`s emphasis] tasks.

Soon members of the community would be compelled under martial law to help and might be rewarded by an allocation of food and water at a level ultimately determined by the Regional Commissioners and their deputies, dependent on local factors and reserves, which *MUST BE HUSBANDED* [again author`s own emphasis].

At most locations and certainly close to the epicentres of the detonations, fires and some firestorms were still raging despite the palliative effect of the weather, that is rain and some snow, however at every location the water supply has been interrupted following damage to the mains and it is impossible in those areas even to attempt to douse the fires which in certain cases are being fed by leaking gas from fractured mains.

Volunteers have been used, under supervision, to attempt to rescue survivors in the outer areas devastated by blast damage, most using their bare hands, for the fire brigades, increasingly with the assistance of army engineers, have used any available heavy equipment to clear blocked roads primarily those that form part of the major communication and arterial network.

Because many of the minor roads are still blocked this has been the reason given why the ambulance service is apparently not attending to emergencies but in any event they would be overwhelmed and unable to cope.

Amongst the immediate urgent duties of the deputy Regional Commissioners is to move their internal forces into every area of the country whether damaged or not and to secure control which means that they are committing up to three hundred and twenty-five thousand men including and supplemented by Territorial Army volunteers."

Prompted by Gerald Kaufman, Harold Wilson drew attention to himself by discreetly coughing and requested, in view of the remarks of the previous speaker, that:

"The Permanent Secretary to the former Minister of Heath clarify the policy regarding medical services."

Unlike the earlier speakers who had spoken with assured but dispassionate confidence, the venerable civil servant was clearly unprepared to fulfil his duties and had to be frequently interrupted by an ever increasingly frustrated and irritated Prime Minister.

"1/   There has been considerable damage to sixteen hospitals in the eleven cities that were attacked, nine of which were completely devastated including St. Thomas' ,diagonally opposite the Palace of Westminster, with the tragic loss of many doctors , nurses and auxiliary staff.

2/   The deputy Regional Commissioners, implementing plans previously drawn up, have halted the potential flow of medical teams from unaffected regions, holding them back in anticipation of further nuclear assaults on their own regions.

3/   Doctors and nurses in the general areas affected by the attacks should have been contacted by the police and by other means and instructed to report to their nearest military establishment within six hours.

4/   Nationwide, hospitals which are still functioning have been instructed to discharge all but the most seriously ill patients and ...

5/   Regard themselves as being under martial law and at the disposal of the military.

6/   Again nationwide, chemists have been served notice *NOT* to issue medicines in response to the presentation of prescriptions *AND* to prepare their stocks for collection.

7/   The pharmaceutical manufacturers have been informed *NOT* to release any stocks to wholesalers and retailers and to be prepared to concentrate on the production of drugs – subject to their facilities - that may be specially required (for example, antibiotics).

8/   In conjunction with the police and the army, I understand that already an embryonic three stage system of medical attention was being set up immediately outside of the worst affected areas of damage consisting of First Aid Posts (*FAPs*), Casualty Collecting Centres (*CCCs*) and hospitals."

It was at this point that he was overcome with emotion and whilst confirming the procedure stressed that ...

"It was inhuman and went against everything that he believed in especially the sanctity of life."

"8A/   Since medical staff were to be forbidden to help 'organise life saving procedures', the new function of the system was to prevent resources being overwhelmed or wasted. The injured would have to make their own way to the *FAPs* and *CCCs*. where they *MIGHT* [author's own emphasis] get some treatment, or not.

It was expected that the sheer number of casualties would overwhelm the available facilities - indeed the reports that he was now continuously receiving confirmed this assumption-and strict, ruthless admission policies were being enforced to sort ,hold and to treat patients till they could possibly be forwarded to hospitals where trained medical staff should be available."

Thus any vestiges of humanity had been stripped from the system of triage which had effectively become brutal and devoid of compassion.

Clearly there was a conflict between his professional and moral values and the amoral necessity of denying help and treatment to the incoming vast deluge of injured and radiated patients.

"8B/   The fundamental criteria, which permitted any medical attention, was that only those who could be of benefit to the State and could reasonably be assumed to have a high percentage chance of recovery were to be given treatment whilst the rest were to be allowed to die *WITHOUT* [once again the author's own emphasis] being given the comfort of pain killers such as morphine.

9/   Disposal of the dead. Where ever and, if possible when ever, corpses were to be identified, logged and their valuables stored for collection by their families, but already the deluge of bodies had swamped those whose duty was to inter the dead and irrespective of their religious beliefs and wishes, were being burned on makeshift funeral pyres and those designated to carry out the gruesome task were also utilising existing fires, therefore prolonging the conflagrations.

10/ The breakdown in the supply of fresh uncontaminated water and the congregation of the survivors in confined, usually unheated, environments such as church and school halls would inevitably result in the spread of diseases such as Typhus and Typhoid especially as sewage was leaking from fractured mains and that people were apparently urinating and defecating in the open which therefore meant that contamination was inevitable [Items 8B to10 inclusive verbatim-author's note]."

(At this point the Permanent Secretary went into a long rambling dissertation explaining the difference between Epidemic typhus caused by lice and Murine typhus caused by fleas on rats and Typhoid fever, a bacterial disease transmitted by the ingestion of food or water contaminated with the faeces of infected people, which contained the bacterium Salmonella enterica enterica).

He continued, with optimism, explaining that the beneficial use of antibiotics to counter 'typhus' and the very recent rediscovery of oral rehydration therapy for 'typhoid' meant that the diseases could be contained and the patients cured however perhaps even he knew that no such treatments would be provided, for drugs and pure water were to be only made available to the few and chosen elite.

Harold profusely thanked him and allowed him to leave the meeting to attend to his responsibilities but he was never to return to a similar conference and therefore did not learn the truth about the comfortingly entitled Special Rest Centres (SRCs).

Another civil servant took the opportunity, during a very brief interlude, to inform the meeting of other further developments...

"My responsibilities encompass the media, which incorporates the press, both nationally and regionally, radio and television and the dissemination of public information.

It is crucial that national morale remains high and that the people understand and support the nation's actions which might be perceived as not in their own short term best interests.

Subversive propaganda both from internal and external sources would be countered and suppressed. Earlier that afternoon, in conjunction with officers from MI5, internal forces closed down the offices of the *Daily Worker* and its staff are currently being interrogated, prior to some of them being moved to an internment camp outside of London, which ultimately will be under the jurisdiction of Mr. Tyndall. Undoubtedly the head of MI5 who is present in this room may be able to give further information (at which point those present turned to him but he moved his head from side to side without speaking).

No national newspapers were printed this morning and none are expected to be published tomorrow or Saturday.

In anticipation of such a situation, contingency plans will be introduced and will recommend and suggest that the two London 'evening' papers temporarily cease publication and the various national 'morning' papers be amalgamated into three publications which would be staffed by employees of the existing journals and of those papers which were to be temporarily closed down.

A meeting is scheduled for tomorrow morning (Friday) with representatives of most of the papers-except the *Daily Worker*- when the suggestion will be aired, however any counter arguments, which under normal circumstances would sway the government's response, can no longer be tolerated and under the state of emergency and martial law, mean that the Regional Commissioners can impose a settlement or even withheld or confiscate the supply of newsprint, as a strategic material.

The cost and availability of distribution will become a vital factor though it has already been suggested that the London Underground system, which I understand, mercifully, has barely been damaged, initially be utilised as a means of distribution.

Nationwide the regional press will be under similar constraints and where again the relevant Regional Commissioners will have the final authority, guided by their civil servants and the availability of newsprint.

We do not intend or wish to impose unreasonable, excessive censorship, however it will be expected that every publication, without exception, will support the government and its actions, without question, and will publish information that is provided to them from time to time.

Freedom of the press is central to the values of our society.

Television programmes ceased yesterday afternoon, conveniently during the mid afternoon break and have not resumed. It is important that confidence and a sense of normality is encouraged and discussions have already begun to resume broadcasting on B B C 1 from Saturday and to utilise the facilities of B B C2 and the Commercial network ,of course subject to the supply of electricity being resumed so there will be an unfortunate and unquantifiable delay .Existing radio channels will continue unaffected as long as possible but for both television and radio, the news and information that we release will be strictly controlled and news broadcasts will end with public information news and instructions. Thus yesterday evening secret plans immediately came into force and the first official notices broadcast confirmed that doctors and nurses report to their nearest military establishment for assignment.

It has also been suggested to the media that great emphasis, in the news bulletins and published news, be placed on the strength of morale and the power of our military forces to unleash a devastating counterblow. I understand that B B C television will show on Saturday afternoon to a limited audience in unaffected areas, the patriotic Second World War film, 'The Way Ahead' and later 'The Dambusters'. The News will show some hospitals which are functioning normally but will not be identified or their locations revealed together with film of the heroic volunteers assisting the authorities both recover and tend the wounded.

In order to strengthen the nation's resolve and bolster the people's patriotism we intend to announce on the six p.m. News on Saturday that Her Majesty will shortly speak both to the nation and also to the Commonwealth and at some point she, or at the end of the statement if she is unable to make the announcement, an announcer will confirm the tragic deaths of the two Royal Princes, Andrew and Edward..."

At which point he would have concluded his statement by also saying that Buckingham Palace had suffered blast damage but his announcement of the two deaths brought an immediate response from those in the room that had not yet been privy to the sad news.

The first civil servant who had spoken again rose, allowing his associate to sit down and began...

"Money has ceased to have any value, though internationally the exchange rate has risen and in New York, in the last hour, was U.S. one $ eight cents. The only currency that now has any value or credibility is the availability of food, water and medicine and they will soon become the final source of survival.

An earlier speaker, who is currently not in this room, emotionally referred to the protocol that is being put into place concerning the facilities that would be provided for the injured. To avoid any doubt whatsoever may I be permitted to both amplify and clarify the situation?

Our resources, in terms of accommodation, available drugs and medicine and above all trained staff is finite and limited. Even now it is abundantly evident that the number of injured has swamped our primary *CCC* facilities. Medical treatment will only be offered to those who can be of benefit to the state and as my associate correctly stated stood a high statistical chance of recovery.

Those, whose conditions are diagnosed as terminal or who are suffering from infections that their own bodies cannot naturally repulse or for those whose injuries are extensive, will be removed to nearby, but isolated, Special Rest Centres (*SRCs*), improvised hospices where they will be allowed the dignity of a decent death (He looked round the room hoping for approval of the arrangement but only noted a general air of cynicism).

The decisions that will be made by the twenty-four Regional and deputy Commissioners, which are absolute, final and not open to question, centre around the primary necessity to maintain law and order and to assist our military forces. They will each have to make decisions that will affect the lives of many hundreds of thousands of innocent men, women and children however they will be supported and guided by teams of civil servants that have recently occupied their headquarters. The twenty-four men will also be able to communicate with their fellow Commissioners on secure - I mean private lines - to share their thoughts and to plan any joint action.

To avoid any doubt or misunderstanding, they may also bring in their own experts and help, provided that they understand that their advices and any actions that they commit on behalf of the National Council are in the best interests of the nation and Her Majesty and that they are personally responsible for their actions."

NINETY-THREE

The Zil limousine sped in the direction of the military airport carrying both Kashkarov and his wife; he was dressed in his finest military uniform, she in one of the pretty outfits that her husband had so cleverly chosen.

It was Thursday evening, snow lay piled on the side of the road and it was cold and dark. Their telephone had been upgraded to make outgoing calls as well as being able to receive incoming calls, and his wife had been treating the instrument like a new toy but she was only able to call a very, very few number of people since the telephone was still a prized luxury and a rarity and it was during one of these outgoing calls, less than two hours before, that the operator had interrupted her and in no uncertain terms informed her that a representative of the Politburo demanded to speak to her husband.

He was to present himself before the First Secretary immediately on his arrival in Moscow.

Also at about seven forty-five p.m. (but Greenwich Mean Time) John Tyndall looked out from the curtained window of his Armstrong Siddeley Star Sapphire, which, later on enquiry, he ascertained had been requisitioned and he was to make this procedure a precedent for his future behaviour. He had ordered the driver to make two special detours on his way to Kelvedon Hatch. First to the site of the 'Imperial War Museum' detonation and then via the 'Ilford' area in order to witness firsthand the devastation, but more importantly to obtain from those in charge their immediate comments and even their suggestions.

His car was accompanied by a substantial detachment of heavily armed troops and a small entourage in a variety of vehicles that had also been either requisitioned or commandeered and the presence of armed troops comforted him because he had been informed, shortly before his departure, that there had been a peaceful demonstration in Ilford, demanding urgent medical help.

Westminster bridge (and incidentally all of the other 'London' bridges) was still functioning and although clear of any vehicle traffic was eerily illuminated by moonlight and fires still burning on the South side of the Thames.

As they crossed the bridge, the convoy was confronted by a pathetic stream of refugees trundling North, who were fleeing the area and the nearby site of the wrecked hospital. As the convoy drew closer and closer to the epicentre, they were just able to discern a vast carpet of rubble and at the epicentre, rubble that had been fused into glass nodules.

Magnetically drawn to the convoy by its incongruous appearance in a landscape of barren rubble, a lone, probably lonely police officer tapped on the curtained window which Tyndall wound down and was informed by the officer in the distinct accent of the area that:

"He aughtn't be around these parts as the villains, or what was left of them, were looting the shops."

The driver, with the navigational skills of a racing pigeon- though he must have either previously reconnoitred the route or had intelligence - crossed back across the Thames at Blackfriars bridge and proceeded East into and through the 'City' and towards the 'East End' where strangely, almost bizarrely, the further they drove from the site of the explosion, the more normal life and events around them appeared, though the streets, offices and other buildings seemed to be lit by candlelight and the occasional piercing beams of a motor vehicle's headlights.

John Tyndall, no, now Mr. Tyndall, was accompanied by an armed army officer and a senior civil servant who had been allocated to him and would assist him in his duties. He was relatively young, in his early thirties, and evidently exceptionally well educated but above all clearly determined to impress the twelfth member of the National Council whose thoughts were palpably concentrated on the current scene of apparent tranquillity - though there was still no lighting- and the ever urgent imperative to make one important telephone call.

As they entered the outer perimeter of the effects of the 'Ilford' explosion, Tyndall later recalled that he first observed what he initially described as the harrowing scenes, not of increasing devastation, but of the signs of social breakdown and distress as the sides of the road were strewn with little groups huddled around fires and improvised cooking facilities.

Thus the vestiges of civilisation were being quickly eroded.

As the convoy accelerated away and moved closer to the epicentre, he was struck by the almost zombie like procession of the few pedestrians who had braved the cold winter evening, for they seemed to be moving at a funereal pace to, he knew not where, and possibly they did not know themselves or the people aimlessly standing about waiting for, what? Clearly they needed a purpose, direction and above all leadership.

Unexpectedly, suddenly, the Armstrong halted and was surrounded by a group of soldiers armed with rifles but they were not menacing in their posture. The officer in charge spoke to the driver in hushed tones and then walked around the front of the vehicle, momentarily admiring the vehicle's emblem, a sphinx, before exchanging places with the armed officer in the front seat, who rather unceremoniously then squeezed into the rear next to the civil servant.

He addressed Tyndall by his new rank and with due deference informed him that:

"The ground burst had left radioactive debris which was still highly dangerous and he would lead them around the danger area. The air burst above the Imperial War Museum had created less radioactive material which was why they were allowed very close to 'ground zero' beneath the actual explosion. Morale was high amongst the troops since they were buoyed by the news as well as informed gossip, that an imminent counter attack was being prepared and would strike emphatically against Soviet bomber bases, missile sites and their key cities, however the local civilians were fairing less well, actually suffering terribly.

Since they had had no prior warning of an attack they had made no preparations or provisions and most, if not all, had not stored any food. Already he and his troops had had to deny desperate, pleading mothers with young children and babies, food and sanctuary. He had also received reports that women were prostituting themselves - not for money - it no longer had any value - but for a loaf of bread, which even if they had such provisions, they could not humiliate themselves to accept such degradation. There had been some looting, attempts to storm at least three petrol station but these, he understood had been repelled, not by force of arms, but by persuasion.

He feared that within a few days, when real hunger set in, that violence would erupt and mobs of starving, desperate civilians would sacrifice many in their midst to secure food at any cost."

They dropped off the officer and proceeded Eastwards towards Kelvedon Hatch when soon afterwards the vehicle and convoy had to make a right hand turn by a complex of factory buildings and the sight that met them was a recreation of hell from an Hieronymus Bosch triptych.

They had already been informed that funeral pyres were being used to cremate the dead but the reality of the work and not an abstract, dispassionate statement shocked them to such a degree that when the senior civil servant left the vehicle and was confronted by the callous, inhuman, almost systematic industrialised operation, but above all the

407

unmistakeable stench of burning flesh and fat that his stomach involuntarily retched and vomit exploded from his mouth. The operation had all the hallmarks of mass production. Adjacent to the side of the wall was a spiralling iron staircase and on the equivalent of the second floor were two men dressed in leather aprons which one might see in an abattoir and they were flinging, by both arms and legs, the cadavers, some of which were still partially or totally clothed, onto a roaring pyre and they were continuously supplied with new bodies by a chain of workers positioned on the stairs and who were similarly dressed. After a period the men changed positions and a new team had the task of flinging the bodies onto the fire. Two soldiers were lazily standing around smoking with their backs to the fire, one with his rifle slung over his shoulder, the other, his rifle at the ready.

Small pockets of civilians were either trying to keep warm or were peering at the piles of bodies awaiting disposal, perhaps in the vain hope of recognising a loved one or to liberate an item of clothing. John Tyndall noted, but made no comment, that no effort was being made to identify any of the bodies or to record the number of incinerations.

The descent from ordered civilisation continued.

Unannounced, a refuse lorry arrived and without ceremony, the tipping mechanism was automatically engaged, the unit raised and a new supply of bodies slid down for disposal. As it departed it was replaced by another tipper but this time its load was of reclaimed wood that had once been furniture or doors or other items that had enhanced the pleasure of existence but now only served to destroy, by fire, the bodies of people, who less than thirty six hours before, lived, breathed, laughed and cried but made up part of the fabric of society and the community.

R.I.P.

Will the survivors envy the dead?

It was an experience which left all those who had witnessed the scene drained and temporarily devoid of the ability to express their feelings, though Tyndall still remembered that he had an urgent, important telephone call to make.

Silence filled the vehicle until a mile or two further on when the driver abruptly called out that there was a large group of civilians ahead of him and that he sensed danger.

They had chanced upon a *C.C.C.* and the enormity of the problem confronted them. Fortunately they were quickly surrounded by armed troops from the convoy and from their posture and demeanour the crowd clearly realised that any violence would be instantly returned by the use of the soldiers' weapons. The three passengers very cautiously exited the vehicle, again surrounded by a smaller detachment of troops and made their way through the crowd to where a small group of doctors, nurses and their assistants were attempting to work but were obviously overwhelmed and the subject of intimidation from frightened, desperate and injured patients, their families and friends.

If these events were being repeated elsewhere, and especially within their own region, it was obvious that the system would soon collapse in anger and violence, but there was no other viable alternative for the medical services and the hospitals would, as the senior civil servant had said in his statement, be unable to cope and there could be no realistic alternative than to deny treatment to patients who would anyway soon die.

Desperate people with little hope, in the depths of despair, will believe what they wish to hear. Tyndall beckoned the crowd towards him, first making certain that he was adequately protected, and made a brief speech which pacified the crowd, even receiving some half hearted cheers and some congratulatory back slapping as he left...

"I am now a member of the new National Council, authorised by the Prime Minister, who I was with less than two hours ago, to supervise the organisation of medical facilities and recovery centres for your benefit, for you are all the backbone of the nation. Emergency food rations are being delivered and you will shortly be fed. You must obey the army and police, who are your own kith and kin, and allow the medical teams, working under difficult conditions, to carry on their good work without interruption or interference. At this very moment, I understand, a devastating blow is being prepared against our enemies!"

Shortly before they reached the safety of the heavily guarded Kelvedon Hatch bunker complex the army officer stated that:

"He was certain that he heard one poor victim call out..."

"God bless John Tyndall and the New Order."

Such was the tension that he had forgotten to kiss his wife goodbye but she still smiled at him as the car drove away from the entrance to the inner sanctum of the Kremlin where he was met by an elite troop of K G B guards and an official who he recognised from his previous visit. He was formally acknowledged by the troops who saluted him but was slightly confused, if not disoriented, when, as the official put out his hand in friendship, he addressed him as...

"Major-General...it is an honour for the Politburo to receive a great hero."

Even though it was about one a.m. on the Friday morning, as they walked through ante–chambers, rooms and along corridors, he glanced at men and women who were still conscientiously and quietly toiling away but did not lift their heads or turn to see who was walking past them. They reached a small, well lit room, which was perhaps a little too warm, occupied by a single table and surrounded by four chairs. It could have been any room in a thousand buildings in a hundred cities anywhere in the world since there was nothing to signify its importance or origins.

He followed his guide's invitation and they both sat down.

"His wife would be accommodated in the best facilities available and possibly he could call her shortly but events were developing at a rapid, even alarming pace, especially as recently as three–quarters of an hour ago when they began to receive, in bursts, a lengthy enciphered message from their embassy in Mexico City which possibly could affect the original plans that he had so carefully constructed and prepared.

He should be ready for an extremely long and vitally important meeting and be available instantaneously when called by the First Secretary and the Politburo, but first a member of the First Secretary's staff would give him an up to date briefing both of the military and political situation. Such was the absolute importance of the decisions that were to be made he had been called in and more significantly the head of North American intelligence which covered Canada, the United States and Mexico - whose identity was so secret that even their embassy in Mexico City did not know - had been flown back via Canada at great risk. They were to be introduced later and assist in the formulation of the ultimatum to the United States, however information in the enciphered message from their embassy might completely alter or even cause the operation to be aborted."

Within an hour, exactly at two eleven a.m. he was both fully briefed and aware of the State's most guarded secrets.

The briefing had begun with details of the attack on Great Britain, listing the targets and the size of the bombs deployed. A series of photographs, taken in the last eight hours by satellite and reconnaissance fighter jets flying at the extreme limits of their performance gave an added dimension to the briefing`s description of the attack. A state of emergency and martial law had been declared by the British government and intercepted and deciphered messages from beleaguered embassies in London indicated that the emergency services were buckling under the weight of casualties and the serious interruption to the utility services such as the water supply and electricity.

Installation of the new generation fifteen point nine megaton thermonuclear devices in the R36s had begun and would be completed within thirteen days.

Their Warsaw Treaty allies were also preparing themselves for a massive NATO counterattack led by the Americans but... (he stopped short as if there was a doubt).

The government and people of the United States had received the news of the attack on Great Britain with the expected shock that such an event would produce. The President had publically expressed his grief and then went through the motions of offering unlimited help, in terms of medical facilities and reconstruction aid, but in reality their analysis and the latest information that was being gleaned, tended them to believe that Johnson would not risk an all out war to defend the much vaunted concept of liberty and freedom though he had, twenty-four hours before their attack, agreed to have lowered the DEFCON level by two notches and interestingly, according to their best sources, only just acquiesced to have the level raised again but by one single notch.

Johnson was either weak or vacillating but this was a matter that had to be weighed by First Secretary Brezhnev and the Politburo and that was why he and the head of North American Intelligence had been brought to Moscow.

NINETY-FOUR

His first act, immediately on arrival at Kelvedon Hatch, which was intended and left no one in any doubt whatsoever that he was the ultimate possessor of power and authority (and it was only later, when the balance between life and death had to be weighed, that he showed both his ruthlessness and cunning) was to give an oral order demanding that, including the Regional and his deputy Regional Commissioner, every section under his authority submit daily reports confirming *THEIR* [author's emphasis] actions.

"I will have a meeting with my new Regional Commissioner once and when I have made an important telephone call."

AUTHOR'S NOTE:

The publishers have again permitted me to include the following paragraphs, which for legal and security reasons have been edited and can only give an outline of the full facts and may hint at other facilities:

The bare room was well lit, perhaps a little too warm and was sufficiently adequate to seat up to four people and only contained a desk, chairs and on the desk were three telephones easily identifiable as they were coloured red, ivory, and jet black.

The senior civil servant was now able to explain each phone's special purpose but above all the web of facilities that supported the telephones' capabilities:

The red phone was his personal access to the ultra secret Federal exchange and could connect him to the Prime Minister, senior officials and most importantly, also to any of the other members of the National Council.

The ivory phone could be used for lower grade communications and would put him in contact with a central exchange linking all government buildings - The Government Telecommunications Network (*GTN*) - the Hxxx tandem which is housed within the bombproof Rotunda citadel below the xxx in xxx Street, xxx, London.

Finally the black phone was connected to the normal telephone system, however there currently existed and had existed from the earliest days of the phone system, the secret Telephone Preference System. When a new subscriber is allocated a phone, they are secretly given a preference category from one to three. Category 1 never gets disconnected in any emergency and covers mainly government organisations and, not surprisingly, the petroleum industry. Category 2 includes the private residencies of the surviving M.Ps. and possibly, for example, doctors whilst Category 3, the vast bulk of the network, would be the first to be disconnected. Subscribers would suddenly find that their phones had gone 'dead', although they could still receive calls from those connected to the service.

The reason that Category 3 subscribers would be excluded from the system was to conserve energy, for if the electricity supply was cut the exchanges could and had to conserve their limited battery power.

Disturbingly, some individuals or organisations in Category 3 might find their phones still operating for the simple reason that their homes or premises had been secretly earmarked for requisition or to be commandeered.

In ascending order he first used the black phone, then the ivory instrument and finally, again without success, the red unit.

"Yes, the bunker has at its disposal motorcycle couriers who would be able to deliver a message."

Such was the confidentiality of the message that Tyndall did not use the facility of a short hand typist who was available and forty minutes later a courier was en route to Central London bearing a hastily drafted, long hand written note addressed to Sir Oswald Mosley, Curzon Street, Mayfair and with instructions to wait for a written reply.

The initial first meeting with the Regional Commissioner and his deputy was most cordial, in fact all three appeared to have found a resonance and bond that contradicted his previous opposition to conventional political practices and policies whilst the latter exhibited their dedication to the procedures of the nation's honourable traditions.

With the approval of the senior civil servant, Tyndall orally acknowledged the Regional Commissioner's authority to oversee the maintenance of law and order and all the other matters that his fellow Commissioners had been planning for some time. Thus, temporarily, outside of the bunker, the Regional Commissioner was in command and had the power of, and over, life and death...

"But it was imperative that he submit daily reports, the format and contents of which they could mutually develop with the help of his senior civil servant; his prime concern was the maintenance of law and order and ultimately the return to civil, democratic government (this went down well with those at the meeting and Tyndall was most insistent that his remarks were recorded and minuted).

The State of Emergency and subsequent imposition of Martial Law was a necessary procedure but he was most concerned that the arbitrary use of the death penalty might be abused and that their intentions might be misunderstood, causing a 'backlash' amongst the community.   He assumed that the Regional Commissioners had already drafted a list of offences that would incur the death penalty and until such time as he received a list of the offences and their consequence and they had been publicly displayed, he could not, would not, sanction such a drastic course and when such authority was granted, each execution had to be confirmed personally by the Regional Commissioner, in writing, or by himself and full particulars had to be recorded in the daily report.

His senior civil servant would therefore immediately communicate with all the Regional Seats of Government to coordinate a uniform policy within the next twenty-four hours and then the proclamation could be printed, distributed and displayed unless, of course, action had already been taken, in which case he would reluctantly approve and agree to the use of the death penalty."

Superficially his intentions and actions were, within the parameters of martial law, decent and fair but his real intentions would remain hidden under camouflage until he was certain of his position and above all the thoughts and suggestions of his idol and putative mentor, Sir Oswald Mosley.

Thus his cunning and instincts imitated the nature and motives of Renaissance Florence politics.

When the door opened - bringing with it the relief of a cooling blast of air-Kashkarov assumed that he was to be immediately summonsed to appear before the Politburo but it was, in fact, the representative from the First Secretary's office and two men that he had not met before but who were well known and formally introduced as Politburo members Gennady Voronov and Sharof Rashidov.

"First Secretary Brezhnev had sent them to talk to him, for they were convinced that the final part of his brilliant plan was now in place and ready to be activated. They had with them the deciphered multi part message sent from Mexico City and he had some forty minutes in which to read the document and make a crucial judgement. "

At the same time Nikolai Podgorny and Mikhail Suslov were discussing the same subject with the head of North American Intelligence but the person had not spoken or read the Russian language for nearly twenty years and he understood that progress was slow as it was necessary to translate the document back into English and for the translator to help with the person's faltering Russian.

The delay transmitting the message was caused by the encypherers following strict protocol with meticulous attention. First the subject had been recorded and the original then transcribed in English, before being translated and typed in Cyrillic, then the whole report was reversed, a relatively simple task, and finally the string of letters was mixed with a previously determined random string of letters of the same number before being encrypted using a special 'one time pad'.

The embassy was certain that their lines were being tapped and that a single long burst would alert the American cryptanalysts who they suspected were aware of their assessment. Therefore the message had been transmitted out of sequence, in short bursts, and the cryptographers in Moscow had to wait until the complete message had been received before putting the parts in their correct order, then reversing the complete procedure and recovering the message.

The Politburo and the political system that it represented did not think or act like the American media and people who expected, and were fed, news and information that their Russian counterparts were deprived of. The power of television, and before that, radio, as a means to disseminate news, opinion and propaganda-government policy - was entirely different. Thus the doyen of American broadcasting, who had cemented his reputation on Friday, November twenty- second, nineteen sixty-three, Walter Cronkite, by his professionalism and desire to publicise the unmitigated facts would create an environment that like Orson Welles` radio adaptation of H.G. Wells` 'War of the Worlds' would soon create fear and irrationality which are the foundation of ...panic.

The message was no more than the transcription of a telephone interview conducted by the highly respected Cronkite on *CBS News* on Thursday morning, March fourth which was syndicated nationally and which was recorded from the Los Angeles stations *KNXT* and *KFMB*. Observant American viewers and readers will, or should remember, that Cronkite normally fronted the evening news, but the studio executives, and Walter himself, sensed a story of the magnitude of the recent JFK assassination and he, with the confidence of experience and ability, helped 'front' the morning show providing as much news of the events in Great Britain as was available.

Significantly, early in the broadcast, before the interview, he referred to an innocuous article in that morning's final edition of the *Los Angeles Times* (Vol. LXXXIV, page 30), captioned:

LIFE NORMAL,

SAYS KHRUSHCHEV`S WIFE

MOSCOW

And read...

Mrs. Nikita S. Khrushchev says she and her husband are leading "a normal, healthy life like other people."

The former Soviet first lady, known to Russians as Nina Petronova, earlier this week made her first appearance inside the Kremlin, since her husband was ousted from power last October. She showed up at the 'Palace of Congresses' the new, modernistic building inside the Kremlin, to hear the opera 'Prince Igor'. Khrushchev, a devoted opera lover, was not with her...(but) a member of the audience said someone asked her how things were going.

"We are now living a normal, healthy life like other people", Mrs Khrushchev replied.

Cronkite`s opinion was that the report was purely coincidental and not a' smokescreen' to mask the Russians` perfidious and heinous intentions and actions but stations, across the United States, were inundated with comments, overwhelmingly negative and generally warning of the Soviets` malevolent intentions.

However it was the chilling and macabre telephone interview, subsequently prominently and widely reported in the nation`s press and other television and radio channels, that must have focused viewers` and the country`s concerns about their own safety and vulnerability and which shortly afterwards culminated in the Soviet 'ultimatum' and the nation`s hysterical panic.

When Walter Cronkite introduced both himself and Herman Kahn, he initially explained to his audience that in view of the tragic news coming from England he had been asked to co-host the morning`s T.V. news programme and they had secured, at very short notice, the assistance of Herman Kahn, a military strategist at the Rand Corporation and a specialist in the field of the nature and theory of war in the thermonuclear age. He then went on to describe Kahn as the author of the nineteen sixty-two work, 'Thinking about the Unthinkable' and his earlier work of nineteen sixty, 'On Thermonuclear War', an academic analysis not only of war itself but of the circumstances and events that could escalate a non military, political confrontation to all out thermonuclear war and more especially the aftermath, an investigation into the nature of a post apocalyptic society and its struggle to recover to its pre-war industrial production level and the enormous effect on the social fabric of the nation.

The telephone interview was supplemented by stock film and stills of the author, a number of test explosions, the consequent physical damage and finally historical film of the aftermath of the Hiroshima and Nagasaki bombings including graphic illustrations of the burns suffered by the population, but there had been insufficient time for the producers to prepare graphs to assist the audience fully understand Kahn`s observations, however, where necessary, they were succinctly and lucidly explained by Walter Cronkite.

The approach and academic style of Kahn to his morbid subject would normally be best described by the descriptions, dispassionate, objective, detached and emotionless, however he seemed at ease, using a style of communication and presentation that the viewers could generally understand.

He could muster a vast array of statistics and facts to prove his arguments but in the limited time available it had to be accepted that whilst the United States (he did not mention or include their allies) still had an overwhelming quantitative and qualitative advantage in military hardware and naval power against the Soviet Union (and again he did not mention their allies) the fundamental basis of their confrontation was the concept of Mutual Assured Destruction ('M.A.D.'), that is neither side would risk all out war because their military planners recognised that both sides would be destroyed and there would be no winner. Therefore both sides, being rational, also feared the other launching a sneak, pre–emptive first strike, if they were able, in secret, to develop and assemble a new generation of weapons which, combined with a vast existing arsenal of weapons and delivery platforms (i.e. bombers, missiles and submarines), could give them such an advantage that a pyrrhic victory was perceived as possible and worth a great, but finite destruction of their infrastructure and loss of a considerable proportion of their population.

The massive nuclear attack, in nineteen sixty-four, by the United States, was launched because the nation had such an advantage in bombers and weapons that they were able to destroy a considerable number of their enemy`s means of delivery (i.e. their own bombers) to halt any further territorial expansion or immediate counter-attack. It had been a carefully planned and soberly considered operation based on the primary consideration to protect the continental United States, however the *REAL* [author`s emphasis] truth which was still a closely guarded secret, was that the President had been incapacitated and that he, Kahn, had persuaded the Secretary of Defence, McNamara, to unilaterally authorise the operation whilst the rest of the Executive and the Judiciary were locked in an intellectual struggle debating the legality of any action.

Had the United States employed the use of thermonuclear weapons then, without a doubt, the Soviet Union, with its few remaining bombers and first and second generation missiles, would have been forced to immediately launch a retaliatory counter first- strike in like kind, resulting in Armageddon, though whilst the Politburo and their First Secretary, Brezhnev, were presumably realists and pragmatists, they might still test the will of the United States 'government and its citizens.

Walter Cronkite then asked his guest to describe the consequences of a single nuclear or thermonuclear explosion and as the explanation unfolded it must have caused the viewers to fear the consequences of a potential Soviet attack...

"There are various factors, such as whether it was an air or ground burst and more importantly whether the device used was a nuclear or thermonuclear weapon. The former are usually between ten and fifty kilotons which means ten to fifty thousand tons of T.N.T. and the latter, hydrogen bombs, which can be anything from one megaton (or one million tons of T.N.T.) upwards.

A five megaton bomb exploded one thousand, six hundred and fifty feet (five hundred metres) above Manhattan, New York would completely wipe out the city and including the immediate and long term dead kill virtually everyone in a ten mile radius, whilst considerable physical damage would be caused within a twenty mile radius.

(He briefly paused before listing the effects of an explosion):

First, within an infinitesimal part of a second, energy would be released in the form of neutrons, gamma and X –rays reacting with the air and creating an electromagnetic pulse which would instantaneously effect the electrical supply and every item of electrical equipment within a large radius (which he did not specify).

The radiation would be absorbed by the air creating an enormous, rapidly expanding, incandescent ball of air and (for a ground burst) as the fireball touched the ground, a crater would be scooped out as the earth and debris were vaporised.

Infra-red radiation from the heat of the fireball would radiate out in the form of a heat pulse generating fires when absorbed by combustible materials and causing burning in various degrees to the skins of those unfortunate enough to be caught in the open (it was at this point that film of the victims of the Hiroshima and Nagasaki bombings was screened).

Then, perhaps twenty or so seconds later, depending on various circumstances, a tremendous shockwave from the sudden heating of the air would move outwards relentlessly destroying everything in its path, gradually abating and diminishing again dependent on the original power of the weapon and the distance from the explosion."

It was, at this dramatic moment, that Cronkite interrupted Kahn and asked about the formation and dangers of radioactive materials...

"Most of the radioactive material would be formed from the debris scooped out from the ground by a ground burst whilst, in comparison, less radioactive material would be formed by an airburst which would substantially decay before falling to earth.

The material scooped up by the fireball following a ground burst would form particles on which the radiation would condense and begin to fall back, influenced by the wind, though the heaviest, most dangerous fallout will drop down beneath the canopy of the now famous 'mushroom cloud' whose diameter could extend for fifteen miles or so, more than covering the areas initially damaged by fire and blast.

Radiation is measured in terms of "Roentgens per hour" and within the central area of the explosion the level would be initially in thousands of units, a fatal amount if a victim was exposed for more than thirty minutes or so.

However radiation 'decays', losing its' energy exponentially, initially sharply and later more gradually which explains why there is latent radioactivity sometime after an explosion.

The symptoms of radiation poisoning have been widely publicised including damage to unborn babies, genetic mutation, loss of hair and incapacity to resist infection because the radiation destroys the ability to manufacture white blood cells leading first to infection and inevitably to death."

CBS were inundated with viewers' comments and questions leading Cronkite to ask the question that would be the catalyst for fear, irrationality and above all panic...

"Viewers have asked if the recently announced Soviet test explosion of a fifteen point nine megaton bomb and the multiple launch of Intercontinental Ballistic Missiles comes within your definition of a new generation of weapons and combined with the attack on our closest ally, England, should we now fear a more aggressive military posture from the Soviet Union?"

For a few moments there was a silence before Kahn gave a confident answer that in itself raised further and unanswered questions.

"A five or fifteen point nine megaton bomb whether dropped on Los Angeles, New York, Moscow or Leningrad will produce the same result. Total obliteration. For the individual there would be no hiding place from the heat pulse or shockwave. The subsequent damage caused by radioactivity will result in a lingering death for the survivors in the outer areas of the explosion.

I suspect that the deployment of such a large weapon would be to destroy and poison the Prairies or if used by us, to irradiate the Ukrainian wheat basin, alternatively a bomb of this size, strategically exploded could effectively destroy most of central England and completely, and I stress completely, overwhelm the combined resources of the whole nation's medical and emergency services.

For viewers of this programme the only salvation that I can offer is to desert the cities and prepare for a long siege in a remote area, however at some point you would need to contact the towns and cities for supplies or medical services where you would find the collapse of law and order and empty granaries, for the production of food and its availability would have, at least, temporarily ceased, been pilfered or exhausted.

Like the British in World War Two, who suffered both The Blitz and attacks by V1 and V2 missiles, the front line has now reached the continental United States which was now no longer shielded by two oceans and mighty fleets."

Kashkarov read, and had time to reread, the document. His argument was not only strengthened, but vindicated by the interview. Europe, and revenge for the attack on Great Britain, would be abandoned by the American government if its citizens put enough pressure on their leaders because the so called freedom for knowledge and information would instil fear.

He would also remind the Politburo, despite the possible consequences to his career, that Khrushchev, on January fourteenth nineteen sixty, perhaps excessively, had stated (in a speech to the Supreme Soviet) that:

"I am emphasizing once more that we already possess so many nuclear weapons, both atomic and hydrogen, and the necessary rockets for sending these weapons to the territory of a potential aggressor, that should any madman launch an attack on our state or on other Socialist states we would be able literally to wipe the country or countries which attack us off the face of the earth."

[Author's note: Please refer to the New York Times, January fifteenth, nineteen sixty].

The only rhetorical question that he dare not directly ask the Politburo was how far they were prepared to confront their enemy in pursuit of the age old policy of territorial expansion.

He felt at ease discussing the subject with two of the most important men in the state when they were interrupted and called into the conference room to join the other members of the Politburo.

NINETY-FIVE

A Top Secret plan, so secret that no documentation was ever produced, code name "Rocking Horse", arranged for Prince Charles, the sixteen year old heir to the throne and Princess Anne, his younger sister, to be temporarily and secretly moved to Sandringham, in Norfolk, where the Queen had an extensive estate set in six hundred acres of woodland and where they were protected both by heavily armed troops and tanks but also by a crack commando unit who had available three helicopters, on permanent standby, in the event of any major development including the improbable possibility that Soviet Spetsnaz troops might launch an audacious kidnapping attempt.

Contingency plans to send the Royal family, separately by submarines, to Canada had already been put in hand but the Queen and her Consort had been most adamant that they would remain in London alongside the titular government but more importantly her subjects, though on the insistence of her advisors she rotated, at night, sleeping either in a secure bunker or being driven to Windsor Castle.

She had summonsed Harold Wilson, at very short notice, to Buckingham Palace to discuss a 'disturbing development' and for him it could only mean one matter, his achilles heel. Whilst the United States were supplying B 52 bombers and thermonuclear weapons, combined with the 'V' bombers that were very slowly being repatriated from South Africa, the R.A.F. could only 'muster' forty-one bombers and it was estimated that perhaps as many as twenty-five percent or ten or eleven bombers would be shot down en route to the Soviet Union. Furthermore the Americans had both the final say on the weapons' use and crucially exclusive knowledge of the bombs' security codes. There was, no longer, any pretence that the United Kingdom had an independent deterrent.

With many of the top civil servants now disbursed to the Regional Seats of Government where the Regional Commissioners were based he was unable to rely on his advisors, even if he was inclined to available himself of their wisdom, and therefore he had to rely on Gerald Kaufman and Manny Gold.

Gold would be his plenipotentiary and arrangements were made for him to meet the United States ambassador at a secret location outside of London and most importantly not close to any potential targets. He would travel to the Palace with Kaufman where he expected to have the usual private audience. Both the Royal Air Force and the Queen were both going to demand an immediate military response and Her Majesty, full details of the progress that had been made by the medical services and other authorities recovering the dead, aiding the injured, clearing the debris and regenerating the various services.

Gold had now reached an undreamed of position of power, and shortly of influence, but his reception and the subject of discussion was not as he had expected.

The country manor house (which incidentally was in Gloucestershire) was exceptionally well maintained and as he entered the long drive up to the house he immediately saw, close by, a cluster of different types of helicopters and like an ant hill, a large contingent of armed troops patrolling the grounds and clearly alert to any potential threat. He was personally welcomed by the ambassador who escorted him to what was and could be described as the library, but they both had to navigate a number of children and their toys and games that littered the floor.

The ambassador apologised for the inconvenience but did not lose the negotiating initiative, stating that, with the force of a thermonuclear weapon...

"Wilson was finished and that the United Kingdom was effectively incapable of defending itself. He, Gold, had only been received, because his loyalty had been bought by the United States some twenty-five years before but he had shown his loyalty to them by supplying them with information.

However, unexpectedly, he could now become a person of great influence and power. He had been personally informed by the President that the United States government had no intention of sacrificing Los Angeles for London and would only launch a first strike against the Soviets if his executive and the Strategic Air Command assessed the situation as absolutely unavoidable. The British Isles were now viewed as an unsinkable aircraft carrier but was ultimately expendable.

Gold was now in the enviable position of being trusted by the British Prime Minister *AND* [author's emphasis] the United States who had, in the present situation, temporarily delegated authority to him."

At that moment, if only coincidentally, but with the effect of lowering the tension, there entered four waiters wheeling trolleys on which were laden a superb selection of plain but excellently prepared dishes including hot and cold Aberdeen Angus roast beef, shellfish and smoked salmon. They sat at a small table and Gold ate sparingly but well as the ambassador outlined Washington's thoughts.

"It was imperative and essential that the current and future British governments be totally loyal to the President and his successors and would maintain, by whatever means, law, order and control over the nation. It was critical that the United Kingdom remain stable and viable to continue hosting United States forces who would act as part of the encirclement of the Soviet sphere of influence but in a potential confrontation that might come to a head they had no intention whatsoever of, as he had said previously, sacrificing a U.S. city to protect London. Shortly, when the circumstances were ripe, they could, would, assist in the fall of Wilson and perhaps the miners` renegade leader, Bill Martin, who was viewed as symbolic of the fundamental problems at the root of British society, however in the meantime, he should report back to Wilson with a statement that was consistent with the Prime Minister`s hopes that he could count on their support both militarily and economically, but they were not ready to launch an all out attack on the Soviet Union and her Warsaw Pact allies."

Gold realised that there was now no reason to ask the ambassador to help satisfy Wilson`s requests and it was only necessary to agree on a series of measures to placate him until he could be deposed of and replaced. Thus Wilson`s future and more importantly, his fate, had been decided.

John Tyndall opened the sealed envelope accidentally partially tearing the neatly folded sheets of expensive notepaper on which were written, in Sir Oswald Mosley`s elegant handwriting, his grateful reply but above all his requests which preceded his suggestions and thoughts:

He desperately needed a pistol, together with a generous supply of bullets and documentary evidence authorising and permitting him the right to carry a loaded weapon. His supply of medicine would only last a further fortnight and he had just learned that he could no longer obtain further supplies from any of the local chemists. There then followed a list of medicines and their strengths with a request for a supply adequate for the next three months or so.

A plaintive request for coal and tinned food, as much as possible followed, and then finally, if almost cryptically, he confirmed that 'CJ' (Colin Jordan) was at his disposal together with his followers but his first advice was to trust no one, and certainly not this adventurer, to delegate the less pleasant tasks to his staff making certain that they were known as the responsible parties and whenever possible obtain and store documentary evidence, including witness details and signatures, formally associating the participants with their acts.

Divide and rule. Whilst it was convenient he should favour one group against another and then shift his support to yet another group against the earlier one, always appearing to support his patron but at the same time secretly 'sounding out' others whose thirst for power was even greater than his, with a view to forming a transient alliance and finally, with duplicity and without conscience, for only the weak have a conscience, inform his patron of the others` disloyalty and treachery when it would be too late for the victims to extricate themselves from their fate.

And, if as an afterthought, Mosley concluded the letter with a post script:

My final advice is that you destroy this letter other than my list of medicines.

Within twenty-four hours Sir Oswald Mosley`s requirements had been fulfilled and Tyndall was able to pursue matters concerning both his duties and his own nefarious plans.

Gerald Kaufman both hoped and expected to meet the Queen again and, perhaps, to play a more prominent role in the future and destiny of the nation.

Unlike their previous visit two evenings before, the short journey was only illuminated by the moon for the local fires had been quenched or had exhausted any combustible material and if the engineers had been able to restore the electricity grid, power was being conserved.

Again, at his trial for treason, Harold Wilson`s recollections were in conflict with the memories of a witness.

Definitely present at the meeting, and not a private audience, were Her Majesty, Prince Philip, Her Principal Private Secretary, Gerald Kaufman and the Prime Minister. Gerald Kaufman, at the treason trial, confirmed that all formalities or even common courtesies were put aside as the Queen opened the meeting with a withering assault on Wilson`s recent actions and in a statement, that Kaufman remembered verbatim, because of the Queen`s near uncontrollable anger, accused him of...

"Betraying the bond of trust that her subjects had placed in her."

Wilson had then expected the Queen to make a direct reference to the impotent bomber deterrent but she requested her Principal Private Secretary to...

"Present details of an alarming and most ominous development that she had first been made aware of some five hours before, though exact and complete details had unfortunately not yet been obtained and collated."

Her P.PS. had before him a small pile of sheets of paper and Kaufman soon noted that some had been typed whilst others had been handwritten, some of which appeared rather hurriedly rushed. With the formality of one who had been bred to serve, whose manners and fastidious grooming were impeccable and who was both erudite and highly educated, he formally requested Her Majesty`s permission to speak which she duly gave not by a word but by a nod of her head.

"A second poster, issued by the joint deputy Regional Commissioners had begun to appear in various parts of the country, usually adjacent to the original poster, from whence (Wilson noted the almost archaic style of his delivery) Buckingham Palace had been supplied with details and he hoped very shortly to receive a copy but he was able to recover, if not the exact wording, the intentions and spirit of the announcement."

It was at this pregnant moment that Prince Philip, with little respect for courtesy, directly and bluntly asked the Prime Minister if he was aware of the document's contents and his negative response was, without doubt, treated cynically by the Royal Consort who then asked the P.P.S.to continue.

[The document was similarly headed as before, but this time without the major spelling error]

STATE OF EMERGENCY

MARTIAL LAW.SECOND EDITION

What now follows is their reconstruction of the document and it should be noted that both Harold Wilson and Gerald Kaufman independently conjectured how and from whom the information had been supplied for it was as if Her Majesty had a secret army of spies and informants which harkened back to the days of the first Queen Elizabeth and Her spymaster, Lord Walsingham.

The proclamation begun with the chilling statement that:

[Author`s note: The following itemised system has only been introduced to assist the reader follow the approximate reconstruction of the proclamation which did not include the section headings. Furthermore certain sub-sections have been rearranged to give the document greater consistency].

PART ONE

It shall be an offence, punishable by death, which may be commuted to penal servitude for no less than five years and not exceeding fifteen years (determined by a Regional Commissioner) to commit, assist, incite, promote or support the following offences or suppress knowledge of the act(s) from a Regional Commissioner, his deputy, and, or, the military authorities acting on their behalf. The definition military authorities is deemed to include the Police or Security forces acting under their authority.

(One)   Commit, organise, promote, support, join or assist in the act of Sedition, Revolution or Treason

(Two)   Withhold knowledge of any intention, act, statement or assistance from a Regional Commissioner, his deputy or the military authorities concerning any individual or body of persons who wish or intend to harm the State by Sedition, Revolution or Treason

(Three)   Commit, organise, promote, support, join or assist in an act or series of acts of terrorism

(Four)   Disseminate information prejudicial to the security and interests of the State

(Five)   Disseminate information, whether true or false, that could be reasonably expected to create public unrest, distress or disquiet

(Six)   Organise, promote, support, join or assist a strike or the withdrawal of labour

(Seven)   Wilfully disobey an order or request from a duly authorised official, whether or not that person or body of persons have identified him/her or themselves

(Eight)   Refuse an order or notification, when requested by a duly authorised official, to take up military service

(Nine)   Refuse a request to billet a member or members of the armed forces or a civilian official or officials, when requested by a duly authorised official

(Ten)   Enter a zone or area designated as prohibited unless permitted by a duly authorised official

(Eleven)	Membership or support of the Communist Party which has been proscribed as an illegal organisation
(Twelve)	Membership of a Trades Union unless that body has been sanctioned by a Regional Commissioner or his deputy
(Thirteen)	Commit, incite, procure, assist or publicise the acts of sodomy or homosexuality
(Fourteen)	Commit, incite, procure, assist or publicise the acts of bestiality or frottage
(Fifteen)	Knowingly transmit a sexual disease
(Sixteen)	Store, hoard, loot, steal (or store for another person or body of persons), food, water or fuel
(Seventeen)	Transport, exchange, sell or buy, unless permitted by a duly authorised official, food, water or fuel
(Eighteen)	Store, hoard, transport, sell or buy medical drugs, unless permitted by a duly authorised official
(Nineteen)	Loot or steal medical drugs
(Twenty)	Acts of hooliganism or anti social or unpatriotic behaviour

[AND FINALLY, AS IF AS AN AFTERTHOUGHT, *PERHAPS* THE MOST EXTREME PROVISION]

| (Twenty-one) | The right of assembly, without the prior permission of a duly authorised official is limited to six (6) persons or twelve (12) persons provided that they remain static and have received the permission of a duly authorised official |

PART TWO

Wilfully deface, cover up, damage, tear down or destroy in part or in full this proclamation or any previous or later proclamations.

PART THREE

After arrest, the accused shall appear as soon as practically possible before a special Court of Protection which may sit in camera or in public, composed of up to, but no more than, three Regional or deputy Regional Commissioners or a uniformed military officer or officers who may be assisted by one civilian expert all of whom have been appointed by a Regional Commissioner or his deputy as competent to judge the defendant.

The accused may only be represented by a uniformed military officer appointed by the Court.

All decisions of the Court are absolute and are not subject to appeal.

It was at this point, that the Queen confronted by the frightening reality and consequences of martial law, turned to *HER* (again author's emphasis) Prime Minister and demanded, in no uncertain terms, what action he intended to take, to protect the citizens of the country and to reinstate the principles that had begun some seven hundred and fifty years before and enshrined in Magna Carta.

With unsuppressed belligerency Prince Philip then verbally assaulted the Prime Minister and with deep emotion accused him, with some foundation in fact, of...

"Betraying the very people he was duty bound to serve."

Gerald Kaufman grasped the nettle, realising that there was little defence to the accusations but he would endeavour to mitigate the draconian terms suggesting that:

"Perhaps the Queen's (Principal) Private Secretary be permitted to complete his presentation and that their combined experience and Her Majesty's wisdom be focused on a course of action that could resolve the fundamental principles of justice."

Despite the tension and anger that filled the room, the apparently unperturbed P.P.S. concluded his presentation...

PART THREE (CONCLUDED)

On receipt of written confirmation of the offence and judgement of the Court, a Regional or deputy Regional Commissioner who did not form part of the Court, in exceptional circumstances, may alter the punishment of the sentence but is unable to change the verdict.

Execution would be carried out by a military firing squad after which the body could be claimed and a notice displayed which should include the name of the deceased, the date of execution and particulars of the offence or offences.

The Prime Minister had been cowed into virtual silence and it therefore became necessary for Gerald Kaufman to defend what for many would be the indefensible.

"May I point out that the deputy Regional Commissioners are all answerable to the Regional Commissioners who were all personally appointed by Mr. Wilson and that their deputies are all, without exception, former distinguished members of your armed forces and have been specially trained and prepared for this most daunting of responsibilities which the Prime Minister is completely confident they will carry out with compassion and integrity."

It was evident that the Queen and Prince Philip were still deeply disturbed however it was agreed on the further intervention of Gerald Kaufman that a schedule be submitted listing the twenty-four Regional Commissioners and their deputies and that lists be supplied every twenty-four hours with particulars of any executions and the charge or charges for which they had been convicted.

Inexorably events, circumstances but above all the poisonous and seductive chalice of power were eroding the diminishing authority of Harold Wilson.

NINETY-SIX

Vasil Mzhavanadze put down the document that had seized his interest and immediately caught both the eye and the attention of Kashkarov as he entered the room behind the two members of the Politburo. Kashkarov was perhaps both unaware of Mzhavanadze`s identity but above all, his reputation and history.

Mzhavanadze owed his position to the ousted former leader Nikita Khrushchev, having been appointed as a candidate member of the Politburo on his patron`s election as First Secretary. Had the political situation and the balance of power within the Politburo been different then Leonid Brezhnev, with the support of a substantial number of its members would have sacked him for Brezhnev and his allies were building a dossier stuffed with evidence of Mzhavanadze`s corrupt and inefficient governance as First Secretary of the Communist Party of the Georgian Soviet Socialist Republic.

The pro Khrushchev adherents were now a minority rump and Mzhavanadze's status as a candidate member meant that he did not have a vote but he was a persuasive speaker and although Brezhnev was confident that his proposed manoeuvre against the Americans would be approved in the imminent vote he wanted to be absolutely certain of an overwhelming vote of support and confidence.

If necessary, unknown even to those closest to him, Brezhnev was pragmatically prepared to disregard the ever damning, incriminating file and make Mzhavanadze a full member, when convenient, in exchange for his total support.

Kashkarov's attention was directed to the man with the 'Charlie Chaplin' moustache though his other senses were strangely, almost magnetically, drawn to an entrancing smell which reminded him of the pleasant coolness of a shaded forest glade in summer where the flowers intentionally broadcast their diverse scents and then, illogically, his mind's eye drew him away from the man's influence and he began to hear the music of Alexander Borodin and in that same mind's eye he could see a caravan traversing the Steppes of Central Asia.

He was about to turn round and locate the source of the beautiful aroma when, like the crack of a whip, he heard his name, preceded by his new rank, almost barked out in anger for it was the second time that the First Secretary had called him.

He stood next to the First Secretary, obedient as a loyal puppy, whilst the sensation of the scent and the aroma evaporated and vanished from his thoughts for he now steeled himself for the task that would confront him.

"Major-General please persuade all those in this room that we should play a dangerous game with the Americans and why you are convinced that we can win without going to the brink and nightmare of all out global thermonuclear war."

He proceeded, with the confidence of his acquired and extensive knowledge and the strength of his case, to present a compelling, cogent argument to the most powerful men in the Soviet Union. It was not initially necessary to dare ask the rhetorical question which he had felt was beyond his status, for the First Secretary had raised the matter in his introduction and clearly understood the consequences of the path that might be followed.

He briefly reminded them, without going into too much detail, of the massive leap in power that had been made to their fleet of Intercontinental Ballistic missiles and their thermonuclear armoury, but he concentrated on the weakness, not of their enemy's massive military hardware, on land, at sea and in the air but on the support that the United States President would receive from the people when they realised that their great cities and towns, scattered across the vast prairies, were all now vulnerable and not as before, only the great coastal cities.

He was about to explain how the American people would react to a Soviet ultimatum, backed by a further demonstration of their military capabilities and their clear intention to move onto a war footing, when he was suddenly distracted by someone, at the back of the room, close to where the beautiful aroma had originated, who was translating his statement into English, automatically making him both verify its accuracy and creating an echo of his own thoughts and words. This most unpredictable of acts made it impossible for him to continue presenting his argument and without hesitation he marched across the room to confront the translator drawing, not unexpectedly, comments of surprise.

But as he reached the man his attention was drawn to a young woman, quietly seated nearby, hurriedly making notes, stunningly, classically beautiful, in her, he estimated, early forties and exquisitely dressed, in vibrant colours, which completely contrasted with the dull grey and dowdiness of the Politburo members and probably of their wives. Having access to the British and American press, or in all truth, pages other than reports of military events and matters it was clear that this woman had purchased her chic and sophisticated clothing from the most expensive and exclusive stores in New York or perhaps even the Beverley Hills suburb of Los Angeles, close to the fantasy world of Hollywood.

She looked up at him and instantaneously a bond was rekindled for they had not seen each other since the camp had been closed over twenty years before and he now realised why the identity of the head of Soviet intelligence in the North American continent had been shrouded in such secrecy.

It was the authoritative and booming voice of Vasil Mzhavanadze that brought them back to reality, demanding an explanation why the authority of the Politburo appeared to be held in such disdain.

She stood up, assured, composed and confident, walked up to the First Secretary, accompanied by the somewhat surprised Kashkarov, and without permission, began to speak fluently in Russian, as she was to admit later to Brezhnev and Kashkarov that the shock of her meeting her dear, old friend and the rudeness of the previous speaker had surprisingly revived command of her beloved mother tongue.

"During the Second World War - what you all, myself included, called the Great Patriotic War - I was personally ordered by Lavrenti Beria to work at a secret camp in the Ukraine where one of my assistants and now good friend was Kashkarov who after more than twenty years of separation stands by my side.

What happened in the camp is still secret but despite the fact that Beria was purged after Stalin`s death his foresight must be acknowledged for the seeds that he sowed have germinated and produced a rich fruit which we are currently harvesting.

I have been head of Intelligence in the North American continent since nineteen forty–nine, less than a year after I graduated from college, and only once, since I was smuggled back into Canada, late in nineteen forty-four, did I speak my beloved mother tongue and that was some eighteen months ago for a few, brief moments. For security purposes a new name and the briefest of histories was created for me and I lost all contact with my parents, who faithfully served you, and were based in California and I have never been able to visit their graves and I am informed, in their wisdom, that they requested their gravestones were not to mention the fact that they had a daughter, solely to protect me.

Never once did the Party show its gratitude to them for organising the plan to infiltrate the home of the Party's most despised enemy which resulted in the execution of the class traitor and enemy of the Party, whose name I dare to raise in this the heart of Socialism, Leon Trotsky.

At great risk to my cover I have returned to my homeland but this time in greater comfort. I do not ask that you judge the life that I have chosen for whilst I have accumulated the material wealth that the Capitalist system worships, because my first loyalty has always been to the Party and the cause of Socialism I have been unwilling and unable to achieve what millions of my fellow countrymen take as their birthright, that of marriage and the right to raise a family. Indeed the fear of ever divulging my true identity and the purpose of my life has left me lonely and isolated, uncertain and cautious about those around me. But ultimately I have both fulfilled my dream and absolutely served the Party.

Now I will explain to you what my old friend was about to say about the American people. They are as brave as the soldiers of the old Red Army and their civilians as stoic as the embattled residents of Stalingrad as they withstood the Fascist onslaught. But no sane person would permit their government to dare risk an assault by the most frightening weapon ever created. Politically you have a great advantage, for the organs of communication are totally under your control so the flow of information means that news can be suppressed or even manipulated. In the United States perhaps too much news and information is available.

Thus a plausible threat to destroy, in a first strike, not only priority military targets but named cities would cause immediate panic, the mass uncontrolled evacuation of those cities, chaos and unimaginable pressure on the President and his Executive to negotiate a settlement, any settlement, to secure a peace however honourable, temporary or fragile.

Therefore you must be prepared to sacrifice tens of millions of your citizens in order to fulfil your plans for territorial expansion and increased influence.

Finally, let me justify my confidence both in your wisdom and political astuteness by informing you all that I live outside the city of Atlanta (which is in the state of Georgia) and I ask, no demand, that you name my home city as one of the civilian targets. I will stay knowing that you will negotiate a satisfactory settlement and that I will not die in the centre of a vast fireball. The American people are already confused and worried why you attacked London and other targets in Great Britain. Your answer will shock and frighten them."

She turned to her dear friend in the pregnant silence that followed and in English stated that:

"I hope that my analysis echoed your thoughts in the matter."

The Soviet Union, whilst ostensibly a Socialist state based on equality, was in reality a male dominated society with a strict hierarchical order and therefore the intervention of Vasil Mzhavanadze was unexpected and welcome. He rose, and if he felt guilty or embarrassed he did not display his emotions, however his words clearly expressed the mood of those present in the room.

The document that he had earlier put down was a current evaluation of their enemy`s latest military capability but did not assess the potential political temperature of the nation.

"I believe that our two comrades have clearly shown us the way forward and we must support the First Secretary."

Within hours the original draft ultimatum, in English and Russian, with the active assistance of the two bilingual speakers had been crafted into a statement that would frighten the American people and end any assumption of isolation or invulnerability. The cities of New York, Philadelphia, Atlanta, Detroit, Chicago, Houston, San Francisco and lastly Los Angeles would be specifically identified as primary civilian targets and were only suggested by the head of North American Intelligence for the banal reason that she was president of a successful company with offices in all these cities and their names were foremost in her mind.

NINETY-SEVEN

The meeting dispersed, leaving only the First Secretary, Kashkarov and the woman in the smoked filled room. She wheezed slightly expressing her physical discomfort.

Leonid Brezhnev could have obliquely thanked them for persuading Mzhavanadze to support his plan to confront the Americans, thus avoiding the immoral act of buying his loyalty, however he decided, when opportune, to discard the corrupt politician, but in the meantime he was deeply grateful (but never that grateful!) to the two loyal supporters for whom he had a surprise gift.

"The people of the Union of Soviet Socialist Republics may not become aware of your contribution to the cause of Socialism during your lifetime or, my dearest, of your parents' help cleansing the stables of the treacherous and perverted Trotsky, but before you both leave Moscow you will each be honoured with the Order of Lenin and the presentation will be recorded so that film will be preserved to inspire future generations.

Now, two questions and two questions only. The camp, what was its purpose and legacy?"

Together, they told him of its history and unique purpose beginning with their original summons, their first meeting and ending in their separate departures, however she withheld any mention of the two 'Sleepers' that had been 'woken' to complete the important assignment that Brezhnev's predecessor had authorised.

Goldburgh of course featured prominently as did the off the cuff comment that Kashkarov had recently met him in Finland and that he was a rising star in the background of the British political scene. It was that brief comment and the amazing story that compelled Brezhnev to have the archives scoured and the files rescued from deliberate oblivion including a hand written letter from Goldburgh to Lavrenti Beria and annotated by him with the prophetic comment...

"File. This might be useful one day."

She was unable to break her cover and the risk of being seen in a public place and being identified was unacceptable. She was staying in a dacha just outside of Moscow with its own indoor swimming pool and chef.

"She would love to meet his wife before she made the lonely and hazardous journey back to Canada (a deliberate lie, intended even for a trusted friend, to avoid giving details of her movements, so ingrained had become her cautious habits) and end her holiday in an isolated and companionless chalet that lacked even a telephone which allowed her the cover to exit and re-enter the country.

Nearly twenty-four hours had elapsed since she had last seen her husband and she sat quietly in the foyer of the hotel that was so exclusive that outside elite armed K G B troops and plain clothes K G B officers dressed as porters and chauffeurs monitored every person who either attempted or was granted entry. Unexpectedly she received a personal visit from the fawning hotel manager inviting her into his private office where she was requested to take a vitally important call and...

"He would appreciate if she could mention to the caller his help and assistance."

When the caller announced himself as the First Secretary she was not unexpectedly surprised but the phone was then handed to her husband who assured her that:

"All was well and that she should be ready for a very special surprise and after many years of silence, an interesting story."

The chauffeur driven limousine arrived at the same dacha that had been his temporary home some weeks before and at the entrance, to greet them, was his dear friend.

After brief introductions, a perfunctory tour of the residence and a breathtaking view of the swimming pool, Kashkarov's wife was informed of the two events that had dominated her husband's life; not his bravery on the Kursk salient but events at the secret camp during the Great Patriotic War and then some twenty years later, after he had been arrested for treason, the amazing change to his, their, fortunes following his meeting with Khrushchev. He was less forthcoming about their joint meeting with the Politburo and he explained that his friend now held a senior position 'abroad' but did not elaborate, however his wife realised that they had been involved in matters of the highest importance to the nation.

"She just had to have a swim in the indoor pool and enjoy the luxury of this most unexpected occasion."

Two female guards were assigned to act as lifeguards and to protect her and shamelessly, hedonistically, she swam naked as she was unable to procure a suitable costume and while she enjoyed herself the other two decided to walk, reminisce and learn more about each other's stories.

His was conventional and boring, only becoming interesting when he had been arrested for treason and he expected to be broken on the 'conveyor belt' and to admit any crime, however implausible, to end the pain and mitigate the consequences of his confession.

But it was her story that was interesting, informative and ultimately to prove that their lives had yet again intertwined.

On her return, in nineteen forty-four to America, she met her parents furtively, for what was to be the final time, but was unable to tell them of Beria's orders or of the new identity that had been created for her (even she would never learn that it had been based on a passport confiscated by the N K V D from a young, idealistic American girl working as a nurse for the International Brigade fighting the Fascist Nationalists in the Spanish Civil War). She was to become head of Intelligence for the North American continent when she had finished her schooling and that her predecessor would contact her soon after graduation.

She obtained a place at an 'Ivy League' college (Kashkarov unfortunately forgot the name) shortly after the war in Europe had ended and obtained an excellent degree in an Arts subject after which she was immediately recommended by the University to a former student, now head of a travel agency, which she took up and since 'never looked back'.

In nineteen fifty-three she became what was now known in the States as the 'Chief Executive Officer' and since then the firm had grown, under her management, to twenty two offices, of which two were in Mexico and three in Canada.

The nature of the firm's business and her status gave her an unrivalled opportunity to travel and the freedom to operate without being responsible to her staff, all of whom were completely unaware of her true status as she had been careful to separate her job from her duty to the Party.

She had moved the company to Atlanta, not on commercial grounds, but on the suggestion some years earlier of her predecessor, not of the firm but the retiring head of North American Intelligence.

Under almost bizarre circumstances she had been contacted in Canada, in nineteen forty-nine, on one of her first business trips. She had rented an auto (he was fascinated by her ability to 'rent' a motor vehicle which was so different from the life that existed in the Soviet Union) in Toronto and was travelling to a hotel for a business meeting when she was 'rear ended' at a stop sign. She had to explain what all that meant.

The driver was most apologetic, a kindly old man who introduced himself with a pleasant smile which exposed well maintained teeth, as a retired American businessman on holiday, who could also have been one of her aged grandfathers had they still been alive, and she took up his offer to have a coffee to relax her as she was rather shaken.

The busy shop served an excellent apple strudel rich in sultanas and dusted in cinnamon. She ordered, rather selfishly, a second slice, this time drowned in thick heavy cream. As the waitress walked away, he gently touched her hand, but not in a menacing way, asked her to take a very deep breath and quietly, calmly as a father would speak to a daughter, told her that:

"We have a mutual friend that you last met in Moscow in nineteen forty-three and..."

"I was about to cry out in shock and surprise when he put his right index finger to his lips which calmed me enormously and he suggested that I enjoy the strudel, for a man of his age was not permitted the pleasure of such an indulgence. He sat with his back to a corner pillar and was thus able both to see outside the window and view the coffee shop, the hustle and bustle and most important of all, the comings and goings of its patrons.

He was well informed of my university career, current work and somewhat rather sinisterly, my quiet, uneventful and uncomplicated private life of which he clearly approved."

"After today we will never meet again and henceforth she had become head of Soviet Intelligence in the North American continent. She was initially to continue her career with the same travel firm and she was to transfer the firm`s Home Office to Atlanta where she was also to personally relocate.

It was unwise that they have an extended meeting and she should continue her routine but that evening they should meet again, for one final time, when he would give her enough information for her to operate effectively. In the meantime she should never directly or indirectly, under any circumstances or pretext approach any Soviet office in the North American continent as they were all, including the Embassy in Mexico City, under permanent surveillance. He was very shortly returning to the Soviet Union where he was to receive the Order of Lenin from Stalin himself.

Later, in about two to three months, she would most unexpectedly receive correspondence from an impeccable firm of New York Attorneys informing her that they acted on behalf of a highly reputable and long established affiliate legal firm based in Berne, Switzerland (what they did not know was that the Swiss firm had been instructed by yet a third firm based in Cologne and West Berlin with connections in Eastern Europe)and that she was believed to be the only remaining living relative of a wealthy Jewish family that had perished in the Holocaust but had prudently transferred most of their assets to Switzerland well before the outbreak of war. She would undoubtedly be invited to visit them with evidence of her identity and she could ultimately thank her college for their cooperation and assistance verifying her location and background.

This surprise windfall which she could, indeed should, make known to her business colleagues and few friends would explain her sudden access to a dramatically higher standard of living far in excess of her not ungenerous salary and future bonuses."

He ended by wishing her well and confirming, for her piece of mind, that her responsibilities would not be hazardous as she would not be responsible for what the American press and the paranoid film makers of Hollywood were depicting as 'Soviet Nests of Spies'. Her responsibilities, which would be fully explained that evening, would be more supervisory and intellectual than administrative and would encompass military, economic but above all social and political matters. Their 'masters' had no objections whatsoever if she maintained a high standard of living which could also explain her frequent travelling and that finally she should remember that if the firm of Attorneys, who were completely unaware of her activities, wrote to confirm that the assets of the Estate had been exhausted she should immediately travel to Europe and cross over to the Eastern block."

They walked back to the dacha and all three enjoyed a meal that his wife would never forget for it included the finest and most sought after delicacies, washed down with wines and spirits that only the most appreciative connoisseur would enjoy.

"He, they, should stay overnight as her guests" and when his wife went upstairs the two dear friends later realised that they both had been participants in some of the dramatic events of the last eighteen months.

"We met that evening in a smart restaurant that specialised in French regional cuisine and he nostalgically, and perhaps inadvertently, referred to his late wife whilst reminding me that it was imperative that my life should never be discussed or mentioned to any of my new contacts, for my identity and indeed of those with whom I would deal with should remain unknown and anonymous and therefore I am confiding in you most of my deepest secrets which should remain so.

He had personally built up and overseen development of thirteen autonomous cells, one in Mexico, two in Canada, more specifically in the Vancouver and Toronto areas and ten in the United States. I still remember, most vividly, what he said and did next. He handed to me a small sealed envelope, which rattled, and then went on to explain how I should operate...

"Everyone must eat, whether frugally or opulently, and nearly always wear shoes!"...

Which I thought at the time was both true and strange. He continued, whilst brushing a slice of bread cut from a fresh, still warm, baguette with a rich, creamy butter which was soft and easily spreadable."

"Inside the envelope are thirteen cards, promoting the same number of restaurants, one in Mexico City, one each in Vancouver and Toronto and ten in the United States, though you will note that there are two in San Francisco.

I began to recruit agents exactly thirty years ago. They were drawn to Communism for various reasons ranging from idealism, cynicism to despair, and you will appreciate that the decade following the Wall Street Crash and during the Depression was a fruitful period. For some, I saw them evolve, their loyalty being formed like the incubation of some great philosophical plan that had to be tested before it could be accepted as true. The thirteen cells are totally independent of each other and its members are unaware that twelve others exist though I suspect that they conjecture that there are others. Even I am uncertain how many belong to each group but undoubtedly each contains no more than half a dozen members who are unknown to each other and only know the head of their group. I am aware that over the decades some of those that I have personally recruited have died and their places have been taken by replacements that they have recruited. Development was purely evolutionary and there was no ingenious plan though their independence is a welcome safeguard against penetration and betrayal.

I leave next week by transatlantic liner for England, then France, when I shall travel by train to Germany where I will be met and be escorted into East Germany and finally, ultimately, into Russia where I will spend my final years, though I suspect that our masters, with great intensity and fervour, will want to debrief me.

There are two cells in San Francisco both totally unaware that the other exists and they operate side by side, in parallel. The thirteen act as independent operations with their own methods and systems to send information out of the country and to receive orders. My duty, which now is your responsibility, is to supervise their work and to deliver funds to them which now explains why you will soon receive an ongoing windfall.

They are all human and I suspect that occasionally some of the funds are misappropriated for some dishonourable reasons however you should ignore this human fallibility.

There are two operations in San Francisco because the second was set up specially to obtain details of the secret Second World War programme to build the Atomic bomb. Their work has been most fruitful and, I understand, continues to bear golden nuggets of information that ultimately reaches Moscow and Lavrenti Beria by means that I do not wish to know.

The friendship and cooperation that existed during the Great Patriotic War no longer exists and I sense a great rift and confrontation between the United States and the Soviet Union. Already a witch hunt is beginning and most likely the American authorities will hunt down our cells, some of which will be exposed and broken.

Along with our attempts to obtain military and economic secrets- such as grain reserves, which might be purchased at favourable rates-it is imperative that each and every cell anonymously supports-and financially contributes to- what is being called 'left leaning' organisations, in high schools, colleges, the weak trade unions, national (and local) newspapers together with their journalists and contributors and finally those who create public opinion and their supporters so that they all promote the ideas and views of the 'left' and throw into doubt the values, opinions and arguments of the 'right'. This will take funds that you will be provided with and will be able to deliver to each cell.

You will never be able to contact a cell directly. They will always contact you. You should be able to organise your business itinerary to coincide with your visits.

Simply make a restaurant booking using the appropriate card in the envelope, a week or so before your visit, of course giving your assumed name (which should be different for each city) and the city of your origin which should always be New York. Never mention your company's name. You will be tactfully and discreetly contacted at some time during your visit to the restaurant. The person, who might be with a woman, but never two men, will each and every time that he meets you, make some comment about your shoes! "Your shoes compliment your dress, the buckle of your left shoe is undone, what a stunning colour are your shoes!", but they must use the word shoe or shoes. If they do not, immediately excuse yourself and leave, choosing a cab or method of conveyance that they have not offered. But if the meeting goes ahead never discuss your private or business life which unwittingly or under duress they may divulge to the wrong people.

At the end of the meeting they will hand to you an envelope containing a new card – cleaned of any fingerprints - it may be the same restaurant or another one where you will next meet, where the rules of introduction must each time be used.

There are other rules that are in fact just common sense such as never giving details of your itinerary, where you came from and where you are going next or even worse forming an attachment, even if it is purely and solely social. Money should be delivered in plain envelopes, certainly none bearing your firm's or a hotel's particulars that you might have used and do not confide in anyone. Perhaps this is the hardest burden to bear.

My dearest, I know instinctively that those who entrusted you with this responsibility have made a wise and prudent choice. Your first meeting will be the most difficult and thereafter it will become a formality.

My last words to you are tinged with sadness for I must inform you of the tragic death of your parents in a road accident some ten months ago. It was an unfortunate incident and death was, according to the police and newspaper reports, instantaneous. They are buried together in a cemetery in San Francisco which I recently visited on your behalf but for security purposes I did not linger and my visit was at a distance, some two rows away but I was able to clearly read the inscription, which on their specific instructions, for your security, did not mention you. I am so sorry. I am prepared to give you the exact location but you must not break your cover which has taken many people and much time and thought preparing."

"I cried and grieved that night in the privacy of my room."

The conversation, since his wife had gone to bed, had been conducted in English, very occasionally tinged with Russian words or very brief intermittent sentences. Then she announced that she wished, for a final time, that they speak in her mother tongue for she did not know when, or indeed where, she would have need, or be able to speak or read such a beautiful language.

Such was her confidence in him and perhaps the necessity to unburden herself of her secret life that she confided in him her two deepest secrets. The task had never been onerous, only the burden of absolute secrecy and that such was the apparent vital importance to Soviet strategic plans that some eighteen months or so earlier, whilst in New York on business, at great risk to her cover, she had been approached by a personal representative of the then First Secretary, Nikita Khrushchev, with instructions to wake two of the 'Sleepers' that they had trained, with the intention to assassinate the American President. She then realised that independent of her operation in the North American continent there must have existed, for some time, a further cell that could be aware of her true and assumed identities but more importantly they had been closely observing the lives of at least two of the sleepers (for others might have survived), one of whom lived in Dallas, Texas where he had built a successful life for himself.

When the name Lee Harvey Oswald was mentioned, Kashkarov realised that his plan had been implemented and that their two careers had intertwined. She conjectured that Oswald had been 'turned' whilst in the Soviet Union but in any case he had been blatantly misled and used as a scapegoat for she then explained that Oswald`s involvement was only peripheral and what had actually been planned, taken place and ultimately happened to the two sleepers after the assassination.

They must have had little sleep in the short period before dawn and morning and later that day the three of them were driven to the Kremlin where his wife witnessed her husband and the woman, addressed by her real birth name, being honoured by the First Secretary, who pinned on each of them the ultimate accolade of the Soviet Union, The Order of Lenin.

Thus their work and contribution to history was recognised and rewarded. Very soon afterwards she returned to the United States, but without her accolade, whilst Kashkarov and his wife did not go back to his previous posting but to the centre of power and influence in Moscow where he was allocated a luxurious apartment together with the trappings of power, and by the side of his bed, in a drawer, were the two Orders of Lenin for one was held in safe keeping, awaiting her return to Moscow.

She regularly wondered how the old man enjoyed his retirement, being able freely to speak the tongue of his birth, then she realised that, in truth, she really knew very little about him, and perhaps he had been born in the United States.

She would never know that he did not reach his Socialist Utopia for on his arrival in West Germany, and before his shepherd was due to meet him and escort him into the 'East', on instructions, he first burned his United States passport and then disposed of all his clothing and few personal effects, including a treasured photograph of his beloved, late wife, and donned cheap, anonymous, second hand clothing that he had bought with the last of his currency and began to walk to his rendezvous.

Death was instantaneous for he collapsed in the street following a massive heart attack.

Western Europe was recovering from the trauma of war and whilst the vast ebb and flow of refugees crossing the continent was visibly decreasing this was just another tragic body that had been washed ashore in the flotsam or jetsam of life`s vagaries.

A cursory report was made of the anonymous, ancient body but they never inspected his teeth and the expensive work on them, which to any professional would have immediately identified the work as having been done in the United States.

NINETY-EIGHT

Following Kashkarov's promotion, a new autonomous Directorate, under his sole authority was created within the structure of the Supreme High Command but responsible directly to the Politburo and primarily, the First Secretary. The 'Department for Research and Development' was given unprecedented freedom and latitude resulting in the publication, some three years later, but of course with an extremely restricted circulation, of an analysis entitled...

'On Potential Trends in the Fields of Global Strategic and Regional Tactical Warfare.'

Such were some of their innovative ideas and concepts that the department, staffed by some of the leading young graduates (all of whom had been chosen because they were fluent in English) in the fields of non nuclear warfare and nuclear and thermonuclear advanced technologies, produced conclusions and recommendations that were immediately accepted and put into place by the Politburo.

Their vision, backed by facts and statistics, mirrored their enemy's view of the future and first of all confirmed (Kahn's work...'On Thermonuclear War') that a global thermonuclear war was unwinnable even if one side was able to launch a pre-emptive first strike, for enough of their enemy's delivery platforms (mainly nuclear powered submarines) would survive to launch a devastating counter first –strike.

It was therefore necessary to maintain parity in terms of the quality and quantity of their weapons, demanding a contribution from the people in terms of a depressed standard of living.

Development costs could be reduced and minimised by the theft of sensitive information and research records from the United States but care should be exhibited for they might be deliberately supplied with false information.

A substantial investment should be made both in resources and finance to cheaply 'buy' information and research records that might cost them billions of Roubles with sometimes no guarantee of success.

Warfare would become regional and tactical, taking place both on the edges of their own and their enemy's empires and could used to dispose of large numbers of unwanted civilians, such as political and criminal convicts, homosexuals of both sexes, Christian zealots,

Zionist-Jewish activists (the worst kind) and trouble makers such as social and moral activists.

The Indian sub continent and Africa, South of the Sahara, were clearly areas where natural resources, including labour, were abundant and that even the United States, for strategic and commercial reasons (to exploit the natural wealth) would wish to impose their presence and no doubt would use their allies, the British, to represent them for their forces were expendable.

Development of space technology was absolutely crucial, both from a propaganda point of view and the now feasible opportunity of having permanently manned space platforms armed with nuclear and thermonuclear weapons that could be targeted against the vital functions of their enemies.

The world would be under the domination of three gigantic superpowers: The United States, China and the Soviet Union. Obviously the Soviet Union had much in common with their political brethren in China, however their perfidiousness and inscrutability might make them uncomfortable allies.

The organisation was also responsible to submit to the military hierarchy plans for clandestine and tactical operations and many such operations were approved and implemented.

Kashkarov often wondered what had become of his dear friend and how she had been able to exit and re-enter Canada. His new status allowed him to make enquiries about her career, but he encountered a brick wall of apathy and evasion, and only discovered that she did not officially exist. That was some five years after their meeting and one day when he was being entertained by some of the nation's leading army officers he was very discreetly advised that his successful and highly regarded career might be in jeopardy if he pursued enquiries about a nonexistent Soviet citizen. But he continued to conjecture how she exited and re-entered Canada.

He obsessively pursued the problem with great enterprise but in intermittent bursts as if it were a tentative military operation that was regularly planned, then postponed, but never executed, even calculating that she had, in fact, flown to Tokyo and then clandestinely, by ship, crossed over to Manchuria and thence to Russia but he concentrated on the assumption that she had legally entered Canada via Vancouver from where she could fly North between the Coast and Rocky Mountain chains through British Columbia to Dawson and then across the Arctic Circle to Inuvik in the Northwest Territories on the Beaufort Sea.

Of course that arduous, hazardous and exhausting flight might have been directed further West and she could have crossed the dangerous Brooks Range and reached Prudhoe Bay, further West in Alaska but in United States territory where her arrival would be recorded.

His theories became less plausible and more porous when he calculated that she could then have travelled by freighter across the Chukchi Sea and South of the Arctic Ocean where a helicopter from the Soviet Wrangel Island could have rendezvoused with the boat and then gone on to Pevek on the Northern shore of the Chukotka Peninsula. The theory was plausible but the distances involved, the seasonal weather conditions, the pack ice and most important of all, the time duration so long that he could not solve the problem which like many solutions in life was far simpler and prosaic.

She had flown, first class, from New York to neutral Sweden and from Stockholm she had been escorted to the Baltic Coast and was then secretly transferred to Poland and then to Moscow!

She had been absent from her office for thirteen days, one more than she had estimated, cross country skiing in Canada with two old college friends, but the world had changed beyond recognition during her absence and more importantly the office was staffed by a frightened skeleton team and on her arrival they all enquired why she had returned to one of the most dangerous places on Earth?

Already the much depleted staff had been inundated with telephone calls from current and former clients and potential new clients desperate to arrange immediate travel facilities to the Midwest, or preferably Canada or Mexico but the airlines were claiming that every flight was full.

The ultimatum (and accompanying appeal) had been conveyed to the American people whilst her flight was en route back from Stockholm to New York and coincidentally, at about the same time, for the British government, two new disasters confronted them. The strategic outpost of Gibraltar, where ships of the Royal Navy lay at anchor, was hit by two nuclear weapons in quick succession, launched by Warsaw Pact fighters probably based in Southern France.

Gibraltar instantly ceased to have any strategic significance and the only survivors were the few military staff that had been working deep beneath the mountain in the subterranean passageways that had been hewn into the rock over many years and decades.

Ten hours later, as the tremors and reverberations were beginning to destabilise the United States, London was hit again, this time the targets were Heathrow, in West London and Dagenham, in East London, which was close to an earlier target, Ilford. It was as if the Soviet Union could assault their enemy with impunity.

The epicentre of the latter attack was the Ford Motor Company factory which formed part of the government's major plans for the country's export drive whilst the capital's number one airport, at Heathrow, West London, was hit by three devices effectively totally destroying the runway complex and rendering the main building and aircraft servicing facilities beyond repair, whilst many civilian aircraft were totally destroyed.

But the overall operation was designed not primarily for military advantage but to create doubt, uncertainty, then fear and ultimately panic in the American people.

The internal flight from New York direct to Atlanta was curtailed and touched down in Philadelphia where she observed what was to be the beginning of the disintegration of confidence which would culminate in panic and, like a plague, would infect the nation.

Every available flight to the Midwest and especially Canada and Mexico was booked solid with flights to certain destinations mysteriously cancelled amidst rumours that the planes were to be used to carry the ever increasing demand for seats on additional flights.

The airport was rapidly becoming overwhelmed with passengers desperately struggling with one another and the impotent airline staff to secure tickets – and seats - on flights that were being cancelled or allegedly being rerouted and the toilets were unable to cope with the deluge of visitors and the stench permeated into the passenger lounges, however after some twelve hours she was able to locate a rearranged flight to Atlanta which, not surprisingly, was sparsely filled and had been laid on to collect passengers from Atlanta (for a flight direct to Kansas City, Missouri).

The ultimatum, which commenced with an appeal, was directed to the people of the United States from the people of the Soviet Union and had been published by neutral news agencies in Stockholm and Zurich. It appealed to the consciences of the United States people, their inherent common sense and values that their ancestors had shown as they went Westwards to populate the Midwest, to build great cities and till the ground until vast swathes of rich, fertile soil nourished seeds that grew into unending fields of wheat which fed the nation.

But their leaders, protected in deep underground bunkers, had shown the most callous, heinous and contemptuous attitude towards the freedom loving and stoic Soviet people who were of the same community as their American brethren. A previous appeal had been ignored as had the suffering of the Soviet nation following the nuclear attack on the Republics of Russia and the Ukraine.

England (sic, but deliberate), who had been in the vanguard of the vindictive attack was now reaping the whirlwind and their innocent civilians were suffering for the callous inhumanity and belligerency of their leaders.

The people of Russia did not demand compensation for their suffering, or retribution, and would not ask that the forces of the Soviet Union mete out justice as the Bible had stated...'An eye for an eye', but they did demand that the menacing ring of fire that was being constructed to surround and throttle them be lifted and dismantled.

Finally, and ominously, the 'people' declared that they would again endure suffering and deprivation to secure their liberty and security and that unless the American President publicly announced a more passive and less aggressive foreign policy they would demand that the First Secretary, the Politburo and above all their patriotic military forces authorise and use whatever force was necessary, at whatever cost, including their rockets which had so spectacularly been recently fired, to secure their liberty and security even if it meant attacking the great cities of the United States including nine which were then identified.

Thus her contribution was succeeding beyond expectation as their office received a stream of telex messages and telephone calls - when the lines were not engaged – from their regional offices who all confirmed the unprecedented demand for travel facilities and the dire lack of available seats. Loyalty to the firm meant that most of the offices, including especially the offices in Canada and Mexico, were fully staffed though some of the offices in the cities named in the ultimatum were, like the Home Office in Atlanta, sparsely staffed.

At noon on Friday, March the twenty-sixth, E.S.T., President Johnson addressed the nation on both television and radio, to an audience which was believed to be the greatest in the country's history, close to one hundred and sixty-five million frightened people, but his hastily prepared statement and more importantly, the lack of confidence and conviction that he conveyed did nothing to assure an overwhelming proportion of the population.

The tone and facts of the statement were essentially true and concerned the nation's military capability and strategic intentions...

"My fellow Americans, I speak to you from the heart of your government in Washington, first to assure each and every one of you that our forces, stationed in the Continental United States and abroad, on land, at sea and in the air have created an invisible umbrella of protection.

The great investment in their training and the weapons that they have at their disposal, combined with confidence in their just cause, is your greatest assurance of security and fear from attack.

Since the tragic and cruel death of my great friend and predecessor, John Kennedy, we have witnessed and suffered devious and vicious acts of warfare perpetrated by the Communist regime in the Soviet Union and by their allies under the banner of the Warsaw Pact. Their latest *communiqué* would leave only the most naive to assume that our enemy has an honourable cause and agenda.

But it is not sufficient to say that our cause is right and just. It must be supported by the will and determination not only to defend our land and the values that we all cherish but if necessary to inflict upon our enemies a devastating blow of unimaginable ferocity that will both render their offensive capability unusable but to finally, once and for all, by action, demonstrate to the leadership of the Soviet Union and their allies that we have the strength of purpose to convert rhetoric into action.

The ultimatum, concocted by bullies, is untrue. I, along with my administration, have not scurried underground to a complex of tunnels to protect ourselves, but we remain, on the surface, continuing with our duties and responsibilities. I understand that some of you have deserted your homes in response to the ultimatum but I warn you that weakness will be followed by further demands. Your government will stand resolute and firm to defend the nation; all we ask is that you remain calm and support our policies and actions."

One hour later Lyndon Baines Johnson signed the first of a number of Presidential Executive Orders, the first one transferring control of the civilian airline fleet to the military authorities.

Less than three hours later, already distressed families at major airline terminals nationwide, hubs and regional airports began to see military forces arriving and being immediately embarked on civilian planes.

Yet again the United States was on the brink of war, but this time of unimaginable magnitude.

Cynical viewers, who four hours earlier had watched the President's broadcast, were already commenting that his broadcast had not been made from the Oval Office or on the lawn of the White House where he would have been surrounded by members of his administration and the Press Corps but from some makeshift studio which was probably underground therefore contradicting his statement.

The Senate Minority Leader and the Chief Justice, Earl Warren, had been present at the broadcast and immediately afterwards had been assured that:

"Despite the fact, for a second time during his Presidency, that the nation was on the brink of war he had no intention of suspending the Constitution and that, as an option, and not as a sign of weakness, diplomatic feelers had been put out, before his broadcast, to clarify their enemy's demands and he felt certain that the crisis could be resolved, however in the short and medium term, it was clear that the 'Cold War' had escalated to a new incandescent level.

He was prepared to concede sovereignty of Western Europe, including France, Holland and West Germany and if needs be sacrifice England (sic) and transfer their forces and facilities to Ireland thereby still maintaining the ring of containment."

In his memoirs, which was permitted only limited circulation shortly after his death, the Chief Justice commented upon the President's palpable vehemence towards their ally, the United Kingdom, clearly blaming them for the chaos and military catastrophes (sic) that had taken place since Friday, November twenty-second, nineteen sixty-three, specifying their disastrous intelligence failure.

At ten p.m., E.S.T. the President signed his second Presidential Executive Order, placing the nation's (privately owned) mercantile fleet (specifically including every oil tanker) under the command of the United States Navy and all crew members under military command.

At eleven p.m., E.S.T. the President again spoke to the nation, this time allegedly from the Oval Office, opening his again hastily and this time, ill thought out bellicose statement, with the comment that:

"I speak to you all for the second time today from the focus of our free democratic society and the seat of power and authority, the White House and the Oval Office. At ten p.m. E.S.T. I signed the second Presidential Executive Order of the day (he briefly paused, clearly exposing his concern for the situation).

With the agreement of the Senate Minority leader and the Chief Justice of the United States, Judge Earl Warren, the nation's civilian airline fleet and naval mercantile fleet have been placed under the control of the government and military.

This is necessary because, on the advice of the Joint Chiefs, all our forces have been placed on the highest level of alert and our planes, submarines and missiles together with their weapon systems are being made ready to devastate our enemies.

Already a tentative olive branch of peace has been waved to our diplomats who will unceasingly work for a lasting, fair, just and secure peace.

I therefore hope that you all sleep peacefully tonight, for a secure peace is close."

But human nature, confronted by the appalling realisation that the Biblical warnings of Armageddon and the Apocalypse were imminent, did not act in accordance with the President's wishes.

What then followed began as a trickle, growing into a stream, then a river in full flood and finally a mighty torrent, as the great cities realised that war on an unimaginable scale could erupt at any moment and that an insignificant incident could be the touch paper that ignited the fuse. The trickle probably started virtually simultaneously in many of the great cities across the nation and not only in the nine that had been named as primary targets.

Families deserted their homes and even their pets in the city centres and the suburbs, beginning an exodus to the country or better still to less hospitable and desolate regions but always avoiding areas where there were military installations that might be potential targets, ignoring the possibility of their own vulnerability to inaccurate targeting. Many, too many, were ill prepared and like some of the inexperienced pioneers that foundered on their way West, they departed inadequately equipped for the task ahead, preparing themselves as if they were leaving for an extended vacation.

The wise and experienced prepared for the unknown more prudently, stocking up with reserve cans of fuel and oil together with drinking water. And weapons! Vaseline and sun cream became a priority as a simple protection against the damage that would be caused following a nuclear flash and the ensuing heat pulse, whilst plain canned food, in volume, was preferred to those who loaded their estate wagons with barbeques! Darwin's theory of the survival of the fittest in the event of a catastrophe might soon be tested.

Initially the road networks were able to cope with the volume of traffic that was streaming from the centres of population but as the sun rose on Saturday March the twenty-seventh the trickle became a river and the gas stations were, at first, inundated and then they began to erect 'closed signs' as their stocks of fuel became exhausted without hope of being replenished.

At nine a.m. that morning, L.B.J. reluctantly signed his third and fourth (emergency) Presidential Executive Orders putting the nation's fuel supply under military (not governmental) control and at the same time declaring a nationwide state of emergency, and, in conjunction with every State governor, called out the National Guard who would ultimately be under military authority.

For reasons that are still shrouded in official secrecy and obfuscation and such was the perceived slide towards what was believed to be the inevitable, the situation was exacerbated by the absence of a Presidential announcement or broadcast of the latest Executive Orders which were released via the media as a 'newsflash'.

This was ultimately seen as a catastrophic error of judgement which dramatically undermined long term confidence in the President and accelerated and widened the plague of fear that now gripped the country.

In less than forty-eight hours the nation had been gripped by a climate of fear that was soon to become panic and was no longer able to function rationally for the population overwhelmingly believed that the only outcome would be, at best, the destruction of their cities in retaliation for the annihilation of their enemies' centres of population. And for what benefit and advantage?

The sheer weight and volume of a nation fleeing its centres of population, manufacturing and commerce was inconceivable. Comparisons with French refugees vainly fleeing the onslaught of the German war machine in May nineteen forty are both inadequate and inaccurate. The naked truth and most damning analogy is of a plague of insanity as waves of many decent, honourable people shed the veneer of civilisation, metamorphosed and descended into primitive anarchy determined, at any cost, to survive.

Thus the nation, by external deception and internal panic could no longer be led by the usual organs of democratic government.

NINETY-NINE

But the crisis did pass and an uneasy peace and calm returned. Many newspapers and books later extensively reported on the events that took place during the eleven days of the crisis, more comprehensive and analytical than this work intends to describe. Looting, on a wide scale, occurred and was only suppressed by the ruthless use of force by the National Guard however to the shame of the nation various incidents took place which exemplified how shallow was the veneer of civilisation and how the rule of law could only operate with the agreement of its citizens.

Some months later the highly respected and authoritative Washington Post published a series of in depth articles, meticulously researched, which charted the community`s response to the political and social pressures that drove many to what was accurately described as social collapse and hysteria. Ultimately the articles were collated and appeared under the title 'A House Divided' *APPARENTLY* [author's specific emphasis] alluding to the famous pre civil war Election speech of the revered Abraham Lincoln but actually referred to the gulf between the people and the Executive.

But it was the confirmed revelations that shocked a shamed nation. Confirmation of five separate lynchings across the country, supported by documentary primary evidence including, in one case, sixteen millimetre colour film. The lynching of two black men who had gone to the aid of beleaguered police officers in Harlingen, Texas (close to the Rio Grande) was recorded by a series of photographs culminating in obscene pictures of some of the participants standing beside the hanging corpses much the same as big game hunters would stand adjacent to their trophies. On the West Coast, in Eugene, Oregon, three police officers were flayed alive in a vain attempt halting a mob endeavouring to (successfully) storm a food warehouse. As a further, final example, in Key Biscayne, near Miami Beach in Florida, a joint emergency Jewish–Christian aid group set up to give hospitality and sustenance to refugees fleeing from the North was overwhelmed and brutally murdered for the supplies of food that they were distributing. Not only that but in a display of moral degradation "Stars of David" in the victims' own blood were painted on each body irrespective of their religious persuasion.

And if the above examples have not satisfied your interest may I refer you to the statistical analysis at the conclusion of A House Divided' (pages 416 to 418). A conservative estimate of the numbers killed by shooting whilst defending their properties or their places of work (specified in this particular example as gas stations, hardware and 'outdoor sports' stores or food sales outlets) during the eleven days of the crisis as *IN EXCESS OF THIRTEEN THOUSAND, EIGHT HUNDRED* adults [author's own emphasis].

Again referring to the book and focusing on one well documented region of the (dis?) United States, that is the desert region in the general area between Southern California and Nevada, which became almost a mecca for Californians, where they believed that they would be safe from the awful consequences of war but they exchanged fear of the unknown for the brutal harshness and deprivations of such areas as the Mojave Desert. Many of the ill prepared and unarmed travellers who had driven off the main highways quickly succumbed either to dehydration or marauders who shot first and then scavenged their victims' possessions.

I would urge readers who require further and better information to read 'A House Divided' and especially chapter seven, pages two hundred and nine to two hundred and twenty three.

Throughout the crisis both the Soviet people and the people of the many nations under the control of the Warsaw Treaty powers were completely unaware of events outside of their own hermetically sealed environment, though a few were able to tune their radios to British, Swiss and Swedish radio stations and were able to piece together a broad canvas of national and international developments.

The Swedish Statsminister (Prime Minister), Tage Erlander, acting immediately at the request of King Gustaf VI Adolf was instrumental bringing together diplomats from both sides and negotiations, at first at arms' length, but later literally across the table, took place well away from the gaze of publicity and in the tranquillity of the Swedish countryside where an agreement, which held, was crafted. The phrase 'hammered out' may be more accurate reflecting the aggressive tone of the Soviet negotiators, but in the end both sides achieved their political masters' perceived demands.

In exchange for acknowledging Soviet hegemony and influence over the former 'occupied' nations of Western Europe, including France, Belgium, Holland, West Germany and Denmark it was agreed that the 'Southern' nations of 'Europe' including Portugal and Spain, Italy and Greece and vast areas of Turkey would remain under the protection of the United States but the Balkans remained an area of dispute, however the matter was postponed for future discussion.

Both protagonists were now formally aware, and had been aware for some time, that the British, under Wilson, had been emasculated and agreed that whilst the United States could continue their 'occupation' of the United Kingdom and could store their own nuclear and thermonuclear weapons there, that any future British government would not be allowed to resume production of these weapons and would not, under any circumstances, be permitted to have their 'finger on the nuclear button'. Thus ended the final pretence that Great Britain was a great and influential power and globally they ceased to be a force of any consequence.

The real winners were the neutral Swedes, for Stockholm was to become the focus of contact between the United States and the Soviet Union, located at the strategic site where symbolically the two great political tectonic plates met and collided. Sweden, at the junction of the two ideologies became the centre of global commerce, far outstripping neutral Switzerland and its trading centre, Zurich, and where entrepreneurs, dealers and 'carpetbaggers' became intermediaries between the Empires and where trade and profit pragmatically regularly superseded political differences and sometimes even war!

That therefore was the background to the geopolitical world that now exists.

ONE HUNDRED

Although the system inherited from the planners had, *de facto,* delegated the internal security and administration of the nation to the twelve Regional Commissioners and their deputies, the National Council was still responsible for the nation's foreign policy and defence, a hollow situation since, as we have seen, the Soviet Union had blatantly launched a number of nuclear strikes which the British government had absorbed without a response, therefore emboldening their enemy.

Chairman Wilson, for this was the title that the National Council had (temporarily) settled upon to replace the inapplicable designation of 'Prime Minister', had been informed by the British ambassador in Stockholm that some form of peace negotiations between his main ally, the United States and the Soviet Union were being brokered by the Swedish Prime Minister and this was verified by the British embassy in Washington which still maintained a few, but still some , excellent connections with the State Department.

An enquiry to the American ambassador in London had been rebuffed and indicated Washington`s and the President`s contempt for the British government.

When it became apparent that talks were imminent, Harold Wilson made clear to those that were in his intimate inner group of confidantes, which included the disillusioned Gerald Kaufman and the increasingly powerful Manny Gold, that he intended, without an invitation, to travel to Sweden and then to actively involve himself but he was confronted by his two protégés with the reality of his, and the nation`s dire situation. The country was under attack, the cities of his main ally had been threatened with destruction, but above all the country was under seemingly benevolent martial law.

Whilst the press, radio and television were subject to strict voluntary censorship, his departure and absence, however much in the nation`s best interests, might be construed as a betrayal of his responsibilities and what might he gain in return for his endeavours? A worthless piece of paper signed by the First Secretary guaranteeing peace as had an earlier hapless predecessor, Neville Chamberlain obtained, which he had waved to the British people on his return from Munich in nineteen thirty-eight, after his visit to Herr Hitler.

He had been ignored by the Americans and was now more isolated and increasingly unable to be an influential force.

Up till then the country had accepted, if only temporarily, the imposition and at that point, the inconvenience of martial law, since the only major change had been a contraction in the number and size of available newspapers and some minor inconveniences obtaining certain foodstuffs such as meat and fish though there was no real shortage as there had been during the Second World War. The draconian penalties announced in the public notices appeared only to apply to those areas that had suffered nuclear strikes and there were no reports of any arrests, convictions and executions. The nation seemingly had come through the crisis.

There was, at that moment, no rationing but common sense suggested that food rationing might be imminent.

The national mood was of resigned stoicism, an acceptance of the inevitable. But underlining this mood was fear and that was being fuelled not solely by the randomness and unpredictability of the nuclear attacks but by a surprisingly single, innocuous action by the authorities. There existed a vast generation that vividly remembered the Second World War and the attacks on the 'Home Front'; the Blitz and later the V1s and 2s. There had been absolutely no defence against the V2s but at least against the bombers and the V1s there was some defence and a wailing warning system, Air Raid Sirens.

The authorities had recently retrieved these items from storage and begun to test the devices but had not notified the nation of their intentions and the wailing sound brought back half forgotten memories, but above all a fear that permeated deep inside the body and into the pits of peoples' stomachs, so difficult to define, an emotion that had to be experienced in order to understand fear of the potential consequences of an impending attack.

At the same time the Regional Commissioners were having private, *ad hoc*, preliminary discussions about the necessary imposition of food rationing but had not confided in their deputies rather relying upon their appointed civil servants, whilst they supervised the reconstruction and revival of essential services.

Whilst the Regional Commissioners, their deputies and those immediately associated with them, were informed of events in the United States and Sweden it is unclear when they became aware that Britain's main strike force was effectively an illusion and that the nation's scant thermonuclear deterrent was now under the control of her ally. It seems most likely that this information had been known at the highest levels of M I 5 and 6 for some time but was not disseminated.

The Regional Commissioners now had a valid reason to dismiss, if it was legal which was doubtful, or at worst, usurp Chairman Wilson and replace him with a more effective leader and, for the good of the nation, facilitate the promised General Election, or...

It was then that certain Regional Commissioners, but not their deputies who had also been selected by the authorities and approved by Harold Wilson, began very discreet discussions about a new national leadership, free from the hindrance of petty, squabbling, short sighted and self seeking party politicians. When knowledge of the nation's impotency began to circulate there was general agreement that Harold Wilson was no longer fit to lead the nation and that those around him should be replaced.

When Manny Gold, a personal appointee of the Prime Minister, became aware of this dangerous and highly invidious scenario, he immediately, and without a second thought, unscrupulously and mendaciously used the situation to his own advantage, citing on one hand his almost intimate relationship with Harold Wilson and on the other, his disgust that the defence of the Realm had been so recklessly mishandled and that he was reluctantly prepared to stand as a witness against his old friend and mentor who had also wilfully misled and misused him.

ONE HUNDRED AND ONE

Dear Reader,

Please excuse this most unusual (and therefore unexpected) digression and interruption of the narrative but it is necessary to remind you of the purpose of this work and if you go back to the original title page you will, or should have noticed, the sub title of this work...

An Alternative True History.

Throughout, I have never used the definition 'novel', always describing the subject as a work or narrative.

I hope that the facts that have been presented to you are convincing because the events actually took place and most can be verified by reference to my source material, listed at the end of the third volume.

You will have read how two great nations, one in decline, the other at the peak of its cultural, industrial and military power were wounded, one almost mortally, by the determined actions and deviousness of their enemy.

In the next part I will describe how the British people were deceived and betrayed by a ruling cabal who seized power and were determined, without pity or compassion, to create a society that perverted the values of democracy and intentionally, by propaganda and the dissemination of lies, undermined and destroyed the individual`s ability to make reasoned judgements, but above all deliberately maintained an environment that by withholding medical facilities and a balanced healthy diet destined its` people to malnutrition and endemic ill health with the sole purpose to subjugate individual and group opposition, therefore rendering them malleable and compliant.

In the meantime what comes shortly in the next and final part of this work, which I repeat is not a novel, are some vivid descriptions of torture *ALL* of which were used on the authority of the Regional Commissioners.

Just remember, if I haven`t shocked you out of your complacency, that the price of freedom is eternal vigilance and the simple, innate common sense to see through the dishonesty and deceptions of some of our (so called) leaders who purport to have *YOUR* best interests at heart. Thank you.

ONE HUNDRED AND TWO

The crisis lasted less than two weeks but fundamentally changed both the attitude and confidence of the people of the United States who overwhelmingly no longer were prepared to countenance the nation`s *de facto* leadership of the so called 'free world', now combined with the risk of the catastrophic destruction of their cities and existence in defence of the interests of their allies.

For the many exhausted, hungry and disillusioned Americans who returned to the virtually deserted cities and towns, a new folk myth was created which became a legend and ultimately the accepted truth. Who are we, yes *YOU* the reader and myself, to judge those who had escaped to the perceived safety of the hills, deserts and forests and had survived, when they had to balance the possibility of death in a thermonuclear Armageddon against a temporary return to the life that their great-grandparents had lived a century before as they built a new nation supported by a mighty Constitution and their own hard work and sacrifice?

Even in that relatively short period significant numbers succumbed to the harsh conditions of an environment that was in total contradiction to the consumer society that had evolved following the industrial revolution and the creation of mass production which had resulted in the wide availability of consumer goods that eased the rigours of everyday life. Most of the casualties were those that had ventured off of the main highways into the deserts between Southern California and Nevada where the fatalities were caused by lack of water, exposure to the vicious, unforgiving and relentless sun (and at night, the cold) and local marauders or other fellow hapless pioneers who were driven to the exigency of theft and the brutality of self survival.

L.B.J. spoke on the radio to the nation and only those close to the President recognised that events, commencing with his predecessor`s assassination, had cruelly and inexorably exhausted his strength and both physically and emotionally damaged his heart. His Presidential term would be remembered not for the deliverance of the nation from its greatest peril since December seventh, nineteen forty-one or the greatest percentage increase in military expenditure ever ordered by any President including F.D.R. but for the apparent feeble lethargy of the administration as they passively 'treaded water' before the next Presidential election.

The President reported that (the following is an abbreviated summary):

Diplomats acting for both the United States and the Soviet Union in Stockholm, Sweden, had agreed significant compromises as both sides recognised that there would be no victor in the event of an all out war.

The drift towards confrontation in the European area would cease immediately and that certain mainland European nations would henceforth be recognised by both sides as being within the political sphere and influence of the Soviet Union and the Warsaw Pact nations. Temporarily, pending a momentous meeting between the United States President and the First Secretary of the Communist party of the Soviet Union, provisionally to be held later that year in Stockholm, Sweden, the United States would call a moratorium on their military encirclement of the Soviet Union whilst the Warsaw Pact nations would reduce their level of combat readiness.

Above all any threat that had been made against the cities of the United States was retracted and in the spirit of friendship, the people of the Soviet Union held out their hands to the people of the United States who had been their staunch ally in the Great Patriotic War against Fascism.

Great Britain was not even mentioned and in any event the message was designed to reassure the people of the United States, however enquiries made by the British ambassador in Washington resulted in a reply some days later from the State Department which confirmed that the agreement covered the termination of a bombing campaign against Britain but made no mention whatsoever about the arrangement to, once and for all, emasculate the British nuclear option and to reduce Great Britain to the status of a 'protectorate'.

It took time for the cities and towns to return to normal as the people gradually and tentatively accepted that the crisis had been resolved and that a secure peace was in place. At first there was a silence as people refused or denied to admit their actions, but slowly, over a period of months, a new, muted confidence took hold as the reality of their flight gave way to the myth of their bravery and resilience, which became the legend and finally became part of the national psyche.

It was into this vacuum that a former Vice- President, Richard Milhous Nixon, chastened by his television confrontation in nineteen sixty with John Kennedy and subsequent defeat at the November polls and a passionate anti- communist, began his long march to adoption as the Republican candidate at the next election where he was elected, winning a remarkable forty-seven States and the votes of their Electoral Colleges. His platform captured and fed on the new national mood which Charles Lindbergh had espoused in the nineteen thirties, Isolationism! Nixon was able to profit from the acumen of his predecessor and Defence Secretary Robert McNamara, promising (and delivering) a new generation of weapons which would keep their enemy at bay, but in the world of the Intercontinental Ballistic missile, in truth, *NOWHERE* was safe or immune.

Events took a different, more sinister course in Great Britain. Perhaps Harold Wilson actually had convinced himself that the British nuclear deterrent was being rebuilt (based on the continuing supply of *SUPERFLUOUS* American B 52 bombers and their weapons) and that he, as the leader of Great Britain, continued to be an influential party at the negotiating table of the 'Superpowers'. He made what was to be his final broadcast and like his American ally, on radio only, but whilst L.B.J`s statement might not have been inspirational it had, at least, steadied the nation. The British people were unaware that the cities of their ally had been threatened with annihilation or that the *TWO* Superpowers had begun to reshape the world without the involvement of the British people in the form of their political leader and Wilson`s statement was assessed by the Regional Commissioners as at best, lacklustre, even soporific, and candidly lacking in credibility for his whole tone lacked conviction, confidence and to use a phrase so eloquently expressed by one of its members, "Just did not ring true".

He was clearly, like President Johnson, an exhausted and spent force whose actions had condemned the nation to an as yet unknown gruesome fate caused by one, rash, hurried and catastrophic error of judgement, creating a calamitous, bitter legacy.

Extracts from his statement were used as evidence at his trial.

Where, when and exactly who first suggested a desire to replace the Chairman of the National Council is now lost in the mists of time and probably the absence of any evidential documentation, if it ever existed, which if it ever existed has, most likely, now been destroyed or if it still exists its authenticity must be in doubt. By the middle of April the National Council MUST have learned of the Regional Commissioners' secret discussions probably through Manny Gold acting on the instructions of the United States' ambassador and behind him the American government, the ultimate instigators.

Action revolved around a cabal of at least seven of the National Council members including, but the order must not be interpreted as to their priority in the instigation of the plan, the two industrialists, the three nominated acting representatives of the armed forces and the two very recently nominated representatives of M.I. 5 and 6,Duggan and Hugh Stephenson, the latter whose career had been prematurely ended by the Prime Minister following the intelligence fiasco and who therefore had personal grounds to gain some form of revenge.

It is perhaps unarguably clear that five of the group represented the conservative 'Establishment' and their historical distaste and distrust of a provincial, Oxford educated intellectual socialist who hypocritically smoked a pipe in public to promote his image, but in private smoked a cigar, but above all was believed, in certain quarters, to be politically unreliable which perhaps, possibly, could explain why he had denuded the country of its nuclear deterrent. He had signed his own death warrant.

Food rationing had to be brought in, without delay, and as for the Regional and deputy Regional Commissioners, whilst their work and integrity was exemplary, their loyalty was to the previous order and they had to be replaced by men who were absolutely loyal to the National Council and a new concept of political power. A majority of the National Council members secretly agreed to sweep away the old failed system and replace it by an organisation where the interests of the State were both paramount and had priority over the interests of the individual and as one of the industrialist ventured to comment...

"That the interests of the Electorate were *ALWAYS* based on self interest and short term demands and did *NOT* consider the long term interests of the state."

Whether it was raised in jest or as a serious option it was decided to ban all political parties except the New Order which brought those present to consider the future involvement of John Tyndall and also Manny Gold which was strange to bracket the two men together. Duggan, the M.I.5 representative, had an 'interest' in both men whose futures would depend on their total support for the new embryonic regime and in respect of the former, his leadership of the 'New Order' which could form a pliant arm of the National Council, but in respect of Manny Gold, Duggan at least temporarily withheld any information or his suspicions concerning the man's still unknown exploits in the Soviet Union during the Second World War and his surprise re-emergence and their meetings in Egypt.

Hugh Stephenson and the two industrialists viewed John Tyndall as temporary and expendable, who could be, and would be relieved of power and influence once he had served his useful purpose but, having learned the lessons of history, for the leaders of post Weimar Germany had viewed Adolf Hitler and his rise to power in the same light, they would be exceptionally careful about his ambitions and exercise of power.

Manny Gold was viewed differently but certainly not affectionately. He was, without using any unpleasant descriptions, a Hebrew (even though he had been observed not to be observant), and *THEIR* loyalties were always in doubt. Furthermore he had been born in Soviet era Russia and his pedigree, as far as could be currently ascertained was hidden in an obscure cloud of uncertainty.

He had *NOT* been educated at Eton or any other respectable school; enquiries were being made about his life and especially his time in the United States and with great difficulty, in Russia. He therefore possessed a most unusual provenance which at that time was not sullied by any observations from Duggan.

But he did possess one vital attribute. He appeared to be a formidable administrator for it was he who had organised and set up the current identity card system which was perceived as the foundation of a scheme to identify and control each and every member of the community. He would be offered the challenge to set up a new and more comprehensive system of state control and if he declined the request, then Harold Wilson's *protégé* and nominee would be the first to be dismissed but in any event his loyalty to them, over Wilson, had to be proved.

ONE HUNDRED AND THREE

MY STRUGGLE

PART ONE-CHAPTER THREE:

POLITICAL CONSIDERATIONS

RESULTING FROM MY TIME IN VIENNA:

"Human rights are above State rights."

The Queen, Prince Philip, Prince Charles and the other members of the Royal family had kept a low profile and few remembered the promised speech they she was to give, for the nation was more concerned with the possibility of further attacks by the unchallenged Soviet bombers and the still unfulfilled promise of an enormous, massive and devastating blow by the British 'V' bomber force in retaliation.

The Queen still received her daily confidential briefing in the form of State documents though now much diminished in volume, sent in the unique and distinctive Red Box but they now usually came some five hours later than pre crisis days for in fact they were despatched from the Chairman's subterranean headquarters in the still unfinished complex at Hawthorn, near Corsham.

AUTHOR`S NOTE:

My publisher has permitted me to disclose details of the location since the site had been known for some time to the nation`s enemies as Britain's war time Headquarters and had become *THE* primary target in the event of an all out thermonuclear war.

The complex could be entered from two sites in Westwells Road, Hawthorn, which incidentally was the former main entrance to the Spring Quarry factory.

Casual visitors to the now redundant complex would be confronted by a dilapidated police lodge outside the main entrance which still prominently displays the sign identifying the complex as a PSA Supplies Division Depot though it is still a 'Prohibited Area' covered under the State Of Emergency - Martial Law. Second Edition (Item Ten).

The National Council (or to give it its original full title, which was soon afterwards commuted to the National Council, the rather dishonestly entitled National Council for Civil Liberties) meticulously, on a daily basis, supplied the Chairman and his Office (which would subsequently be forwarded to the Queen) the latest lists of executions.

Statistically they were broken down by each of the twelve areas, the nature of the offence(s), the date of arrest and date of trial concluding with the verdict.

Up to April fifteenth nineteen sixty–five (incidentally Maundy Thursday) the total number of executions nationwide totalled thirty–one and there is every reason to believe in the integrity and accuracy of this figure and more importantly the distribution and 'breakdown' of the committed offences which were:

(Sixteen)   Store, hoard, loot, steal (or store for another person or body of persons), food, water or fuel

NINE MALES and FOUR FEMALES

(Seventeen)   Transport, exchange, sell or buy, unless permitted by a duly authorised official, food, water or fuel

TEN MALES and ONE FEMALE

(One)   Organise, promote, support, join or assist in the act of Sedition, Revolution or Treason

TWO MALES

(Eighteen)   Store, hoard, transport, sell or buy medical drugs, unless permitted by duly authorised official

THREE MALES

(Ten)   Enter a zone or area designated as prohibited unless permitted by a duly authorised official

ONE MALE and ONE FEMALE

All but two of the offences had taken place in areas devastated by nuclear attacks and in four further cases the defendants were found not guilty, but peremptorily warned and then discharged.

Additionally, in two further cases both in the East London Ilford area, the defendants were found guilty of wilfully disobeying an order or request from a duly authorised official however as they were both underage the deputy R.C. used his discretion and the two males were confined in a military prison for twenty-one days as punishment and as a warning to others.

Having due regard to the circumstances and situation of those areas where most of the offences took place and the traumas suffered by the local communities, it is not unreasonable to accept that the deputy R.Cs. were apparently even handed dealing with these offences though in respect of certain items these acts had been treated as 'Black marketeering' during the Second World War and only then, at worst, resulted in imprisonment.

Thursday, April fifteenth appears to be a crucial date for then onwards the number of arrests and convictions dramatically increased and the nature of the offences widened.

There is every reason to believe that on the fifteenth, final plans were laid and put in motion to arrest Harold Wilson on various charges and the twenty-four Regional and deputy Regional Commissioners on other various (spurious) grounds but specifically gross dereliction and abuse of their responsibilities.

In reality this was a *Coup D` Etat.*

ONE HUNDRED AND FOUR

John Tyndall`s only loyalty was to himself and to his own future. Colin Jordan, who will feature later, was currently an irrelevance, whilst Sir Oswald Mosley was a convenient mentor though fate was to ultimately change history and reverse their roles.

John Tyndall was approached by Duggan and Stephenson and surprisingly approved of, and welcomed the coup, also agreeing, though he was astute enough to suggest that his organisation be both subordinated to and ultimately controlled by the National Council, but that it would be permitted both an increased role in the control of the civilian population and ominously, superficially in the GOVERNMENT (author's specific reference) of the nation. Judiciously, he was not informed that the organisers- whose number and identity temporarily remained secret-intended to proscribe all the other and relatively long established parties. His venality and moral corruption was exposed when he asked to be included in the party that was to carry out the arrest of Wilson. It was clear to Duggan and Stephenson that the man had no ethical values and was to be given unbridled power at their peril.

The plan, in common with the best plans, had the hallmarks of simplicity, cunning and execution and was scheduled for early May when the organisers intended to entice Wilson from his subterranean lair and divide him from any of his loyal supporters and more importantly from his armed guards whilst at the same time inviting the Regional and deputy Regional Commissioners to a 'Conference' at which Wilson would attend and speak.

The Coup had to remain secret at least until after Wilson had been arrested and the twenty-four Regional and deputy Regional Commissioners had been 'processed', however Saturday, May the eighth, V.E. day was the earliest when all the parties could be assembled.

Control of the press, radio and television was absolutely essential and it was arranged that once the Coup had been completed, those who controlled the 'media' would be invited to an urgent meeting at which time the arrest of the Chairman would be announced and the fact that he had been charged with High Treason, explaining the charge on the grounds and giving outline details that the nation no longer had a viable strike force.

Then details would be given listing only the current number of executions carried out and finally expressing their contrite regret, the discovery that the Regional Commissioners and their deputies had abused their position and that they were in protective custody pending urgent investigation of their offences (whilst in reality they had been immediately 'processed').

Because the media were to become privy to two of the nation's most important secrets and, it would be hinted, supplied with further highly confidential secrets, it was to be decided, with their agreement and with immediate effect, that temporarily there had to be greater, more intense supervision of the media for if news of Wilson's treachery became public it would be impossible to anticipate the outcome of the people's anger and wrath.

Interestingly, on May tenth, the Monday when the meeting actually took place, no one present mentioned, or raised, the fundamental right of the British people to have a General Election and to choose their representatives and a new leader.

Democracy, R. I. P.

Duggan was directed, by one of the two Industrialists, who had previously lived in the general area, to a pleasant residential and semi rural area in South Hertfordshire reached by the A1000 and A111 from London, and the A1 from the North and Central London. He was also attracted to the existing infrastructure for the area was well served by public transport.

The Northern underground line ended at High Barnet, the Piccadilly line ended at the quaintly named Cockfosters and the 'over-ground 'railway line was on a direct route to the 'City' terminating at Moorgate, stopping at the strangely entitled Potters Bar and after that Hagley Wood. All the public services were within no more than ten to twelve minutes of each other by car and a number of locations which, when combined, seemed ideally suitable for his embryonic plans which the National Council would have to approve.

Furthermore there was a small private aerodrome at Elstree, some twenty minutes away. Indeed Harold Wilson could be flown to the aerodrome and then, to lull his suspicions, the final stage of his life, (Duggan promptly corrected himself) complete his journey by helicopter to the discreet and private Wrotham Park Estate where he would be welcomed, offered a whisky and soda and then formally advised that he was under arrest on charges of High Treason.

Adjacent to Cockfosters underground station was a large cemetery and next to that the well known and conveniently secluded Trent Park Estate which during the Second World War had, amongst other responsibilities, been a prisoner of war camp for captured high ranking German officers and later, Italian troops.

And it was pointed out that on the perimeter of the Trent Park estate was a hotel, which was not as palatial as the private golf club where

John Tyndall had, it seemed, a life time ago, been seduced by its luxury, but was more than adequate for overnight stays.

Duggan's guide was surprised by an unusual enquiry from him and confirmed that indeed another local cemetery, at Brunswick Park Road, no more than ten to twelve minutes from Cockfosters tube station did have a crematorium with the 'usual' facilities.

Thus the instruments to install the totalitarian state were now in place but above all it required the single mindedness of a group, a class who were prepared, without scruples, to deny the existence of common justice, habeas corpus or Magna Carta and finally of the laws and procedures that had been built up over centuries to defend the rights of the individual.

The purges and then the terror was imminent and there was no longer a bulwark to defend freedom.

The approach to Manny Gold took place, over lunch, at the Dorchester, Park Lane, by the two Industrialists accompanied by Hugh Stephenson and Duggan who later remarked that such was Gold's composure and equanimity that he realised Gold possessed a formidable personality which went, some way, to explain his meteoric rise but still did not open a window into as yet, aspects of his obscure hidden earlier life.

The Roast Beef at the Dorchester is superb (and can be personally recommended) and is usually generously served with an accompaniment of homemade horseradish sauce. Gold continued to enjoy his excellent portion only answering the forthright questions once he had digested each mouthful. The betrayal of his mentor was complete and total. If they intended to deceive him then their plans were thwarted and diplomatically handled. The scenario was both dangerous and highly invidious. Immediately, but slowly, he mendaciously and without scruple used the situation to his own advantage, citing, on one hand his almost intimate relationship with Harold Wilson, and on the other, his disgust that the defence of the Realm had been so recklessly mishandled and that he would reluctantly be prepared to stand as a witness against his old friend and mentor who had also wilfully misled and misused both him and the nation.

Finally, with flair and an initiative that caught the other National Council members by surprise because of its subject matter and urgency, he stated that he saw the absolute necessity for rationing as the nation's second most important priority but primarily to resolve the defence of the Realm.

He, personally, on the instructions of Harold Wilson, had devised the Identity Card document and system and brought in its use but, to be fair to Wilson, because of constraints on costs, paper and above all photographic paper and equipment he had not been able to see the job through to the end that he had been capable of achieving and above all, was necessary.

He had conceived a combined identity card, internal passport and ration card offering the facility, for example, to increase the allowance for heavy manual workers, pregnant women or new mothers.

He even raised a chorus of laughter when he emphatically stated that it would certainly not be embossed on the front cover with the letter J.

It was only later that he realised how convincingly he had swayed and captured the confidence of the National Council members, that even greater power was now within his grasp and that he had effectively written his own 'Carte Blanche'

ONE HUNDRED AND FIVE

MY STRUGGLE

PART ONE - CHAPTER TEN:

THE PREMONITORY SIGNS OF COLLAPSE IN THE OLD EMPIRE:

"In all these things the aim and the method must be governed by the thought of preserving our nation's health both in body and soul. The right to personal freedom comes second in importance to the duty of maintaining the race."

The meeting was the first official contact between the United States ambassador and representatives of the National Council and took place in the privacy of his office, buried deep within the embassy, and his guests should have inferred that his presence in Central London confirmed that the threat from Soviet nuclear attacks had ceased.

The delegation, led by Hugh Stephenson, included Manny Gold and the two Industrialists and had been arranged, at short notice, by Gold primarily to obtain certain facilities from the United States which would enable him to set up the organisation to nationally issue the new joint identity card, internal passport and ration card but also to gauge the Americans' support for their domestic policies without disclosing their intention to imminently depose Wilson.

What the other members of the delegation did not know was that Gold had already discussed the subject with the ambassador and had yet again repaid their faith in him by disclosing details of the impending coup, which was scheduled for the following Saturday.

Wednesday May fifth marked what was to become perhaps the formal, if not official understanding of the new long term relationship between the two nations. When Stephenson, who previously had excellent contacts with the' Intelligence Community' in the United States, began speaking on behalf of the National Council and confided in their imminent plans and intentions but not the coup, the ambassador was able to respond, with apparent authority and confidence, ensuring that his visitors would leave having received an imprimatur of their plans.

"The internal affairs of the United Kingdom are of no concern to the government of the United States provided that our military and commercial interests in Great Britain and the rights *OF THOSE WHO HOLD UNITED STATES PASSPORTS* [author's emphasis] are not, under any circumstances, infringed upon or interfered with and that they are permitted free movement and are not hindered."

Gold, and perhaps his fellow Council members, realised that the brief statement had demanded and created a self contained independent state *WITHIN* their own borders but he did not understand the personal ramifications of the rights of American passport holders.

The agreement made in Stockholm was mentioned in passing as if the United States considered that the agreement did not concern their ally and its contents were not disclosed other than the statement that the Soviet diplomats, under pressure and counter threat, had formally agreed to end their attacks on Great Britain.

"The good faith and friendship of the American people and government towards their English (sic) partners was confirmed by their continued support and the ongoing delivery of B52 bombers and their weapons to defend freedom and democracy.

Wilson, as the representative of the British government, would have been welcomed as an observer or a participant in the recent talks that had taken place in Stockholm but unusually he absented himself and there were no British diplomats present and it was left to Britain`s ally to obtain a concession and an apology from their Soviet counterparts and their agreement to immediately discontinue their acts of aggression."

Washington was already aware that a request was to be made for photographic equipment, photographic paper and hundreds of tonnes of paper suitable for the new documentation but the ambassador allowed Stephenson to make the request and then to introduce Manny Gold who would (again, but now openly) explain its urgent and specific use.

A most sympathetic and apparently cooperative ambassador confirmed that an answer would be ready by the following Monday but he saw no reason why the order could not be promptly met since, for example, the Kodak company had vast resources and he believed a factory or facilities in England.

ONE HUNDRED AND SIX

MY STRUGGLE

PART ONE – CHAPTER TWELVE:

THE FIRST PERIOD IN THE DEVELOPMENT OF THE NATIONAL SOCIALIST GERMAN WORKERS` PARTY:

"The objective of a Movement of political reform is never attained by laboured explanation or by bringing influence to bear on the powers that be, but only by seizing political power."

John Maxwell Edmonds (1875-1958):

Went the day well?

We died and never knew.

But well or ill,

Freedom, we died for you.

The Times, February sixth 1918, Page 7, Column 4. The Second of Four Epitaphs headed:

On Some who died early in the Day of Battle.

A reconstruction of the dramatic events on that Saturday would have been impossible to fit together had I not been informed by Joel Ben Yitzhak that a first hand primary source report, now stored in the National Archives in Washington, had been compiled by Manny Gold the following Tuesday in the comparative tranquillity and safety of an office in the United States embassy on the pretence that whilst he was waiting to see the ambassador he was suddenly informed that a complete submission of the identity card programme had to be submitted when, of course, the requirement had already been sanctioned by the U.S. government. Seven pages of A 4 paper, poorly typed and double spaced, bore corrections of words and even whole lines and sentences, inserted either by hand written annotations or a series of typed crosses and attest to his attention and perhaps undoubtedly remain the only factual report that can be relied upon.

Indeed, when permitted, I have relied upon subsequent clandestine written reports to the ambassador or the ambassador's reports to Washington, based on information passed to him by Gold which have been declassified or in certain instances have been very kindly, if discreetly, been made available.

Furthermore access to reports in neutral Swiss and Swedish newspapers, when they appear to be primary source information and not secondary source transmissions of 'official' government statements has been used whenever possible to verify my narrative.

Therefore, in some ways, we are observing the events through the eyes, ears and experiences of Manny Gold.

It also marked the momentous day when the policy of revisionism - the 'rewriting 'of history - to conform with the current *status quo* first was used and later was to be a tool of propaganda and history thus enabling its authors to pervert the truth of historical events both by denigrating those who had fallen from grace and enhancing the reputation of those who were now in favour.

It was perhaps the ultimate irony that Harold Wilson was ceremoniously transported in the same Bell 204B helicopter that had very recently been the mode of transport that had impressed the vast crowds that attended John Tyndall's rallies and was being supplied, along with the pilot, by the same shadowy Industrialist who was now part of the conspiracy. Although capable of holding up to seven passengers, the helicopter only brought the Chairman of the National Council together with a senior civil servant and their luggage and arrived at ten forty-five to be met by a small party comprising Gold and Tyndall (who he both knew) and the acting National Council members for the three branches of the armed forces who were each individually introduced to him and were attired in combat uniforms and not ceremonial dress.

Although there was more than adequate space for the helicopter to safely land within the Wrotham Park Estate the pilot had been instructed to land at Elstree aerodrome on the basis that his charts were inadequate to land in a private area and of course where perhaps Wilson might spot the hidden troops that had been deployed.

The three officers were separately driven to Wrotham Park in a camouflaged military registered Jeep, followed by Gold in the Chairman's former Prime Ministerial official car whilst the Chairman of the National Council and the civil servant travelled with Tyndall in his official Armstrong Siddeley Star Sapphire.

Readers will, or should observe that Wilson had, for the good fortune of the plotters, not been accompanied by a private detective and that the pilot automatically remained at the aerodrome.

Wilson, who had previously lived in North London, vaguely knew the geography of the area which was verified when the convoy passed the well known landmark of the Thatched Barn hotel on the A1 near to Borehamwood and Arkley and within a further ten or so minutes they had arrived at the Wrotham Park Estate where the troops, and their vehicles, had been secretly deployed and were hidden out of sight.

The troops had been specially selected and formed part of a new unit (a template for the future), the description elite being inapplicable since their primary qualification, other than their individual records of active service, was their recorded animosity to the previous government for the perceived betrayal of their fellow troops who, having suffered the vicious experience of chemical warfare, had apparently been abandoned and apparently the only prisoners of war who had been returned were those whose lives were ruined and were beyond treatment. They would be excellent and reliable jailors when, very shortly, the purpose and nature of their task was announced.

Stephenson and Duggan would soon be exposed as the catalysts and engine behind the day`s actions but they had delegated the actual arrest and imprisonment of Wilson to the two as yet untested co-conspirators on the basis that Wilson would be lulled into a false sense of security because of his misguided trust in Gold`s presence and that Tyndall, who had already expressed his personal feelings, would have the ruthlessness and self interest to support Gold.

The three representatives of the military chiefs were lightly armed and had agreed that any failure to perform the arrest would result in the immediate execution of Gold and Tyndall as a warning to Wilson.

But, according to Gold`s report, there was no indecision or hesitation, indeed Gold needed no incitement from the other four present to announce (according, verbatim, to his report) that:

"James Harold Wilson, you are now under arrest on a charge of High Treason, and you will be shortly removed to a place where a military tribunal will convene and by due process will reach a verdict. In accordance with the State Of Emergency - Martial Law Second Edition you will be defended by a uniformed military officer."

Wilson, who was still wearing his famous Gannex raincoat, even though he had had adequate opportunity to take off the coat, for the group was indoors and the weather outside was pregnant with the warmth of imminent summer, was most unpredictable in his response. Gold looked into his eyes and felt certain that the now deposed politician was in fact relieved that the burden of power had been removed from off of his shoulders and that the deeds of his premiership would be positively analysed with the critical forensic objectivity of a trio of historians in the guise of a military tribunal.

Perhaps almost paternally, Gold without prompting, explained that he would have the freedom of the estate and that by the end of the day staff would be brought in to maintain his style of living and status but regretfully he would not be allowed to communicate with his immediate family, friends or staff.

Within minutes, almost like autumnal mushrooms appearing overnight, the estate was flooded with soldiers ordered not to allow any visitors into the estate or to communicate with their prisoner whilst the senior civil servant was removed to...

The journey from the Wrotham Park Estate to the hotel on the perimeter of Trent Park took no more than ten to twelve minutes but during that brief period allowed Gold some time for introspection for his report confirms that absolutely no oral communication with made either with John Tyndall or the two Council members representing the Air Force and the Navy, for the third of the trio remained behind to organise and supervise the luxurious incarceration of the prisoner.

They arrived at the hotel, parked adjacent to a coach and entered first the front door before going straight to the lounge where the unsuspecting Regional Commissioners and their deputies were being entertained in anticipation of the arrival of Harold Wilson. Those who were privy to the plan realised that the initial phase had succeeded, solely by the very presence of the perpetrators and their confident facial expressions and then Stephenson announced that there had been a slight change to the agenda and timetable and they were to travel to the nearby Wrotham Park Estate where the Chairman of the National Council had decided to stay and where he was to announce his plans once martial law had been terminated.

Instead of turning West towards the announced destination, the coach, filled with the unsuspecting victims and followed by a convoy of some

half a dozen assorted vehicles, turned South towards Cockfosters and shortly before the underground station turned left into Trent Park Cemetery whose signs had been temporarily hidden or disguised.

For some the day went well, for others, death was to be soon, swift and summary.

It was somewhat of a contrived and callous conclusion for as the victims exited the charabanc they were confronted by a brace of lorries around which milled a number of soldiers enjoying the late spring sunshine.

The welcoming smile had dissolved from the face of Duggan and his tone and appearance became menacing. Facing the startled twenty-four men he announced with a coldness and unconcealed venom that:

"James Harold Wilson had been arrested and charged with High Treason on the grounds that the defence of the Realm had been imperilled by the wanton removal, to South Africa, of the 'V' bomber force along with their weapons and that they - the Regional Commissioners and their deputies - *in absentia*, had been found guilty of gross abuse of power including the unnecessary and excessive use of the death penalty and moral corruption."

The execution of the mass execution was over within a minute or so therefore not enabling the victims either the time or opportunity to plead their innocence or to query the charges and within ten minutes or so the senior civil servant had also been dispatched.

Shortly afterwards an unsuspecting George Woodcock arrived and was immediately welcomed by Duggan with the sincerity of an old and trusted friend before strangely walking away, after which the troops performed the execution and *Coup De Grace* using pistols at very close range, and not rifles, as they had used on their previous victims.

The first of what was to be the forerunner of many mass 'military' graves awaited the victims and the anonymity of the bodies was ensured by a temporary notice which identified the deceased as twenty-six unidentified noble dead who had valiantly given their lives on the battlefields of Germany in November nineteen sixty-three.

The following day, with the connivance and knowledge of those who ultimately controlled the media, photographs and T.V. film were published and broadcast showing Harold Wilson enjoying the spring display of flowers and greenery in the garden of 'Number Ten' whilst concurrently, and retrospectively, documentation 'signed' by the Chairman of the National Council was drawn up impeaching the twenty-four Regional Commissioners and their deputies together with the judgement of the (Military) Tribunal. The official court report of the tribunal was shortly thereafter either lost or possibly accidentally destroyed or shredded.

END OF VOLUME TWO